A MOUNTAIN IN THE AIR

— A TRILOGY —

LAURA KOERBER

Copyright © Laura Koerber 2024

All rights reserved.

No part of this publication may be altered, reproduced, distributed, or transmitted in any form, by any means, including, but not limited to, scanning, duplicating, uploading, hosting, distributing, or reselling, without the express prior written permission of the publisher, except in the case of reasonable quotations in features such as reviews, interviews, and certain other non-commercial uses currently permitted by copyright law.

Disclaimer:
This is a work of fiction. All characters, locations, and businesses are purely products of the author's imagination and are entirely fictitious. Any resemblance to actual people, living or dead, or to businesses, places, or events is completely coincidental.

Author's Note

The three novellas in this book are Coyote's Road Trip, Raven Woman's Tavern, and A Mountain in the Air. The first two were published separately and Coyote's Road Trip is still available as a standalone novel.

The three connected novellas are based on the old Celtic tradition of "pucas." The pucas were shapeshifters that played tricks on people and occasionally helped them. The Celtic pucas took the form of wild animals native to the island we now call Ireland. For my purposes in this book, I used Raven and Coyote. Although both appear in Native American traditional spirituality, my Coyote and Raven are quite different and shouldn't be confused with indigenous concepts.

The first novella, Coyote's Road Trip, describes an indigenous hunting and gathering community. The community is imaginary and similarities to the real indigenous communities is co-incidental. Readers should not assume that they are learning anything about any real tribal societies. I urge readers who are interested in Native American cultures to go to Native American sources.

All three novellas are entirely fictional.

Contents

Author's Note iii
Coyote's Road Trip - The First Novella ix
    Prologue 1
    Chapter One 5
    Chapter Two 8
    Chapter Three 12
    Chapter Four 16
    Chapter Five 20
    Chapter Six 23
    Chapter Seven 26
    Chapter Eight 31
    Chapter Nine 34
    Chapter Ten 37
    Chapter Eleven 42
    Chapter Twelve 47
    Chapter Twelve 50
    Chapter Thirteen 55
    Chapter Fourteen 62
    Chapter Fifteen 66
    Chapter Sixteen 71
    Chapter Seventeen 77
    Chapter Eighteen 84
    Chapter Nineteen 88
    Chapter Twenty 90
    Chapter Twenty-One 95
    Chapter Twenty-Two 98
    Chapter Twenty-Three 102
    Chapter Twenty-Four 105
    Chapter Twenty-Five 109
    Chapter Twenty-Six 113
    Chapter Twenty-Seven 118
    Chapter Twenty-Eight 126
    Epilogue 131

Raven Woman's Tavern - The Second Novella 133

- Prologue 135
- Chapter One 138
- Chapter Two 142
- Chapter Three 146
- Chapter Four 149
- Chapter Five 157
- Chapter Six 160
- Chapter Seven 166
- Chapter Eight 168
- Chapter Nine 172
- Chapter Ten 175
- Chapter Eleven 178
- Chapter Twelve 181
- Chapter Thirteen 184
- Chapter Fourteen 188
- Chapter Fifteen 192
- Chapter Sixteen 194
- Chapter Seventeen 199
- Chapter Eighteen 201
- Chapter Nineteen 205
- Chapter Twenty 210
- Chapter Twenty-One 215
- Chapter Twenty-Two 220
- Chapter Twenty-Three 224
- Chapter Twenty-Four 227
- Chapter Twenty-Five 233
- Chapter Twenty-Six 235
- Chapter Twenty-Seven 237
- Chapter Twenty-Eight 241
- Chapter Twenty-Nine 244
- Chapter Thirty 249
- Epilogue 254

A Mountain in the Air - The Third Novella 257

- Prologue 259
- Chapter One 262

Chapter Two 265
Chapter Three 270
Chapter Four 275
Chapter Five 280
Chapter Six 283
Chapter Seven 286
Chapter Eight 290
Chapter Nine 293
Chapter Ten 297
Chapter Eleven 301
Chapter Twelve 304
Chapter Thirteen 310
Chapter Fourteen 315
Chapter Fifteen 318
Chapter Sixteen 321
Chapter Seventeen 329
Chapter Eighteen 334
Chapter Nineteen 338
Chapter Twenty 340
Chapter Twenty-One 345
Chapter Twenty-Two 349
Chapter Twenty-Three 355
Chapter Twenty-Four 360
Chapter Twenty-Five 365
Chapter Twenty-Six 370
Chapter Twenty-Seven 374
Chapter Twenty-Eight 378
Epilogue 382
Other books by Laura Koerber 385

Coyote's Road Trip

The First Novella

Prologue

Most of the humans who pass through the Valley of Dry Bones have their eyes on the horizon and see very little of the desert outside the windows of their cars. Bored, they count off the miles left to get somewhere else. They calculate speed-to-distance, estimate their ETA, and grind out the hours of white line fever by fiddling with the car radio, tossing cigarettes out the window, eating junk food, or yelling at the kids in the back seat. Four hours to Reno. Three to Salt Lake City. An hour to Ely. They have no desire to be where they are. They want, often very badly, to be somewhere else.

A long time ago, Coyote saw some strange people passing through the valley in a wagon train. They had their eyes on the horizon and dreamed of California, but they figured distance in terms of footsteps and diminishing water, while calculating how long their cattle were going to hold out. They wanted very, very badly to be somewhere else.

Coyote was not in the habit of watching humans die, but he was present when Old Man Hardkoop finally gave up and lay down in the dirt in the meager shade of a sagebrush bush. The old man had been a passenger on the wagon of the Keseberg family—Mr. Keseberg being the guy who later became notorious for eating Tamsin Donnor. Mr. Keseberg had to lighten the load for his half-starved oxen. He'd already tossed furniture overboard, and he and his wife were afoot, carrying their young daughter. He told Old Man Hardkoop to get out of the wagon and walk, knowing that the old man wouldn't be able to keep up.

All of the settlers in the wagon train knew that Old Man Hardkoop wouldn't be able to keep up. They didn't discuss it, at least not while Coyote was in earshot, tracking their progress through his territory. They just trudged onward, eyes on the distant mountains, dreaming with increasing desperation of California. To them, the desert was an obstacle, a dreadful passage, a trial that tested their moral and physical strength. They saw nothing in the desert to sustain their lives.

The sustenance was there. After all, the People had been living in the desert for generations. Their ancestors had wandered into the Valley of Dry Bones hundreds of years previously. They'd looked around, learned what they needed to learn, and found what they needed to find. In the landscape of soft grays and beige, delicate pinks and vivid greens, of thorns and insects, of drought and torrential rain, they found rice grass and jackrabbits. They found springs of fresh water and a river. They found pinon nuts on the slopes of the mountain, reeds in the marshes, and antelope out in the sagebrush. In other words, they found the necessities of life: food, water, shelter, beauty.

The valley's name came from the tendency of dead animals to hang around forever as white bones, cleaned by the vultures and insects, and scoured by windblown sand. Strewn on the ground were the tiny bones of mice and the slightly more robust bones of rabbits. Coyote often stepped on bones of hawks and antelope as he patrolled his territory. Once he found the bones of a desert tortoise rattling like castanets in the shell. He'd seen bones of snakes, bones of people, and bones of his brother and sister coyotes. All those bones were constant reminders of how everyone's story ended. Like the tangy taste of dried ants, death flavored life.

The valley is a wide, flat plain between sudden mountains that climb up abruptly, not bothering with foothills, straight to the sky. Often hazy from the hot dry air, washed out by the glare of the sun, or obscured by thunderheads, the mountains are like a distant dream. The best time for you to see the mountains, dear reader, is on an overcast day when the sky is a dark, cloudy blue. Then your eyes can see across fifty or so miles of flat land to where the pinon forests cover the mountain slopes with a soothing patchwork of dark green. The bones of the mountain are easy to see on those days: steep slants cut by ravines. The forces of erosion have been in action since long before Coyote came into being, and certainly before you, dear reader, were born. The mountains are another way that death spices the lives of the living. All you have to do is look at the rocks and ravines to know that life is short.

Coyote didn't pay much mind to the People who lived in his valley. They lived by their accumulated years of experience and weren't in need of his magic. Nor did he need much from them. They co-existed side by side, foraging and feeding, procreating and dying. Coyote didn't pay much attention to their deaths either. He knew that individual humans lived and died—just as the animals and plants lived and died—but the web of life in the desert remained constant.

Old Man Hardkoop's death was intriguing to Coyote because the wagon train people had turned their backs on one of their own. The People of the desert were never indifferent to the suffering of one of their own. They moved seasonally, but they carried those who needed to be carried as best they could. If they were starving—which happened every now and then—and they couldn't carry someone with them, they mourned those they couldn't save. Coyote was baffled by the ways of the new people. They seemed to be stupid, incompetent, and cruel.

Old Man Hardkoop didn't die right away. He tried to keep up. His feet were swollen and bleeding, and his boots were worn down to rags. The wagons—wearily dragged along by thin, thirsty oxen—didn't move fast, and neither did the thin, thirsty women or the dusty, frightened children. Everyone shuffled and stumbled. Mrs. Keseberg held on the side of the wagon to keep herself on her feet.

No one spoke except to yell. Mostly they yelled at the oxen, but sometimes they exploded at each other with voices raw and ragged from the dust. When not yelling, they trudged in silence. Old Man Hardkoop didn't ask for help. He staggered on, first only twenty feet behind the Keseberg wagon, then forty feet, then behind so far that he couldn't see the wagons anymore, just the dust.

Coyote tracked him from the brush nearby. He watched the bony shoulders and limp, dusty hat; the swollen hands dangling; the tear tracks on the dirty cheeks. The old man's eyes weren't on the horizon and any dreams of California were dead. His steps slowed. His head bobbled at the end of his skinny neck. He was wondering which step would be his last one when his knees gave out.

Coyote watched the old man collapse into a heap on the ground. There he slumped, his head dangling on his neck, his gnarly old hands laying in his lap. Maybe he thought about the home of his birth in Belgium. Or maybe he remembered his farm in Ohio. His wife, God bless her, was in her grave. He had dreamed of California, but he knew he would never travel any farther than a sagebrush bush in the desert of Nevada.

Coyote watched the old man wipe the sweat off his face and look around one last time. Old Man Hardkoop couldn't see any way to sustain life. Slowly, gently, he lowered his shoulders and his head so that he was laying on his side. Then he covered his face with one of his thin, spidery hands.

Coyote trotted away. It was all very confusing. For millennia, only the People had lived in the desert. Now these new people were passing through and they didn't know anything, didn't seem to want to learn anything, and they didn't take care of their own. He didn't like them.

THE DESERT

Chapter One

Two customers, one staffer, and one guy at the hookup. I didn't like those odds, so I strolled outside and around to the back for a long piss in the weeds. The truck stop had a bathroom, but people are disgusting.

Nope, better to piss while enjoying a landscape of weeds and dust. The air stank but not as bad as the toilet. I smelled some asphalt mixed with herbicide, though why anyone would bother spraying for weeds was beyond me. The town was nothing but ramshackle trailers, each with a front yard decorated with discarded washing machines and vehicles that didn't run. A chained-up backyard dog barked out his neuroses, making my insides cringe.

I zipped up, and headed back to the store. It was the only store in town, kept alive partly by passing vehicles but also by selling necessities like cigarettes, beer, hot dogs, and potato chips to the locals. The guy who'd been using the electrical hook up was at the counter, boring the crap out of a teen-aged clerk with some long, involved story about why he was on the road. Something to do with looking for work in California, which meant that he and I were going to be driving down the same highway all the way across Nevada. I decided to wait until he was gone.

One of the other two customers had disappeared, leaving a bulky guy with a beer gut and no hair. He had a gun shoved down the back of his pants. That right there's something I don't understand at all. Doesn't the gun ride up or slide down with each step? Isn't it cold and scratchy? I wouldn't want a trigger digging into my backside. And how do guys sit down with guns back there? What keeps the gun from popping out and falling on the floor? Shit like that just baffles me.

His body language was showy and stupid too. He had a wide-legged stance, as if trying to impress the display of pop cans with his machismo. The pop cans just glinted out reflections of the overhead strip lights, uninterested. I decided to wait until he was gone, though chances were some other gun-toting asshole would show up.

I drifted past the chips and jerky, down toward the sundries. The store sold needles and thread, patches for worn out jeans, decks of cards, and batteries—boring stuff but useful. That kind of crap had a reason for existing, unlike the aisle with twenty different kinds of potato chip. The end cap had some car stuff and some tools for people who had work to do while snarfing their very favorite brand of chip. The store was trying to stock everything—even guns and ammo—in spite of the constant supply chain fuck ups. Meanwhile, Mr Macho had finally picked out the pop of his choice and was sauntering toward the clerk.

She looked to be about sixteen and wanted badly to be a thousand miles away. Her head was decorated with multiple ear piercings, a gold nose ring, and a beaded headband of the fake Native American kind. Dishwater blond hair was rasta'd into snakes that bounced around her shoulders. I kind of admired her, and I wasn't surprised to see a tattoo of a flower blooming on her cheek.

I *was* surprised when Macho Man pulled his pistol and told the girl, "I want the cash." He hadn't noticed me standing in the chip aisle at the back because I'd been using a mild "don't notice me" spell. I looked around for something heavy.

The girl squeaked, "Okayokayokay." I heard the cash register ping cheerfully. The only handy heavy object that I could see was a wrench. It was tied to a piece of cardboard advertising its fantastic durability. I hefted it, aimed my mind at Macho Guy, and fired a spell at him: *Ignore me, ignore me, ignore me.* Then I ripped the cardboard off, took the five strides down the aisle fast, and swung that wrench like Babe Ruth hitting one clear out of the stadium. Blood exploded on Mr. Macho's face. The gun went off. I knew it would, but the odds were greater that he'd hit the ceiling than me. I aimed my work boot at his hip and kicked him over. He landed on his back with the gun still in his hand, so I pounced on him and sank my teeth into his wrist. I have a good, strong bite. My mouth filled with blood, and my ears filled with his screams. The gun dropped. I grabbed it and jumped to my feet.

The girl was leaning over the counter watching, wild-eyed.

"You call the cops yet?" I asked.

"Un, no sorry, not--"

"Well, don't," I interrupted. "Put that cash in a bag for me, will you, hon?" I watched the corners of her mouth jerk into a grin of delight.

"Are *you* going to rob the store?"

"That's what I came for."

"Okay." Working with both hands, she quickly filled a small paper bag. "Sorry I can't get into the safe."

"It's okay." Mr. Macho was curled up around his bleeding hand, moaning. I stepped up to the counter. "Toss in some butts, please?"

"What brand?"

"Them." I pointed. She dropped two cartons in on top of the money and held out the bag.

"Thanks." I set the gun down on top of the money. There was yearning all over the girl's face, and I wasn't magicking her at all. She wanted to come with me.

"Have a nice day," I told her. "Give me a five minute start?"

"Sure." She was solemn, a promise made.

"Thanks."

I took a look out the door. No complications out there. "Good luck," I said and left. I've found that it doesn't hurt to be polite and sometimes helps. There's a lot of miserable humans in this world and many have larceny in their hearts. She was going to be questioned by the police, but she didn't know what my truck looked like because I'd parked it alongside the building. I hopped in and hit the road.

I thought about the truck stop girl as I piled up the miles. I wondered if she would ever escape the dingy little town. Where would she go? Climate change had fucked up a lot of things for humans too. Ironic that she wanted to leave but was stuck, and I, who wanted to stay, was fleeing—also with nowhere to go. The Valley of Dry Bones was in my rear view mirror, and I was headed toward the Backbone Range to go up and over and be gone.

Chapter Two

The driving conditions were perfect; an overcast sky of blue clouds blocked the sun glare. The dirt of the desert floor was almost luminous with glowing layers of gray, bronze, and gold. The highway lay out flat and straight for over thirty miles. Far ahead of me I could see where the road dodged the highest part of the mountains by shifting northwest toward Ely. A flock of wind turbines, white as sea gulls, fluttered up the valley along the road to a distant ranch. Too late—the world was already fucked by fossil fuels. But I didn't want to think about that. Instead, I counted colors in the landscape to distract myself: ultramarine in the distance; sage green, lime green, and silvery green along the road; shimmering layers of gray, silver, and rose on the rocky mountainsides.

Miles of sagebrush. Miles of dust and sand. So flat that I could see the roundness of the earth. A long blue highway, straight and unchanging, ahead of me. Something big and lumpish lay sprawled out on the shoulder maybe five miles down the road on my side.

I squinted through my sunglasses. What the fuck? Two thick sticks stuck out of the brown bulge. Maybe something had fallen off a truck? As I stared, the lump gradually became a dead cow. It'd been hit several times already, though how any human could be dumb enough to hit a cow on a straight stretch of road with thirty miles of visibility was beyond me.

Poor old cow. I looked around but didn't see any herd out in the sage. They died of heatstroke sometimes in the summer. It wouldn't surprise me if they died of thirst sometimes too, but that cow had been hit by something big enough to survive the experience and drive away. Maybe a semi-truck.

"Lot of meat," said Joseph, and I nearly jumped out of my skin.

"Goddamn it!" I yelled, as I yanked on the steering wheel and got us back on the road. I took a quick look in my rear view mirror at the skinny old man in the back seat. He was wearing a battered red baseball cap and a plaid shirt washed to a faded mix of gray and rust.

"Sorry," he mumbled. "Just sayin' that was a lot of meat to just leave."

"I ain't in the mood for roadkill." I swerved again at the sudden appearance of Janey in the passenger seat. She had a round face like her dad's, and his same tired, rounded shoulders and bad teeth. Unlike her father, she was well padded. Too much junk food, too many beers.

"Shit, you guys!" I hadn't known they could become ghosts. They'd startled the hell out of me.

"Sorry I surprised you," Joseph said. "We've been riding with you since…" his voice trailed off. His mouth went slack and his eyes got an inward look.

"Since we died." Janey had always been the forthright one. She met my eyes in the rear view mirror. "Surprised, huh? We got in a while back."

"I had no frickin' idea." I got the truck aimed down the highway again. Since I wouldn't have to turn the wheel for ten minutes at least, I took my eyes off the road and checked out my two passengers. They looked reasonably solid, almost real. Maybe a bit faded, but Joseph had looked faded in life. Janey, on the other hand, had always looked unhealthy but very much present, like pizza and potato chips.

"So when did you get in?"

"We followed you to your truck after your sweet little funeral." Janey rolled her eyes.

Sweet little funeral, I grumped to myself. I'd done my best; I wasn't used to mourning for humans.

"Burning sage was a nice touch." Janey grinned.

"I didn't know what kind of funeral you'd want." The service I'd made up had been more for me than them.

"You did a nice ceremony." That was Joseph from the back seat. He was a nice guy, or he had *been* a nice guy and now was most likely a nice ghost. Janey threw her arm over the back of the seat and twisted around to smile at him. The affection on her face made her look like a holy icon. She never radiated that look at anyone but Joseph. I was thinking about that when I noticed that Janey was wearing a seat belt.

"Hey, you don't need that." Weird how I hadn't noticed the seat belt bulging out before she got visible.

Her sudden laugh rang out. "You're right." She unclipped and shook her shoulders, enjoying the freedom of movement. "After all, what's going to happen to me?"

"Good question," I said.

That surprised another laugh out of her. "Yeah, you're right about that too, Coyote Jim. What's going to happen to us now? We're the undead!" She twisted around in her seat again. "Hey, Dad, you can smoke now all you want. Go for it! I won't nag no more."

I'd introduced myself to her as Jim, but she'd started calling me Coyote Jim right from the get-go out of some instinct. She didn't know I was a nature spirit. She just meant the nickname to be an insult because she thought I was a bum. Seriously. She thought I was a long-time squatter who lived out in the bush somewhere due to not being able to hold a job or not being willing to hold one.

Which was kind of true, but why would I move to town and work when I could get by on jack rabbits and mice? If I needed a little cash, I went down to Jackpot Wash or drove to Salt Lake and tricked the money out of someone. I have some special skills that keep me in coffee, beer, books, and power ups for the truck. One: I can put ideas into someone's head—or keep ideas out of their head. Two: I can make a person feel obligated toward me or like me. With those skills, I can rob a store, cheat at poker, or do odd jobs and get people to overpay me. And three: If I'm really pissed off, I can stick a human on a different timeline and stash them there for a while.

None of my skills were ever going to get me rich, especially since I could only leave a person wondering why their wallet was empty so many times before they started realizing that I must've had something to do with it. People don't trust me. It's instinctive, I think, but also maybe has a bit of prejudice to it. I don't look white enough to be white and not anything else enough to be anything else. Humans don't like that because they want to put each other into boxes with labels. If they can't label someone easily, they feel uncomfortable. Besides, the irises of my eyes are sometimes yellow.

Other than scamming them, I hardly ever spent time around people. Well, except for Janey and Joseph. Janey's ranch had always been a good hunting grounds for me. With that thought, I got back mentally to my two passengers, Janey-the-snide and her sweet old dad. She was sprawled in her seat, her eyes on the desert. I checked my rear view mirror. Joseph was asleep. I didn't know ghosts did that.

"Did you guys know you were going to become ghosts?"

She gave her head a quick shake. "Nope. First I knew of it was those flowers."

I think I may have had something to do with the sudden appearance of flowers at my funeral service for them, but it wasn't intentional. Maybe some force of creation had been working through me. But what do I know? To me, holiness is seen by its effects: growth, death, birth. I don't see God as a super person, or an animal, or a mineral, or an easy answer to a shallow question. I'm a god of sorts, the spirit of a place, but I don't claim to understand creation.

I'm a homeless god. That sucks.

"You were clueless and didn't see us," Janey was still back on the subject of the funeral. "We watched you walking away. Then I said, 'Let's go.' and we ran to the truck and got here before you did." She waved a hand. "We went right through the doors."

"That's handy," I said. "Maybe you guys can help me rob stores?"

Chapter Three

About that funeral...
I don't get premonitions very often, but I had one about Janey and her dad. I had a vision of them standing side by side out in the brush, holding hands. They had their backs to me and were looking out across the flat lands toward the west where the mountains formed the edge of the world known by me. A turkey vulture circled overhead, black wings out flat against the sky. My visions aren't subtle.

They'd been neighbors of mine for years. My place was out toward the base of the mountains and theirs was by the highway, with about five miles of sagebrush, rabbits, and mice in between. In the Valley of Dry Bones, that counted as next door. They were just about the last hold outs since the toxic leak.

Bothered by the vision, I skipped my morning coffee, climbed into my truck, and bounced down the dirt track to the highway. Their house was nearby but hidden behind a windbreak of ratty dried-out Russian olive trees. I shed my boots and clothes and tossed everything into the cab. Leaving the keys under a rock, I trotted off into the sagebrush. The morning had been heating up by then, even though there was a smooth layer of cloud from horizon to horizon. No sign of rain, though. Even the sagebrush was parched.

Then I spotted them, a dumpy woman and a bent up old man out in the sagebrush behind their house. Janey was carrying stuff, plus propping her dad up as he inched his way along. They picked a random spot and dumped their stuff—well, the spot had looked random to me. The land all around their house was flat and any one sagebrush bush looked pretty much like another.

She shook out a blanket, and they sat down and disappeared from my sight. I crept through the brush until I got a glimpse of Janey's red T-shirt through the gray-green sage. After inching a little closer, I settled into the sand and listened. I could hear Janey pretty well, but Joseph's voice was just a wisp of sound, dry as the air.

He whispered something, and she said, "Wait a goddamn minute, will ya?" I shoved my nose between the twisted branches of sage for a better look. She was struggling with the child-proof lid on a pill bottle.

They'd carried a blanket, some bottles of booze, a lot of pills, and a photo album with them. Janey poured a few pills into her palm and handed them to Joseph. Then I saw her pop a few herself and wash them down with a slug from a bottle of red wine. That done, she dragged the photo album on her lap and started flipping through the pages.

"Look at this. Mom sure was happy about her canning." Joseph mumbled something. I couldn't see him because Janey's lumpy body was in the way. "Here's me when I graduated from high school." Janey's voice had the forced cheerfulness of an adult talking to a kid. "Goddamn, my hair was long." Her dark hair was still down to her waist.

Joseph mumbled something, and she said, "Okay, Dad, here's two pills more for you and two for me." More mumbles. "Oh look, that's the day I was in the rodeo over at Ute Creek. Remember, Dad? You probably took that picture."

A hawk was riding a thermal way up in the dark blue sky. No breeze stirred the air. My nose was full of the scents of sage, dust, and rabbit turds, but I could smell the wine too. I wondered why were they out in the sagebrush when they had a front yard and some trees for shade.

"Some more?" The wine bottle got more action. Janey dumped the last of the pills into her hand and counted them.

"Here, Dad." I shifted position because a twig was sticking me in the ribs. "You gotta drink more of that wine."

That's when I figured out what was going on. I pulled my head back to give them privacy. Death is something to do alone or with someone you love, so I settled myself down in the sand to wait.

After awhile, they put the photo album away and lay down. Janey sang a pretty country song, then a lullaby. They weren't, as far as I knew, religious. I'd never heard Janey mention God or Jesus except in the context of swearing at other drivers or grocery store prices. "Goddamn, if that old boy drove any slower we wouldn't be moving at all." Or "Jesus H. Christ, if prices go up much more, we're gonna give up eating."

After the singing stopped, I crept closer and listened to the breathing. When I no longer heard any breathing, I tiptoed up close and sniffed around the bodies. Then I sat back on my tail and howled. After that, I trotted back to my truck, went to my human form, and put my clothes on. Then I returned to take care of the bodies.

They didn't look peaceful in death. Joseph had died with his mouth open and his chin wet with saliva and snot. Janey's face, unlit by her personality, had looked shapeless and dull. I rolled them both face down and pushed their bodies close to each other. Then I spread Janey's long brown hair out over her shoulders and over Joseph's too.

In the many seasons of my long existence, many lives have come and gone. Many rabbits died because I killed them. I've seen animals dead from disease, or by road kill, or murdered by humans. A long time ago, I saw the original People fight for their home and die. I've seen the new people die, too, mostly from car crashes or something stupid like that. About fifteen years ago, I started seeing animals and plants die from drought and heat because humans had fucked up the climate.

Seeing Janey and Joseph dead did something to my insides. I felt a jagged, ragged tear right up through my guts to my heart. I knew I wasn't mourning them. Well, them a little. I was mourning all the other deaths too.

To a human, driving one of their death machines down one of the highways that killed the world, the desert probably didn't look much different post-climate change than it had before. That's because most of the humans hadn't cared much about the lives in the desert before climate change, so why would they care afterwards?

Janey and Joseph had known about the silent, unseen deaths out in the sagebrush. Like me, they'd been watching the deaths pile up since around 2020, when it started getting really obvious that the desert was changing. They knew about the radiation leak, too, and they'd known about Joseph's cancer. So I guess they'd decided to get it over with.

I wasn't ready to just walk away, so I got Janey's lighter out of her pocket and lit up a bit of sage. While the smoke curled up toward the hot blue sky, I whispered a litany of goodbyes. Yes, a desert can be too hot and too dry.

Goodbye, I whispered. Goodbye to the marshes and the ducks. Goodbye to the antelope and the sage grouse. Goodbye to the migratory birds. As I chanted, Janey and her dad began to fade and flatten into the ground. Their clothes became rags tangled with whitened bones. Janey's long brown hair wound its way into Joseph's vertebrae. By the time I'd reached my goodbye to the wild horses, their bones had disintegrated and settled into the sand, leaving nothing behind but their clothes, faded and flattened as if by years of heat and dry air.

I sat back on my heels and contemplated. I'd never seen decomposition happen so fast. Did my litany of goodbyes do that? Was creation trying to tell me something? After grinding the burnt sage into the dirt, I climbed stiffly to my feet.

That's when a decision made itself inside me. Looking around out over the flat land to the mountains, I said goodbye one last time. A tiny sparkle of quartz in the sand burst into a beam of light, catching my eye. The sparkle morphed into a thin, fragile sprout. I watched as long, slender, sliver-green leaves wriggled loose from the stem and tilted themselves to catch the sun. Creamy white petals appeared, and a mariposa lily smiled up at me.

I tossed Janey's lighter down onto the rag that had once been her T shirt. "Plastic is forever," I whispered. "Goodbye, Janey and Joseph."

Chapter Four

G oodbye, hell. I'd gotten all sentimental and sad over my goodbye to two humans, but there they were, back in my life again. I felt sort of pissed off at them.

"You can plan your own damn funeral service for the next time you die," I told Janey.

She grinned and said, "I'll burn some sage for you when you go. Since you like that sort of thing." Then she quickly turned her head to stare out the window.

I knew Janey and Joseph better than I knew any other humans. Actually, a lot of what I know about people comes from books. I read a lot of history, which is why I have a great deal of faith in mankind's ability to rationalize selfishness and to justify killing each other. Mostly I try to stay the fuck away from humans. Don't ask me how I learned to read, by the way. It just came to me, like the change from the old language of the People to the new language of the new people. In the old days, I hardly ever looked human, but now I passed all the time. Adaptation, I guess.

I'd been living in the desert near Janey's house since before she was born, so I'd known her and her dad by sight for years. Her great-grandparents were Basques who started out as sheep herders before buying their own bit of desert and running their own sheep. Joseph got out of the sheep business when his wife died and he got sick.

The news of the radiation leak came out the same summer that super-heat waves made it unsafe to land planes in Las Vegas, and cows died of heat stroke out on the flat lands. After the toxic leak from whatever they were doing on the military land, most of the humans moved away. Janey and Joseph had been the only humans left in my territory, so I started paying more attention to them.

I often saw them while I was out hunting. Janey was always trying to garden, and her sad rows of carrots and onions attracted rabbits, and the rabbits attracted me. Joseph set snares out for the rabbits and smoked them in the backyard. I ran then down and ate them uncooked. One thing about rabbits; there's always plenty of them. Janey would shake her shovel at them and swear, but they just couldn't resist sneaking in to nibble on her lettuce.

Janey and Joseph lived in a house that had been slapped together on the cheap and had deteriorated into a shapeless worn-out husk, the paint blasted away by the wind, the measly front porch askew, the back steps made of concrete blocks. Janey'd done what she could for the place. The roof was solid, none of the windows were broken, and the electric bill was always paid. She'd kept geraniums in pots out front.

After their car died beyond all hope of resurrection, I got in the habit of driving Janey into Jackpot for supplies. I benefited because she paid for the power up. We chatted on the trips back and forth, just casual conversation about how Joseph was doing and bitching about food prices. Sometimes she'd mention something about climate change. She told me once that she was glad she didn't have any kids. Well, she said she didn't think she could stand living with any goddamn kids, a comment she made after switching through the radio channels hunting something to listen to, but I think she meant more than just not liking that godawful noise they call music.

I helped her get supplies for her horse, too. Her name was Alice and she'd been a barrel racer back when Janey was in high school. I don't know if Alice and Janey got any medals or anything. Alice was pretty contented, as horses go, but really old. Janey always kept the shed in good repair and made sure Alice had food and water. Janey got a goat to keep Alice company—an only horse is a lonely horse.

I got my first clue that something serious was up with Joseph and Janey when I saw her lead Alice outside the fence to the open range. I was out hunting mice in the sagebrush, so I didn't let Janey see me. The goat noticed me though—her head jerked up at my scent. All three gathered in a little group and stood for a while looking out over the wide, flat expanse of grayish, greenish desert. Alice and the goat fidgeted, uneasy, but Janey just stood as immobile as a rock. I noticed a pair of vultures sailing in slow circles overhead, looking for the dead.

Then Janey said, "Go on, go on." Way far in the distance three cottonwoods stood together, green against the hot, gray land. On the far side of the trees, an old windmill still pumped water. It was left over from the neighbors. They'd cleared out after the mother got cancer. We couldn't see the windmill, but all of us—me, the goat, Janey, and Alice—knew the water was there.

"Go!" Janey's voice ripped out raw, serrated like a knife. Alice and the goat shuffled their feet, their heads up, eyes rolling.

"Go," Janey whispered. She pointed. "Go that way." Then she turned her back on the animals and stomped up the dirt trail to the house. She had to hoist herself up to get in the back because the wall and door were missing, swept away by the flood.

Yeah, it was weird to have a flood in the desert. The arroyo ran alongside the yard in the back. It was shallow and nearly always dry, since mountain run off usually sank into the ground long before it got to Joseph's house. But the pinon forest in the mountains had burned, and there weren't enough trees left to hold the soil or water. The winter snow, followed by crashing thunder storms in the spring, had dumped far too much water on the mountain sides all at once, and the water came roaring down and out onto the flat land. Along the way the water had picked up dead wood, old bones, and a ton of dirt. It blasted its way down the arroyo like a giant bulldozer and spilled out over the sides. The roaring and tumbling was done by the time the flood reached Joseph's house, but the water was over the bank, spread out on either side, and still pushing a load of mud, sticks, and bones.

The debris got jammed up on Joseph's back steps. The steps held long enough for more debris to pile up, grinding and poking and dragging at the back of the house until a big hunk of the back wall tore out, leaving the kitchen plumbing dangling like the eviscerated innards of a road-killed animal. Janey and Joseph were out in the front yard with Alice and the goat when it happened. When Janey and Joseph went back into the house, part of the kitchen wall was gone and their plumbing was fucked. It was a couple of days later that she sent Alice and the goat over to the neighbor's spread. A little after that I got my premonition, and then they died.

"So, how was it? Dying?" I asked. I startled Janey into a laugh.

"It was like being in high school again." She grinned. "Drunk on my butt. I haven't done that in years."

She wasn't really answering me, but that was okay. If she didn't want to share, she didn't have to. I was curious, though. I've seen a lot of lives come and go, but I've had never had the chance to talk about it with a human. I assumed that humans went from their living molecular structure to being distributed throughout creation, dissipating like a fog in the sun. But that doesn't explain how it feels, does it?

Chapter Five

We were coming up on the Backbone Range when Joseph suddenly started speaking in the old language of the People. To my surprise, since I hadn't heard the old words in years, I understood that he was saying: "Be careful now. You're leaving our territory." All Janey heard was words full of clicks and round vowels. Both Janey and I turned to stare at him, and I had to yank on the wheel to get us back on the road.

"Hey, Dad?" she asked. Joseph snorted and his head rolled. He was still asleep.

"That was the old language." I told Janey. "I mean from the tribe that lived here before you white people."

"Weird," Janey frowned. "He doesn't know any of that."

She turned back to look out the window. The road was making a long, slow, slanting turn up the shoulder of the mountain. We both watched as the sagebrush gave way to the dense, dark pinon pines. It felt odd to be rising up from the flat land. A few more turns of the road and we would arrive at the top of the grade.

"Mom used to come up here for the berries." She spoke quietly. I could only see the back of her head, but I wondered if she was crying a little.

"Wanna stop?" she asked.

"Okay." I think we were both feeling our insides get knotted up. I slowed and started looking for a wide spot on the shoulder. The road leveled a bit, then headed due west into the sun. I squinted. Even with the cloud cover, the sun was baking hot. I saw a a thin trail leading off into the pinons.

"Here we go." The truck bounced off into the soft, sandy soil. I stopped as soon as we had a tree or two between us and the road. My door creaked as I opened it; it needs oil or something. I'm not really a car guy, and it was an old truck, one of the first electric ones. I got it second hand. I let my boots hit the ground, stood up, and did a few stretches. I hadn't been driving long enough to get really cramped; I was just procrastinating before we took that long, last look.

Janey had her head poked into the backseat while I looked around. Pinons are small trees. Densely green, they stand at a distance from each other so each tree has its own little territory of sandy dirt. There was no view out over the valley. Janey withdrew her head, shoved her hair out of her face, and said, "He's dead to the world, heh, heh."

I grinned back at her. "Zonked out, huh."

"Could be hung over." She walked around the truck and joined me. "Let's see if there's a view down that way."

We moseyed through the pines down a gentle slope. It became clear after a while that we weren't going to find a good view spot unless we headed back to the road, so we cut on over. The pines had a thick resinous scent that I liked. I inhaled deeply, as if I could suck the scent in and keep it with me. Janey walked heavily. I was surprised. I guess I thought a ghost would float.

We left the trees and walked out on the shoulder of the road. The far side had a short steep bank that would give us some elevation, so we crossed the road and scrambled up. I noticed that Janey seemed to have as much trouble getting traction as I did.

I said, "I thought ghosts would float."

She shrugged. "I thought ghosts were fiction."

We stood side by side and faced east. The Valley of Dry Bones lay out flat as a table top. The clouds had thinned, letting more sun in and washing out the colors of the sage and soil, but making purple shadows. The faraway mountains on the east side of the valley caught the sun and were grayed out like a faded photograph. I let my eyes follow the road, flat out across the valley with a little bump in the distance for the Sandy Creek arroyo. Farther away, the raggedy cluster of metal and wood of the truck stop and the trailer court was visible mostly as glints off the metal roofs embedded in the dull gray-green of cottonwoods. The main road headed northeast and eventually got to Salt Lake. Joseph's house was forty miles south on the secondary road. I could see some of that road, but I couldn't follow it all the way back home.

It used to be that, even in the summer, the desert was a land of contrasts between wet and dry. The run-off from the mountains pooled and sank into the soil, making spots of vivid green reeds and rushes where water birds nested. The desert itself flowered, sometimes so densely that the land looked like it had been painted. Even in mid-afternoon on a sunny day the valley had been full of life. Sleepy life: ducks snoozing in the reeds, antelope with their fluffy white cloud-butts snoozing in the shade of cottonwoods along an arroyo, the People napping in their brush shelters, and the slow sleepy circulation of hawks riding thermals. A snake's eyes unblinking in the darkness under a rock. The silent sparkle of dragonflies over water.

In the old days, my time had been ruled by the sun. I hunted at dawn or dusk when the air was cool enough for small mammals to be out and about. Like everyone else, I found shade during the day and slept the heat away. After sleeping, I'd go to the nearest spring or run-off pond and have a good, long drink. But always, always, always I was out in the desert, my feet on the soil, my nose full of the tang of sage, my eyes skimming for movement, and my heart full of beauty.

My home had been gone for a long time.

I wondered how Alice and the goat were doing.

I felt Janey shift position from one foot to the other. We caught each other's eyes, and she grimaced quickly, then turned away.

"Let's go," I said.

Chapter Six

I frowned at the beer selection. Grocery stores were getting more and more hit and miss on what they had in stock, and the prices justified crime. It had dawned on me, while driving over the mountain, that I was probably not going to be living on rabbits for awhile and needed to do some foraging in a grocery store. Janey and I had brainstormed a shopping list even though neither of us was sure that ghosts could eat.

Beside me, Janey was bouncing on her toes impatiently because she didn't care what brand of beer I got. I frowned at her, and she frowned back at me. "Hurry up!" she said. "It's all just beer." An old rancher wife shot a glare at me, thinking I was talking to her. I hissed, "Shhh!" at Janey which didn't help.

Janey had figured out that she could make herself invisible to everyone but me, and she was enjoying the opportunity to freak people out. I don't usually give a shit what people think of me, but when you're setting up a flimflam, it's best not to draw attention to yourself. I dragged a six pack out and loaded it into the cart. Then the cooler case opened and a second six pack of a different brand made the short trip to the shopping cart. The rancher wife stared, her mouth a round red hole. I kicked Janey in the ankle as I pushed past her, and she snickered.

The grocery was big and busy. Not too far off the highway, it was the go-to place for Ely and everyone else within a drive of two or three hours. Even though it was just about the only place to stock up on food, there were empty shelves in every aisle. I saw two white ladies arguing over the last can of tuna. This is the world you made, bitches, I thought.

Janey and I cruised the aisles, tossing grab-and-fix foods into the cart. After hunting down some big wooden campfire matches, I stopped to inventory the stuff in our cart. Food, check. Pan to cook in, check. Beer. What else? Maybe a cooler and some ice, if they had it. We needed all that life support stuff because I'd left with next to nothing. Just took off from the funeral with no stop by my cabin.

Suddenly, standing there in the grocery surrounded by all those women buying stuff for their families, I had a vision of my cabin. I saw it empty, the door hanging open and banging in the wind. It wasn't much—just a shabby wooden shack—but it had been my home for many, many years.

I felt hollow, as if the wind could blow right through me, and so sad that my boots were stuck to the floor and I had no energy to push the cart. I was never going to do my home rituals again. No more fixing a meal for myself and eating it while sitting on the steps and gazing across fifty miles of air to the mountains. No more deciding whether I felt like sleeping in bed in the cabin or sleeping outside under a sagebrush bush. No more enjoying the beauty of the desert. No more watching as seasons came and went, as births were followed by deaths. The cycles were broken and there was nothing left to watch.

In that moment I really hated humans. Then I blinked, my eyes focused, and I saw Janey standing by the cart—bored, fidgeting, probably worrying about Joseph out in the truck—and she was homeless too.

"What's wrong?" she asked.

I shook my head. "Nothing. Just thinking about what we need to buy."

I got in line for the cash register, and Janey walked around to the doors. Another one of those middle-aged rancher ladies was in front of me. I watched her pile her stuff on the conveyor belt and watched the cashier's busy hands process it all through. The cashier gave the white lady a practiced smile and a "Have a nice day" to send her on her way. I piled my purchases on the counter, mimicking the speed and the actions of the rancher lady, and strolled causally up to the cashier. She was a hefty young woman with thick black hair. Her smile was perfunctory.

I got two tens out and waited.

"Off the grid?" she asked as she swept the matches across the reader and dropped them into a bag. It was pretty common for people to more or less camp in their homes. A lot of humans were just barely getting by.

"Yep," I said. I groped around in my mind to get the magic working. It takes some concentration. The cashier was on autopilot, which was helpful to me.

"I have cash," I told her. "Can you break a hundred?"

"Yep, sure." That's when I got really busy. *Hundred hundred, hundred,* I thought at her, *those are hundreds.*

She held the bills up to the light and frowned. *Hundreds.* I bore in on her with as much force as I could, but my mind felt scattered and my power was weak. She set the bills down next to the till, punched two hundred into the cashier register, and started pulling out change.

"You take care now!" She handed me the bills and change with a big smile, and I grinned back at her, relieved that my scam had worked. I stuffed the money in my pocket, grabbed my cart, and aimed myself at the door at a fast walk. Janey, sniggering, joined me. I was almost trotting by the time I got to the parking lot, half expecting the cashier to come running out of the store, yelling. Joseph saw us coming and opened the truck's door.

We crammed the grocery bags into the back seat, leaving just enough space for Joseph, and we all piled in. As I drove for the road, I asked, "Janey, anyone chasing us?"

She swiveled around in her seat and looked back. "Nope."

"No one screaming and waving their arms around?"

"Not that I can see."

"Okay."

Janey settled herself into her seat and dug a candy bar out of her pocket. I headed out of town, watching her from the corners of my eyes. I was real curious about the eating habits of ghosts, if they had eating habits.

She peeled back the wrapper and sniffed. Took a cautious nibble. Swallowed.

"Good?"

"Naw. Weird." She grimaced. "I used to love these." Twisting around to look back at Joseph, she asked, "Hey, Dad, you hungry?"

He answered in the old language, "Not yet." Janey's eyes widened.

"Did you understand that?" I asked.

"Yes," she whispered. "Dad?" But he had fallen asleep again. To me, she said, "There's something weird going on with him."

I laughed. "Yeah, he's a ghost."

She glared at me, so I added, "Yeah, it's weird. But being a ghost is weird too, isn't it?"

Janey huffed out her breath, turned back around, and contemplated the candy bar. She took another bite and said, "It's okay. It just...not as much flavor somehow. Still..." she shrugged. "Whatever."

Chapter Seven

I found a National Forest access road that led off to the south. After turning off the highway, the long dirt road lay out in front of us, dusty and hot in the glare of the late afternoon sun. Janey moved the sun visor over, but the heat was cooking her ear anyway.

"I can feel hot and cold," she griped. "It's gonna suck if I can get wet too." We'd been speculating about destinations, and I'd suggested the coast up around Oregon or Washington, mostly because oceans and rain were about as opposite as you could get from hot and arid.

"Yeah, that would suck," I agreed. "Getting wet."

"It doesn't always rain in Washington though. Did you know I went to Seattle once?"

"No." I was surprised. I thought of Janey as being like me, a creature of the valley.

"I went there to visit my grandma. This was back before she died." She had her window down and the hot breeze was blowing her hair around her face. "I went up there just for a few days. There's this mountain." She sketched a mountain shape in the air. "Really big. Comes up out of nowhere."

"We have mountains," I reminded her.

"Yeah, but this one was different." She frowned, searching for the right words. "It's so big, out of proportion to everything around it. You can see it from anywhere. It looks like it's floating in the air."

I tried to picture a mountain floating in the air.

Janey shrugged. "Anyway, that's what I remember. That and the traffic is hellacious."

We ground along the dirt track through the sagebrush, making maybe fifteen miles an hour. I let my eyes roam and thought about rabbits. Usually this time of day, the time of long dark shadows, was good for hunting. Get my back to the sun, look for movement, creep up on the rabbit and pounce. But I wasn't feeling it. I was tired from being in the truck, tired from being around humans—but not ghosts. Ghost humans weren't tiring me out. It was the grocery store ones that drained my energy. But really the dragged-out feeling was from too much emotion. A funeral. Deciding to leave. The last good bye. I was tired.

"What's that over there?" Joseph was awake and speaking English. He pointed across the sage to a large rock and a clump of cottonwoods.

"Must be a spring or something."

There was no turn off but also no fence, so I gave the truck wheel a spin and we bounced off the road into the scrub. I kept the accelerator down and steady as we plowed through the brush, the stiff grass scratching and clawing the underside of the truck. I stopped about thirty feet from the cottonwoods because the vegetation was getting thicker and bushier. The sun, coming in as a long horizontal beam, hit the big rock and burnished the brown to gold.

We piled out, stretched out our backs, and looked around.

"Looks like a good place to camp," said Joseph. He headed straight for the cottonwoods.

When you have lived as long as I have, you lose your sense of time. As I watched Joseph shuffling through the rice grass and dirt, his moccasins scuffling along, his long hair coming untied from a leather thong, I thought: Wait a minute. That's not Joseph. His bronze shoulders were as leathery as an antelope's hide, and his sinewy brown legs were dusty. In one hand he carried a bow.

I cut my eyes to Janey to see if she'd noticed anything.

"That's weird," she whispered. She still looked like Janey: dumpy in her over-sized T-shirt and worn jeans. Really worn, not bought that way as a fashion statement.

"That's one of the people from long, long ago," she said, her voice thinned by disbelief.

The old hunter heard us. Moving stiffly, he carefully reoriented himself to face us, smiled, and called in English, "Hey, look, there's some water."

He was Joseph again. Old beat up, bent up Joseph with his sweet smile, his eyebrows lifting in question as we stared at him speechlessly.

"Water?" he repeated. "Maybe camp over here."

Janey cleared her throat. "Yeah, Dad, we'll take a look."

I wondered if Janey and I would fall through a hole in time if we went too close to the cottonwoods, so I kept an eye on her as we wound our way through the brush. Which made me realize something: Joseph seemed to be slipping into the past, but I had gone a long ways toward slipping into the present. I felt like something in me had broken. I wanted to get off myself and think about it, but Janey had her hand on my arm, tugging gently. "Look."

We were on the edge of a marsh that wasn't really there. The thick scent of mud hit my nose. Blue water, rippled by the breeze, lay deep and full of life under a haze of bugs. The reeds and rushes around the edge of the pond rustled softly, seed heads bobbing in unison. In a flutter of wings, ducks took flight, black against the white of the evening sky. Janey's fingers fumbled for mine.

"This isn't real, is it?"

I snorted. "We're having a mystical experience."

She laughed. "Ghosts in a ghost landscape."

And with that, the landscape became solidly real, stinking of cow shit instead of mud, with messy cottonwoods instead of reeds and rushes. Joseph, back to normal in his old plaid shirt, was pointing at the big rock.

"See that? Petroglyphs."

It used to be a good life, for the most part. The People were hunters and gatherers in the old days. They lived in extended family groups that usually got along with each other pretty well. There was a lot of bickering, the occasional shouting match, and a fight that did real harm every now and then. Humans are humans after all. Their claim to superiority over other creation is mostly a failure to be honest with themselves about themselves. I've never see a group of humans who didn't act like a wolf pack—concerned with ranking inside the group, concerned with holding territory, and concerned with being mean to those outside the group. But the humans of long ago didn't have the capacity to do lasting harm to the valley or the mountains or to the other species, and what harm they did to people was minor and intermittent. They didn't do genocide and didn't fuck up entire planets.

For example, they were careful not to over-hunt the antelope. They only had hunts every three or four years, depending on how well the herds were doing. They had an elder who studied the herds and advised on whether or not there would be a hunt.

They got along day by day, finding food, eating, fixing up their huts, raising their kids, making their baskets and arrows, dancing, celebrating the life-giving valley, and mourning their dead. Sometimes they'd get in fights with the next group over or a raiding party from far away. Sometimes the fights were pretty bad and a lot of humans killed each other, but mostly life went on day to day with the People minding the business of survival. I liked them, even though they competed with me for rabbits. They worshiped rabbits too, so that made it alright. They worshiped the sun and the rain and the dirt and the seeds and many of the animals. They didn't worship me, but that was okay.

But that was long ago. Their whole world was destroyed when they were invaded by people who did do genocide, though they did it slowly over about two hundred years. And over that same two hundred years, plus or minus some decades, those new people killed damn near everything. Mass extinction events, they call it.

I'm not sure I want to be around for the next two hundred years.

We puttered around making a little campsite for ourselves on the sunset side of the cottonwoods. Sitting in the dirt, we used an old blanket that had been in my truck forever as a picnic cloth, and we set out the food. I ate mostly with my hands.

After Janey was through bitching about ghosts not being able to taste stuff—which didn't stop her eating—we sat with our backs to the petroglyph rock and watched the sunset. The temperature was just right: not too hot like the day had been, and not as cold as the night was going to get. Joseph got his tobacco out and chewed, making the occasional spit off to one side. It's a gross habit, and I tried not to see the spit. We were quiet together until Janey said, "Well, it turns out that ghosts have to pee. Whodathunkit?"

She got up, brushed the dirt off her butt and looked around.

"We won't watch," I said.

She laughed and headed off into the sagebrush.

Joseph watched her and, as soon as she was out of sight, he whispered, "Maybe I should've talked her out out of it."

I was trying to keep our fire going, so only gave him half of my attention. "Out of what?"

"Dying."

I'm not the type to have human friends. Or friends at all, really. I've always been pretty content with my own company. If I felt like hanging out, I'd go find some coyotes. Real ones, I mean. So I felt really uncomfortable when he started crying.

"It's just," he wiped his nose on his sleeve. "It's a lonely thing, death, and she said she wanted to come with me."

"Her call," I told him.

"I have cancer. I was going to die anyway."

"All of you humans are going to die anyway." As soon as the words were out of my mouth, I realized that I wasn't being comforting. "I mean sooner or later, right?" I added.

Joseph's eyes were leaking, and he snuffled, "But she still had years."

"Why are you thinking about this now?"

"The sunset I guess. Look how beautiful."

The sky was lemon yellow and orange over blue mountains. Yes, beautiful as desert sunsets usually are. The air was still and scented with sage.

"I used to sit out on the back porch and watch the sun go down. It was like a meditation or prayer. I did it every day, even in the winter," Joseph said.

I knew that. I'd seen him.

"Janey said it was boring, and besides I was going to catch my death of cold sitting out like that."

We heard a crunch and a muttered swear word. Janey was on her way back.

Janey and I put Joseph to bed in the back seat. We sat out for a while longer, then argued about whether or not she should sleep in the passenger side. I insisted and she finally climbed in the truck. I walked back to the cottonwoods, waited, then checked. In the darkness, I could see a dim gleam on the metal of the truck but not Janey. I took my clothes off and headed out into the desert.

Chapter Eight

I wanted to be alone.

I wanted to hunt, too. Jack rabbits are really hares. Like me, they mostly are solitary, but they will group up sometimes, mostly for sex. The males fight. A lot. But only at certain times of the year. Humans think of jack rabbits as nuisances, but actually they're very smart and aggressive as hell. They're super fast too. I respect them. I'd say that when I hunt jack rabbits, I only catch one out of every four tries. Mice and ground squirrels are easier, especially if I have a badger's help.

I sniffed. A warm, dusty, musty smell floated in the air. Definitely the scent of a badger. I trotted off into the sagebrush, following my nose. Pretty soon I could hear her. She was digging up a gopher tunnel, always a noisy activity. Badgers are big weasels. They are very single-minded, determined animals, the only animal that reminds me of a machine. They remind me of rototillers.

I found her after about a quarter mile of trotting between sage bushes. She was rototilling away at the dirt, flinging clods over her shoulder while grunting and snuffling to herself. I gave a brief yip to let her know I was there. She paused her digging, pulled her head out, and glared at me.

I can communicate with animals but it isn't like talking to people. We don't use words. I sent a thought about sharing over to the badger. Her beady eyes gleamed with wrath.

"Seriously, I will," I whispered. I used to share with a badger over in the valley on the other side of the mountains.

She grumped at me, not in words, but still a clear "fuck off" message.

"I'll share," I repeated aloud, while trying to radiate goodwill at her. I like badgers. They're hardheaded, suspicious, and smart. She rumbled at me a mixture of threats and complaints.

"You'll see," I said and I put my nose to the ground. I found the other end of the gopher tunnel about six strides away. People think that gophers are just wild rats and a nuisance, but they're smart little beasties. They have to be, since everybody eats them: me, badgers, foxes, snakes, hawks. Badger was drilling down into their plunge hole, a straight drop down to their hallway system. I planned to lurk at their exit. In between, they had a bathroom for pooping and peeing, a living room for hanging out with mate and kits, and a turnaround space since their tunnels were always a pretty tight fit.

I could hear badger making scary sound effects. She was probably down in about as far as she could go. I listened. Oh yeah! Here they came! I got the first one, a nice plump mouthful. The other turned around and shot back down into the tunnel. Badger stomped through the sage and snarled out a whole long string of insults about coyotes in general and me in particular.

I said, my mouth full, "You'll get the next one. Where there's one gopher, there will be more." I tried to send an apology her way, but I wasn't really sorry. She grumbled and grumped her way around a bush and stuck her head down a different hole. I trotted along, nose down, and found the other end. No sound from badger, though. I have excellent night vision, so I could just make out her furry butt on the far side of a tuft of grass. She wasn't moving.

I fidgeted impatiently. She let me know that she was waiting for me to go away. You'll get the next one, I thought at her. The distrust she sent my way was as thick as the stink of a skunk.

I tried to radiate trustworthiness at her and got a shitload of disbelief back. I understood her position. I've messed with badgers before, promised to share but ate everything they scared out. They don't like getting tricked the into doing all the work while I got the food. Tricking badgers is stupid in the long run because you can only trick a badger once or twice, and after that you have a enemy for life. Share, and you have a partner for life.

"I promise," I told her out loud, hoping my tone would reassure her. "I promise on the stars and the moon. The next gopher goes to you."

She curled her lips back from her teeth in a sneer.

That shut me up. I tried to think of how to convince her. Then I had an idea. I pictured the food back at my truck. I wasn't sure what she'd eat. Did badgers like peanut butter or corned beef hash?

She got the image of the truck and froze, rigid with suspicion.

"Yeah, sometimes I can take human form. I can get you..."

She was running, gone. Left me alone in the dark.

I sat down on my haunches and listened. No gophers out and about. We'd scared them all way down into their underground bunkers. Oh well, I wasn't hungry.

I was homesick. I'd joined in the gopher hunt for old time's sake, to feel like I was back home. Tipping my head back, I howled out a long, lonely cry of the heart. I could almost see my howl as it rose up to the sky and disappeared in the darkness between the stars. Every star in the universe was out and sparkling in the black sky. From horizon to horizon, they glittered against the infinite darkness of the universe. I've always loved the stars because I like to be reminded of the vastness of reality and the smallness of our little lives on our little rock. I usually find that perspective comforting. But that night, in the silence after my howl, I didn't feel comforted. I just felt lonely.

Chapter Nine

I slept curled up on the ground by the cottonwoods and woke to the sounds of people talking.

"Is it rabid? Should we get into the truck?" A woman's voice.

"It looks pretty healthy to me. For an ol' coyote." A man's voice.

"Why is it laying there like that? I have never seen a coyote sleeping. I mean I know they sleep, but sleeping near people and staying asleep while we stand here and talk? That's real strange."

I sat up. Both humans stumbled back, clutching at each other and babbling.

"Don't panic! It's me." I glared at them.

"What?" Janey leaned forward, squinting. "Jimmy?"

"Yeah," I sighed. I'd waken up too fast and felt shell-shocked.

"You're a..." She frowned, digging in her mind for the right word.

"You're a huachitua!" Joseph's face lit with amazement, at least partly because he was using a word he'd never heard before.

"A what?" Janey asked.

"Huachitua." I sighed again. I really didn't like being sociable first thing in the morning. "It's a word from the old language of the People who lived here before you guys."

"What does it mean? Where are these words coming from anyway? We never knew any of their words before!" Janey glared. She didn't like stuff that she didn't understand.

"It means a spirit. Well, it really means someone who can be two spirits, like coyote and human."

They stared at me blankly. Then Joseph asked, "Are you the reason we're ghosts?"

I hadn't thought of that, but maybe he was right. "Look, I'm getting dressed," I told them. "If you don't want to see a naked guy, then go away."

Neither left. They stood right there, Janey gripping her Dad's arm, their mouths open like idiots, while I changed to human. I found my jeans and T-shirt and hunted around for my socks. Then I got dressed and headed for the truck.

"Where are you going?" Joseph quavered.

"Coffee," I said.

No planning meant no cook stove, which meant no coffee unless I could get a fire going. I sent Janey and Joseph off to look for anything burnable while I broke twigs off the lower cottonwood branches. There were a few small branches on the ground and a very old, very dry cow patty.

The ghosts found a few sticks and, together with my offerings, we got the bare minimum of a fire. We made hot water and added in the instant coffee from our shopping spree. It was the worst coffee I'd ever tasted. I took a sip made a face and set my cup down. Janey and Joseph were staring at me, tracking every move with fascination.

"Look," I snapped, "being a nature spirit isn't any weirder than being a ghost."

"I just didn't know that any of the old ghost stories were true. I mean you're a shapeshifter." Janey sounded almost pissed about it. "So what else is true? We've got ghosts and a shapeshifter..."

"Well, don't get carried away believing stuff. Mostly stories are just stories. People don't understand even half of what they think they understand."

"So what," she hesitated, glanced at Joseph and asked, "what else is true? Werewolves?"

"Not around here." I tried another sip and made another face. "Look, people believe all kinds of crap. I just know that most of it's BS. Nature spirits are real. There used to be water spirits around before so many of the marshes dried up. Stars are just stars but there's something holy about them too. Bones. Mountains. I don't understand all this religious stuff either."

I shrugged. Janey and Joseph were still staring at me, so I said, "Why do you expect me to have all the answers? You're ghosts. That hasn't given you any great insights, has it?"

"No," said Janey. "It hasn't."

Joseph said, "I never believed in ghosts, or fairies, or any of that but I always sort of thought that all of the religions were true. I mean at the center. God. Creation. Being good, as good as you can be. Do no harm."

Janey's mouth twisted into a strange, sad smile. Her glance at her dad was both fond and mocking. "And I've always believed that all of the religions were equally wrong."

"Well, I believe in creation." I stopped and thought a bit. "And that we shouldn't fuck up creation."

Joseph nodded. "I believe that."

Janey just shook her head at both of us, smiling sadly.

Chapter Ten

We drove and drove across the desert. I never got tired of watching the flat land, the long distances, or line of mountains on the horizon. At Winnemucca, we charged up and paid real money, but we scammed another grocery for supplies. Then we turned north on the two-lane blacktop road. I can't abide the interstate, and Janey and Joseph weren't in a hurry to get anywhere.

In fact, I could feel something dragging at them. You know how sometimes you can feel that a decision has been made even if you don't know what it is? You just know? Janey and Joseph had started talking the old language more than English. They chatted in that intermittent way traveling people do:

"Just look at that!"

"An antelope. All alone."

"Yeah."

Or, "They have hot springs up here. I seen pictures."

"Yeah."

Just chat like that. But always to each other. Never to me. I said once, "You know you guys are talking the old language, right?"

Janey laughed. "I'm getting used to it. I guess it comes with the deal, like a computer that has programs already installed." Then they went back to chatting with each other.

The road meandered north sometimes, west sometimes, then ambled north again. It was a road that invited slow speeds. The landscape was lumpy and rolling, grassy with breaks of sand and dust. We rambled along, going only about thirty miles per hour, slow enough to watch the dried grasses and silvery sagebrush go by. The mountains were closer, near enough to see the dark covering of conifers. Jagged peaks scraped the hard blue of the sky. The peaks looked harsh and unforgiving, eternal.

My foot just couldn't make the truck move any faster, as if some force was on the brakes. In fact, I got such a strong drag that the wheel almost turned itself, and the truck bounced off the road and onto a small playa. Not the one where they used to do Burning Man. Just a small playa surrounded by low hills with a bright green reedy spot tucked into a ravine.

We piled out and gathered on the edge of the playa. It looked like an old lake bottom, but the dun-colored expanse of cracked, dried mud was perfectly flat. There was nothing growing out there. It was as strange a world as the surface of the moon. The silence was loud in my ears.

"It's weird." Janey tried to shade her eyes with her hands.

"I think it's kind of peaceful," Joseph commented. He let out a big sign of contentment.

"It's kind of hypnotizing," I said. The cracks zigged and zagged out over the surface randomly. Or maybe not random? Maybe there was some order to which part of the playa dried up first and which dried up later. I couldn't decide if the playa was really beautiful or really ugly.

"What's that over there?" Janey, squinting in the sun, pointed across the bare brown ground. Next to the green patch at the foot of the hill we could see some odd white shapes like melted candles.

"Let's go look."

The sun beat down on us as we hiked along the edge of the playa. All three of us were hot by the time we got close enough to see what the weird melted candles were.

We'd found a hot spring. They bubble up all over the northwest corner of the Nevada because of something geological going on under the earth's crust. Our spring was hot and poisonous and had made strange white statues of mineral material. Beautiful and alien, not life-giving to us mammals.

"Looks like sculpture of something. I don't know what." Joseph fanned his face with his hat. The white shapes twisted up in towers about six feet tall.

"Ghosts," Janey said. "Like us."

Now that we were closer, I thought they looked like the memory of herons.

The spring was oozing stinking mineral water that spread out over mud and sank back into the ground. A fresh water spring nearby leaked a thin trickle that wound its way down through the rocks and merged with the mineral water, forming a small pond. There was enough fresh water to nurture a few rushes and reeds. It was the kind of place that used to provide shelter and forage for the migratory water birds.

There were no birds, but a wisp of breeze brought the sound of singing. All three of us turned as one and stared. Janey gasped with amazement, clutching Joseph's hand. I was pretty surprised myself.

Out on the playa, a ring of dancers was preforming a ceremony. They were dressed in costumes made from whatever they could find in the landscape but so cleverly shaped that I saw the dancers as antelopes, jack rabbits, and sage grouse. The jack rabbits and antelopes were male, but the sage grouse were female. They formed a single line and moved in a circle. Each species danced its own way, stomping, twirling, leaping. A small crowd, maybe as many as a hundred people, stood on the hillside, chanting and playing flutes.

Dust stomped up by the dancers got in my eyes, making them water. Janey and Joseph were transfixed, holding hands. I coughed from the dust, and Janey turned to check on me.

"Ooh, you'd better get behind some bushes." My clothes had fallen off and I was in coyote form. She was probably right; the dancing people or the watching people might not like to see a coyote at their ceremony. I retreated behind a stunted pinon and watched from between the gnarly branches.

I knew what was going to happen, but it didn't play out as I expected. Janey and Joseph got each other by the hand and approached the dance slowly. Janey had one hand up in greeting and suddenly the the whole vision disappeared, leaving Janey and Joseph standing on the edge of the playa, her hand up, greeting the silent air. And I wasn't a coyote any more.

I walked out from behind the bush, wincing a bit from the sticks and little rocks, and put my clothes back on.

We sat on the truck and ate some lunch, me on the top of the cab, Janey and Joseph on the tailgate. "They aren't our ancestors." Janey said. She added for my information, "We're Basque on one side and Irish on the other."

I was eating corned beef hash cold from the can, which grossed Janey out. She was eating one of those little cakes that comes wrapped for sale next to a cash register or in a vending machine, which grossed me out.

She wiped her mouth on her sleeve and asked, "Why don't you live more in that...time travel world or whatever it is, Jim? It's real, isn't it? I like it over there."

Yes, I'd thought about staying in that other reality and, yes, I did like it over there. "I want to find out first if there's some place for me here." Besides, I wasn't dead like Janey and Joseph.

We munched on our lunch for a while. The playa felt very lonely and empty without the dancers.

"Dad, could you understand what they were singing?" Janey asked.

"Some of it." He licked his fingers clean.

"It was that language that we've been speaking," Janey said, "but I had trouble making out more than a word or two." She paused, then chanted softly, "In beauty I walk."

Joseph didn't answer. We all knew that somehow Janey and Joseph had learned the old language, and we knew what that implied. I ate more than I needed because I felt empty inside. Janey started packing the food away. We'd picked up a cheap cooler and a box for the canned goods and can opener. She fit things together methodically while Joseph and I watched. Then she slid down off the tail gate and turned around.

"Jimmy?"

"Yeah."

"I guess we just don't want to go to Washington. All that rain."

"We're desert rats," Joseph said apologetically.

"Yeah." I got off the cab and jumped down, making a little puff of dirt. Janey helped her dad get off the tail gate. Saying good by can be real awkward. We all just fidgeted and looked at each other. Then I stuck out my hand to Joseph and said, "Good luck, old man."

He smiled and said in the old language, "In beauty may you walk."

Janey grimaced, the closest she could get to a goodbye smile, and said, "You take care of yourself."

"I always do."

She was blinking back tears, which surprised me. She got her dad by the shoulder and turned him away, and they set out across the playa. They got about halfway before they vanished.

THE OCEAN

Chapter Eleven

The ocean didn't look anything like the pictures I've seen. Like the desert, it was mostly flat, but there were no distant mountains. No distant anything except the faraway line between water and sky. Between that line and me what I saw was mostly textures in silver and blue, ever-shifting in patterns that repeated, ever-changing but always the same, row on row of shades of blue splashed with froth in the front and silvered with the reflections of the sun way out on the horizon. The froth splashes got big near the shore and rolled over and spilled out on the sand, surging up the beach to my feet. The repetition was hypnotic. I don't know how long I sat staring at it. Well, I can make a guess: a couple of hours. The sun moved from overhead to part way down toward the line between sky and water. The movement of the sun changed the colors, deepening the blues and brightening the silver into gold.

That was just the surface. The ocean boomed and boiled with underwater currents that I couldn't see, but I could hear and feel. Scary, and full of eternal power. But not eternal life. Under the waves, the ocean was as fucked up as everywhere else. The fisheries had crashed, and the seabirds and sea mammals were starving. I thought about their vanished lives as I listened to the boom and boil. I'd only been on the coast for half a day, but I'd already seen places where the ocean was getting revenge.

I'd arrived at the ocean that morning after driving down out of the mountains. Feeling stunned by all the green of Oregon, I found myself in a world of blue at the ocean's shore. I kind of missed Janey and Joseph. What would Janey have said at the sight of the ocean? Something rude. Too noisy? The ocean was loud.

Down the beach, something screamed. My eyes tracked the

meandering line of sand at the base of the bluff. Far away a little family huddled, the parents with towels, the kids coated with wet sand. The beach was out for us that afternoon, but at other times the ocean slammed into the bluffs, biting off big chunks. There were warning signs posted alerting people to the danger that the bluff might suddenly give up and slump over, burying anyone who was too close.

I wasn't seriously worried about it. In fact, I felt almost good to be alive. Maybe I'd made the right choice back at the playa. In my head I kept a running commentary to Janey: You'd hate this place, girl! Too fucking wet! I grinned. My skin was coated with salt from the spray.

Well, time to hit the road. I was curious about what I'd see. So far Oregon had been oppressively green. The plant life abounded, crowding the forests, making it impossible to hunt rabbits—assuming there were any. I couldn't even get off the road in most places because the dense tangle of plant life was impenetrable. No ground was visible through the mess of leaves and forest litter, and no sky visible through the crisscross of branches and the layers of leaves. Even the places where the timber companies had scalped the land or places where fires had burnt life into charred stumps, plants were relentlessly taking over. Growing growing, growing. Burgeoning like the ocean but silently. I felt trapped between the mountains of plants and the pounding ocean, but I was interested too. Not my home, but somebody's. There had to be some spirits around somewhere.

I headed north on the coast road, a bouncy cheerful ride. The desert was mystical because death was only a whisper away, making life precious, but the coast of Oregon was abundant with life, disguising the deaths. Each turn in the road revealed sudden views of green valleys dotted with black and white cows under a blue, blue sky. I caught glimpses of dappled shade beneath enormous mossy trees. Tall flowering plants decorated with double rows of lilac or white bugle-shaped blooms grew in masses in sunny spots beside the road. The first time I saw them, I was so astonished I nearly lost control of the truck. Foxglove. The name just popped into my mind. The plants along the road gave the impression of joyful life.

Yeah, but darker data points about the coast had been popping into my head ever since my arrival. The coast was talking to me, introducing itself, and most of the news was sad. Shore birds used to fly up the coast in the millions, but all were gone now except for a few stragglers. I could almost see the huge flocks of tiny gray and white birds skimming in for a landing just ahead of the waves. Squadrons of pelicans used to wheel in over the water. Long strands of black scoters used to bob in the breakers like bathtub toys, imperious to wave action. Their populations had crashed, but I could sense them like ghosts out on the water.

Gone, too, were the otters, the seals, the dolphins, and the sea lions. First, the babies starved. For a couple of years, the beaches had stunk from the little bodies that washed ashore and rotted. Then, as the fisheries crashed, the parents starved too.

Still, the landscape seemed to be happy under the sun. Bushes flung out sprays of tiny blossoms as delicate as froth. Pink miniature roses bloomed along the fences. Arcs of spiky dangerous-looking vines loaded with white flowers crowded the roadsides. Those were bad, the landscape told me. Invasive blackberries. They killed native plants.

That was the pattern for the coast: pretty and full of life, but also darkened by the memory of the dead. Then I rolled into the first town since I'd hit the coast, and it was weird. The left hand side of the town had fallen into the sea.

They'd set out concrete blocks to keep drivers from going over the cliff while rubbernecking. I parked and got out to walk so I could gawk. I could tell that the town had once been a tourist destination and was still trying. Crammed between the mountain and the water, the businesses and houses were strung out along the road, barely hanging on and frantically advertising Seafood! Seashells! Art! as if aware that the water was coming for them. Not many people were parked to shop for the shells and nautical knickknacks. Not many walkers or browsers, no one headed in or out of the coffee shop.

I strolled across the road to the cement barricade. The beach below was a jumble of boards, roofing tiles, and chucks of house. I could tell that the catastrophe hadn't happened all at once because some of the houses were almost intact, though laying sideways, while others had been wave-pounded nearly into driftwood. A few tenacious pines grew at a crazy angles, still alive with their roots hanging out exposed to the sea.

I didn't know what I felt. Almost satisfaction—that's what you humans get for screwing up the climate! Knowing man, intelligent life created in the image of God, but not smart enough to heed decades of warnings. Yet the sky was blue, the mountains were green, and on the other side of the street a coffee shop was open in case any tourist like me wanted to stop, view the wreckage, and spend a little money.

So I drifted back across the street to check out the remaining businesses. A bank was still open. Next to it a couple of cottages built back in the twenties were now used as stores. One sold fish. Not real fish. Pictures of fish on flags, T-shirts, mosaics for your garden, sun catchers of fish, stuffed toy fish for the grandkids. The cottage was painted pink, and the fish were turquoise, orange, red, yellow—every color, like a box of crayons.

A more sober weathered gray cottage next door was a home. I could tell by the potted petunias on the porch and the fat old woman slumped in a deck chair out in narrow strip of unmowed yard. She caught my eye and gave me a little wave of one hand.

"Hello, sailor." Her grin made her words a sly joke which I didn't understand.

"Hey." I slouched over, not sure I wanted to talk, but not sure I wanted to ignore her either. She was a beached white whale. A vast T-shirt covered the lumpy terrain of her chest and thighs. Fat red feet strained against her pink flip flops. A tiny dog peaked out from her armpit and yipped.

"Oh hush!" she rebuked the dog. She smirked up at me. "Coyote, huh?"

I nodded my realization. "Seal."

"Uh huh, but I don't go out in the water much anymore. No point."

So this is how the local nature spirit lives, I thought. She had pink plastic flamingos sprouting out of a flower pot on her porch.

"Whaddaya think of our beach front?" she asked with a grin.

"Looks like it's closer than it used to be."

She laughed. "Yeah, those people from outside with money, they bought up the shoreline to be close to the water views." So I wasn't the only one enjoying the karmic forces. And I could see what she meant. On the remaining side of the street, the buildings were all older, dating back to the fifties and back even farther to the twenties.

"Used to be summer was the time to be here. Now it's the winter." She saw my skeptical look. "No, I mean it. I got a front row seat. You should see the storms come in. Waves has high as that barricade over there. The water comes right up on the road."

"What are they going to do when the road goes?"

She laughed. "Block it off. No more coast road. So drive it while you can." Then she sighed heavily. "They'll fix it up nearer to Portland."

She gazed out at the sea, shutting me out. I took that as a signal that our chat was over, so I said, "Well, nice meeting you."

"Drive safe." She kept her eyes on the ocean. "Say hi to the real world for me when you get there."

"Will do."

Real world? She was firmly rooted in her little bit of shoreline, even if her territory was just a funky little village, already halfway into the sea, and a stretch of water with no fish. I wondered if she was the force that was keeping people there when the sensible thing to do was to pack up and leave. I got in my truck and I left.

Chapter Twelve

I saw a hitchhiker up ahead. She was standing in one of the rare wide places on the road, a slender female with a huge pack propped against her thighs. The wide spot was the drive back to a farm, so maybe her last ride had been the farmer. Or maybe the farm was her home and she was running away. I caught a glimpse of her face as I went by. She looked tired and annoyed.

The countryside was really working that bucolic theme with low green mountains mounded up in the near background and farm houses and cows nearby. The road had turned inwards from the sea and we could've been in the Midwest. Or at least my idea of the Midwest since I've never actually been there. I was curious about the farms; they seemed to be getting by. Not prosperous. I saw some tarps on roofs and some trucks that looked older than mine, but the farmers were still farming.

Then the road took a turn back to the sea and once again I was rolling along between the drama of mountains and shoreline. I saw an overlook that still had some pavement on it, so I pulled over and turned the engine off.

The sea had taken a big bite out of the overlook parking lot. I parked back about fifteen feet back from the edge, got out, and approached the cliff cautiously. The tide had come in and big blue and white waves were slamming into the base of the cliff as far north and south as I could see. The air was damp and salty. A little ways up the coast, a row of vacation homes were on their way down the cliff. Jagged bits of plumbing stuck out into the air, windows were long gone, and planks of cedar siding either desperately hung on to nails or popped out in defeat.

Weird feeling. Surreal, I guess. The happy blue sky; the greenery everywhere; and the tilted, broken, abandoned homes that had once been someone's pride and joy. I didn't feel sorry for the owners. Unlike the migratory birds, they were probably still alive somewhere.

I got back in the car, still balancing my contradictory feelings, and aimed myself northward. I was tired of the strange mixture of life and death. I was getting tired of the sticky, salty air. I was getting tired of my own thoughts. I was getting lonely.

I should've picked up the hitch hiker.

I needed somewhere to stop so I could sleep. I was getting tired of sleeping in the truck, but I didn't want a motel room. Too claustrophobic. My truck had a roomy front seat, but the backseat was only big enough to serve as a place for me to toss stuff. Books, coats, boots, whatever. I could squeeze in back there, but the fit was tight. I was tired of sleeping bent-kneed.

I was tired. Not the good kind of tired from running across the desert. A bad kind of tired from sitting too damn much and listening to the boring cycle of the same thoughts digging the same groove into my brain until my head ached. I was tired of driving, tired of sitting, and tired of me.

I pulled off at another overlook. The bluff was more or less intact because someone had put in a cement wall along the bottom. The tide was on the way out, but the summer waves were slapping cement. I could tell that winter waves went over the top; the dirt and clay was scoured back and the overlook, right where I was standing, was getting under cut.

So no jumping up and down here, I told myself. I'd stopped at enough of these places along the ocean road to be as savvy as a local, so my truck was parked back a ways from the concrete barricade at the cliff edge. Having nowhere else to sit, I climbed into the truck, propped the door open, and settled in to watch the sun set.

Late evening by the ocean was an annoyingly sunny experience. The beams of sunlight shot across a thousand miles of water, unimpeded by anything except the curve of the earth, and slammed into me full force. Despite the salty breeze, the inside of my truck heated up. The sky was stubbornly blue overhead and had no intention of darkening until the sun finally reached the horizon. I dug the map out of the glove box as much for something to do while I waited as for the information.

I had a ways to go before crossing the Columbia into Washington state. I was kind of interested in the floating mountain, but I was headed that way more by default than anything else. The alternative was to go back over the mountains to a valley dominated by an interstate highway designed to suck people either north to Portland or south to San Francisco. I had no interest in any metro area.

There was another choice. Why not turn around? But I clamped down on that thought. I had come this far, and I might as well complete the trip. I could always go back to Nevada later on if I wanted. Or go see the Rocky Mountains. What was left after all the fires. Maybe go to Canada.

The light changed, making my map harder to read. I folded it up and tossed in onto the passenger seat. Out across the ocean, the light show had finally started. Overhead the relentless blue was still holding on, but the distant clouds were gathering shades of color from mauve to ultramarine. The light hit the hillside behind me and lit the trees with gold.

Pretty shabby, as sunsets go, I thought. I liked the desert sunsets better, especially the backside opposite to the sun. That's where the real color show was, the lovely shadings from pink to rose to purple. However the mountains blocked the view to the east, so all I had to look at was the burning ball in the west, still glaring out at full wattage over the orange line of the horizon.

"Heh," I grinned to myself. "Critiquing sunsets." As if in response, the sun dropped a few degrees and the entire surface of the ocean was transformed into a field of silver and then, just as suddenly, into a field of gold.

"Now that's just plain garish," I said.

Then, just like that, the lights went out. The sun slid down out of sight and darkness settled in as soothing as a cool drink on a hot night. I sat up for a while, enjoying the cold breeze off the water and waiting for the stars to come out. Only a few appeared. I guess the stars were blurred out by all the moisture in the air.

The summer seas were relatively calm. Calm for an ocean, I mean, but still noisy. The roaring went on all night. Every time my legs cramped and I changed position, I could hear the roaring. It seemed a lot louder when out of sight. It was still dark when I gave up on sleeping, dragged myself behind the wheel, and rolled off in search of coffee.

Chapter Twelve

I found coffee up around a few bends in the highway in another village where all the ocean front property values had plummeted. The other side of the road wasn't prosperous, but the businesses were open. The little town had a fifties look with lots of one or two story block-shaped buildings with big windows and no charm whatsoever. People had added tackiness to the gracelessness by hanging signs painted with nautical imagery everywhere. I pulled into the parking lot of a restaurant where a sign assured me that I would "Have a Whale of a Time!" in Port Whatever. I'd missed the town's name on the way in and didn't care anyway. Coffee was my focus.

I stumbled in to a hot, steamy interior full of hunched-over old people, scrambled eggs, and the stink of old fryer oil. Clearly in command, a large woman in a tight waitress outfit signaled to me by rapping her knuckles on the counter. I complied mostly because a quick glance around the room proved that all the tables were occupied.

"What'll you have?" she asked with professional briskness.

"Coffee."

"Need a menu?"

"Nope."

She plonked a cup down in front of me and left. Lone coffee drinkers probably weren't big tippers. I took a cautious sip. It was good coffee. Life seemed possible after all.

Four sips later, I had regained enough consciousness to be slightly bored. By the time I got to the bottom of the cup, my brain had reactivated, and I'd started wondering why the cafe was functioning as an old folks' home. Maybe all the younger people had left town? The waitress kept herself busy, clumping heavily from table to table, teasing back when the old men teased her. The old women out numbered the old men but didn't seem to like the waitress.

I tried to catch her eye, but she wasn't going to look my way. Not for a lone coffee drinking out-of-towner who probably wasn't going to tip. I sighed. Then the door banged open and yesterday's skinny female hitchhiker pushed her way in, hauling her backpack by its straps.

Everyone in the room stared at her. I took advantage of the opportunity by holding up my cup and calling out, "Any chance of a refill?" The waitress gave me a blank stare. Then, to show me where I stood in the hierarchy, she moseyed over to another table of old guys. But she was headed my way, so I set my cup down.

The girl dragged her backpack to the counter and propped it up against a stool. She was young, a little stray cat, breathless from wrangling her baggage. With a whole row of stools to choose from, she'd picked the one next to me. She wiggled her butt onto the stool and gave me a wink.

I didn't wink back. The waitress lumbered up, carrying a coffee pot and a cup. I think she assumed that me and the hitchhiker were connected somehow because she poured coffee for the stray cat unsolicited and asked me, "Ready to order now?"

"No, but I want a refill." Pouring me another cup, she asked the stray cat, "Howabout you, hon?"

"Not just yet." The stray cat flashed a grin full of crooked teeth. "Give me a minute, okay?"

"Sure, hon." The waitress gave me a skeptical look—I was still too much trouble to serve—and stumped off. The girl scanned the menu. I planted my elbows on the counter, aimed my eyes straight ahead, and thought grumpy thoughts. I didn't want this stray cat.

"Hey," she whispered.

"What?" I gave her a brief glance

"You drove right past me. Didn't you? Yesterday? I know cause I saw the Nevada plates."

I really looked at her then for the first time. She had large gray eyes, but otherwise her face was plain and not improved by dirty, stringy blond hair. I liked the way her chin and her shoulders asserted themselves, but I didn't like her thin, brightly painted lips.

"Yeah, I saw you."

"You're headed north? I'm going to Rainier." She made her red lips expand in a slow smile and batted her eyelashes at me. "Give me a lift?"

I looked her straight in the eyes and said, "You're too young to be out hitchhiking."

Her mouth dropped open in outrage. "I'm twenty-one!" she lied.

"Twelve," I said.

She glared. "Fuck you. There's lots of guys. I'll get a ride with someone else." She turned her back to me then and got her elbow out on the counter, fencing me away.

No problem. I didn't want a stray cat. I decided to mess with the waitress's expectations by over-tipping her, so I dropped a ten on the counter and got up. The girl shot a look of hurt feelings at me, then quickly ducked her head.

I walked out into a gray day with low white clouds and weak beams of sunlight. Kind of like my mood which was gray and drab. I walked along the sidewalk past the shops selling tourist junk, a decaying motel, and the gate to a hillside of weather-beaten pink condos. The road arched up onto a high bridge. I drifted up the sidewalk while peering over the railing and watched the ground fall away to a river. The tide was coming in and had backed up the river water, making angry whirlpools. I lit a cigarette and leaned on the rail.

The water looked like I felt: conflicted. Back home I sometimes saw dogs out in the desert that people had dumped. I picked them up, if I could, and drove them to town and left them there. At least in town there was the chance that they'd find some human to latch onto. No dog was going to last long in the desert.

I didn't want a stray cat. I didn't want the stray cat to get picked up by some creep. On the other hand, the truck sure felt empty, and I was going her way. I'm an introvert most of the time, but ever since I'd left Nevada I'd felt like a tumbled weed bouncing out of control in the wind. But not a tumble weed that was tumbling to spread seeds. A tumbleweed careening down the beach, and what the hell was a tumbleweed doing near the ocean? I wanted to go home.

But I didn't want to go back to Nevada. Home was the Nevada of fifty years ago or one hundred years ago. That thought left me feeling bleak and lonesome. Face it, I was depressed.

I smoked and watched the battle in the water below. Both sides of the river were barricaded with piles of driftwood and busted up building materials which probably got rearranged every time there was a storm. Part of a faded sign stuck up out of the tangle. I tilted my head and read its message: "open eight to eight." I wondered if the owner of that failed business still lived there and could see the sign every day. Then I dropped the butt on the sidewalk and walked back to my truck.

The girl was standing outside the restaurant. She saw me coming and held her chin up. She'd made a trip to the bathroom to comb her hair and reapply her make up.

"I can give you a ride," I said.

She grinned, a sneer in her eyes. "Okay." With a huff of effort she shoved her backpack up against the side of the truck. I helped her boost it over. We climbed in our respective sides of truck, and I took off. We went over the bridge to a straight stretch of road. Since the meager sun was heating the truck up, I said, "Hold the wheel for me." She did, and I pulled my jacket off. She made me wish I hadn't because me taking my jacket off acted as a signal for her to take hers off too, and she used the opportunity to give me a look at the profile of her chest. Maybe it'd been a mistake to pick her up.

"Where are you headed?" I asked.

Her laugh had a jeer in it, "I told you. Rainier. I'm going to stay with my brother."

I took a quick look at her. I was getting mixed messages. She'd said "yes" to the ride, so what was all this veiled hostility about? Why the smug knowingness, like she had me all figured out?

"I just wanted to know how far you needed to go." I let myself sound annoyed because I was annoyed. "So where the hell is Rainier?"

Another sneer. "It's just up the road. In Washington. Basically, you drive straight up the road, and cross the river at Astoria, and keep on going." I was so totally stupid for not knowing this, of course.

"So how long would it take to get there?"

"I dunno. Four or five hours? We could get there today without much trouble."

"Okay." So I'd devote the day to the delivery of the bratty stray cat to her sibling. She was making me regret letting her into my truck, but now I had a destination and that was a good thing. I shifted into travel mode: sped up a bit, focused on the road ahead.

"There's a map in the glove box. Use it to figure out how far away we are."

She huffed with with annoyance, but she dug the map out and bent her head to study it. We rounded a few more bends in the road, crossed another small river, and she said, "It's about one hundred and fifty miles." She looked up at me and finally her expression was sort of almost neutral. "That's probably more like four hours than five."

I nodded. With just coffee in my stomach, I was going to need food. "We'll stop for lunch somewhere." For some reason her cynical, calculating look came back. "And we'll need to charge up the truck." She smirked.

I decided to just ignore her presence in the truck. She slid down in her seat and parked her boots on the dashboard. With an elaborate sigh, she settled into watching the scenery roll by. On her side that meant tree, tree, tree. I had the ocean view.

The ocean was gray and white, the same colors as the cloudy sky. All of yesterday's cheerful blue was gone, replaced by sullen, hostile clouds, and the sea water looked cold.

The landscape had changed too. The mountains were back farther, the road was flatter, and the human presence had increased with more houses, more roadside tourist traps, and more traffic. In places the highway had been rerouted inland because of incursions of ocean, while in other places they'd built the road up to act like a dike.

It was a jumbled landscape, a jarring and unpleasant mishmash of seaside pines and ticky-tacky houses. Each outbreak of housing was followed by a little stretch of windswept pines followed by ugly boxed-shaped structures selling chainsaw sculptures of whales or seagulls. Very little seemed natural anymore. I wasn't enjoying the drive with little Miss Stray Cat.

Which reminded me that I'd forgotten to ask for her name, and I hadn't given her mine. Well, she hadn't brought up names either.

Chapter Thirteen

An hour later, after miles of chewed up scraps of coastal forest between summer homes and tacky shops, Stray Cat suddenly spoke up.

"So where are you from?"

She'd startled me, so I took her question at a much deeper level than she'd meant it. I said, "I think I just grew out of the sand."

"Desert rat?" she joked knowledgeably. "I saw your plates. I just wondered if you were from Las Vegas."

"Nope. Been there, done that." And cheated, too, at the high stakes table. I really hate the casino atmosphere of humans frantically trying to convince themselves that they're having fun. The high rollers are even worse because they don't gamble for fun. To them, it's warfare. A pissing contest. I can out-piss any human, but it's not my idea of a good time.

"Oh? I'd like to go there. Just to see it."

I shrugged, "You can always look at pictures."

She made a disgusted noise. "So where are you going?"

I huffed a short laugh. "Rainier, apparently."

She frowned. "I mean for real. Where are you going?"

It was my turn to sigh loudly, "I don't know. I just thought I'd try somewhere different, but I don't know where that is yet."

She let some landscape roll by and asked, "Ever been to Washington before?"

"Nope." I decided it was time for me to interrogate her. "So where are you from?"

"Crescent City, California." she answered promptly. Too promptly, like a rehearsed lie.

"Why are you hitchhiking by yourself?"

"I told you. I'm going to see my brother." She gave me a side glance to see if I was buying it. I had my doubts. "He invited me to come up and live with him because I don't get along with my stepdad."

There was probably a little truth somewhere in that. Plus an implied admission that she was younger than what she claimed to be. She lifted her chin and shoved a lot of irritation into her voice. "Besides there's no jobs there and no one has any money."

I believed that. Lots of humans were having a tough time. She reached for the radio, saying, "We need some music."

I covered the knob with my hand. "No, we don't."

"I've gotta stop to pee," I told her. About an hour of silence had passed while I stared at scenery I hated, and she hunkered over on her side of the truck with the back of her head aimed my direction. We were in one of forested stretches. I saw a wide spot and pulled over. Stray Cat gave me a furtive glance that I didn't like. I got out of the truck and scrambled behind a tree. A quick pee later and we were off.

Ten minutes later she said, "Now I need to pee." Why hadn't she said so back when I was peeing? We could have used different trees. Stray Cat studied the map and said, "There's a town in about ten miles. It looks pretty big. I mean, big for around here."

"Okay." I could use a charge up for the truck. I was getting low on cash again, too. I hate to pay the real cost of things if I don't have to. On the other hand, I was reluctant to scam anyone with Stray Cat in the truck, especially on a road that ran north and south, trapped between the mountains and the sea. I decided to pay for the charge and wait on the scamming until we got to this Rainier place.

Rounding a bend in the road, I slowed down for another funky little town with fallen down buildings on one side and tourist crap on the other. Stray Cat was right, the little town was a bit bigger than most, though all that meant was more houses up the hillside and a few more businesses that looked to be on the skids. I spotted a EV station attached to the kind of grocery that sold junk food and probably had a public bathroom.

Stray Cat made a beeline for the john while I got out and plugged in for the charge-up. A seagull made a mewling cry and a big splat of white shit appeared on top of the truck. I glared skywards. Stray Cat came back and slammed her way into the truck. The clouds were darkening, settling down for the long haul. Gloom suited my mood, and the wet, salty air was making goosebumps on my arms.

"Hand me my jacket."

She shoved it out the window, and I shrugged my way in. After finishing the charge up—in my mind I still think "pumping gas" and "gas station"—I headed into the store. That's when a little paranoid thought wriggled to the forefront, and I decided to check my wallet.

I had complete official paperwork for my existence as a human, all of it based on the birth certificate of a male child who died about forty years ago, but a peek in the money section showed that my money was missing.

When did she do it? I ran my mind back over the morning's events. I'd had my wallet out in the restaurant, but little Miss Stray Cat had no opportunities to get her thieving mitts on it then. Oh. Back when I got out to pee. My wallet had been in my jacket pocket which I'd left in the truck.

Bitch.

The store clerk was watching me suspiciously. I held up one finger in a "I forgot" gesture and headed back out. Stray Cat couldn't get far.

She hadn't. I found her frantically pleading with an old guy driving a van. I marched up, set one hand on her shoulder, grinned at the old guy, and said, "Good morning." Then to Stray Cat I said, "I want my money back." To the old guy I explained, "She stole the cash right out of my wallet."

"I did not!" she yelled. Lousy liar. Defensiveness in every line of her body, shrill anger in her voice.

"Give me my money, and I won't call the police."

"Leave me out of this!" The old guy started rolling his window up. From the passenger side, I heard the thin whiny voice of another old man. "Tell those people we don't want nothing to do with them."

"I am telling them that!" he whined back.

"Well, call the cops, then!"

"I will! Give me a minute!"

Leaving them to argue, I snapped at Stray Cat. "Give me my money. I gotta go pay."

She dug the bills out of her pocket and threw them on the ground.

I said thanks with maximum sarcasm and headed back to the store. There was a line at the cash register, so I had to stand around while the cashier rang up a drunken woman in a T-shirt that said "Ask Me About the

Paradise Club" and a couple of teens getting pop and candy. I didn't even think of trying to scam because I was too pissed off to concentrate. Out of the corner of my eye I saw Stray Cat hoisting her backpack into the bed the of the truck. Then she stomped around to the passenger door which she slammed with all the self-righteousness of martyrdom.

I growled, "Thanks," at the cashier. She glared as if there was something fishy about me. I stepped outside the door and lit a cigarette. Then I climbed up into the driver's seat and exhaled a big cloud. Stray Cat leaned back and fanned her hand in front of her face. I put the truck in gear and rolled out on the road. A few puffs later I was out of town. I asked her, "Why are you here?"

"Those old farts were going to call the police." She softened her voice and lowered her head so as to look like a victim.

"Yeah, but why are you here?"

Setting her face in a cute smile, she wriggled, "You're a nice guy. I can make it worth your while to help me. Please?"

"Huh?" The ocean road was to curvy too allow me to really get a good look at her, but the glimpse I got showed her turned toward me, her chest stuck out in an attempt to show off her boobs.

"Aw shit!" I threw the cig out the window.

"What's wrong?" A quick glance told me that she was going for pouty now. "I can give a blow job while you drive. You won't even have to stop. A good one."

"Fuck, no. I don't do sex with kids." I didn't do sex with any kind of human, but I didn't tell her that.

She withdrew as if I'd slapped her. Made herself smaller, like a snail contracting itself into a shell. She even got her boots tucked up under her butt. A little kid act. Or maybe not an act? Maybe the real her?

I was driving too fast, so I made myself slow down. The landscape had changed again, becoming much more interesting, not that it mattered to me. The road swung up through a forest, out of sight of the ocean, and wound around the side of a big hill. I saw a place to pull over, so I did.

She unfolded herself slowly, eyeing me, not sure what I was up to.

"Lunch," I told her. "That's all. Food. You eat food, right?" She had the hostile eyes of a dumpster-diving raccoon. "But before I get the food out," I said, "I want to get something straightened out between us."

She made a small involuntary noise.

"I'm tired of your drama. Stop bullshitting me."

Her mouth opened but nothing came out.

"My guess is you ran away from somewhere. Home maybe with that evil stepfather. Nod or something."

"Yes!" She glared.

"I was planning to take you to your brother. Is there really a brother in Rainier? Or was that a lie?"

"He's real." It was getting hard for her to maintain the glare.

"Does he know you're coming?"

Her eyes dropped.

"No?"

"I had to just leave! He wasn't listening to me! I had to leave!" And now the tears were about to start.

"Okay, whatever. I'm not getting in the middle of that fight." I let my breath out in an exasperated sigh. "Look, I got no problem driving you to your brother if he's a real person who is really there in Rainier."

"He's really there. He'll take me in." She sniffed. Then she turned her back to me and muttered to the trees outside the window, "I'm sorry I stole your money. I shouldn't of done that."

"Okay." My anger was just about gone too. She was pathetic. "Okay. What's your name?"

Still talking to the trees, she said, "Tamar Jean. TJ." Then, "It's a stupid name. My mother made it up."

"TJ. I'm Jim."

She turned halfway back and started talking to her hands clenched in her lap. "I really did have to leave, but I wasn't living in Crescent City. I started hitching in Eddina."

I didn't know where that was, but I understood she meant she'd been on the road for a while.

"Most guys want something. You know. Something." And suddenly she was making eye contact. "And I *have* done it before. *Lots* of times. I can pay for my ride and lunch and anything else that comes up. I'm not a kid."

Humans are so damn weird about sex. "You don't owe me anything for the ride," I said. "There's no obligation." She kind of shrunk a bit at that, and I thought, well, maybe she did owe me something. "You owe me for trying to rip me off. You can pay me back by phoning your brother. Let's make sure he's going to be home when we get there. I don't want to be dropping you off on the front steps like a Fed Ex package."

She went back to glaring but not with any real heat. She dug her cell phone out, jabbed it a few times, and showed me a number displayed on the screen. The ringing was interrupted by a voice.

TJ jammed the cell phone up against her ear. "Gayle?"

I listened to her side of the conversation.

"Is my brother there?" Pause.

"Can I have that number then? It's an emergency." A female-sounding babble from the phone.

"It's an emergency! If you won't give me the number, *fine*. I'll just get it from directory assistance." She mouthed "bitch" at me. "Yes, I do know what his business is called. It's called Craig's Auto Supply."

"Okay." TJ chanted the phone number at me, as if I could help her remember it. She did some more quick jabs at the phone. Then she waited, eyes rolled in exasperation. Suddenly she said, "Hey, oh, Craig, it's me." She hunkered over and all the acid disappeared from her voice, leaving it shaky and vulnerable. "I have to tell you something."

I could hear a male voice mumbling.

"I know you're at work," Tj told the phone. Then, after a pause for more male mumbling, "Craig, I'm sorry, but I had to leave and I'm coming up on the bus."

Another pause and TJ shrilled, "I already left!"

After listening intently she said, "I'll be in Rainier at about one o'clock. You don't have to meet me at the bus station." Her voice wavered. "Okay, I'll see you at two. I love you." She waited a few seconds, then gave the phone a last poke and slid it into her pocket.

The corner of her mouth jerked in a sad smile. "Is that good enough for you?"

"I take it we need to get to the Rainier bus station by one." I opened my door. "Let's get something to eat."

We crossed the river at a place called Astoria. The Columbia River was so wide that it was like an inlet of the ocean. Halfway across the bridge, I nearly hit a flying seagull. The seagull wasn't flying low. I was driving high because the bridge was built way up in the air to allow container ships to wallow their way up river to Portland. I drove and drove and drove and was still on the bridge, still driving, before we got close enough to the far side to feel safe. Too much water for me. TJ noticed and grinned, "Not your element, huh?"

"Nope." I was curious about her at this point "Do you know this area?"

"Yeah, I grew up in Rainier. Then my mom got married and we moved to Eddina which is a shit hole." She grimaced. "So I'm coming home."

I hoped life would be better for her but suspected that it wouldn't.

Chapter Fourteen

It started raining for real once we got into Washington state. TJ told me that it was unusual to get rain in the summer. "Just the other three seasons," she'd told me. "Rains all the fucking time." We didn't talk much as we drove through the green forested hill country. I could tell she was getting anxious, though. She started fiddling with the radio again, skipping from one station to the next until I told her to just shut it off.

"You get along with your brother?" I asked since talking was better than the screeching and banging she called music.

"Yeah, pretty good." She didn't look at me when she said that. "He's a lot older than me. And he's married and has a baby." Then she did give me a quick glance. "I can help with the baby," she added, as if to convince me or maybe herself. "I'm more mature than I was last time I stayed with them."

"So you've stayed with him before?"

"Yeah. Rainier's a drag." She made a face and we lapsed into a silence that stretched until an intersection suddenly appeared in a gap between trees.

"Left," she said. She perched on the edge of the seat, her back stiff and her eyes on the road.

I turned onto a narrow paved road that meandered a few miles and then morphed into an on-ramp to a four-lane highway. A sign said, "Rainier 15 mi." I laughed. "They named the town for the weather?" There were probably towns in Nevada named Hot or Dry.

TJ frowned, puzzled. "It's not named for the weather. Oh! You mean 'rainier'! No, it's pronounced like 'Ray Near.' It's named after a really beautiful mountain. You should go see it sometime. The mountain I mean." She was twisting and fidgeting as if the seat was electrified.

"A mountain around here?" I asked, just to keep the conversation going.

"Uh uh. It's..." she waved her hand vaguely. "A long ways away. Over by Seattle."

Oh, the mountain Janey had talked about. The one that floated in the sky. I couldn't think about the mountain, though, because the highway had gotten crowded with vehicles, all packed together in a thundering herd. Then suddenly we all rounded a corner and got sucked down into a downtown of mostly empty red brick buildings near a decaying harbor. After a few blocks of stop and go at traffic lights, she said, "Left," again. I pulled into the bus station parking lot.

The rain had diminished to a drizzle that suited the town. It looked like a place for meth, booze, suicide, and rain. Everything—the parking lot, the bus station, nearby stores—was shabby and gray. Behind the bus station I could see a harbor where decrepit boats were tied to docks that looked unsafe.

She climbed out of the cab and stood next to me. "Armpit of the universe, huh?"

Not a town I wanted to live in. I pulled her pack out of the back, feeling a knot of dread in my belly. I felt like I was dumping a cat or dog off by side of the road. Not that I've ever done that, but people do it all the time. I've seen the desperate animals running along the highway, trying to catch up to whoever the asshole was that abandoned them.

"Let's go inside," I said.

"You'd better not be here when my brother shows up." TJ was dancing nervously on her toes, shooting anxious looks around the bus station lobby. "He's going to jump to conclusions. "

I snorted a laugh. "Okay, I'm just going to hang out over there like I'm waiting for the next bus. Just to make sure someone comes for you." I didn't think she was lying about being met; I just wanted to make sure that someone actually showed up.

We both shifted around on our feet, and she said, her head ducked down, "So...thanks. For the ride."

"No problem. Good luck." I was pretty sure she'd need some. I did a fade out toward some benches, picked a spot, and sat. She fidgeted by the door and stared out into the rain.

We were between buses, evidently. I was the only one in the waiting room, except for TJ, of course. I tried to look bored instead of looking how

I felt, which was nervous and pissed off. Nervous that no one would show and pissed off because what the fuck would I do with her then?

Tj stationed herself by the big glass front entry doors and kept up her anxiety dance, one foot to the other, back and forth. Then suddenly she stuck her arm up in the air and waved. She took a quick look back at me, then grabbed her backpack and started hauling it through the door and out to the curb. A red truck with a business logo on the door pulled up. The driver was a blond woman with a tight, annoyed expression. She didn't get out to help TJ wrangle her pack up onto the bed of the truck. TJ climbed into the cab and closed the door. The truck took off immediately. I thought TJ wiggled her fingers at me as she left but I wasn't sure.

I didn't miss the stray cat. I didn't miss the annoying messing around with radio stations, the constant role-playing of sex kitten or "I'm so grown up" or the pouting and the anger. I was thankful that she had a brother and was now his problem. But I felt bad anyway. Hollow. Pointless. What the fuck was I going to do now?

Other than leaving Ray Near, the town not named for the shitty weather, I didn't have much sense of destination or goal. I climbed into my truck, turned on the engine, and sat there watching the clouds leak rain all over the grimy gray of the harbor. A wet seagull hunched and shook its feathers. Then it shit a huge glob of white goop onto a piling. That's about how I felt about Ray Near, so I got moving, edged the truck out into the traffic, and started down the main thoroughfare on my way to somewhere else.

Four lanes of traffic lurched from one traffic light to the next through the dead downtown of empty buildings. No, not completely empty—there was a pawn shop, a loan shark, and a rent-to-own furniture store. Used clothes. No one on the sidewalks, though. The main drag took a sharp turn and arched up over a bridge, giving me a view of a harbor full of half-sunk boats and rotten pilings. More seagulls wheeled in the gray sky, shitting on the boats. The rhythmic swishing of my wipers smeared up my windshield, making everything in sight merge together in a mush of grayness. How the hell did people live there without being suicidal? Or drinking themselves to death? I had a little bout of self-destructiveness by lighting up a cigarette. Not that I'll get cancer; I don't get human diseases. I just know it's a nasty habit, but sometimes I want to be nasty. Me and the herd of other drivers finally extricated ourselves from the dreary town, and everyone stomped on their accelerators.

I drove until I got beyond the raggedly sprawl of ugly houses and rundown trailer courts and escaped out into the countryside of cow pastures and forested hills. Then I started looking for an exit ramp and took the first that came up.

The exit shunted me onto a beat up black top road that threaded its way through forested hills. I saw a sign that listed the distances to a series of towns with odd names: Humptulips, Queets, Quiliacum. A second sign said, "Olympic National Park." Somehow I had gotten myself headed north. Well, that's okay, I thought. I'll go see a national park. Maybe go look for that mountain in the sky later on.

Chapter Fifteen

The drive north from Ray Near wandered through a butchered landscape of clear cuts and tree farms of young Douglas-fir. I couldn't see any mountains even though I was set on a course around the Olympic Range which had, according to the map, peaks as high as 10,000 feet. I could only see the degraded, chewed-up sides of the foothills.

So I was feeling kind of depressed when the highway suddenly crossed a big river and veered west to run alongside the ocean. Between the road and the ocean was a thin strip of Sitka spruce forest that had never been cut. Thick scaly trunks grew up out of a luxurious green undergrowth of salal, elderberries, and Indian plum. I got glimpses of the ocean between the wind-blown spruce trees. Then, abruptly, I arrived at a resort. Out of curiosity, I turned into the parking lot.

The resort consisted of a row of small cedar-sided houses—too fancy to be called cabins—along a cliff overlooking the ocean and a lodge with a grand entry way for valet parking. The lodge was built out of stone and wood combined to look natural in the fake way that pleases the kind of people who want to enjoy nature from indoors. Lots of big windows.

There was an EV station. The price was sky high. And it was the automated kind that didn't take cash. I heard a soft whirr and a miniature van loaded with bulging bags of laundry shot by. The driver had brown skin and a long black braid. She stopped at one of the small houses.

No matter how hard life gets for the ordinary person, there will always be rich people looking for ways to spend money on themselves. And there will always be playgrounds for the rich, with the rest of us relegated to trespasser or servant status. That's the way of humans. I felt out of place just driving into the parking lot, and I knew I'd never see the inside of any of the resort buildings. Of course I didn't *want* to see the inside, but that's not the point.

The point is them that has keeps, and the rest of us do their laundry or take out their trash.

I let my truck roll slowly down the row of rental houses. They were all built to face the sea with no windows on the back. The architect had gone for a windblown style with slanted roofs and odd angular decks. Most were empty, but two had Lightening Bolt SUVs with black reflective windows for the gangster look, though the owners probably weren't criminals. Maybe banksters or some other legally sanctioned criminal. I'd seen rigs like that in Las Vegas, and the owner was usually a man accompanied by an expensive-looking woman.

The second Lightening Bolt had its back open, and a big fat cooler was plonked in the grass in full view of the road but conveniently out of sight of any windows. No people. I rolled up and looked around.

The maid in the minivan had vanished somewhere. There were no pedestrians out enjoying the cold, wet ocean breeze. Probably the expensive woman was inside with the bankster, taking in the view from behind a picture window. The resort probably employed some serf to lug in their stuff.

I left the engine in neutral and set the emergency brake. Then I slid out of the truck, leaving the door open, and strolled over toward the cooler. The best way to steal stuff is to be very casual and open about it. People notice furtive behavior but they don't notice ordinary behavior. I kept my shoulders relaxed and kept my eyes moving. Just a tourist here taking in the gray sky, the tasteful architecture, the neatly mowed grass, and the big fat cooler. I added a little magic: *Don't notice me. Don't notice me.*

I grabbed the cooler by the handles and heaved it up. Wow, Rich Guy and Expensive Woman were really planning a party. By grabbing the handles, I'd entered the danger zone. There was no way to explain why I was carrying a cooler that didn't belong to me. It only took six or seven steps to get back to my truck, but the whole time I felt like I had a target between my shoulder blades, waiting for a bullet. *Don't notice me.* I kept my steps casual and tried to look bored. Nothing to see here but a guy lugging a heavy cooler. There were no yells of outrage as I dropped the cooler into the bed of the truck.

I kept my pace brisk but not frantic on my way around the truck to the driver's seat. Still no one yelling. Off I went, but slowly, minding the ten mile and hour speed limit. I checked the review mirror and a dark-haired young man in a uniform was walking briskly toward the parked Bolt. The help, I realized. I made the turn into the EV station and took one last look back. He was dragging a suitcase out the back of the car and hadn't noticed the missing cooler yet.

With a gleeful stomp on the accelerator, I shot out onto the highway and got up to speed.

The rich will always be with us, the Bible says. At least, I think the Bible says that. If it doesn't, then it ought to. After all, they run everything. I was grateful, almost, to the bankster and the expensive woman for making my day. Nothing like a little theft to boost my mood. Plus I really wanted to see what was in that big fat cooler. But I was also feeling a little paranoid as my truck and I bounded up and down the seaside hills.

It was a beautiful stretch of road. Hills dark with Sitka spruce slanted down to cliffs that dropped down to sandy beaches interspersed with boulders. Offshore, ragged miniature islands of rock were topped with more spruce trees. They had to be super tough trees to live out there, blasted all winter by storms and soaked all summer by salt spray, with nothing to nurture their roots but the cracks in the rocks.

Even with my little pinprick of paranoia, I was really enjoying the drive. It was fun to curve around the corners, dive down the hills, and bound back up again. But that cooler sat in the back of the truck, my secret horde that someone might want to take away from me.

Mr. Bankster was going to call the police as soon as he saw the cooler was gone, and that probably happened just about when I got out on the highway. No. He'd call the manager first. He'd blame the staff. He'd spend some time shouting at the maid. Maybe he'd seen a glimpse of my truck or maybe someone else had. At any rate, once the they got around to calling the police, I'd be easy to spot. There was just one road up the coast and mine was one of the very few vehicles on it.

The road ran all the way around the Olympic mountains. On the ocean side there was only one town of any size and a few tiny villages. So some bored cop, sitting somewhere while hoping for a speeder, might break up the monotony by keeping an eye out for me. I slowed down.

Yeah, I'd been speeding. Some of the fun went out of the drive when I slowed but not all of it. After all, I assured myself, no matter how bored the cop was, he or she couldn't arrest me for stealing a cooler if I didn't have it. The time had come to get rid of it. I saw a sign that said "Beach Access," so I hit the brakes, made the turn, and swooped into a parking lot.

The sky was clearing and tentative sunlight was warming the asphalt, making the pools of rainwater steam. No one else was parked there and, from the looks of it, no one had been there for a long time. The bathroom roof was covered with needles and forest debris thick enough to support a growth of ferns and small foresty plants. The parking lot was getting fuzzy around the edges from accumulations of leaves and branches. There was even a young Sitka spruce growing through a crack.

I wrangled my funky cooler out of the back seat and set in on the ground. It smelled a bit, so I checked the insides. Nothing worth eating. The cheese looked soggy and the veggies were left over from Joseph. I hurled the celery off into the landscape and followed up with some brown lettuce and a few radishes. Then I tipped the cooler on its side and let the water drain out. My ice was long gone.

Now for my treasure chest! I heaved the rich guy's cooler out of the truck and set it down next to mine. Too bad I couldn't keep the rich guy's cooler since mine was crap. Oh well. So let's see what's in here, I told myself gleefully. I opened the cooler up and stared, astounded. Booze. He had a cooler full of alcohol. Some beer in bottles, some whiskey, some red wine. The only food was a boxed selection of cheeses with French names, some fat sausages, and some boxes of fancy crackers. And a cake. A huge double layer chocolate cake swathed in swirls of dark chocolate icing and decorated with red icing flowers, probably cherry or raspberry flavor.

I lifted the cake out reverently. I pictured the cooler sitting on the grass and decided that the rich guy deserved to lose that cake. Even on an overcast cool day, only an asshole leaves a cake outside.

Since his cooler was bigger than mine, I had to stash some of the contents in my truck. The cake was inside a clear plastic cover, so I set in on the floor in the back seat and lay a blanket over it. No way it was going to get over-heated on my watch. The sausages I ate while I wrapped the bottles of wine in my T-shirts to keep them from clinking and shoved them under the passenger seat. Everything else I packed into my cooler which I shoved into the back seat. Then I hauled the rich guy's cooler off into the woods and dumped it.

A few more big bites out of the sausage and I was feeling pretty happy. I'd eat the cake for dinner. Meanwhile I wanted to go for a run. I moved the truck into the shade—not that it was exactly sunny, but there was some blue showing between the clouds. I left the windows cracked to keep the interior cool. Then I stripped down, stashed my clothes in the truck, and hid the key under a rock.

Chapter Sixteen

God, it felt good to be a coyote. I took off in a run and bounded down the steep tail to the beach. The tide was out and miles of wet sand gleamed in the pale sunlight. The sky was a mix of gray and blue and so was the ocean. Waves rolled in, crested, and pounded the beach, sending long sheets of lacy froth up to my paws. A wet wind was blowing and the clouds shaped and reshaped themselves in ever-changing patterns—very much like the waves. I was surrounded by the movement of air and water. I leaped up on a driftwood log and flung myself into movements of my own.

Leaping from log to log was fun. I kept up a fast pace and really pushed myself. In fact, I made a game of it by pretending the sand was poisonous. Don't touch the sand! Most of the time I had only a short jump from log to log, but sometimes I had to jump five or six feet, and once I climbed up a pile of logs and made a huge bound across the sand to land on what used to be a small boat.

Stripped of their needles and gray, I couldn't tell what species the trees were. They were big trees, though. Since all of the branches had been battered off, they must have traveled a long ways through the ocean to get to the beach where I was having my run. I could tell the sea was using the trees as battering rams against the cliff. Like the waves and the clouds, the cliff was ever-changing, just at a slower rate. I stopped to catch my breath and looked around.

I had miles of beach to myself except for the seagulls. They wheeled overhead, making their lonely, sad cry. Long tangled skeins of seaweed had washed up along the driftwood piles. They smelled of salt and rot. I breathed in and out, enjoying the scented air.

Down the beach I saw silvery blue stripe across the moist beige of the sand. A stream! Good timing because I was getting thirsty. I abandoned my poisoned sand game and ran up the beach to the water. The stream was only an inch or so deep but had scoured the sand off the beach, revealing a mosaic of colored rocks. It was too shallow to drink, so I followed the water up to the bluff and made a discovery.

The stream had made an arroyo in the bluff by cutting its way under and through the roots of a Sitka spruce tree. I climbed over the drift wood to get a closer look.

The tree was suspended in the air, hanging on to the edges of the arroyo by its roots. Somehow the water had made its way under the tree. Over the years, as the tree grew bigger, the water had dug its stream bed deeper and deeper. Now the tree was huge—its trunk a good three feet across—and the arroyo was deeper than a human man holding his arms over his head.

The tree had been hanging at an angle for so many years that the trunk had grown in a curve as if it was dancing. The branches gracefully lifted skyward, balancing the curve of the trunk. The tree seemed to be frozen in the moment of movement like a photograph of a ballerina. But the tree didn't represent one moment in time. It had taken years and years for the stream to dig while the tree grew into the graceful, fragile configuration I was staring at.

"About three hundred years," said the tree. "But this is probably my last year."

"What?" I literally didn't believe my ears. I'd never heard a tree speak out loud before. I'd heard plants and rocks speak inside my head lots of times, but never out loud. "Did you just talk to me?"

"Yeah," said the tree.

I waited for more but that's all it said. Just one word. A silence stretched out. I sat back on my butt and contemplated the situation. What does a coyote say to a talking tree? "You're pretty impressive."

"Thanks," said the tree in a very dry tone. Another silence.

The tree had started the conversation but wasn't helping much to keep it going. "Is it getting hard to hang on?" I asked. My question seemed a bit personal, but what the hell.

"Harder every year." The tree sounded resigned. "The waves come farther in than they used to. I don't think I'll make it past the next winter storm."

I didn't know what to say to that. The first tree that ever spoke out loud to me was expecting to die soon. It was a shame that something so wonderful was going to finally give into erosion. Now the silence came from me.

"They used to call me the Tree of Life." There was a ghost of a smile in the tree's voice. "I mean back when more people came out here. People took pictures of me all the time. People got married in front of me. Heck, one woman came here to die. She planned it out. Lay down about where you are and cut her wrists."

I don't know what to say to that either. Pretty awesome.

"People still come out every now and then. Mostly checking to see if I'm still here."

I finally found some words. "So where do trees go after they die?"

"We don't die." The tree sounded annoyed. "We take another form."

Okay. But that was true of everything, wasn't it? We all got recycled. Still, the tree was a monument to persistence and endurance, so I wasn't going to dig for a better answer.

"If I had some wine, I'd toast to you," I told it.

The tree laughed.

"I didn't know trees could talk out loud."

The tree didn't answer. I waited. The breeze off the ocean ruffled my fur, cooling me off and making me realize that the sun was out and heating things up. My cake might be getting hot in the truck. Sunlight lit the golden rocks and sand of the bluff. I noticed a bright spot of red—some kind of wild flower that had sprouted on the face of the cliff. I waited for the tree to tell me what the flower was called, but heard nothing.

"Hey, you still there?" I asked. Stoically, the tree hung by its roots. I wondered if having curvature of its trunk was painful, like an unnatural curve is in the spine of a human or a coyote. More silence.

"Well, thanks," I said. "Nice meeting you."

I waited a bit more but something had withdrawn from the tree, leaving it not lifeless but not alive in the same way it had been. Or maybe I'd just imagined the whole conversation.

I felt like I should honor the tree in some way. Leave something for it. All I had to give was pee, so I gave the tree some nutrients. Actually I gave the base of the bluff some nutrients which ran down into the sand, but it's the thought that counts, isn't it? I mean in one way communion wafers are just crackers and sage smoke is just sage smoke, but just because something is symbolic doesn't mean it isn't real too.

I wandered back along the beach while thinking about the tree. And thinking about being dead. I'd lived for a long, long time. Most of what I cared about was gone, so death didn't seem like a bad idea. I could understand why that lady had killed herself in front of that tree, though wrist-slitting wasn't a method I'd choose. I liked the way Janey and Joseph had killed themselves better. Of course, they didn't seem to be all that dead. Not totally dead.

I started the steep climb up the trail toward the parking lot, still thinking about Janey and Joseph. Maybe they'd finished dying when they disappeared. I had assumed that they'd gone to live with that tribe on some other timeline. Didn't someone famous say that the past was never the past? Something like that.

I was riding a wave of nostalgia for the past as I crested the trail, but there was my truck, still in the shade, and a chocolate cake was waiting to be eaten. I shook off my meditative mood and unlocked my truck. It was still cool inside. My cake was fine. Good. I was looking forward to that cake. Time to go.

I wasn't as chipper driving north as I had been before meeting the tree. Even with chocolate on my mind, I'd sobered up. Besides, I was in human form again which meant my lower back ached. The road turned north and followed a river. The forest alongside the road was old enough to be interesting. It didn't seem like the timber companies had fucked things up as much as they had in other places. I liked seeing the thick trunks and mossy branches as I rolled by.

Then I rolled by an airfield, a couple of derelict buildings, and chainsaw-carved sign that said "Hell." Someone had taken an ax to the sign and whacked the "o" off. I was in the biggest of the little towns on the west side road.

I drove slowly down the main drag, past empty store fronts. The town's heyday must've been back in the fifties, judging by the graceless architecture. Most of the buildings were one story boxes with big windows. Most of the big windows were covered with plywood and decorated with obscure graffiti messages. I saw an EV station and stopped for a charge up.

I paid inside, plugged in the charger and froze, realizing that I had picked the wrong place to stop. Across the street was a brick building that had some style to it—wood and stone. It was the town's municipal building and had been built back when the community had some pride. Now it sported a red, white, and blue sign that said. "Patriotic Protection Force." Their police force had been privatized, outsourced to the local militia. Lots of small towns had done that and the results were scary. Shit. Since I'd pre-paid, I didn't want to leave before the charge up was completed, so I spent the next five minutes trying not to look fidgety and furtive. As soon as I got charged up, I headed straight for the driver's seat and fired up the engine.

I rolled slowly to the street, elaborately checked both directions, and pulled out cautiously, a model citizen and careful driver. But sometimes luck just sucks; I caught a red light which put me stationary right in front of the militia headquarters.

I told myself that there was nothing to worry about. If the rich guy had called the police, it would've been hours ago. And he probably didn't have a description of my truck. He was probably still blaming the maids. Most likely, the police never got a call about a stolen cooler. If they did, would they care? Besides, I didn't have the cooler any more.

Finally the light changed. I drove two miles per hour under the limit until I got out of town.

THE FOREST

Chapter Seventeen

Picking up speed but still minding the limit, I headed out. The road turned east. I was now north of the mountains but still couldn't see them. Back in tree farm country, the scenery alternated between clear cuts, dense masses of young trees, and stands of maturing Douglas-fir. A sign said, "Growing trees for the future." Next to it a broken down truck was parked off the road. Two sad humans were leaning against the truck bed. The man raised his thumb as I passed by.

My foot hovered over the brake pedal. A picture of TJ formed in my mind, and my gut tightened up at the thought of how she'd paid for rides. My foot went down on the brake and I pulled over. Then I backed up, keeping to the shoulder. A big semi truck blasted by, followed by a couple of pickup trucks. I stopped and got out.

The two humans turned out to be three because the woman was holding a baby. The father and mother had that half-feral look people get when they don't have regular access to a shower. It isn't just the build up of dirt in their fingers or oil in their hair; it's an attitude of alienation. Being dirty all the time is the stigmata of the rejected outsider in the same way that bad teeth is the stigmata of poverty.

They were also pathetically young, barely twenty. The young man shoved his hand out at me and said, "Thanks for stopping. I'm Micheal." A jerk of his head: "That's Patty."

"I'm Jim."

Micheal looked like he hadn't smiled in a long time. He had the thin, tough body of a wild animal. Even when he wasn't looking at the woman, his body language was protective. Patty gave me a pleasant smile that revealed her missing front teeth. She was generically pretty in a white girl way with an oval face, small nose, smaller mouth, and big eyes. Her thin light brown hair was pulled back into a pony tail. Like many poor women, her shape was bulky and bulgy, the effect of living on pasta and mashed potatoes. She snuggled the baby against her chest.

Her husband gave one of the tires a kick and said, "Flat." He glanced at me and added, "Bald. I knew they were going to blow sooner or later."

"We drove all the way up from Texas." Patty bounced rhythmically for the benefit of the baby.

"I got work doing roofing but haven't made enough to get tires yet." I could see that his responsibilities were weighing on him; his eyes were almost feverish, as if he was desperate to convince himself that the bald tires, the old truck, the new baby, and the move to a new state was all stuff he could handle.

"So where are you headed?" I asked.

"Well, what would be really cool is if you could drive us and our groceries about ten miles that way." He pointed the way I was headed. "I can get some guys I know to come back for the truck."

"Sure." The back of his truck was full of bags and boxes. He explained that he and Patty had been doing a grocery run for several families.

"We take turns," he said and gave his tires another look of disgust.

Once we got the truck loaded, I moved all my back seat shit into one side to make room for Patty and the baby and we got out on the road.

"It isn't far," Micheal said. "There's a mailbox on the right."

We drove in silence. I was curious so I used a little magic on him to get him to talk. *You can trust me,* I thought at him. Which was true. I had no reason to harm him.

He relaxed a little and asked me, "So why'd you come up here from Nevada?"

He'd noticed my plates. "No reason. I'm just driving around."

He nodded. "We're from Houston, but we got flooded out."

"Every year," said Patty from the backseat.

Micheal corrected her, "Not every year but over and over. And no one has flood insurance because the companies won't sell it anymore."

She corrected him, "They sell it, but they charge the earth and the sky. Only rich people have insurance."

"So where are you living now?" I asked

Even with the magic working on him, he hesitated. "Just a place. Private property."

"It's safe," Patty told me.

We drove in silence while I thought about safety. They didn't seem like the armed-to-the-teeth-bunker types. Abruptly, Micheal said, "Slow down. Turn right there."

I pulled into a dirt track and stopped at a gate locked with a heavy chain.

Micheal said, "We'll unload here."

"How far back is your safe place?" I was really curious now, so I kept up the *trust me* magic on him.

He glanced over the seat to Patty, and she said, "You promise not to tell anyone?"

"Who would I tell?"

Micheal shrugged, got out, and opened the gate with a key he wore on a string around his neck. He waited until I pulled through, then locked up behind us. I realized that I wasn't going to be able to leave without an escort.

"Militia," said Micheal as he climbed back into to the truck.

"Government," said Patty from the back seat.

"Not the county so much," Micheal disagreed. "It's those militia assholes always looking to bust someone. We just want to keep ourselves to ourselves. It's better that way. We don't want nobody coming in and being...you know, trying to..."

"It's against the law to be homeless in this state." Patty said. "Even on private property."

The community was back about a quarter mile through the woods on a narrow rutted track that was probably hell to drive on in the winter. We crossed a stream on a little bridge and pulled into a clearing. I didn't need Micheal's directions to see where to park; the village layout was obvious. All the vehicles were parked to one side and the housing—mostly tents but a couple of trailers and a camper—formed a half circle around a large fire pit. People were lounging in plastic chairs around the pit or hanging out around the tents. Some kids were playing on a makeshift swing hung from the branch of a huge leafy tree. A puppy pranced around, barking. Meager sunshine lit the scene.

A bulky man with a hobbit beard separated himself from the rest of the community and strolled over. Micheal and I helped Patty and the baby get out of the back seat. Somehow I ended up holding the baby, but I gave it to Patty right away. Before it could pee on me or something.

"This here's Jim. My truck broke down." There was subservience in Micheal's body language. "He helped us get all the groceries here."

"Thanks for helping," The hobbit said, without sounding thankful. His eyes were watchful. "My name's Carl." His handshake was firm, almost aggressive.

"Glad to help," I said, looking around. The village was as neat as a campground could be. From the smell I could tell they shit in the woods off to the left, away from the stream that flowed down the right hand side of their clearing. Some gardening was being attempted, and they were mulching their garbage. The other trash, the stuff they couldn't mulch, was accumulating in the back of a pick up truck to be hauled away at some point. Carl was mayor of a well-run little town.

"No drugs," Carl said, almost as if he had heard my thought. "Except weed. Drinking's okay unless you're the type who turns into an asshole when you get over the limit. We got kids here."

"I'm an asshole all the time." I said, "but I'm just here to drop off your stuff."

Carl smiled, but briefly. Already the adults were unloading the truck and dispersing the groceries. Lots of pasta and potatoes, of course, along with boxes of canned goods, loaves of sliced white bread, and cans of soup. The kids had abandoned their swing and were hanging out in a little groups, staring while trying not to look like they were staring. They were all skinny, pasty-faced, and wary.

"Did you get any doughnuts, Mom?" whined a little girl in a teddy bear sweatshirt.

"Baked beans suck." That comment came from a red-headed boy of about twelve. A girl I took to be his older sister asked their mother, "Why to we always have to eat baked beans?"

"That's what the food bank gives away," their mother snapped. The food bank also seemed to be giving away a whole lot of mushroom soup and peanut butter.

I thought of the chocolate cake. My luscious, dark, dreamy, chocolate cake.

"Here, carry this," Like all the women, the mother had the look of chronic stress. She handed a box of cans to the sister. The girl was willing, but the box was heavy. The red-headed kid shoved his arms under the box, and they staggered off toward the trailer.

"I got some stuff I can give you," I told Carl. "A lot of it's booze though."

He raised his eyebrows. "Like I said, we allow drinking here. Just no obnoxious drunks. No fighting. No scaring the kids."

I shrugged, "If you want it, you can have it."

"Let's see."

I think he was expecting one or two bottles. His eyebrows shot up at the sight of a cooler packed with booze. In the shuffle of getting Patty and the baby in and out, the blanket had gotten pulled off the cake. It sat on the back seat, gleaming with dark chocolate luster. A small boy peeked around Carl, saw the cake, and whispered, "Who's birthday is it?"

"Not yours." said Carl. "Scoot."

"They can have it," I said.

"He has a cake!" The little boy was tugging on his sister's arm. The kids gathered around, big-eyed. I counted heads. Ten, no eleven kids. And two more off lugging a box of canned goods.

Fuck. Those kids were going to be on that cake like a plague of locusts. I wasn't going to get any of it.

"Later," said a dumpy woman. She frowned at the kids. "Go back to playing. Go on."

As the kids retreated she stepped up and we went through that handshaking ritual that's so important to humans. "I'm Sarah," she told me. I could tell that she was Cart's wife. Like Carl, she was probably in her thirties but looked older. She said, "The kids will enjoy that cake. We can't afford treats."

I shrugged.

She leaned over the cooler and started digging around. "Ooh," she laughed. "Where did you get this?" She held up a bottle of whiskey. "Did you rob a liquor store?"

"No, I robbed some guy back at Kalaloch. I guess he was planning a party."

All the wariness dropped out of her face and she laughed heartily. "Well, shoot!" She waved the bottle at Carl. "Let's have a party!"

"Well," Sarah observed with satisfaction, "you are the bringer of good fortune. We haven't had a blow out like this in quite a while."

It wasn't that much of a blow out. No one lost their manners or got stupid drunk. No fights. No puking. All of the adults got a bit tipsy, but no one forgot about looking after the kids.

They made the eating of the cake into a ritual with a protracted build up. First came the making of the soup, a communal activity that involved a huge iron pot and a fire. They mixed eight or nine cans of mushroom soup with water from the stream and a mix of canned vegetables and canned stew. Then all the adults had a round of their choice of drink while the kids tried to contain their eagerness for desert.

Once the soup was hot enough, they dumped in a ton of pasta and produced a thick, calorie-rich glop. They made the older kids run back and forth carrying bowls of glop out to everyone. The adults had dragged the lawn chairs around the fire so everyone ate together. After shoveling down their glop, the adults had another round of drinks. I skipped the glop and just drank.

After the glop was gone, they sent a trio of older kids off with the pot to clean it in the stream. Meanwhile, Sarah got the cheeses out and passed around the cracker selection. At this point all the adults were lubricated enough for them to start telling funny stories. About half of the men worked together on a roofing crew, and the others did yard work. Most of their stories were about idiot rich people, but some were about dropping hammers on each other and other adventures in manual labor.

The grown ups made the kids wait until after they were all on the third round of drinks before they held the great cutting of the cake. Sarah did the honors with a huge steak knife. First she took a quick glance around, counting heads. Then she eyed the cake and planned out her cuts. The kids managed to keep their eagerness disguised by good manners, but there was some foot shuffling and a lot of frantic whispering.

"Line up." Sarah used her knife to indicate where to stand. After some jockeying for position, the oldest girl pushed the youngest child, a boy in the toddler stage, to the front.

Five minutes later, the thick dark icing had been transferred from the cake to their faces, their fingers, and their t-shirts. Sarah grabbed the toddler and kissed him all over his face, "You are just yummy," she told him. "Umm, boy."

After that, the party started to wind down. The adults made the kids say "Thank you for the cake, Mr. Jim," one at a time which was embarrassing. Then the women herded the kids down to the creek to wash their faces. The men started yawning while they finished their drinks. No one wanted to be doing hard labor with a hangover, so they headed off to bed shortly after the women put the kids to bed. I stayed up late because it didn't matter if I got hung over or not.

Chapter Eighteen

The EV station-plus-grocery store was just what I wanted. It was open but, since it was only around six in the morning, there were no customers. Just south of the parking lot the road split. I knew from studying the map that there was another split about five miles down the road.

I'd been up since dawn because Carl's people were all early risers. The women and kids got up and started the coffee for the men. Then they all pitched in making a huge pot of oatmeal. Everyone stood around morosely stamping their feet in the morning chill and slurping up their breakfast. I was hungry, a little hungover, and caffeine-deprived, but I was also way past my limit for being sociable. I slammed down two cups of coffee without making eye contact with anyone, then asked Sarah if she could unlock the gate. Sarah rode with me down to the gate, unlocked it, and walked back. She didn't make a big deal out of saying good bye, which was fine by me. I drove a little ways down the road and pulled over to look at the map. An hour later, I was in Ryan checking out the little quick stop grocery store.

I needed more cash, but I didn't want to do a hold up in a place where the cashier could just say, "He went thataway," and send the cops off after me. The place on the map called Ryan was perfect. For one thing, the whole town consisted of five houses and three were boarded up. For another thing, the EV station store had parking both in the front and in the back with lots of access to the main road and to a secondary road that led off toward a larger town and another little paved road that probably didn't go much of anywhere. I pulled in around back and parked. I tried the back door and it wasn't locked. Then I walked around front and came in like any customer would.

The cashier was a pimply young guy with short beige hair. I put out some *ignore me* magic and it worked. He stayed bent over his cell phone, scrolling through social media, while I drifted around shopping. I stuffed my pockets with lunch meat and helped myself to a couple handfuls of beef jerky. Then I sauntered up to the counter and pulled the gun out of my belt. The *ignore me* spell was working so well that I had to clear my throat to get his attention.

At the sight of the gun, his mouth and eyes got round. Then he shot a glance down to his right to the place where store keepers sometimes have an alarm button or a shotgun.

Cooperate, I thought at him. *Go along. Cooperate.* Out loud I said, "Drop your phone and hold your hands up. There's nothing here that's worth dying over. Is there?"

"Uh." He was too scared to answer.

"Say it," I told him. "Say that there's nothing here worth dying for. You don't get paid enough to defend any of this shit."

"I don't get paid enough." Then something clicked in his brain and he said, with real feeling, "The pay is shit, but this is the only job around here."

"Okay." I didn't want his life story. "Give me the cash. Put it in a bag,"

"Sure. Can I reach over here to get a bag? It's really shitty working here. My wife's got a baby on the way." Maybe my *be cooperative* magic was working too well because he was babbling like we were friends. "We can't afford to move because you need first and last rent," he told me while he flapped a paper bag open. His nervous fingers jumped around on the cash register, and the drawer pinged open. "Here. That's the ones." His hand bumped on the edge of the drawer, and the bills showered down on the floor. "Oh shit!" He looked like he was going to start crying. "I didn't mean to do that!"

"For fuck's sake." I took a quick look out front: no traffic, no one walking around. Then I set the gun down and leaped over the counter, shoving the clerk out of the way. "Gimme that bag."

I scooped up the fives and tens while he cowered against the racks of cigarettes and whined, "Please don't be mad. I've a wife and a baby coming."

"I'm not mad." I was annoyed.

"This is a shitty job and the pay sucks."

"Then why don't you take some money for yourself?" He was really pissing me off. I dug out the fifties and split the handful in half. "This is for you."

He recoiled. "What?"

"Help yourself," I told him, "but be quick about it. We don't have all morning before someone walks in."

I grabbed a carton of cigarettes. He fumbled for his stack of bills, hesitated, then stuffed them in his pocket.

"You might as well get some food while you're at it," I told him. "Just get it all out to your car before you call the police."

"Call the police?" Clutching a carton of butts against his chest, he looked completely confused.

"Yeah," I explained, trying to be patient, "as soon as I'm gone, you gotta report this. Or, actually, as soon as you're finished robbing the place, you need to report it."

"Yeah." His eyes darted around. "I'll just get some beer and maybe..."

Idiot. He was going to get himself caught. "Be quick," I told him, "or some customer will show up."

"Yeah."

"I mean if you want some beer, get it now."

"Okay."

"Hey!" He jumped. "Snap out of it!" I told him. "Get your shit together. Grab your beer, hide it in your car, and call the cops!"

"Yeah, right, okay." He scurried around the counter.

I picked up my gun and the bag of cash, and I headed for the back door. He was stuck at the beer display, hesitating between brands. Sheesh, what a moron.

"Move your ass!" I yelled. He grabbed a six pack and came running. We charged through the back room and out the back door. "Put your stuff in your car," I told him as I headed for my truck.

"Okay. Thanks." He looked a little less hysterical. *Calm down*, I thought at him. *Hide your stuff and go back inside.*

I waited to make sure he'd actually hid his stuff and headed inside before I drove off. The last I saw of him he was waving good by to me from the back door.

I didn't get much cash because of sharing with the idiot, but I'd scored some beef jerky to gnaw on while driving south. My journey around the mountain range was almost complete, but I hadn't seen any mountains. Not real mountains like in California or Nevada. No snow capped peaks or rocky crests. Lots of green slopes that disappeared into mist. I was probably too close. One of the ironies of mountains is that you can't see them unless you're either right near the top or pretty far away.

I drove through a series of valleys with farms that looked like they were hanging on pretty well. I'd started measuring the prosperity of people by their roofs. Obviously people in tents were poor. People who had houses with tarps on the roof to keep the rain out were probably poor too. People who lived in houses with good roofs were probably doing okay. The road swooped around a corner and suddenly I was in a little town with a lot of tarps on the roof. I just passed on through and out the other side.

The road was like a green tunnel through old trees. It wound along between water—an inlet of Puget Sound—and the green slopes of the mountains. My kind of road: winding, hilly, empty of other traffic. I wanted to enjoy the drive. I lit up a cigarette, rolled down the window, and stuck my elbow out. I turned on the radio, tried to find some music, and turned it off again. I just wasn't enjoying the drive.

Why not? I wanted *to get* somewhere. I wasn't enjoying the traveling because I wanted to arrive. Where? I didn't know. In an hour or so, I'd be back on the four lane highway with a choice of driving towards Olympia and the metropolis of Seattle or going the other way out toward Rainier. And maybe head back down the coast. Maybe go home.

Did I want to go home? Not really. The feeling I had of impatience, of needing to be somewhere, wasn't about being in Nevada. TJ? Was I worried about her? I ran that thought around in my head for a while and decided that I *was* worried about her, but I definitely didn't want to do anything about my worry. I couldn't help her. I just hoped her brother could.

So go back to the coast? Maybe visit the seal? But that didn't feel right either. I'd been on the coast for…I'd lost count of how many days. Not that many, really, but enough. I didn't need any more salty air, wet wind, and sand.

Maybe the mountain in the sky was calling me? I didn't think so. Too far away, too much of an abstraction. Besides, other than turning east, I didn't know how to get there. So I wasn't feeling a call from Mr. Rainier.

But I sure as hell was feeling a call from somewhere.

Chapter Nineteen

When I reached the four lane highway, I turned east. I hadn't decided to go to the metro area or mountain in the sky. I'd just decided against going back to the wet, dinginess of Rainier. Not going west meant going east. I drove numbly, hating the sudden increase in traffic and the stink of asphalt and tires. Hating the billboards and the trash along the road. Then a sign popped into sight that said, "Warrentown next right." Someone had used the sign for target practice. I made the turn, swooped down the exit ramp and suddenly I was on an old potholed road that led off into a forest.

Huge trees leaned and loomed overhead, making the air green with filtered light. Their trunks were embroidered with thick pads of green moss like trees in a Walt Disney movie. I half expected to see gnomes or trolls. Every now and then, through the thickets of underbrush, I glimpsed the heavy, slow flow of a river. Rolling down my window, I let the thick scent of leaves and moss surge in and drive out the stink of asphalt and engines. The frantic striving to move on, move on, move on that had been churning in my chest eased off, and suddenly twenty miles per hour was just fine. I looked for a wide spot and, finding one, pulled over.

The air was wet. I looked up through the layers of emerald leaves at tiny glimpses of a gray sky. All those trees respiring, all that moss, and all that river water made the air feel nearly as damp as a mist.

I wanted to see the river, so I walked along the roadside, looking for an entry point through the bushes. Now that I was out of the truck, I noticed a second type of tree that had gray trunks encrusted with patches of lichen. The lichen trees seemed to grow in groups, the trunks leaning outward. The leaves were fluttery, serrated ovals. Alders, the forest told me. I found a deer trail that led off through a grove.

The trail didn't amount to much. I had to watch my step because the ground was knee deep in ferns, fallen leaves, and a matrix of fallen branches. Underneath all the forest litter, the ground was wet. After thrashing my way though a tangle of salmon berries, I found a mossy spot on a muddy bank overlooking the river.

I stood on the bank and watched the water flow. Little leaf boats spiraled in an eddy under a tangle of tree roots. The water was clear but colored by reflections of the sky and the trees. I wondered what Janey and Joseph would think of such an abundance of water. Kneeling down on the mossy bank, I scooped up a handful and lapped. It occurred to me that I hadn't been a coyote in a long time. I looked at the river with coyote eyes and saw it as too big to cross. Any territory of mine would be on the same side of the river as the road.

My territory? No. It was somebody's though. I could feel it.

I got up, turned my back on the river, and thrashed my way through the brush to the truck. My boots were wet, and my jeans were soaked and muddied from the knees down. The wet cloth rubbing on my skin was chilly. I had a sudden memory of getting into the truck after a walk in the desert and kicking the sand out of my boots.

"Janey," I said aloud, "I'm homesick."

I climbed into the driver's seat, stuck the key in the ignition, and sat paralyzed. In my mind I was back on the freeway, heading back through Rainier, making the turn to the road that led out to the ocean, retracing my trail down the coast of broken houses where the sea gnawed on the road and the salt air blew onto the land from across thousands of miles of water. I turned the key and heard the engine turn over. As I eased my boot down on the accelerator I almost, *almost* turned the steering wheel to make u-turn.

A raven croaked out a warning. Behind me, a branch gave way from one of the big maples and crashed on to the road. Chunks of bark shot out like soggy shrapnel. There was a sudden rainfall of moss.

I opened the door and leaned out to assess the damage. The branch sprawled over the road, broken into damp chunks. I thought: Well, if someone *really* wanted to stop me from leaving, they shoulda dropped a bigger tree. The branch wasn't too big for me to drag out of the way.

But I didn't. I just pulled out on the road and aimed myself onward through the forest.

Chapter Twenty

I rolled along the potholed road through the green tunnel of mossy trees for what seemed like a long time, but really was only about an hour by the dashboard clock. The whole time I kept my eyes aimed forward, peering around each bend in the road, as anxious and fidgety as TJ had been.

It was weird to feel someone waiting for me. The forest receded a bit, pushed back by a rusted and busted old sawmill with a parking lot full of weeds. One last remaining logging truck was slowly disintegrating, so decayed that wildflowers were growing from the buildup of dirt and debris in the nooks and crannies of the trailer apparatus. The chain link fence around the property had become a trellis for wild honeysuckle.

Past the old saw mill, the road joined the river and ran alongside for a short stretch. Then suddenly I was rolling into a small town that looked nearly as decrepit as the old mill. And there she was, waiting for me.

She was short, stocky, black-haired, and a raven. I pulled the truck alongside the curb and turned the engine off. The main street of the little town was silent. A glance up and down told me why. Only one business, the Raven Tavern, was open. The others looked to have been looted—busted windows, doors askew, nothing inside or on display. I couldn't even tell what kind of businesses they'd been. There was a new looking electric truck parked in front of a Quonset hut across the side street from the Tavern and, moving with painful slowness, an old man and his dog were inching their way along the river side of the road, watching the water.

I got out of the truck. "Raven?" I asked.

"Coyote?" Her eyebrows arched upwards and she smiled. "Hi, I'm Rachel and this is my bar."

"Jimmy," I said.

"Come in and have a beer."

She wasn't beautiful or even pretty by some standards, but she was sexy. Not the deliberate sexiness of a show off. She wasn't trying, she just was. I watched her backside all the way into the bar and up to a bar stool. Then I looked around.

Light from the big front windows spilled patches of dull yellow on the table tops, making the shabby interior look homey. The small space was crowded with the kind of glittery junk that attracts the corvid eye. Dream catchers twinkled in the window, and the walls were decorated with framed mirrors—all sizes, most with frames that over-dazzled the mirrors. Every table had a colorful vase of some kind, but most didn't contain flowers. I saw a Mexican-looking ghost peering at me through peacock feathers, while across the room a wiry guy with a sulky expression had shoved the vase of balloons to the far side of his table.

The overall effect was more of a shop for third hand junk than a bar, but behind the counter there was an old lady barmaid who propped herself up on one elbow and asked what I wanted.

"Whiskey?" I asked.

"Sorry," she said without apology. "Just beer. And just this beer." She pushed herself upright and gestured. Behind her along the wall, under the sink, and on shelves were boxes of canned beer. None cold, I saw. Oh, and Rainier was a brand too. A mountain, a town, and a beer.

"Ray Near," I said, pronouncing it like a local. I accepted the beer and glass and introduced myself.

"I'm Valerie," said the old lady. She had delicate features, a long thin neck, and a body that was worn out and breaking down. All of her movements showed pain and exhaustion.

"How much?" I asked.

"On the house," said Rachel with an through-the-eyelashes glance at me. She saw my reaction and laughed. Rachel poured herself a beer and said, grinning, "We'll find out if you rate the good stuff." It was a challenge and a tease. Valerie didn't seem to approve, or maybe she was just too tired to be friendly. She had a chair behind the bar and collapsed into it. I guessed that the bar didn't get much business because she had a sewing project in a basket at her feet. I took a big gulp of the beer and looked around for a more comfortable place to hang out than the teeter-y bar stool.

The front door banged and Valerie moaned, "Oh, God."

"Annnddd here's Mary!" yelled a ugly old drunk from the doorway. She was already legless and had to grab tables to steady herself on the way to the bar. A skinny woman, her gray hair was stiff with grease, and her jeans were blotchy with grime. She packed a powerful smell too.

Rachel popped a beer open and plonked it down on the table.

"Aw hell, I don't want that! I want the good stuff." The drunk waved one arm in rejection of the beer and nearly lost her balance.

"Not today," Rachel told her calmly. "That's all you're getting."

Mary stuck her chin out, slapped her hands down on the counter, and leaned forward into Rachel's face. Rachel wrinkled up her nose. "Go away, Mary. You stink."

"I stink?" Mary swayed with exaggerated outrage. "I stink? Me?"

"Yes, you. Go sit at a table and get out of my face." Rachel didn't seem pissed off, just bored, like it was a conversation she'd had before. Mary didn't seem offended either, just theatrical, hamming her part up to the max.

"Well, excuse me, your highness!" She grabbed the beer, and hanging on to one of the bar stools for balance, attempted a bow.

"Careful," Rachel warned. To me, she added, " I don't want to have to clean up after her if she falls on her ass."

Mary gathered her flailing limbs, got her feet underneath her body, and made the short distance to the nearest table without falling. An old man backed up to get out of her way. None of us had noticed his entry because of all of Mary's noise. Mary greeted him, "Hey! Siddown and have a beer with me."

He moved slowly toward the counter. It was the old guy I'd seen outside walking his dog by the river. The dog, a pit bull with a head the size of a basketball, was following closely behind him.

Rachel saw Valerie put her sewing aside and said, "No, I'll take care of things." To the old man she said, "Have a seat. I'll be back." She disappeared to through the door to a back room.

The old man gave me a friendly nod, got himself turned around, and aimed himself at the ghost's table. That got me wondering how much these people knew about ravens and ghosts. The ghost got up and helped the old man to his seat. He greeted the dog and settled himself back down. Mary swayed back and forth in her seat, unhappy with not being the center of attention anymore. She called to me, "Hey, stranger."

"My name's Jim."

"Hey, Jim, whatcho doing here in this...this outpost of civilization?"

"I'm not sure," I told her.

"Well, that's not good, sonny boy. You ain't gonna get nowhere if you don't know where you're going."

"Jesus H. Christ, pearls of wisdom from a drunk schizophrenic." It was the scrappy guy sitting by himself near the door. He had a face like a fist, all clenched up. He was speaking past Mary to me. "It was okay in here until that smelly old goat came in. Hooboy!" He pinched his nose and invited me to laugh with him. I didn't. Instead I picked up my beer and walked over to the crazy lady's table. She reeked but I could tell that if she didn't have anyone to talk to, she'd be yelling at all of us.

"Mind if I join you?"

"I do not. Be seated by all means." The close up view didn't improve her much. Her eyes were blue but pale and watery, and the skin of her face was gray from dirt and bad health. She had been cute once, petite and playful like a young fox, and she still tried to be flirty.

"So, seriously, what brings you here to our neck of the woods?" Her eyebrows waggled at me. "No one comes here for no reason."

"Just driving around."

She shook her head. "Nope. Rachel controls the road. People don't get here by accident," She took a big slug of her beer. "Now I ain't saying she watches that road every damn minute of every damn day. Someone could drive up when she wasn't paying attention. But you ain't no accident." She paused meaningfully. "Are you?" She waggled her eyebrows at me again. I looked her over thoughtfully. I've met crazy humans before, and they weren't any better at recognizing me than the regular people were.

"If she controls the road, why did she let him come up here?" I nodded toward Fist Face. He was sprawled back in his chair, surveying the tavern as if he owned it.

"Oh, him. He's an old timer. Owns that business across the way. Not that he makes any money here. He's got other places in Rainier and Aberdeen. But he owns that Quonset hut, and he comes out here to keep an eye on his property. And on us." She tipped her beer at him in a salute.

"Is that what you all are? Old timers?"

"Me. Rachel. Old Man. Haysus is new." She shrugged.

Rachel appeared carrying a tray. She set a plate down in front of the old man and a bowl on the floor for the dog. Then she added a big glass of water. "Jesus?" she asked the Mexican ghost. "Anything for you?"

"No, no." I could tell by the embarrassed way he shook his head that he didn't speak any English.

Fist Face snorted with derision. Rachel snapped out, "He's welcome here. You don't like him, you can leave."

Fist Face rolled his eyes with contempt. "Hey, all I'm saying is he needs to learn English." He shook out a cigarette and lit it. "He wants to live here, he needs to talk like the rest of us, right?"

Rachel turned her shoulder to Fist Face. Picking up her drink, she joined me and Mary. "I can fix you a meal. Just fried chicken and peas tonight."

"No, thanks." To my surprise, it was getting on toward dinner time. The sun had moved down to the tree tops, and the tavern was shadowed. Valerie hung an oil lantern on a nail, and called out, "Anyone want a light for your table?"

Old Man said, "Over here please, Val, if it isn't too much trouble."

He began the slow, painful climb to his feet while Val, carrying a lantern, started around the counter. Rachel intervened by taking the lantern away from Val and carried it over to the Old Man and Jesus. Then she rejoined me and Mary.

"Dark's fine with me," I told her.

Rachel grinned. "Me too."

"You're one of them, aren't you?" Mary asked.

Rachel patted Mary's hand. "Now you know if you talk like that people think you're off your meds, right?"

"Yeah," said Mary, "but he's still another one like you."

Chapter Twenty-One

We sat around for the length of one beer. No new customers came in. Rachel's tavern reminded me of the restaurant where I'd picked up the stray cat; it was more of a hangout for old people than a functioning business. Fist Face was the only customer who had a job, and it looked to me like he was the only one paying for his drinks. Well, maybe the rest were running a tab. At any rate, I couldn't see how Rachel was going to stay open. I asked her about it, and she said, "Let's take a walk."

We went past the bar counter and through a jumbled up store room that had a kitchen Jerry-rigged on one wall. Just a Coleman stove, a cooler, and some jugs of water. She didn't have any electrical power. We walked to the side street in the misty drizzle, and Rachel pointed at the Quonset hut. "That's Harry's place. He's hanging on just to be spiteful."

His place didn't look like much; weeds were invading the parking lot, and the sign announcing Scot's A-One Auto Repair was faded and moldy.

"I'm thinking about getting rid of him. He isn't helpful, and I could get someone better to live in that Quonset hut."

Rachel started up hill and I followed. The houses of the little town were scattered on a hillside against a background of larger hills where dead cedars stood like gravestones among the brush. To the north along the river, the hills were catching the evening light, gold on green. The distant mountains were blue. The little houses of the town had mostly been painted white, but were now faded to gray and greened with mold. We hiked up the hill about a block and Rachel stopped.

"This is the house Valerie uses." So not Valerie's house. She was a squatter. Someone had once cared for the yard; fat pink roses were fighting for their lives against an invasion of weeds. The blossoms were badly chewed by bugs. About half of the front porch was stacked with firewood.

Rachel started walking again. We climbed up another two blocks to the edge of town, and she stopped again to point. "That's the old man's house. We just call him 'Old Man.' He used to run the grocery here." Old Man's house had been a cute cottage once, but was now a grim demonstration of the effect of rain on wood. Probably a good thing he was so old because he was unlikely to outlast his roof.

We turned to look down hill toward the river. "I've been here all of my existence," Rachel said. "Never traveled anywhere."

"I used to be like that," I responded.

The river was beautiful in the evening light. Gleams of gold lit the reflected colors of sky and nearby trees.

"There's been a lot of change, obviously," Rachel said. "The people here now are either the very last holdouts since the sawmill closed or refugees from somewhere else."

I let my breath out in a long sigh. "You don't have to beat around the bush. I'm a refugee from somewhere else. I don't know where I'm going to go next. Maybe that mountain I've heard so much about."

"Mt. Rainier? It's beautiful." She let out a sigh that matched mine. "I won't beat around the bush either. I could use some help here. I have a place you can stay."

I let my eyes roam around, taking in the colors. The sunset looked like the inside of an abalone shell—don't ask me I how I knew that. The sky was pearly white and gleamed with blue and silver. The sun was just over the horizon, but smothered in cloud. In between the horizon and me and Rachel was a wet landscape crowded with vegetation, a lot of it non-native. The fir trees were third or fourth growth timber, and someone had been putting in ponderosa and lodge pole pines. I was looking at an illusion of nature; in all that greenery most of the native animals were either gone or nearly gone. There were coyotes, though. I could feel them out there hunting mice and squirrels. Some were eating domestic cats.

"Why are you helping these humans?" I wished the stray cat well, but I was glad not to be around for the train wreck her life was likely to be.

Rachel shrugged. "They're company. I like them. Most of them."

"What do you do for them? Besides beer and fried chicken."

"Beer and fried chicken is hard enough. It takes money, and money is hard for me to get."

So she'd sensed a coyote near her territory and pounced. It was an evening for long sighs. I said, "I'll stay a couple nights and see how it goes, okay?"

"Sure." She tossed her head to get her hair out of her face. We were both damp from the misty air. I wondered if I'd get moldy if I decided to live there. Everything else was moldy, so why not me?

"It really does rain for nine months out of twelve," she warned me. "but it never gets really cold, so there's that. I mean if you decide to stick around."

I didn't say anything. I didn't think I was going to stick around.

Chapter Twenty-Two

I woke up to sunshine. Rachel had given me a small apartment over the tavern. Once upon a time the building had hosted five or six apartments, but now no one lived there but Rachel—and now me. Except I wasn't planning to stay long. Still, I got up to look out to see what sunshine was like in Washington state.

Very green. That's what I saw out the window. Somewhere out in the distance was the bay that connected the harbor at Rainier to the ocean, but I couldn't see any of that. Just miles of green, the trees making a mass of woolly texture.

The river was wide, deep, slow, and brown in the sun. Old Man and his dog were on the bank, soaking up the morning warmth. Both slumped as if tired, their heads hanging low, companions in old age. In the desert, the nearness of death makes the ordinary moments of life more vivid. Maybe dampness of Washington did that for Old Man. I tired to feel appreciative. It was sunny after all, and likely to get hot.

But I didn't feel appreciative. I felt lost.

Shit. I got dressed and headed downstairs. The tavern was empty; apparently they served dinner but not breakfast. I walked out into the sun and lit a cigarette. Coffee. I needed some.

I went back inside and poked around in the backroom until I found a bag of Seattle's Finest. Finally something not named Rainier. After firing up the Coleman, I got a pot going. Rachel had told me to make myself at home, so I did. While waiting for the coffee to perk, I snooped into the stuff stored in the back room and found a cache of prescription medications that must've been liberated from a pharmacy because no one could legally have a stash that size of Oxycontin. I didn't think Rachel was an addict. She also had stores of over-the-counter medications, first aid supplies, shampoo, soap, and toothpaste. Stacked up by the wall, she had piles of dog and cat food. Someone had thievish habits. I was getting an idea of what Rachel meant by taking care of Warrentown.

The back door opened and Rachel came in. "Found the coffee? There's some bread around somewhere. We don't have a toaster, but you can grill the bread if you want."

"Thanks, but I think I'll go hunting later."

"Okay." She poured a cup for herself. Then she propped elbow on the counter and looked me over. "How're you doing?'

"Fine." I felt defensive for some reason. "The room's nice. Thank you."

"Oh, sure." She took a sip of the coffee. "Well, you can see what I need help with." Ravens are scavengers, so foraging comes naturally to them, and I could tell that she was a powerful spirit. On the other hand, hitting pharmacies and feed stores for supplies had to be a constant hassle for her.

I poured myself a mug full of the hot brown brew. Coffee was one of the few things I'd miss if civilization collapsed completely. I told Rachel, "I'm going out for some sun."

I got a glimpse of disappointment, quickly covered up with a smile. "It doesn't rain much in the summer. We can go all summer sometimes with no rain."

We went outside together. There was a bench in front of the tavern, handy for early morning coffee. We sat down. Across the road, Old Man and the dog were making slow progress toward the corner. He gave a little wave.

"Good morning," Rachel called. "How are you for dog food?"

"I could use some."

"Maybe Jimmy can carry some up the hill for you later on."

He stopped and leaned on his cane. "I'd sure appreciate that."

"Sure," I said. "This afternoon okay?"

"Any time. Thank you." He nodded a farewell and got himself in motion.

"He walks down the hill and up every day," Rachel explained. "It's his exercise routine."

I finished my coffee and dropped my cigarette butt on the sidewalk. I had a feeling that Rachel had a whole list of chores for me, but I wanted to get out and run in the woods. Standing up, I said, "I'll help the old guy out later today."

Then I walked back inside. It seemed like the best way to end the conversation.

I started climbing the hill. It felt good to stretch my legs after so long in the truck, but I could tell I'd been smoking too much. An end to cigarettes would be another benefit from a complete collapse of civilization, I thought, as I chugged upwards. As it was, civilization had only part way collapsed. Humans were hanging on to what they valued most, and it was interesting to see what that turned out to be.

I climbed my way past Valerie's house. Cats lay sprawling in the sun on the porch and a pig was munching thoughtfully on a rotten cabbage. All the animals lifted their heads and watched me with cautious, unfriendly eyes. I heard a shout from the interior. The door slammed open, and a kid goat bounded out. He paused on the top step, then ping ponged down the steps and around the house toward the back yard. Valerie poked her head out the door.

I stopped and nodded a hello. Her hands flew to her hair, fluttered in effectually, and dropped into her apron pockets.

"That dratted goat has learned how to open doors."

"Goats are smart."

"Well, he'd better get smarter and stay out of my kitchen, or I'll let Jesus and Maria put him in a soup pot."

I could tell she didn't mean it. She was upset and tired, but there was no real threat in her voice. "We don't need a billy goat," she added sadly.

"You guys farming here in town?" I asked. So far, I'd seen goats, pigs, and chickens.

"Sort of." Valerie tried and failed to flatten her crest of gray hair. "By accident." Then her eyes sharpened. "If you aren't too busy, could you help me with something?"

I tried not to sigh audibly. "What?"

"Wood." She nodded toward the wood pile. "I have a bunch in back that needs splitting. I can fix you a real nice meal, if you're hungry."

The Mexican ghost was rolling sections of a fallen tree into Valerie's back yard, watched by two kids, the baby goat, and an array of chickens. He stopped when he saw me, straightened up, and gave a little wave.

"Want some help?"

He shrugged apologetically. "No English." Up close I could see that he probably wasn't a Mexican ghost. More like Guatemalan. Short and broad-shouldered, he had a face that looked like it had been carved from rock. Behind him in the unkempt weeds, two silent children stood side by side, the boy holding the girl's hand. They had round faces, big round eyes, and hard round potbellies, but their arms and legs were skinny. Ghost children.

I pointed. "Yours?"

"Mis hijos." He smiled with shy pride. I wondered if ghost children were ever going to grow up. With sudden animation, Jesus began waving his arms like a tour guide. The commentary was all in Spanish, so I only got one word in ten. I could tell he was explaining his work project.

The house behind Valerie's had been stripped of siding, and the planks were stacked neatly in Val's back yard. The wads of old insulation were packed down under a tarp weighted with bricks. I could see right through the studs to the interior where bits and pieces of kitchen remained: stained linoleum, a broken table, cabinet doors hanging askew.

I followed Jesus on his tour. They had rolls of plastic piled up in the driveway. Jesus mimed nailing the plastic to the studs, and I realized what they were up to. They were converting the old cottage into a green house.

"That's smart."

A pleased grin spread across Jesus's face. The kids gathered at his side. With their swollen tummies and scrawny arms and legs they looked like spiders.

"Hey, Jesus," I asked. "Do people here know you all are ghosts?"

He frowned, puzzled. I tried gesturing toward Val's house. "Val, you, espirito?"

He pointed at himself. "Espiritu. Si'"

"Yeah, but..." Oh well, I thought. I'll ask Rachel. But Jesus was on a roll. "Espiritu," he repeated, pointing at each kid. "Espiritu." He waved his hand toward the house, probably indicating his wife, not the stripped cottage. "Frio. Mucho frio." He hugged himself, shivered and closed his eyes. He was telling me that he and his family had died of hypothermia out in the woods.

Then he shrugged and grinned. "Espiritus ahora."

Chapter Twenty-Three

I took over Jesus's job of spitting wood, and he took the kids back to the house they were stripping. I hefted the sledgehammer, aimed it at the mallet, and slammed it down, pushing the swing clear past the mallet and into the heart of the tree round. With a loud crack, the round split, revealing the raw pink and orange interior.

The tree had been a Douglas-fir. Jesus had cut the branches into chunks and had them stacked up under a tarp for Valerie. That must have taken him hours, I thought. I set my half round of fir up on end, switched to the ax. Another heft and swing and the wood split. My shoulder started to ache but I didn't care. Hard work felt good.

After slamming out more half rounds, I whacked them into quarter rounds. Between the ringing bangs of the sledge hammer on the mallet and the whacks of the ax on wood, I heard the bumps, clangs, and ripping noises of house demolition. I got the murmur of Jesus's voice every now and then, but I never heard a sound from the kids.

I kept at it, swinging the mallet to spit the rounds, swinging the ax to spit the halves. After a while it stopped being fun, and both of my shoulders ached. I could feel the slam of the ax clear up my arms as a burst of elbow pain and a throb in the shoulder. A radio fired up in the greenhouse playing bouncy, cheerful, and annoying Mexican music.

I hauled another round up on end, tapped the wedge into the wood to get it started, and hefted the sledged hammer. Valerie opened her door and called out across her backyard, "Jim, you want something to eat yet?" She stepped out and looked around, "Oh Jim, I sure did put you to work."

Her hand resting on the rickety railing of her back porch looked like a worn out piece of fabric, wrinkled and faded. The porch wasn't in good shape either. Sooner or later, she was going to step out her back door and drop right through the rot into the dark world of spiders and weeds under her steps.

I had spit eight rounds. The firewood I'd produced was scattered all over her back yard and mixed with sawdust and and goat poop. It all needed to be cleaned up. She wouldn't even be able to walk around without tripping on wood or stepping in poop.

"Come on in and rest." She smiled at me, but the smile didn't reach her tired eyes. I tossed the sledge hammer aside and worked my way to her porch, stepping over and around the obstacles. I followed her in through her kitchen which was, I noticed, a weird combination of old-fashioned dishtowels, frilly curtains, and camping equipment.

Lunch was set out on her coffee table in the living room, which also was odd mix of respectable spinster and survivalist. She had a big soft couch—which I sank into until my butt was almost on the floor—an armchair piled with crocheted throws, and some wooden bookshelves and end tables made of maple in the early American style that went out of fashion way back in the 1950's. All of her stuff was probably salvaged from wherever she'd lived before being exiled to Rachel's last stand.

The survival stuff included a Coleman lantern and a stack of firewood by a wood stove that had been Jerry-rigged into the living room. The pipe went out a window, so it was obviously not part of the original design. She had stacks of homemade canned goods, jars of home dried fruit, and boxes of food bank mushroom soup stored up all along the walls. My guess was she lived on soup plus canned veggies.

All of that survivalist activity made me more appreciative of the food she'd served than I would've been otherwise. She'd given me the best she had: slices of bread with peanut butter and jam, a bowl of lettuce with some kind of dressing that looked homemade, and coffee.

"It's peanut butter and jelly." Her eyes blinked at me apologetically "I get a lot of peanut butter from the charity food bank in Rainier, and we make our own jelly. I really appreciate the work you did."

It was on the tip of my tongue to say I'd finish up tomorrow, but I managed to say instead, "Peanut butter and jelly is great."

Just like grandma made, I added in my head. Not that I had a grandma, but I was sure getting that vibe from old Val. She hovered, twisting her fingers in her hands. "Water? I should've given you a glass of water. You're probably dehydrated." She turned toward her kitchen, nearly stumbling in her worn-out shoes.

"No thanks! I'm great." I was dehydrated, but I could drink out of a puddle after lunch. I smiled right into her eyes and did a little calming magic: *Sit down and calm down.* "I'm fine. Really." She groped for the arms of the arm chair and almost fell into the seat. I added out loud, "You should take a nap."

I almost felt like taking one myself, but first I had to get the firewood stacked near the porch handy for her or she'd break a leg trying to do it herself. And after that, I probably needed to go back down the hill and get Old Man's stuff.

Chapter Twenty-Four

"Here ya go." Rachel had the job all prepped for me. All of the Old Man's supplies were piled in a wheelbarrow. In answer to my unspoken question, she said, "We don't use my truck unless we have to because the nearest charge station is clear in town." I glanced across the street at Harry's Quonset hut, and Rachel added. "He doesn't have power over there anymore."

She chewed her lip thoughtfully as she gazed at the Quonset hut. Not my problem, I told myself. I grabbed the wheelbarrow by the handles.

"Come by for dinner later," Rachel said. She squinted up at the meager sunshine. "We might have a barbecue."

I wondered if the humans would let Rachel get away with cooking roadkill over a campfire. Then I remembered the greenhouse and decided that they probably would keep themselves a bit above that level. I personally didn't mind road kill, and I'd eaten it both raw and cooked.

It was hard work shoving a wheelbarrow uphill. The weight wasn't a problem, but the wheel wanted to veer off to one side or the other all the time. I couldn't set an even pace and had to keep lurching left or right to counter the wheel's lurching. I arrived at the top of the hill feeling sore and annoyed.

Old Man's house was on the corner with a good view out over the decay and disintegration on the hillside below, backed up against the rise of the hill behind him where the dead cedars stood like monuments to a war they'd lost. I dropped the handles of the wheelbarrow and just looked for a while.

The sky couldn't make up its mind what kind of afternoon we were going to have. Fat billowy clouds blocked the sun, but between the clouds, the sky was blue and bright. I'd worked up a sweat from pushing the damn wheelbarrow uphill, but my skin prickled with chill in the shadow of the clouds. The top of the rise behind Old Man's house had dissolved into mist. The day looked like it might get rainy, or might clear off and get hot, or maybe was going to do both at the same time depending on where you stood on the hillside.

A woof greeted me. Old Man's old dog, square and bulky as a wrestler, was standing at the top of the porch steps. A string of drool hung in a necklace of drops from one corner of her smile.

"Hey, girl," I said and I grabbed the handles of the wheelbarrow and shoved it into motion.

His house gave me claustrophobia. I've never had a problem with allergies, but two inhales of his living room air and my nose was crying for help. Mold, dust, dog hair—the trigger could've been anything. The couch stank and was stained with spilled food. Rings of sticky liquid covered his coffee table and end tables. Even with his Coleman lantern was smudged with sticky fingerprints. Old Man had covered the windows with newspapers for some reason. Maybe insulation? In the grayed-out filtered light, I could see dusty cobwebs in the corners. I coughed and mumbled, "Excuse me," and coughed again.

"Can I get you something?" The poor old guy could barely stand up, but he was trying to be a host. I didn't think I could eat anything in his house without getting food poisoning, and I've eaten roadkill so ripe I could smell it half a mile away.

"No thanks," I told him. "I just got food from Valerie."

He blinked his faded eyes. "Valerie. She feeds me too."

"Siddown," I told him. I was afraid he'd fall down. "I can put your stuff away." It took me four trips up the steps to haul his supplies in. I heaped everything on the floor. Most of the supplies were for the dog unless he ate Rainier's Best Crunchies and rawhide strips.

"Right there's okay," he said as he eased himself carefully down on the soda. Puffs of dust haloed around his bald head.

I shifted the bags of dog food over toward the wall and out of the line of foot traffic. Then I picked up the box of canned soup and carried it through to the kitchen.

I'd braced myself for disaster, but the kitchen was actually fairly clean. Someone had tracked mud all over the floor and the windows were moldy, but the counters were washed, the dishes all put away, and dishtowels were draped neatly over the edge of the sink which was full of gallon containers filled with water. The camp stove sitting on top of the oven was spiffed up and ready to go. I set the box of soup on the counter near the stove to be handy for him.

In answer to my silent question, he said, "Val cleans in there for me sometimes. Sometimes it's Rachel that cleans."

"Mind if I smoke?" I asked.

"No, go ahead." I sat down on the edge of the armchair and disturbed dust and large spider. The spider skittered along the arm of the chair, stopped to waggle its eye stocks at me, and disappeared toward the floor. I lit up, exhaled, and felt grateful for the smell of burning tobacco.

"I've lived here all of my life," Old Man said. "Born here."

"Really? So you know the story of this place, huh?" Maybe he knew about Rachel.

"We used to be a busy town. Sawmill." He made a weak gesture with one hand. "This was all timber country once. Rachel hates us." He grinned and for second I could see him as a much younger man. "She's a tree hugger, but that's how we made a living."

"How long's she lived here?" I asked.

"I dunno." He frowned, trying to think. "Seems like she got here a longtime ago. I think I started seeing her around here about the time the sawmill closed. She didn't always run that tavern, you know. It used to be called Timberman's. But old man Riley took off when business got so bad that it wasn't worth trying any more."

"A lot of people left," I commented.

"Yeah, I used to run a grocery store, but there was no point in that either."

I looked for an ashtray and decided that I wasn't going to hurt anything if I ashed on the carpet. So I did.

Old Man didn't notice. His eyes were faraway. "We were really different when I," He broke off and grinned ruefully. "I almost said 'when I used to live here' but I still am living here. Sort of. I'm a little more alive than dead."

"How old are you?" I asked.

"Over eighty. And feeling every day of it." He needed to take a nap. I pinched the cigarette out with my fingers and dropped the stub on the floor.

A little stale tobacco smell would improve the atmosphere.

"Thank you," he said. "Thank you for hauling my freight uphill."

"Hey, no problem." I had an impulse to say I'd bring him some fire wood later, but managed to shut myself up. Instead I said, "See you later," which was almost as bad.

The weather was working its way up to rain, but slowly. The clouds had bunched up into a swollen gray mass that hovered ominously overhead, yet in the distance, out past the river, bursts of sunlight still gleamed down on the trees.

I studied the hillside of shabby cottages with their mossy roofs, weathered paint, and their half-dead roses and rhododendrons. The pig was munching on garbage behind the Tavern. Chickens gossiped on the sidewalk. The bratty baby goat had climbed up on top of an old pickup that had suck into the weeds. Like everything else, the truck was moldy and mossy. The village looked like a scene from a post-apocalypse movie about life after the break down of civilization.

Come to think of it, it *was* a post-apocalypse scene. The human assault on nature had fucked up many aspects of human civilization too. Weird how easily I had gotten used to changed circumstances. Adaption, I suppose. The desert was too hot and dry for life; towns were falling into the sea; the ocean was dying; and the forests were on fire everywhere except right where I was. Weather problems had screwed up the supply chains, and crops were failing, making prices high for human food—for people who *had* food. Many had none. Millions of people like Jesus were desperately migrating way from the hottest areas of the world and mostly being rejected wherever they sought refuge. Animals had starved out everywhere. It was apocalyptic, but somehow the death and loss had all become normal in the way that a person can get used to an amputated arm or a broken heart.

Chapter Twenty-Five

I dithered about going for a run. I might get caught out in the rain. It wasn't the right time of day. At least it wasn't the right time for desert hunting. I didn't know what the right time was in Washington. I didn't know what I'd be hunting either. Deer? It was probably past the fawn season. On the other hand, I'd waken up wanting to go for a run and felt like I should make good on my plan. Instead of heading down hill to the Tavern, I walked across the road, through some scrub and grass, and shoved my way through a wall of huckleberries into the hillside forest. As soon as I was out of sight of any humans, I took my clothes off and dropped into my coyote self.

The forest above the town was dead. Beside the town and stretching out toward the highway miles away, the forest was Douglas-fir on the slopes with maples and alders in the valleys. The Douglas-fir had been planted sixty some years ago and had been thinned once so the trees were all the same age, the same height, and stood at equal distances from each other. It was a lifeless timber farm. There was no trail, and I suspected that coyotes didn't come up the hillside much. I angled down slope.

Walking wasn't easy. The huckleberries came in dense crowds that were easier to walk around than through. Otherwise, the ground between the trees was a mixture of low-growing Oregon grape and lots of rotten branches jack-strawed all over the mossy ground. Every now and then I encountered a stump from the timber company forest that had preceded the current crop. The original forest had been cedar but even the stumps were gone, all cut down one hundred and fifty years ago or thereabouts. I wondered about the dead cedars above the town. For some reason the timber company hadn't cut up there. Maybe the land belonged to the government? Or someone had wanted to save the cedar forest? If so, that someone failed. Climate change hadn't killed all of the cedars, but it had changed the boundaries of where they could live. The cedars above the town were in the die-off area.

The third-growth Douglas-fir forest whispered all this to me as I wound my way downhill at a slant away from town. Squirrels and mice can live here, the forest told me. Sometimes rabbits. Ruffled grouse, but not here. The forest is too deep for grouse, it said in a voice that had thickened into a sound like running water. This is where the owls live and the pileated woodpecker.

Wait a minute. What the hell is an pileated woodpecker? I stopped and looked around. Oh. Another time travel event. I was standing on the soft ground of a very different forest: one deep, dark, and silent. The trees were cedars and immense. Solemnly they stood, the trunks at ground level larger than the distance from my nose to the tip of my tail. Long mossy branches swept down from the sky, making a thick lattice overhead, filtering the light into a greenish haze.

The giant trees were close enough to each other to have intertwined roots. I started off to explore, but walking was darn near impossible. The ground humped up into ridges choked with tangles of bramble and fell into hollows full of ferns and moss. I scrambled up and down between the huge trunks, looking up every now and then at a burst of light between the branches, but mostly minding my footsteps to keep from tripping.

The hollows between roots were often full of murky water and ringed by strange fungi and gardens of moss. I leaned down and sipped from one pool. The water tasted of soil and bugs. Down deep under a black tangle of roots, tiny orange mushrooms sprouted. A snail oozed slowly through its miniature world under the tree roots. It seemed odd to me that the forest was made of plants so gigantic on one hand and so tiny on the other, with so little in between.

It wasn't a forest for a coyote. I heard squirrels skittering overhead somewhere up in the crisscross of branches. I sat back and stared up wards until my neck got sore, but I never actually caught sight of one. After a while I noticed a small accumulation of sticks poking out of a hole in the tree trunk. The hole sprouted three ugly little heads. Baby birds. They were very young, their throats pink and wrinkled, their meager feathers sticking up like spikes. Then their mouths opened impossibly wide like they were going to turn themselves inside out. With a whisper of wings, mom arrived. The pileated woodpecker.

The damn thing was the size of a chicken. Red, black, and white, with a long neck and a crest, it was Woody the Woodpecker only for real. Well, not for real because I was in the memory of a forest, not a real one. They'd been real once.

Woodpecker drilled her beak into each baby's mouth in a way that looked fatal but didn't bother the babies at all. Or satisfy them either. She no sooner dropped a load into one voracious maw when the chick demanded more. With a flap of her big black and white wings, she took off to scout for more food.

I watched her navigate between the trees and thought again that the forest was no place for a coyote. It was a forest for creatures that could run up and down the trees and jump from branch to branch. Or fly. But not walk. I struggled onward, climbing up mossy piles of half-buried roots and scrambling down into dense wet tangles of greenery latticed over pools of rainwater. I got up on top of one root that was as massive as a grown tree and had to jump to get down the other side—and landed neck deep in salal and ferns. After fighting my way up to the root pile of the next tree, I searched with my eyes for an easier route. There wasn't one. I could see a sunny spot, but it was clogged with the armored arcs of salmon berry branches, waiting to tear the shit out of any creature that got too close. In the shade, crisscrossed stacks of fallen branches had rotted together into a mossy mass. The moss was emerald green and almost luminous in the gentle half-light of the forest.

I wasn't going to get very far in a hurry in this forest. I sat down on a mossy rotten log—everything was mossy and rotten—and let my breath out in a long sigh. There was no point in pushing on. Sooner or later the forest would disappear and I'd be back to the hillside of Douglas-fir and huckleberries, where the walking was easier. Meanwhile, I wished for a cigarette and let my eyes roam around.

The most common moss was the emerald green stuff I was sitting on, but there were plenty of other kinds. Bumps of soft fuzzy lime green competed with small carpets of wiry brown threads. The strangest moss was made of threads of green with orange tips.

Long grayish greenish strands like an old woman's hair hung from branches of a young tree. The little tree was encrusted with scabs of lichen too. I realized that the tree was not a cedar. Something else. I squinted at it. Hemlock, the forest told me.

Okay then. Across from me, where a root twisted over a rock, the moss was growing in feathers of green, like a miniature forest. A shiny black and purple beetle struggled along, and I knew how it felt. I watched it crawl out from the feathers and onto a patch of lumpy lichens and wondered if beetles had enough brains to feel relief. Or any emotion. It was moving faster.

A distant caw snagged my attention. A raven up on a branch high above my head took the air, twisted like an acrobat, and landed on a root pile, black and shiny against the background of moss. She cocked her head, and I said to one beady black eye, "What's up, Rachel?"

In answer the raven took flight. I pushed myself up to my feet, human again, and cold without my clothes. The old growth forest was gone, replaced by the timber lands with the straight, uniform trees and the lifeless silence. I trudged back up the slope until I found my clothes. One of my socks had rolled under a huckleberry. I extracted it and, dancing on one foot and then the other, I got my jeans and boots on. After shaking the needles out of my shirt, I put it on and headed downhill.

Part way down, it occurred to me that I hadn't seen a single bone. Any walkabout in the desert, in real time or that other reality, would be a walk among bones. They were everywhere. But here? Moss. Mold. Rot. Was that a bad thing? I decided it wasn't, just weird. Something else to get used to.

Chapter Twenty-Six

"I'm going to throw Harry out tonight," she said. "I can get someone better in that Quonset hut."

Did she mean me? Or was she thinking that I was going to leave, so she needed to find someone else?

Rachel and I stood side by side and surveyed the interior of the tavern. Val was fixing some fried fish for Old Man and his dog. The salmon were gone from the river, but some other species remained. Old Man had caught a lamprey which everyone said was inedible, but Rachel said, "You killed it, you eat it." Old Man was sitting at his usual table, knife and fork at the ready. If he found the fish inedible, he'd just feed it to his dog.

Jesus had brought his little family in. He and his wife had beer, and the kids had pop. They were sharing the table with a skinny old white guy wearing a rain jacket and jeans. The old guy's face had a fading bruise and a wound on one cheek. The only other customer that evening was Harry, the fist face guy.

"Why tonight?" I asked. "You been putting up with him for years."

She frowned, thinking. "I don't know if he's getting worse, or if I just don't have the tolerance anymore. And we need more help out here. He isn't helpful. I mean, look at Al." She nodded toward the old white guy at Jesus's table. "He's got Parkinson's. He's getting worse."

Al was trying to lift a glass of water, using both hands. Jesus was watching him, ready to grab if Al lost control of the glass.

Meanwhile, Harry was sprawled in his seat, legs wide, his crotch aimed at the rest of us. He wasn't saying or doing anything overtly obnoxious, but there was a sneer in the corner of his mouth and his eyes were unkind. He saw me and Rachel looking his way, so he tipped his beer at us, a gesture that would've been friendly if anyone else had done it.

"Most of the houses here are too far gone for anyone to live in them. I need that Quonset hut."

She turned away to watch Old Man. He was carefully picking the bones from the fish, a finicky process since his eyes weren't good. His dog sat, taut with anticipation, at his feet. Her big head was spit by a huge, sloppy smile full of drool.

"Just wait," he whispered, "I'm trying."

"And here I am!" Crazy Mary announced from the door. She arrived in a flourish of scarves and coats and began peeling off the layers, flinging her rainy weather clothes over a nearby table. I could smell her from twenty feet away.

Harry made a gagging noise and pinched his nose. Mary drew herself up in a dramatic display of offense. "You got a problem, Harry? Your nose bothering you?"

"God, woman, you're enough to gag a maggot. Take a shower before you come in here." Someone else could've said that as a pointed but friendly tease or maybe as a tired chronic complaint, but Harry's words were meant to hurt. Mary planted one hand on her hip and vamped her way across the room. She aimed her butt at Harry as she passed and farted at him.

I grinned and Valerie slapped her hand over her mouth. The bruise face guy set his glass down shakily and called out, "Hey, Mary, you drunk yet?"

She sauntered up, not as drunk as usual and able to keep herself upright without hanging on to the furniture. When she got close enough, she pointed at the bruised spot and asked, "What the hell happened to you, Al? Your girlfriend hit you one?"

He shrugged. "I was trying to not hit a deer. I hit a tree instead."

Mary guffawed. "Hit a tree instead. You dumbass. You're supposed to hit the deer."

"Knocked my teeth right though my cheek." He poked his cheek from the inside with his tongue. "Ttee tha ho?"

Jesus leaned forward to get a closer look. Well, we all did. Sure enough, in the middle of the faded yellowish-green bruise on his cheek was a ragged round red hole. Mary threw back her head and howled with delight. "I bet you could smoke through that!"

Al held the cigarette up to the hole, and we all made gagging noises.

"Watch this," he told us. Then he stuck the cigarette in his mouth, sucked in the smoke and, with his lips pursed closed, blew the smoke out his cheek.

We all cracked up and Mary called out. "Give the man another beer!"

Harry sneered, "Jesus, that's sick. Get to a doctor before you get gangrene."

Rachel snapped, "What the hell do you come in here for?"

And Mary said, "He thinks he oughta be the mayor of this town, not you, Rachel."

In the sudden silence, we all realized that she was right. Harry wanted to be the one everyone looked up to. He laughed as if Mary's remark was stupid, but we all knew it was true. He was jealous of Rachel.

Rachel frowned at him and spoke quietly, "I've made a decision, Harry. You're banned." Her voice was so gentle and calm that her words didn't register with him.

But they did with Mary. She let out a shrill cackle. "Hoo, she told you! Out on your ass, asshole!"

"She wasn't talking to me." Harry's glare took in all of us: me standing a little behind Rachel; Val leaning on the counter, her mouth slightly open and her eyes afraid; Jesus huddling next to his wife, the kids too scared to make a sound. Harry was confident and his confidence was intimidating.

Rachel said, "Harry, no. I meant you. You're banned. Now go on back to Rainier."

He couldn't believe what he heard. I saw the disbelief on his face plainly. He picked up his beer as if it was his admission ticket and took a long gulp. Then he set it down and said, "You need me in this crummy dump. I pay for my drinks."

"I don't need you," Rachel told him. "That's kind of the point, actually. And you don't need us."

He stood up. "I ain't going nowhere. Them, they need to leave." He pointed at Jesus and his family. "You think I can't tell they're illegals?" His voice accelerated into a shout.

Maria made a soft moan, and I stepped forward to Rachel's side.

"*She* belongs in a mental institution." He meant Mary. "This used to be a nice town, and this used to be a good bar. And *you*," Harry narrowed his eyes and glared at Rachel, "whatever you are. Indian? Get back to the reservation, squaw."

"Get out," Rachel whispered.

He laughed and I exploded. Just like that, my arms shot out and grabbed a chair. My legs took three steps, and my arms swung the chair through the air and down on Harry as if to hammer him through the floor. He yelled and fell. I kicked the chair out of the way and jumped him with every intention of ripping him into a bloody rag. I was going to bite him and tear him to shreds and gnaw him to pieces, but Rachel grabbed my shoulder and yelled into my ear, "Stop it, Jimmy."

I stood over Harry, teeth bared, ready to bite, and panting like a sprinter.

"Jimmy," Rachel tugged at my sleeve, "enough. You made your point."

Harry rolled to one side stiffly. He shot a glare at me and, moving carefully, climbed back to his feet. His face was brick red and his voice was choked with anger. "You're lucky I don't have my gun with me."

"You're lucky I don't have mine," I growled. Which was totally true. I would've shot him, not just once but over and over and over until the gun was empty.

Rachel patted my arm, but she spoke to Harry, "You better go now. Go on."

He flicked a glance around the room and sneered, "When I come back, I'll have Immigration with me. I'll get this place closed down."

"Okay, you try that," Rachel said.

He gave us a glare of disgust, picked up his baseball cap, and headed for the door, limping a bit. At the door he stopped for one last look at us. He had his chin up to show us that he wasn't intimidated. "I'll be back. This is my town too."

Rachel pinched my arm to keep me from responding. She waited until the door slammed behind Harry, then she whispered to me, "I won't let him come back." Waving her hand at her friends, she called out, "Hey, show's over. Let's all get back to eating and whatever."

"I coulda killed that fucker," I said. I was still shaking with pent up rage.

Rachel gave my shoulder a pat. "It's okay. I almost feel sorry for Harry. I mean he isn't the most obnoxious person around."

"That's Mary," said Al. He needed to see a doctor for his face but probably didn't have any money. "But Harry's an asshole. No loss."

"I have plans for that Quonset hut," Rachel explained.

"Here you go." Val set a plate of fried potatoes down in front of Al.

Rachel frowned. "Can you eat?" We all had visions of potato coming through the hole.

"Yeah, I can." We watched fascinated as he shakily stabbed a chip of potato with his fork. The potato bounced up and down on the way toward his mouth. He kept moving his head and his hand around until finally he speared the fork into his open mouth. Then he maneuvered the potato to the other cheek—we could tell by the bulging as he chewed. After swallowing, he said, "See?"

Chapter Twenty-Seven

I woke up when the windows were gray with dawn light and the stars were gone. Rachel was curled up like a kitten, hidden beneath her blankets and her tangle of hair. I slid carefully out of her bed and gathered up my clothes. After tiptoeing across the hall to my room, I tossed the clothes on the bed and went to the window. Her window looked across the road to Harry's Quonset hut and down toward the sawmill. Mine looked out over the slow, dark river and the miles of forest, still gray and black in that space between moonfall and sunrise. I wondered why she'd saved the room with the best view for guests. I lit a cigarette, and watched the sun come up. Well, watched the light come up. The sun was around behind the hills and wouldn't be up until ten or so. The sky lightened first into white and then into a fragile, gentle blue. Yellow touched the tree tops, followed by all kinds of green from the dark needles of the firs to the solid, almost oily green of the madrona trees. I saw the Old Man and his dog appear, shuffling slowly along the river bank and I knew that the day had begun. I went down stairs and made the coffee.

Out on the bench in front of the tavern, holding my coffee, I waited for Old Man. "Good morning," he said and carefully lowered himself on to the bench. I waited for him to ask a favor of me, but he didn't. Instead he fumbled a piece of jerky out of his pocket for the dog.

"Her name is Angela," he told me. "I found her out in the woods, oh, maybe eight years ago? Before my arthritis got so bad and I could still hike around in the woods."

Old people look like they have always been old. I couldn't picture Old

Man as young and spry. "I used to go out in to the woods a lot," he said. "Fishing in the streams or picking mushrooms."

I wondered if he'd ever been married. He'd let a lot of snippets of his life out but so far no mention of a woman.

"I don't know how she got herself lost out in the woods." He rubbed the dog's head. "But I sure am glad I found her."

"Man's best friend," I said, trying not to sound sardonic.

"That's for sure."

I wondered why he was sitting next to me. Trying to keep me from leaving? I had leaving on my mind, but at the same time I felt a reluctance to leave right then. As if in response to my thoughts, I heard the sound of footsteps and Rachel appeared in the doorway. She was wrapped in a blue shawl with a long fringe and her feet were bare.

"It's gonna be sunny today," she said. "Good day for driving." She smiled at each of us in turn.

Old Man glanced at me, startled. "Who needs to be driving anywhere?" he asked.

"Jimmy is." She was watching me through the steam rising from her coffee.

I shrugged. I was trying to not feel the little pain in my chest. "I thought I'd go see that mountain I heard about."

"Mt. Rainer?"

"Yeah." I didn't give a fuck about the mountain. Every word I said felt as heavy as a rock. But I wanted to leave, right? This place was a black hole. A place to get stuck. I'd told Rachel that coyotes did a lot of one night stands. I had told her not to count on me.

"It's beautiful." Old Man said. "I haven't been to see it in years and years." He reached down to fondle Angela's ears. "I guess you take things for granted if they're close by."

"It isn't that close," Rachel commented, her eyes on me. "To get there you have to drive through a couple of hours of city and suburb. Then turn around and drive back through it all again to get home." Took a sip of coffee and added, "I'll pack some snacks for you. For the road."

I drove down the shady green tunnel to the highway while trying to enjoy the sunny patches between tree shadows. Leaving was what I wanted to do, I told myself. Staying meant spending all my time toting dog food up the hill or fixing Val's back porch. I'd get roped into the greenhouse project. And hadn't Rachel sort of told me to get on my way? I tried to feel happy about it. Or at least not unhappy. I got to the highway faster than I wanted to.

Rachel's comment about it being a good day to drive kept replaying itself in my head. Was she pissed? She hadn't looked like she was. In my experience, spirits and coyotes weren't as clingy as people. We don't act like sex is some kind of contract, a transaction of a more binding kind than TJ's deals. Rachel might've enjoyed another night of making love, but she wasn't the type to treat one night like a promise of more. She hadn't made any kind of big deal out of saying goodbye.

But she'd done it. She'd said goodbye. She said it before I said anything about leaving. Before I had even finished my coffee.

I drove up the on ramp to the four lane highway and immediately crashed into a mood of grim irritation. Everything was ugly. The trees along the highway were just a fringe, not enough to mask the houses here and there and the junkyards and fields. Blackberry vines, dusted with highway dirt, choked out any native shrubs. I passed a huge vacant lot for some kind of failed business. Traffic wasn't heavy but still the air reeked of machinery, asphalt, and cow shit.

Some bastard in a truck was hauling cows, and they were desperately mooing, terrified. The truck caught up with me and hung beside me, the driver too oblivious to either slow down or speed up. I could smell the stink of piss, shit, and fear. I wanted to kill the driver. Instead, I took my foot off the gas, let the damn truck get ahead of me, and kept my eyes on the road.

I couldn't help the cows. Could I? I imagined myself passing the truck and forcing it over on the shoulder. Then shooting the damn driver and letting the cows out. There was no place for them to go. They wouldn't even be able to get through the blackberries to the properties on the other side. Besides, most likely the valley properties were farms where people had other cows they were going to use up and kill. The hillsides were timber lands with no place for cows.

There's no place in the world for you, I thought. I'm sorry. Yeah, I know, I killed rabbits all the time. But I didn't torture them first.

Rachel hadn't sent me off to save cows. I wished that she had. I would've liked to save their soft brown eyes. I liked their heavy awkward shapes, and they way they lived in groups, always near each other. I knew about cows because they lived in the desert. They didn't belong there and they ate the forage needed by the pronghorns, but it wasn't their fault. People sent them out, and they did the best they could to get by. I'd never bothered them, and they hadn't bothered me except as another way humans fucked up the desert.

Sheep, now. I ate lambs sometimes. But there's a difference between being a predator and being cruel on a large scale for money. The truck's brake lights came on, and it slowed for the turn lane. I aimed my eyes ahead and swept past, not looking. I'm sorry cows, I thought. I gripped the steering wheel as if it was trying to run away.

The highway curved to the south, was joined by another highway, and turned into one of those multi-lane monstrosities that sucks you relentlessly into an urban area where more cars and trucks crowd and compete and intimidate each other. I don't mind saying it was no place for me. There wasn't really a lot of traffic, but I was used to Nevada where there usually wasn't any. I had some cars ahead of me and some behind me. One was lurking in my blind spot, and there was one broke down by the side of the road, poor sap. An old man huddled by his vehicle, buffeted by the dirty wind kicked up by the passing traffic. I was headed south, and he was stuck on the side headed north, but going nowhere.

The trees thinned until both sides of the road were lined by box-like buildings. Rows of boxes for apartments, lines of boxes around parking lots that used to be malls, stacks of boxes along the city streets. Everything had the look of old plastic—the boxes were from back in the nineties, probably, and looked worn. Here and there a tree fought for survival. I hated it all.

Traffic picked up from entry lanes on both sides. We all rounded a corner in a herd and suddenly, hanging in the sky over the urban area, I saw a mountain. Just one magnificent snow-covered peak that seemed to be floating on a cloud, disconnected from earth. The slopes of the mountain were a slightly darker shade of blue than the blue of the sky. It rose up like a dream, like a fantasy of lost beauty, like a rebuke to the ugliness of the city.

Someone honked and I jerked my attention back to the road. Four lanes had become six. Traffic was converging from all directions and I couldn't take my eyes off the road to look at the mountain anymore. Big signs warned of intersections approaching. One said "Portland South one mile." I did *not* want to get shunted onto a highway to Portland. An exit ramp opened up on my right and I took it.

The ramp swooped down to a traffic light, and I made a sudden transition from fast to stopped. On the corner, a skinny young woman held up a sign that said, "Anything helps God bless." Her small, dull eyes peered out from under a sweatshirt hood. At her feet, a brown dog crouched.

The light was red. I rolled my window down. "Over here."

She lumbered off the curb and between cars. I gave her the change that had accumulated in the coffee holder. She said, "God bless you," but not like she meant it. The dog's eyes tracked her hand. I hope you spend that money on your damn dog, I thought.

The light changed to green. With cars backed up impatiently behind me, I almost panicked because I had no idea where I was going. The parking lot next to an EV station offered refuge. I drove straight across the intersection, turned in, parked, and turned the engine off.

Then I just sat there for a while. Cars and trucks drove by. I was surrounded by asphalt, concrete, metal, and plastic. The only plants were weeds that had bravely shoved their way up through the cracks in the pavement.

Ironically, I could still see the mountain. It floated serenely above the city, oblivious to the traffic and the noise and the smells. All in shades of blue and white, it didn't seem real.

My truck had one of those gizmos that gives you directions, but I'd never set it up. Back in Nevada, I always knew where I was and how to get where I was going. How lost can you get when there's hardly any roads? Besides the only cities I ever went to were easy to get in and out of. In Las Vegas, I just drove in on the one main highway, looked for some casino towers, and parked in a parking garage. Salt Lake was more complicated, but I rarely went into the city itself. I got what I needed in the suburbs. I remembered what Rachel said about getting to Mt. Rainier. Hours of urban driving to get there. Hours of urban driving to get back where you started from. I dug my map out of the glove box and took a look.

I didn't even know where I was except that I was on the west side of Olympia. The highway from Rainier snaked its way into town before it disappeared into a tangle of merging and separating highways and city streets. There were at least thirty different ways to get confused in that mess and get headed the wrong direction. Assuming that I got through that...I tried to follow the lines to Mt. Rainier. Get on I5. Turn onto 512. Turn again in a place with the improbable name of Puyallup. Then turn again onto a different road and then again and again and I still wasn't at the mountain.

No way. No way I would ever get through that scramble of red, black, and blue lines.

I looked up at the mountain again and, unexpectedly, I remembered a quote from the Bible. Something about lifting my eyes to the mountains from whence cometh strength. But I'd never find my way there. I'd just get lost or get in an accident. And if I did finally get there, would it turn out to be just another place where I didn't belong? Would it turn out to be all fucked up from climate change? Did I even want to go there?

What did I want?

Fuck. My thoughts were as scrambled as the roads on the road map. I didn't know what the fuck I wanted to do. I couldn't sit there in the parking lot all day, surrounded by traffic and noise. I had to go someplace. Fuckfuckfuck.

With a snarl, I got the truck moving and shoved my way out into the traffic, making a little coupe brake and honk. I didn't care. I just intimidated some more drivers until I was in right lane for the on ramp. After driving under the highway, I hit my blinker and waited impatiently for the traffic to clear. Once the street traffic unclogged, I shot up the on ramp. Fuck all of this. I'm getting out of here.

I had a yearning for the desert where I could see for thirty miles and not see a single vehicle. Back to where the animals I saw on the road were dead already and not dying, begging at me with their despairing eyes. Back where I could see lots of mountains and could go visit them anytime I wanted.

But I'd left for a reason. It wasn't my home anymore. It was a place of used-to-be. Loss. Sorrow.

I shoved my way onto the highway by making a small truck cringe and change lanes, and I headed north. The retail and apartment boxes rolled by, followed by a shabby neighborhood of trailers, some miserable ratty fir trees, and a big sign advertising a casino. And there was the old guy with the dead car. He waved at me, and we made eye contact. As I passed, his arm fell to his side, limp with defeat, and I muttered to myself, "Shit."

Shit, fuck, damn. Okay, so that's what Rachel had planned. She was some powerful spirit. Sneaky bitch. I didn't know if I was pissed or impressed. I put my blinker on and pulled onto the shoulder. He's not going to be my stray cat, I told myself. He'll be Rachel's problem. She will get whatever kind of help another old man can give her.

The old guy looked as frail as spiderweb. He was wearing jeans, a T-shirt, and an over-sized wool shirt that was going to be too hot in an hour. In spite of the old clothes, there was something respectable about him—maybe the sad eyes blinking behind his glasses.

"I need some help," he said as I walked up. A truck roared past us and blasted us with hot air.

"Broke down?" I asked, stating the obvious.

"Yeah, it's an electric and they...I don't know anything about them. I could sort of diagnose what ailed the old kind but these new ones baffle me." He gestured helplessly with one hand. Rachel, I thought, are you sure you want this one? The world was full of people in need, and most of them would be more help than this guy.

"I take it you didn't just run out of charge?"

"It isn't that. But I let my phone charge run down, so I can't call anyone." His eyes asked for understanding, but his mouth showed that he was mad at himself.

"You can use mine. You can either call for a tow in Olympia or you can call for one to Rainier. I'm going that direction, and I know of a place you can stay while the work's getting done." I waited to see what he would do.

He hesitated. "I don't have towing insurance."

"Do you have anywhere to stay in Olympia?"

"No." His shoulders were rounded with defeat.

"Well, the place I know of is free. I know the landlady. It's gonna cost you for a tow either way."

Still dithering, he looked around as if an answer was hiding in the scotch broom along the road.

"Your call." I could've used my skills to make up his mind for him, but I didn't.

"Okay," he said, finally. "If you're sure it's okay with the landlady."

"She'll be glad to have someone staying in the place she's got. It's empty now."

He stuck his hand out. "I'm Charlie."

I was caught by surprise. I always forget about these little rituals people go through. But I got my hand out, gave his a brief pump, and said, "I'm Jim. Let's go."

"I'll need some of my stuff." Apologetically.

"Oh sure."

He opened his car and I could see that he had all of his worldly goods in there packed into boxes and suitcases. I let him rummage through and pick out what he wanted. We hauled two boxes and two suitcases over to my truck. His stuff went in the back and we climbed in the front.

It was easy to get on the road because we were going north and all of the traffic was headed south. He let a mile or so go by and started talking.

"I used to be a college professor." He spoke wistfully, as if he had no current identity, only the identity of what used to be. "I retired a while ago."

I didn't know what to say to that so I just grunted.

"I had to retire even though the pension isn't much because my wife got sick. I took care of her."

I could tell where his story was headed. "She passed away?"

"Yeah. It took two years." And probably cost him a bundle, judging by the experience of Janey's dad. "I sold our house." His voice trailed off.

I said, "So you need a new life."

"Yes, that's what I need. A new life." But he sounded doubtful.

"You'll like Warrentown." I told him.

Chapter Twenty-Eight

The trip back went fast. So fast I almost missed the turn.

"Aren't we going to Rainier?" Charlie asked, bracing himself on the dashboard as I took the turn hard.

"Your car can go there," I said. "I'm taking you to Warrentown. It's kind of a ghost town, but there's a few people still living there."

"Okay." We slowed down for the run up through the green forest. Charlie perked up a bit as the trees closed in. "I like the old big leaf maples," he commented. "Is that a river over there?"

"Yeah."

"It must be..." He thought about it. "It must be the Wishnacum?"

"I don't know."

"A lot of the rivers have names that come from white people not being able to pronounce indigenous names correctly." He grinned. "Humptulips. Dosewallup. Lilliwaup."

Ahead of us on the right I saw an over-sized pickup stopped with the hood up. A runty guy with a pissed off expression waved his arm at us. I gave him the finger as we passed.

Charlie looked at me in surprise. "Friend of yours?"

I checked the rear view mirror. Harry was shaking a fist at me. "He had something the mayor needed," I told Charlie "You'll meet her. Her name is Rachel and don't piss her off."

"I'll try not to do that," he said, eyebrows up. "What kind of behavior pisses her off?"

"She wants people to be helpful."

"Okay." He went quiet, thinking, I suppose, of how he could be helpful. And suddenly there we were back in Warrentown. Afternoon sun gleamed on the slow river, where the grayish-green water was nearly the same color as the weathered wood of the tavern. Old Man was sitting on the bench with his dog beside him. An ancient gas-fueled truck was parked halfway up on the sidewalk as if it was drunk. The right hand side of the front was bandaged with layers of duct tape. Al, the guy with a hole in his face, was propped up against the hood. And there was Rachel, standing outside the tavern waiting for us.

I parked and we got out of my truck. Charlie followed me toward the tavern. He hung back a bit. Shy, I guess.

"So who is this?" Rachel asked. She was teasing because she knew.

"Charlie," I said. "He's a retired college professor."

"Oh?" Rachel lifted one eyebrow in inquiry. "What did you profess?"

Charlie blinked behind his glasses. "I taught poetry." He shrugged, embarrassed. "I've published a few books of poetry. Out of print now. I don't know if I can be helpful."

"Oh, I don't know. Having a poet around will lift the tone of the place." She nodded toward the tavern. "Come on in. I'll introduce you to some people."

The party didn't really get started until after a crew of old used-to-be bikers hauled in. Big beer-bellied guys with long gray hair and long gray beards, they parked themselves around one of the tables and slapped a deck of cards down in challenge to all comers. The leader, I discovered, was named Vulture.

I took the challenge. Since we were playing poker for pennies and nickels, I didn't cheat. Much. Just a little. Meanwhile Crazy Mary kept up a running commentary on the game, emceeing like a sportscaster.

"And Jimmy throws down an ace that he'd been hiding up his sleeve! That beats Sammish Bob's one pair and the round of five card draws to a close. Get it? Five card draw draws to a close!"

Sammish Bob muttered something rude, but Vulture glared him into silence. I scooted the pot of loose change over to my side and accidentally elbowed an empty beer bottle off the table.

"Ca—rashh!" Mary shouted, "As the liquor takes hold, will the game get more exciting? How will we stand the excitement when the stakes are so high, right?" She laughed like a crow. I saw Sammish Bob start another mutter and Vulture stop him with another stare. The other three gang members were solemn, quietly determined guys who studied their cards with the intensity of Russian chess players. One pulled in a pot every three or four hands, with no change of expression at all between winning or losing. The other two were getting silently intense about their loses.

"I need another beer. Anyone?" I asked.

One of the tense ones growled, "You paying?"

I said, "Sure." Why not? I was paying with their money. Vulture said "I'm good. For now," and took a big slug.

Val was leaning on the counter, trying to chat with Maria. Charlie perched nervously on a bar stool, looking like he was trying to fit in and failing. Maria's pretty golden brown skin glowed in the light of the Coleman lantern and her thick braid gleamed blue black. I thought about asking her how she liked being a ghost but I didn't know if Val was aware. And Charlie definitely didn't know about ghosts.

"Cerveza," said Maria, holding up her beer.

"I know that one," Val told her. "Cerveza." She tapped her finger on her glass. "How do you say this?"

Maria laughed, but shyly like someone not used to laughing. "Sorry. Please."

"Maybe your husband could tell me?" Maria just looked confused, so Val pointed. "Husband? Jesus?"

Charlie cleared his throat. "If I may interject...The word for 'husband' is 'esposo'."

Maria's face lit up. "Si', esposo. Mi esposo, Jesus."

"Oh, you know Spanish?" Val turned to Charlie. "That'll be helpful. We're always playing charades with Jesus and Maria."

"Well, sorry, not really. It's just that some words in Spanish are very similar to some words in English. Esposo and spouse, for example." His voice had the rhythm of a lecture. "Or lavar and lavatory. Spanish words that end with 'iudad' are very similar to English words that end with 'ty'. Cuidad and city, for example."

"Huh," Val responded, "I guess you could give us lessons."

Charlie's shoulders hunched and he contracted his head like a turtle. "Sorry. I used to be a college professor, and I guess I'm still in the habit of lecturing."

"Never mind," I said, "Rachel thinks she traded up, and that's all that matters. Val, gimme couple more, okay?"

I ignored Charlie's look of confusion. I'd brought him to the lake. It was up to him to learn to swim.

"I like this song," Rachel emerged from the back room, her head tilted as she listened. There had been music in the background all evening, country mostly, some country rock, and the melodic kind of pop. Old music from back in the 1980s or even earlier. I hadn't been listening but Rachel's comment made me tune in. A sad, tired, wistful voice sang that whatever the the fight was about, it could wait 'til the morning. Melissa Manchester. I'd always liked that song too.

I kept listening as I carried the beers back to the table. Rachel intercepted me before I could sit down.

"Waltz?" she asked with a definite leer in her eye. The music changed to a lush drunken country song about waltzing across Texas. I set the beers down and Rachel grabbed me. I swung her around into a dip with her head thrown back and her hair falling nearly to the floor. Someone whistled, probably Mary. I pulled Rachel back up and we leaned into the music, swaying back and forth. I had a vision of me and Rachel dancing under the star-encrusted desert sky. She was grinning up at me, and my vision morphed into the two of us in bed together.

Rachel was just the right height to fit her head under my chin. My fingers got all tangled in her long black hair, and I could feel her warm breath against my neck. When the music changed, we stopped waltzing across Texas and instead began a tuneful, sentimental waltz across Tennessee. Jesus and Maria joined us, smiling into each other's faces. Their kids watched and I thought about TJ. I wished she'd find someone who could teach her that sex wasn't a commodity for transactions.

But I didn't think about her for long because Rachel had started kissing my neck. She worked her way up to my ear, and then pulled me down and kissed my mouth. The jukebox was playing "Slow Hand" as we headed upstairs.

Later, in the moonlight, we talked. "I can drive you to Mt. Rainier," she said. "It's nonstop urban for a long time between here and there."

"I dunno." Besides, I'd realized that I'd rather keep the mountain as something precious in my mind. A mountain of my imagination. Rachel had mellowed me out so much that anger seemed like something some other me had felt.

"How do you do it?" I asked.

"Do what?"

"Keep on living here when so much is gone."

Her head was deep in her pillow, and her black hair was sprawled over both of us, reminding me of Janey and her dad and how they had looked in death. "I just...am still taking care of this place. I just take care of different living beings than I used to."

"Humans," I said, and I felt the old, sad anger creeping up on me.

"Look at me." Rachel got up on one elbow, so I could see her face. Her eyes and hair were black in the darkness, but the smooth skin of her face was a pale as the moon. "I know this isn't your place," she said.

"No, it isn't."

"But neither is anywhere else."

I let that comment sink in. She was right. She fell back on her side with a soft sigh. Pulling the blanket up to her shoulder, she cuddled against me, her head on my arm. "So maybe instead of a place, you could have friends."

The flat silvery disc of the moon glowed through the misty darkness. Her room was a cozy nest, but high up in the air, giving a feeling of possibility, a place for launching into flight. I dragged my imagination away from Janey and her dad and instead pictured myself pushing the wheelbarrow up the hill to Old Man and Angela. I saw myself nailing plastic sheeting around the greenhouse, watched by the silent ghost children. Eating dinner with Rachel's friends after a day's work. Going for a run down the river road to see what I could find. Rabbits, maybe. Maybe I'd meet a fox and get some local info about the food in the valley. My arm was getting tingly from the weight of Rachel's head.

"Maybe," I said, but after such a long pause that Rachel had fallen asleep.

"I don't know," I said to the dark room. "I'll try it for a while."

Epilogue

Rachel slipped quietly out from under the covers. Coyote kept his breath deep and regular in imitation of sleep. He felt the bed shift under Rachel's weight and heard the gentle thump as her feet landed on the floor. She let the blanket slide down from her shoulders. Coyote, peeking through narrowed eyes, admired the way her long black hair spilled down her back.

The room smelled of warm bodies and sex. Rachel sniffed, enjoying the scent, then stood up. Pearly gray moonlight lay on the floor and illuminated the windows. Coyote watched as, barefoot and naked, she walked the moon's path. Then she slid her fingers under the latch and pulled the window up. It rose easily; she'd made sure of that years ago.

Rachel stepped onto the window sill, first one bare foot and then the other. Already her body was collapsing, her toes changing into claws, her elbows into wing bones. She shook her long black hair into a cascade of black feathers, flapped hard, and launched herself into the night sky.

Coyote lifted himself up on one elbow. He, too, enjoyed the smell of warm bodies and sex. He was also enjoying the warmth she'd left behind under the sheets and the moist, cool air that touched him lightly on his shoulders. Rachel had left the window open.

In the moonlit darkness, Rachel's collection of precious objects glinted and gleamed. It didn't matter what the objects were; she collected things for their shine, not their shape or utility. It amused Coyote that her found objects lit the shadows of the room like stars, as if the night sky had sailed in through the open window.

Stars. Coyote considered getting up to look out the window but decided not to bother. He knew there would be no stars visible. Back home...back home stars had been a nightly source of delight. Every star in the universe was visible from the Valley of Dry Bones. Bones, stars, and the mountains had framed his life, but now he lived in a place of rot, trees, and clouds. Everything dies and feeds the ground, Coyote reminded himself. There was a floating mountain he could visit someday if he wanted to, and the stars were still shining somewhere on the other side of the clouds. Maybe he'd pick up Rachel's love of the moon.

She was out there sailing around in the black air, rejoicing in the moonlight. Looking over her town, her people, and her animals. Maybe Valerie's light would be on. Val was an insomniac. She sat up all night reading by her Coleman lantern while her animals slept. The obnoxious baby goat was probably curled up against the warm belly of the pig, and the chickens were most likely cuddled together somewhere, maybe under Val's back porch. Rachel knows where everyone sleeps, he thought.

She wouldn't see any light at Old Man's house. Probably wouldn't be long before she wouldn't see an old man, either. Coyote wondered who would take care of Angela after the old guy died. Someone would. Angela wouldn't be left to starve.

Meanwhile, Jesus and Maria were probably zonked out, tired from working all day. And Mary would be face down somewhere, passed out. Charlie? For some reason Rachel had wanted a poet for the community. Well, she had one now. Maybe he'd be useful and maybe he wouldn't.

Coyote rolled over on his back and closed his eyes. Rachel would be back soon. They'd snuggle together in her bed. He wasn't home, but he didn't feel like moving on either. Maybe she was right about looking for friends instead of looking for a place. Maybe he could grow to love looking after Warrentown the way he had once loved living in the desert. It wouldn't be easy, but he had adapted to change before. He decided to stay. For a while anyway.

Raven Woman's Tavern

The Second Novella

Prologue

Most white people think the story of Warrentown started with the loggers, but that isn't true. The story started with Raven. Well, if you go back far enough it started with Creation, but it was Raven who, many millennia ago, lit on a tree branch overlooking the curve of the river and gave the place a name. She called it home.

That's it. That's the whole story: Raven landed in the river valley, found it good, and called it home. That's not much of a story, but she didn't call the valley home because anything in particular happened there. She just found what she needed: food, water, protection from the weather, and companionship. She was able to raise raven babies there from her series of relationships. (Raven loved deeply but in succession.)

She was happy most of the time in her home. Not singing and dancing and laughing her head off, of course. Just content and sometimes more than that. Sometimes she experienced the most precious of all emotions, grateful delight.

She was delighted by the first silly flights of her children. She was delighted by the long golden beams of evening light that made the meadow grass glow with orange on green. She was delighted by the feel of wind under her wings and by the silvery glisten of raindrops on the needles of the cedars. She was delighted by her lovers for as long as the love lasted. Many things delighted Raven, even the relentless pounding of winter rain.

She shared the bend in the river with people who had their own name for the little meadow in the valley. They called it Fish Camp because they came up in the fall for the salmon. Raven delighted in the fish guts they left on the grass. She also liked to eavesdrop on the stories they told their children and, to her delight, some of the stories were about her.

She wasn't delighted by death, but she knew it was the price paid for life.

People came and went. Animals came and went. Fish came and went. Plants came and went. Raven watched and loved and said goodbye when the time came.

And so, her daily story repeated for many, many years: days of eating, procreating, raising children, feeling delighted, and sleeping with a grateful heart. And saying goodbye when the time came.

But then one day, strangers pushed a dirt road up the valley and chopped down the trees. The cedars were ancient, some as much as five hundred years old, but it only took a team of timber beasts a couple hours to saw one down. They attacked the trees in teams, chopping and sawing until, one at a time, the great cedars were murdered.

If Raven had known what was coming, she might've chosen to die. Instead, she fought. She caused accidents. She led loggers into the woods and left them to die of hyperthermia. She made them careless, encouraged drunkenness, and led them to whorehouses so they'd get diseases. But the timber beasts just kept coming. The bosses didn't care how many got chewed up by accidents or died; the men were replaceable. No matter how many of them cut off their own hands or dropped trees on each other, the bosses always found more to send into the woods.

And the loggers got more organized. The company built a sawmill and improved the road. A collection of little cottages appeared to house the sawmill workers. Little businesses moved in. Horses were replaced by trucks, power lines replaced the old oil lamps, and a school was built. They called the place "Warrentown" after the man who owned the sawmill.

After a millennia of living, the ancient forest was killed in less than one hundred years. It was replaced by a forest of young trees, cut on a cycle of mere decades. The first people, the animals, the plants, and the birds were pushed into smaller living spaces or died.

Meanwhile, the people of the town were proud of what they'd accomplished. They had lots of stories about the old days—by which they meant when the loggers first appeared. They had tales of fights, accidents, and deaths, but also of building, growing, and settling. Their lives were, in many ways, like Raven's: they ate, they procreated, they slept, and they sometimes felt delight. They prayed with gratitude to a god that they believed was on their side. They didn't see destruction. They thought they were building a future for their children. They weren't.

Raven watched them from her retreat in the woods. Unlike many of her friends and neighbors, she had the choice of staying because she was adaptable. She hated the raw, boring, sterile, new forest, but she could survive.

So Raven watched the town and, after a while, she got to know many of the town's people. She even grew to like some of them. However, she didn't like any of them well enough to follow them when they left–and leave they did, most of them, when the mill closed. The trees had been over-harvested, the corporation sought profits elsewhere, and the town died. The people, after killing everything around them, had brought destruction on themselves. Raven got a bitter satisfaction out of that.

But the death of the town was only a symptom of a larger problem. Changes came, an accelerating cascade of changes set in motion by the people over a hundred years previously. The climate grew warmer and threw everything out of whack. The winters were more rainy and the summers hotter and drier. Fleas proliferated. Many of the remaining cedars and hemlocks died. The migrant birds no longer arrived, and the spring was nearly silent. The forest animals–ravaged by fleas, disease, and hunger–could no longer raise families and died out. The orcas starved as the fisheries collapsed.

Raven watched the devastation with the courage of despair. Her world, the world of delight and gratitude, was driven away by chaos. But she could fly, and when she flew high enough into the sky, she could see that the river remained, as did the hills, the rocks, and the rain. The sunset still sent golden beams across the meadows and glowed on the skeletal forests. The night, soft and comforting, obscured the sins of the people. The valley of the river bend was her place and remained her vantage point for watching the world. Animals, plants. and people came and went, but Raven stayed.

Chapter One
Rachel and Jimmy Go into Rainier to Shop

They did a drive-by, rolling along just beneath the speed limit. There wasn't much traffic in town: just a few bicyclists, a motorcycle, and an electric delivery truck. Their old-style hybrid car stood out, which was bad, but there was nothing they could do about it.

Jimmy drove while Rachel checked out the pharmacy parking lot and the parking spaces in front of the adjacent stores. They saw no sign of the militia. Jimmy popped the blinker on and they turned the corner, giving Rachel a view of the pharmacy's solid, windowless wall. He hit the blinker again, and they turned into the grocery store parking lot behind the pharmacy. It was six o'clock and near closing time for most businesses. Jimmy navigated through the grocery parking around to the far side of the pharmacy and parked where their car couldn't be seen from the pharmacy's back door.

They got out and strolled casually around to the front of the building. Though they were trying to look inconspicuous, they were a striking couple. Rachel was short, lithe, and dark, while Jimmy was as lean and sharp-eyed as a sheep-killing dog. They ambled together through the front parking lot the pharmacy shared with its neighbor businesses. The one functioning shop, a secondhand store, was just closing. They picked up their pace and hit the door of the pharmacy just as the clerk inside was preparing to close up.

Jimmy strong-armed the door and strode in. The clerk, a young woman, startled but friendly, almost staggered to get out of his way. Jimmy took a quick scan of the interior as Rachel flipped the sign to "closed." The clerk stuttered, "Can I help you?"

"We're the last customers," Rachel told her. She smiled into the clerk's confused gaze and repeated firmly, "You're closed now, and we're the last customers."

"All clear," said Jimmy. He pulled his gun out from the back of his jeans and pointed it at the clerk. Her wide-eyed gaze went from startled to frightened, and her mouth opened. Before she could scream, Rachel locked eyes with her and stated firmly, "You are going to close your mouth and stay calm. And you now are going to lock the door." She backed up her words with a focused thought: Shut up and lock the door.

The clerk swallowed hard and clamped her mouth shut. Still round-eyed, she fumbled the key in the lock.

Rachel and Jimmy knew that the pharmacy had one clerk out front and a pharmacist and tech in back. They also knew that the front door was out of sight from the back, blocked by stacks of shelves loaded with sundries, over-the-counter medicines, and candy. Rachel took the young woman's arm and told her, "We're going to the back now. You will not speak. We aren't going to hurt you if you follow directions."

"Yep," Jimmy told her. "This is a stick-up. So, get moving." They marched to the back of the store.

The pharmacist, a thin white man of middle age, was frowning at a computer screen on the far side of a counter. Behind him in the stacks of medicines, someone was whistling aimlessly. They heard the rip of a cardboard box being opened. Jimmy held the pistol up and barked "Hey!" to get the pharmacist's attention.

"Uh, what?" Understanding dawned on the pharmacist's face, and his mouth dropped open.

"Be calm," Rachel told him. "Don't resist. Call your help to come out here."

"There's no one," he stuttered, his eyes darting around.

"Yeah, there is. Do it," Jimmy's voice was knife-sharp.

The pharmacist cleared his throat and called, "Joanie."

"Huh?" Joanie emerged, a short, round, white woman with grey hair and thick glasses. She saw the gun and came to an abrupt halt.

"Okay, everyone," Rachel said. "I've got a simple direction for you to follow. Place your hands on the counter and keep them flat. Got that, everyone?"

They all just stared, too scared to move. Jimmy snapped, "Is there anything in this place worth dying for?" Three pairs of frightened eyes blinked at him. "So, get those hands on the counter."

They complied, the two clerks shakily, the pharmacist with his lips compressed in disapproval.

Rachel pulled a black garbage bag out of the pouch of her sweatshirt. Moving briskly, she worked her way down the aisles toward the front of the store, scooping band-aids, toothpaste, over-the-counter pain killers, and vitamins into her bag. She hit the cash registers and cleaned the money out of the till, her fingers quick and efficient. Then she paused, her attention snagged by the glittering display of Halloween-themed key rings and jewelry draped over a plastic statue of a witch. Rachel's hand hovered over the witch. Then she snatched it up, shook it until the necklaces and key rings fell off, and dumped it headfirst into her bag. Conscious that she was taking too much time, she headed at a trot up the personal hygiene aisle, tossing shampoo and soap into her bag on her way.

Jimmy watched his three hostages while she worked. The older clerk's fingers trembled on the counter, and the younger one's mouth worked incessantly as if she wanted to speak. The pharmacist worried Jimmy a bit; he was visibly seething, and he was clearly planning his call to the militia. Jimmy's mouth was tight with irritation when Rachel finally joined him, hauling her heavy bag.

"Now we're coming around to your side." Rachel grabbed the young clerk by the arm and marched her around back. Jimmy followed, keeping the gun aimed in their direction.

"Okay, almost done," Rachel told them. "We need some antibiotics, some pain killers, and some of your meds for crazy people. Then we're going out the back door. Lead the way." They pushed the pharmacy staff along in a little herd through the maze of stacks while Rachel grabbed bottles and boxes and tossed them into her bulging bag.

"Done now!" Rachel sang out cheerfully.

"Back door," Jimmy told them. "Move."

He made the staff sit on the floor along the wall beside the back door. Rachel pulled a roll of black electrician's tape out of her pouch and taped their hands and feet. They'd get free in a few minutes; all she really wanted to do was slow them down.

Jimmy stood by the door with his hand on the knob. He shoved the door open the minute Rachel finished taping the last pair of hands. Rachel directed her black eyes at each frightened face in turn and stated firmly, "You will not remember what we look like. You will not be able to describe us." Then, black bag bouncing on her heels, she followed Jimmy out the door. They walked briskly but calmly along the back of the pharmacy and around the corner to their waiting car. Rachel tossed the bag in the trunk and climbed into the back seat. She ducked down out of sight while Jimmy got the car started. He drove carefully right below the speed limit down the main drag.

"That was fun," Rachel called from the floor of the backseat.

"Stay down, we ain't out of town yet," Jimmy told her.

Chapter Two

Meanwhile, Valerie and Charlie the Poet

I*, Valerie the Crazy Cat Lady, do bequeath my cats, chickens, and pig to Charlie the Poet.*

Valerie set her pen down. The will required a date, so she sat back and examined her calendar. A splotch of mold was creeping across a picture of geraniums and bouncy playful kittens. The year was 2031.

Val's stomach clenched with an emotion she did not want to name. Instead, she made a decision not to estimate how many years had passed since she'd nailed the calendar to the wall. She didn't count years. She didn't count days. Sometimes she didn't count minutes. Instead, she wrote *"Right now"* on the line for the date in carefully formed italics and stabbed a period down with a flourish.

Then she sat back and smiled to herself, thinking about Charlie reading those words. He would understand the mixed blessing of the burden. He was the right choice; Charlie was old, vague, and inefficient, but he was the only person that she knew for sure wouldn't eat Pig as soon as money ran out. He'd eat the eggs. He'd eat a chicken if it died of old age. But he could not look Pig in the eye and shoot him.

Of course, in the long run, he'd have the same problem she had: who to care for the animals after he left. But some problems were not hers. No, she was going to take her problems and dump them right on Charlie. Val grinned; revenge, sort of. *That's what you get for being a nice guy, Charlie*, she wrote. Then she sighed and leaned back in her chair. *That's what I get for … her thought trailed off.

Outside the last of the sun was gleaming through fat clouds gently tinged with rose and orange. Between the clouds, the sky was a deep evening blue, as smooth and solid-looking as a plastic bowl. She squinted and thought about her metaphor: the sky as a plastic bowl. Plastic will inherit the earth, she told herself. It will outlive us all. Her pen was plastic, too. What would happen to her pen after she died? Val threw the pen down, impatient with herself and her maudlin introspection. She shoved her piece of paper–her draft will or plan or whatever it was–to the back of her desk and set a rock on top of it.

Then she sighed again and climbed to her feet. To be human, she thought, is to get used to things. That's what people did to survive. The world was on fire, millions were refugees, species were going extinct, but she needed to keep plodding along, coping and hoping, but mostly ignoring what she could of the savagery of the world. She was grateful for Rachel and Jimmy because it was their protection that allowed her to obtain food for herself and the animals. She was grateful to Jesus, Maria, and their kids for the garden. And she was grateful to Charlie for the friendship. So, buck up, she told herself.

Besides, no matter what kind of mood she was in, the animals had to be fed and watered: her cats, her chickens, and Pig. And when she got done feeding the animals, she'd head down to the tavern to fix dinner for whoever showed up later that evening. Jimmy and Rachel would be back soon with a delivery, so most of the neighborhood would be dropping by. Her neighbors, too, were on her list of those to be fed and watered. Life goes on, she thought, grinning ironically. In the midst of death, we are alive. For now.

Charlie was fully aware that poetry would not keep him from starving. Some days he thought nothing would. Some days, heck nearly every day, he told himself that he was glad to be old, widowed, and childless; it was better to experience the end of the world on his own. Still he was a writer, and writers write. So, he wrote:

We are experiencing the rare blessing of sunshine. The sun that is burning up the rest of the world with drought and fire is nurturing us. The veggies in the greenhouse will lift their fragile leaves in gratitude and process that light through their cells.

I wonder how that feels? Does it tingle?

Charlie climbed to his feet, a slow process given his arthritis. With one hand on the shaky railing of the Quonset hut's battered front porch, he held his other hand up to the sun. He did not feel like a young plant. Plants were pliable and full of promise. He was elderly and teetered on the brink of a despair so deep it was like a black hole to oblivion. However, despite his sorrow, he still could feel a tentative warmth on his palm and the light touch of the breeze on his wrist.

Carefully Charlie lowered himself back onto the plastic lawn chair. He took up his pen and wrote:

The little plants are growing, and to the extent possible for a plant, they are probably enjoying themselves. To the extent possible, each day I try to experience some joy, even if for only a moment, because I can't stand the alternative. Today, I can feel a tiny wisp of joy while thinking about plants.

That wasn't much. Charlie leaned back in his chair and surveyed the landscape of his life. His porch had a view of the Raven Tavern's dumpster and the associated raccoons, rats, and stray cats. He could see a little way up the hill to Valerie's cottage, one of the three houses still occupied. All of the lawns had reverted to weeds and Scotch broom, with a desperate rose or camellia hanging onto life here and there.

The view in the other direction was better. From his porch, Charlie could see across the road to the river. He picked up his pen.

Looking around, I can feel a touch of joy in the reflections on the river water. Water is not blue, except to people who are not really looking. The river is a deep dark green on the far bank where it is shadowed by the alders and willows. Mid-river there are ever-changing shapes in off-white, black, blue, and silver: sky and clouds.

And the clouds sail overhead, oblivious to all suffering. I can feel a faint stirring of delight in the lovely randomness of their cottony shapes. And my heart is lifted by the shadings of blue and the tinges of gold, the very first beginnings of evening. Heaven-like. If I was a painter, that's what I would love to paint.

Charlie set his notebook down on the other lawn chair, the one he kept for guests, and gazed up Main Street. He saw the sad, bent shape of an old man inching his way along the sidewalk, accompanied by his ugly dog. The dog stopped for a sniff and pee, and the old man waited patiently. *There's something to cherish,* Charlie wrote. *Their love.* The old man chatted with the dog as they bumbled along, and the dog appeared to be listening.

Then a whomping sound caught Charlie's attention. Valerie had stepped out her front door and was shaking out a throw rug. Her curly gray hair bounced around her face, and he could see the sagging muscles of her upper arms flopping around with each jerk on the rug. Valerie gave one last shake and disappeared back into her house.

Val would be heading down to the tavern soon, Charlie knew. It was an odd tavern, more like a hangout for the locals than a real business. Rachel must keep that place open as a public service, Charlie mused. She couldn't be making any money. Not with so few regular customers. How many? He counted: Jimmy, who maybe didn't count since he was Rachel's boyfriend; the old man and his dog; Crazy Mary; Jesus and Maria; himself, and who else?

Charlie thought about it. The crazy meth tweakers never came in, not since Rachel and Jimmy ran them off. Sometimes people from Rainier came up, people who still owned property in Warrentown that they couldn't sell. Al, who owned the defunct gas station, came up every now and then. He owned a string of electric fill-ups in Rainier and was one of the few people who had successfully made the change to the new economy. He could be pretty smug about that.

There was Vulture and his crew of old vets, all big hairy men who'd decided that it was too much bother to bathe or wash their clothes. They had a ramshackle compound of homemade shacks up in the woods someplace. In the past, they'd supplemented their disability checks with meth sales, but they'd kind of aged out of crime. They came in every now and then to sit around the tavern, drinking with silent determination. Everyone left them alone.

The young couple who'd inherited Mrs. Allen's house came up to keep the place in repairs, and they dropped by for a beer sometimes. Charlie grinned, thinking of how potential buyers might see the town: a dump with a few half-starved old farts eking out a survivalist existence.

Speaking of half-starved and eking out an existence, he still had an existence of his own to work on. Besides, Rachel and Jimmy would be back soon from their run into town, so they'd have some Tylenol to hand out. Old Man would need some. Bent, creeping along, the old man and his dog were within a block of the Raven Tavern. It made Charlie's back hurt just to watch their slow progress. Charlie wrote:

I have no reason to feel worry for myself. In fact, I am one of the luckiest people on the planet: born at the right time, dying at the right time. None of the real tragedies of the world are mine, so my sorrow needs to be given to others. My role is to keep myself sane while I bear witness.

Chapter Three
Old Man and His Dog

"I don't know which of us is slower," he mumbled. A dust-colored pit bull glanced up at the sound of his voice, then returned her concentration to walking. Arthritic shoulders made her steps painful. Knee, back, and neck problems made the old man's steps painful. Side by side, they hobbled down the sidewalk. They had only traveled five blocks total to reach the Raven Tavern–three blocks from his house to Main Street, and two down Main–but the distance seemed much longer.

Five blocks. That's what his life had narrowed down to. Not that his life had been overly broad before. He'd never wanted to know much about affairs beyond his own life; neighbors and friends and family had been enough for him. It seemed like every time he paid any attention to the wider world, all he got was an earful of bad news. Disasters everywhere. Refugees and illegal immigrants. Apocalyptic weather. People shooting other people at political rallies. War. No, it was better to not see much farther than the next step, he thought. And the next step. And the next one.

A fragile warmth from the evening sun touched his shoulders, but he knew it wouldn't last. Maybe he'd sit for a while when he got to the tavern. Sit out on the steps with Angie and let some warmth seep into his bones, if the sun was still out when he got there. Seemed like he could never get warm anymore. The old man squinted at the sky. Nope, by the time he got to the tavern, the sun would be behind a cloud. It was October, after all.

"What do you think?" he asked the dog. "Do you think I'll live to see another summer?" Her big brown eyes met his with a worried look. She always looked worried because her coat lay in wrinkles on her big blocky head; however, when she grinned, her smile was as wide enough to swallow a basketball, and no one could help but smile back.

"So, smile this evening for me." He grinned at the dog. "Look, it isn't raining and we are still moving! Out and about! Give me a smile there, girl!" And she did, an ear-to-ear grin accompanied by a stiff hop or two. The old man laughed.

Then he straightened his back and looked around. They'd arrived at the corner of Alder and Main, not that street signs meant anything anymore. The old town sure looked different from when he was a kid. For one thing, there used to be four blocks of businesses along the main street opposite the river. Now only one business survived: the Raven Tavern. The gas station had been decommissioned. The Warrentown Family Diner's windows were busted out and the innards–the tables, chairs, dishes and so on–had long ago been looted. The other storefronts were open to the ravages of winter rains and showed the damage in mold, broken gutters, and peeling paint.

"Looks like the set of a movie about life after nuclear war or something," he told his dog.

He could remember what most of the stores had been. On the corner, the old grocery. His grocery. Just one room stocked with the kinds of stuff that people needed but didn't want to drive all the way to Rainier to get: toilet paper, pop, ice cream, 3-in-1 oil, potato chips, sundries. Next, a building that had housed at various times a women's dress shop, a bookstore, and a soda fountain. There had once been a secondhand store after that, followed by an antique and curio shop, and then the Tavern.

Past the Tavern, Main Street degenerated into ramshackle storage rental units full of stray cats and a Quonset hut that had once housed a repair shop. The old man remembered Harry, the repair shop guy–he'd been pretty handy at fixing machinery, but had been kind of harsh, not neighborly. But Harry was gone and now a poet lived in the Quonset hut. The old man couldn't think of any skill less useful than writing poetry. Maybe the poet wrote about decline and decay.

Actually, the town had looked pretty rough before the mill closed, he remembered. Warrentown had always looked like a village thrown together in a hurry. The residents had kept up a respectable appearance, but there'd never been money for anything fancy. But, at one time, they'd had a sort of defiant community pride. They were the descendents of pioneers! They were rough and hardy survivors! They'd built a town where none had existed before!

Old Man lifted his chin and looked across the river at the rolling hills. They had built a town out in an untouched, untamed forest. At one time the logging trucks had rolled down out of the hills all day long, and other trucks had hauled the milled logs away down the road to town and beyond. They'd existed as the transfer site where the forest was turned to construction materials.

"A slaughterhouse. That's what Rachel says," he told the dog. "She says we killed the forest."

He hadn't been a logger. He'd been the grocery store guy. He'd spent years selling bubble gum and pop to the children of loggers and cigarettes to their parents.

And the streets were haunted with his memories of those days. Good memories, for the most part. The time before the mill closure had been almost idyllic from the perspective of the town's people. Picnics. Hunting and fishing. Hanging out with neighbors. Everyone had known everyone else's business. If someone was sick, half the town showed up with casseroles. If someone was in trouble financially—maybe injured and couldn't work—they'd all pitched in to help out. His counter at the store had been the center of that kind of organizing many times. He'd used a gallon pickle jar over and over, every time someone needed a fundraiser.

So, we were a good town, he thought. We were good people, even if Rachel doesn't think so. She was a funny one. Mexican or Indian or something. He could remember when she first took over the tavern. There was a little trouble in the beginning with people not accepting her. "But she has a way of saying things straight out to your face without hurting your feelings," he told Angie. "She just tells people what she thinks and lets them take it or leave it. She's our local eccentric." Besides, she had the only tavern in town and no one wanted to drive all the way to Rainier for a beer.

The old man stopped to catch his breath. He let his eyes roam around. He saw the town in layers: the present obscured by images from the near and far past. "Funny now things can be both good and bad," he told Angie. "Maybe Rachel is right about us. I don't know." At any rate, the town had died and he was going to die soon, too.

Chapter Four
The Raven Tavern

Rachel and Jimmy leaned companionably against each other in the doorway to the backroom and watched Valerie tend the bar. Val ran the tavern in exchange for a little cash. There wasn't much to the job; they only had three kinds of hard liquor on the premises, a few bottles of red wine, and a stack of cases of beer. Val cooked for the regulars, but mainly her job was to keep Rachel from being nailed down to the place, which Rachel appreciated since she and Jimmy needed to be freed up for thieving. Besides, Rachel didn't like to cook.

Val was behind the counter snarling at the customers who occasionally snarled back. Rachel did a quick inventory: one outsider—the former gas station guy—and four of their regulars. Jesus and Charlie were sharing a table while trying to converse with a stunted vocabulary of mixed Spanish and English. Old Man was hunkered protectively over his drink, his bony back a wall of sticks, and Mary was cackling over a joke that no one else thought was funny. Rachel studied Mary thoughtfully; she'd need some Lysol to spray the stool after Mary left.

Not that Rachel was any kind of clean freak. The tavern was irredeemably dusty. The upstairs was Rachel's home, but the downstairs was as much a place for her hobby as a place of business. Rachel's hobby was collecting colorful bits of nonsense that caught her eye: pieces of glass, old store or traffic signs, license plates, dishes and placemats that she'd scrounged out of abandoned houses, framed prints of cartoon animals. Spidery dream catchers dangled from the ceiling, occasionally catching a customer by the hair.

The tavern boasted a row of booths along one wall and three tables.

Before the town died, she'd kept her found object collection under control, but now her colorful glass bottles and tacky nick-knacks had overwhelmed some of the booths and were spilling out on the tables. She'd find a place for the witch when she got the chance.

A sudden burst of voices startled Rachel, and she craned her neck to see through the dim interior to the front door. A quartet of strangers shouldered their way into the cramped, dark interior. They were remarkably similar in appearance: all in skinny jeans and jackets with oversized shoulders, all with brutalist buzz cuts, even the lone female. They stopped together and all four surveyed the room, three disdainfully and one with curiosity. The tavern's regulars stared back in silence.

"Assholes." Rachel felt Jimmy's body stiffen. She scanned the room. Jesus had vanished, probably by hiding under the table. Charlie, with elaborate casualness, was sliding Jesus's beer over to his side.

Rachel said, "They're militia, aren't they?"

"Yeah."

Militia members, Rainier's privatized police, but out of uniform for a spree. They moved in a unit, heads up and shoulders back, striding rather than merely walking, and hit the counter next to Old Man. He gave them a quick glance, picked up his drink, and retreated to the opposite side of the room. Mary, grinning toothlessly, greeted them. "Well, look who's gracing our humble abode with their presence tonight!"

The militia gang ignored her. The biggest one, a self-consciously muscular white guy, leaned on the counter, putting himself in Val's personal space, and asked for a shot of Scotch. Val stepped back and gestured toward the packing crate shelving behind the counter. "That's what we got. What's your choice?" The girl snorted, but the guy just said, "All you have is beer?"

"There's your choices," Val told him, "That's what we got right now." They kept the hard liquor and wine out of sight, so as not to be wasted on assholes. Val set the beers and glasses on the counter without making eye contact with anyone. She was relieved when the guy got his wallet out and paid willingly.

Rachel gave Val a tiny nod on her way to the storeroom. She edged past Jimmy, who gave her butt a pat and exhaled cigarette smoke into her face.

"What?" Rachel asked.

He ducked down to kiss her forehead. "Don't worry."

Rachel stepped around him. She had work to do in the back room, and the presence of the militia made the work imperative. With brisk efficiency, she began shoveling the contents of the black garbage bag into plastic bins. The medicines went into an opaque red bin, and the OTC drugs into a brown cardboard box. She mixed the red bin and the cardboard box in with all the other boxes and bins in their crowded storage room. The remaining sundries she left in the garbage bag, which she hid by shoving it into the corner next to a bag of real garbage.

Then she popped the lid to a bottle of Percocet, shook out some pills, and started grinding them to a powder on a scrap of paper, using the butt end of a screw driver. Val peeked into the storeroom, then hurried in. Her hands fluttered around her face.

"Here." Rachel handed her the paper scrap. "Mix it with water, then see if you can get it into their drinks."

"You think that's enough?" Val peered anxiously at the powder.

Rachel hesitated. She didn't like using the supply up too fast, but it was a waste if they didn't use enough. "I think so. That's one each. Plus, the alcohol."

"Okay."

Rachel's mouth twisted into a grimace. "Well, let's see if they buy enough booze to be worth it."

Val snorted. There was a shout of laughter from the bar and the two women's eyes met. Val hurried back to the bar, the Percocet tucked into her hand. Rachel ambled after her and took a quick look around. Jimmy met her eyes and they shared a thought about the militia.

The militia pals were leaning all over the counter, crowding Crazy Mary, who was crowding them right back with her body odor and sprawling arms and legs. Propped by her elbow on the counter, she had spun around on her stool to face the gang and was entertaining them with one of her disgusting stories. Well, fine, Rachel thought. The militia had probably come to see the wildlife, and Mary was about as wild as their lives got. Rachel parked herself against the doorjamb opposite Jimmy, where she could watch the room.

"So, I said, you know what a Rainier girl does on Sunday morning? She puts her clothes on and goes home!"

"I've heard that one before," sneered the militia girl, bored.

"Yeah, but you don't know what we do Sunday morning." Crazy Mary's eyes glinted. "We ain't Rainier girls, now are we?"

The militia gal snorted her contempt. The three guys were only listening with half an ear each. Their eyes roamed the room, lit briefly on Old Man, skimmed over his dog, and drifted through Rachel's treasures. Not much to see at the Tavern that night. To Rachel, that meant they might gin up some trouble of their own, if the Percocet didn't slow them down. She pushed herself away from the doorjamb and drifted in the direction of the bar where Val was standing. Val had her hands below counter level and was softening the Percocet in a little water.

"Buy me a drink and I'll tell you a story," Crazy Mary bared her toothless gums at the three militia men. The leader waved a hand at Val, who gave Rachel a quick smirk. Then, using the shelf that ran along below the counter, she poured beer into glasses and slipped a shot of water/drug in each.

"She's full of shit," Val told the guys. "Her stories are shit."

"Hey!" Mary reared back in her chair with faux outrage. "I am full of stories, good ones! Like, you wanna know why that road is called Brody's Wife Road?"

"Cause someone named Brody and his wife lived here," drawled the shorter, pudgy militia guy. Rachel noted that he was leaning on the bar, well into his second beer.

"I guess that's part of it." Crazy Mary knocked back a slug. She could drink the militia under the table even when their drinks weren't spiked. She took her time lighting a cigarette, making them work for it. The gal broke first. "So, what was the other part?"

"Part what?" Crazy Mary asked, fake blankness on her face.

"What was the other part of why–I don't give a shit! Don't tell us if you don't want to." The militia girl turned her back on Mary. "My aunt used to live up here, and I never heard her call it nothing but the Rainier road. There's no story." She was nearly done with her second beer but hadn't mellowed any.

Rachel eyes narrowed and she snapped at Mary, "Just tell the damn story."

"Alright then." Mary swung her legs idly to let everyone know that she was acquiescing willingly and not at all rushed. Rachel hissed with impatience.

"It all started, well, I suppose way back in the day long, long ago like most things start, huh, Rach?"

"She means back before the mill closed down," Rachel told the militia.

"Yup," Mary agreed. "Before you were born when lots of people lived up here in the woods. Anyhoo, this is how it went down:

"Brody MacIntyre was one of six brothers all born right here or at the hospital in Rainier. Their dad worked at the mill, and they had a nice little house in town. Brody was the oldest, so he moved out first. Everything was cool as long as the mill was running. Then the timber industry turned to shit and Brody got laid off and couldn't get a job. His first wife took the kids and skedaddled. So, Brody started selling meth from that trailer that used to be right down the road from here a little ways."

"Tweaker," sneered the pudgy militia guy. The other two males lounged against the counter, barely listening.

"Anyway, Brody was cute, so he got himself a new wife. And they played house together in their little trailer. But Brody had all those brothers, and the next one down in age was always out here to pick up some crank or some weed. Anyway, Brody started to get suspicious because it seemed like every time he was driving down that road he'd see his little brother driving up. And when he asked his new wife about it, she'd always said, 'Oh, he just made a buy.' But Brody's little brother sure was buying a lot, which was weird because he actually had a pretty good job on a construction crew and they do drug testing.

"So one day, Brody is driving down that road and he sees his brother and he just waves–you know, like it's no big deal–but as soon as he can, he pulls over and turns around. I bet you think you know what happened next."

She paused, wriggling her eyebrows dramatically. With an elaborate display of boredom, the militia gal said, "He caught his brother in bed with his wife."

"Oh no, that would be too easy. That would be no story. He gets out of the truck and starts walking up the road because he wants to sneak up on them, right? But it was raining. And he was wearing a sweatshirt over a flannel shirt over a t-shirt, which you don't do in the rain unless you're stupid because cotton don't keep you warm. So, pretty soon he's wet. And then he's getting cold. And he's shambling along, and his knees are getting shaky. You know you can die from the cold in sixty-degree weather if you get wet, right? He's getting shaky and trembly and really having a hard time…"

"How far did he have to walk?" the gal interrupted.

"Well, that's the funny thing about that road. It's longer than you'd think sometimes. You'll have to ask Rachel about that." She nodded meaningfully, and Rachel rolled her eyes.

"Anyway, he wasn't that far from the trailer, but he was walking and walking and walking and not getting anywhere, and then he heard the sound of a truck, and he thought it was probably his brother leaving, done with visiting, you know?" Mary leered at the militia guys, who didn't leer back.

"So he just stands there and, sure enough, it's his brother, who says, 'What the fuck, Brody? Why're you out in the rain?' And he says, 'My truck broke down.' He can't tell the truth, right? He can't say he was trying to sneak up on his brother and catch him in the act. So, his brother drives him back to the trailer, and his wife gets him all dried off and into bed, and gives him hot chocolate and basically saves his life. Her and his brother saved him."

"So that's the end?" the militia girl asked, her voice rising with annoyance. "They lived happily ever after?"

"No," said Crazy Mary. She paused, grinning, stretching the moment out. "The wife disappeared."

"What do you mean disappeared? Did he murder her or something?" The militia gal glared.

"I mean she walked out the door and was gone. No one ever saw her again."

"No." The militia girl slammed her drink down. "What kind of stupid story is that? He must've decided to kill her and hid the body."

"It's not stupid." Mary thumped her glass down, too. "It's haunting is what it is, 'cause no one knows if she just left or if he killed her. But *I* know."

"Oh, God," moaned the big blond militia guy. "Here it comes, more of this interminable story."

"I know because I am her." Crazy Mary smirked triumphantly.

Militia gal made a long snorting noise, and the big blond guy honked out a laugh. "Oh, bullshit."

"No, I did. I just up and left." Crazy Mary leaned back against the counter and fluttered her hands. "I walked down that road—and for me it was a short walk—and I caught the freight 'cause it goes really slow up the grade there before the road gets to the highway. You saw the place coming in. I just up and left."

The militia girl stuck out her chin and sneered a challenge, "Why?"

"Why what?"

"Why'd you leave if he wasn't going to do nothing about you fucking his brother?"

Mary grinned, showing a mouth empty of teeth, "Why, little girl?

'Cause I could tell that if I didn't, I'd be taking care of that man all my life. A man so damn stupid he couldn't come in out of the rain. And such a goddamn whiner that all he can say when he catches his brother with his wife is 'I'm cold.'"

The militia girl didn't look impressed by any of this. The three guys were beginning to sag.

Val asked, "Ready for another round?"

Mary, cackling, slid off her stool. "I gots to pee." She headed toward the door, rocking side to side not because she was drunk but because one leg was shorter than the other. On her way past, she bumped the pudgy militia guy. He didn't notice.

The militia girl called after Mary, "I don't believe a word of that." She turned to Rachel. "Was any of that true?"

Rachel shrugged. "Some of it."

The big blond leader guy plonked his glass down loudly. "So far this place hasn't been worth the drive. I thought it'd be more fun, not just a few old geezers." He raked the room with a sneer but kept his eyes away from Jimmy.

Rachel shrugged again. "Depends on who's here."

"Isn't it boring living here?" the girl asked.

Rachel turned her back and pretended that the sink needed to be wiped. But the girl was persistent. "Isn't it boring? How come you don't move away?"

Rachel tossed her rag in the sink. "I don't get bored. I know how all the stories end."

Later, after the pudgy member got so groggy that he could no longer stay upright, the militia finally got bored and left. Val watched the door close behind them and gave the counter a short, sharp rap with her knuckles. Rachel grinned sourly. Out in the darkness of the tavern, the locals stretched their legs and lifted their drinks. A spate of conversation broke out. Crazy Mary reached into the depths of her over-sized sweatshirt and extracted a wallet.

Charlie tapped the table to signal all clear, and Jesus crawled out. He climbed awkwardly up on to his chair and shook the stiffness out of his shoulders, grinning sheepishly. His black hair was festooned by spider webs, which startled Charlie into a laugh. Jesus ran his hands through his hair and patted himself all over. "Hay muchos bichos." He crawled his fingers across the table like a spider.

"I drank your beer," Charlie told him. He mimed with Jesus's beer glass. "I'll get you another." But he didn't need to; Rachel appeared over his shoulder with a bottle of Jim Beam.

"Hit me too," Mary yelled.

"Not unless you pay," Rachel told her.

"I can pay!" Mary waved the wallet aloft.

Rachel stared at the wallet. Then she said, "You shouldn't have done that, Mary. You might've brought trouble on us."

Chapter Five
Baylor's Sunday Morning

Baylor hefted the bag of trash and lugged it down the steps. He got a sense of satisfaction out of de-trashing his apartment just as he got an odd sense of satisfaction out of trashing it. There was something solid and reassuring about the routines of life, the way food ebbed and flowed in and out: hot steamy pizza in and yummy pizza eaten, pizza box crumpled up on the coffee table in front of the TV, pizza box on its way to the dumpster. More pizza would come in the near future. Repeat with fast food chicken, takeout Chinese, whatever he was in the mood for. Sometimes he even went to the grocery, bought stuff for himself, and carried his purchases home to put away on his very own shelves to cook later.

Probably a pretty fucking stupid thing to get satisfaction out of. He swung the bag into the dumpster and watched it settle with a *thunk* into the pile of other peoples' trash. But, whatever–it was a pretty, sunny day, and he intended to be in good mood. So there!

Baylor stepped back from the dumpster and observed the sky: a flat, smooth, cloudless blue. Unusual. Puddles of water glistened on the asphalt of the parking lot from the night's rain. The leafless trees behind the fence were dark and dank with moss, witchy-looking even in the sun. The sound of a truck surfing through a wet patch on the road caught Baylor's attention. People were up and moving around, going about their Sunday business. Time for him to go about his.

Of course, that left the question of what exactly his Sunday business was going to be. He was only a little hung over. Probably Randy and Melissa were still asleep. He would not call Pete, of course. Pete was an officer, but Baylor and Randy and Mel were just recruits. Lowly auxiliary members.

He'd known the others in high school, where they hadn't been friends, but it was different now that they served together. They were companions now, so in theory he could call them to make a plan for the day. But, better not. They were probably still sleeping in from the previous night.

So, Baylor headed back to his apartment. He wasn't going to call Randy or Mel to go out for target practice or anything like that. He could go by himself, of course. That's a plan, he thought.

He ran up the steps to his apartment and headed straight for the coffee pot. Then he stepped out on his tiny balcony, sipped his drink, and let the sun warm his shoulders.

Life was looking sort of good to Baylor. He wasn't in the war and didn't have to join up. Most guys either joined up and got sent off somewhere or got into some kind of crime or got boring, low-wage jobs. But he had managed to get into the militia auxiliary, so he had a respected job: defender of the homeland! His mom was proud of him! Well, sort of. He had a place of his own, an electric motorcycle, and a job–which was more than most people had.

And he was young, healthy, and not ugly, so a girlfriend was a real possibility. Not Mel, obviously. She was cute, but he suspected her of being a real bitch. She was all sharp edges and prickliness, a real suck-up to Pete, and when Pete wasn't around she acted like she was the officer. He wanted to like her and wanted to be friends with her, but it was hard.

Like last night at the tavern. They'd gone out to Warrentown on a lark because the tavern out there had a bad reputation. Supposedly a place full of weirdos. Turns out that on a Saturday night there was no one there but a crazy old woman and the bartender who was also an old woman. Well, there was the younger black-haired woman who looked like she might be part foreigner of some kind and that guy, the guy who just stood in the doorway and watched. He looked pretty shady. But, anyway, the point was all that evening Mel had hung onto Randy and wrapped herself all around Pete but had shown no special friendliness toward Baylor. She'd barely made eye contact with him at all, except to give him side glances just before being especially flirty with the other guys. Story of his life. He had always been the one on the side, since birth. Always the watcher, never a participant.

But that would change. He was stepping up and stepping out. And if she didn't like him, that was fine because in truth he didn't like her much, either. So there!

Baylor knocked down another slug of coffee. So, what to do with the pretty blue-sky day? Go out to the shooting range? He was a good shot. A very good shot, actually. He pictured the holes in the red circles of the target and imagined the satisfying *thunk* of a bullet hitting a hay bale. Yeah, he could do that. He swallowed the last of the coffee and poured the dregs off the balcony into a puddle on the parking lot.

Chapter Six
Sunday for Charlie and Valerie

I'm sad, she thought. This is what sadness feels like: a bite wound. Teeth sunk into my side, my blood drained out all over the floor. I am limp and empty and immobilized because any movement will hurt too much. So, I sit hunkered over to protect the wound. I just sit. Even my eyes don't move. I stare at the wall.

I have that wallpaper memorized because I have been staring at just like I used to stare at the wallpaper in my mother's house. I stared at her wall paper for fifty years. Fifty years! How the hell did that happen? Decades spent watching TV, only moving every now and then when Mom needed me to change her diaper or roll her over. All those goddamn fucking years of cowboy shows and reruns and nature shows while Mom was asleep.

I wanted her to die. People said things to me about how nice it was for me to take care of my mom and I'd get this shitty little glow. That was my reward, that shitty little glow because people thought I was such a good daughter.

I walked to the mailbox every fucking day just to get the hell out of the house. Sometimes I'd see someone and they'd say "How's your mom?" And I'd say, "Oh she's doing okay." I could tell they were thinking what a noble and good daughter I was, and at the same time thinking, "Thank God I'm not trapped in a life like hers." And they had to ask me about Mom to find out how she was doing because they never came to visit. Well, maybe not never. But only once or twice a year like before Christmas or Easter. We ate alone, we watched TV alone, we were alone. And no one ever asked how I was doing.

And that loneliness took a big fucking bite out of me. No, that's wrong.

I got this wound before the loneliness. I might've been born with it. My very earliest memory–so far back it's like a story someone told me–is of lying pressed against the wall in my bedroom with my stuffed mouse, Mousie, gripped in my arms, and I was vibrating with fear. The walls were vibrating. The whole house was vibrating. I had puked in the bed, and didn't want to tell anyone, so I had scrunched over as far as I could get and just lay there awake, feeling the house shake and my legs shake, and I clutched my Mousie tighter and tighter.

The house was always vibrating. Sometimes the vibration was the wind, and I actually liked that. I used to pretend that the wind would lift the house like in The Wizard of Oz and blow us away to somewhere different and beautiful. Most of the time, the vibrating came from Dad. He could make the air tremble just by being in a shitty mood. Mom tip-toed around, always careful not to drop anything or bump into anything. Our cat hid under the bed. And I'd just made myself small. The house was always vibrating because of him.

I promised Mousie that someday I would escape, and I'd take him with me, but the truth is, by middle school I'd forgotten him. Mousie must've gotten thrown away at some point. I don't even know when he disappeared or when I last thought of him. I just forgot him.

But I kept on dreaming of running away. But that's all I did: dream. The only real change for me was I moved down the road to the highway, took a left into town, and stopped there. I got a job at the door factory, which I liked. My own money. My own place, a little house that I shared with three other girls. We went to bars in a little herd, each of us looking for a guy. And if one of us found a guy, then off she'd go for the rest of the evening, or the night, or even the next couple days. I thought my roomies were really brave for that, for going off with some guy. The only time I tried it, it turned into a really shitty experience I don't like thinking about.

And so a few years went by. Not many. I kept working, even as my job got boring, and I ignored my mom. I ignored her until I got a call from a neighbor that Mom was being taken to the hospital in an ambulance. Dad had given her a concussion. Her head hit the corner of the oak table in the kitchen. It was square and that corner had always stuck out belligerently, a weapon we'd always been aware of. Usually her head hit a wall, which had some give to it, but those corners on that table had always been there, and he finally did it, decked her just right so the corner got her on the way down.

But she didn't leave him. She didn't divorce him or press charges. He left on his own and I moved back to take care of her. It's our minds that trap us. Our thoughts. Our thoughts limit what we can conceive of doing. There are layers of words in a person's head. The loudest words are out in the front of your mind. Those words you know about and you can hear—the self-talk, it's called. Those words aren't the important ones. They're just the drug that lets you get through each day. My drug words were, "I'm leaving, I will get out of here." I drugged myself with that promise every fucking day of my life, but I never left because there were other words deeper in my head that didn't let me go.

Charlie pushed the wheelbarrow up the street to the tavern. He could feel the weight yanking on his elbows and shoulders. He was like a skeleton, bones clanking and rattling, barely held together by thinning strings of cartilage. A skeleton covered with rags of old flesh.

Rachel heard the wheels squeaking and poked her head out the door. Her long black hair was unbraided, thick, and would have been a delight to Charlie's eye if he'd had the energy to feel delight. If he'd been thirty years younger, and if Jimmy hadn't been around, he would've let himself fall in love with Rachel's hair.

"Come for some water?" she called. Her smile, too, was a potential delight.

"Yup." Charlie dropped the handles of the wheelbarrow and tried to straighten up.

"Jimmy's here. He'll give you a hand."

Behind Raven Tavern, the dumpster overflowed. There was no garbage pick-up anymore, so every now and then Rachel invited the town folk down for a garbage-burning party. Free beer, chocolate, store-bought cake. Charlie wasn't sure how she acquired stuff, but was pretty sure her methods weren't legal. However, after the way the government had screwed him out of his pension, his ideas of respectable behavior had been turned inside out. A pension-less college professor who had no income beyond the remnants of Social Security couldn't afford to ask where a cake came from, or where the meds Rachel kept in her back room came from, either.

The water was also appreciated. They all saved rainwater and used river water, but as long as the Raven Tavern still had Warrentown's well water, it was everyone's preferred drinking source. Jimmy opened the back door and Charlie handed him two of his plastic jugs. Jimmy disappeared inside to use the utility tap in the back room.

He's a strange one, Charlie thought. Lean as a coyote, ageless, one of those guys who kept their hair forever. One of those guys who stayed sexy forever, too. Charlie had never been charismatic, not even in a poetic way. He had been loved–and had loved his wife, who lived on as a bittersweet pain in his heart–but he'd never had the animal magnetism that made Jimmy the focal point in any group, even when he had nothing to say.

Jimmy, his brown arms ropy with muscle, slung the two jugs into the wheelbarrow and grabbed the second pair. Charlie watched with envy; he'd never been athletic, either. In fact, he'd never been anything like Jimmy. We're hardly the same species, he thought.

Jimmy dumped the second pair of jugs into the wheelbarrow and grabbed the handles. Realizing what Jimmy was up to, Charlie protested, "You don't have to do that. I can make it."

Jimmy grunted something around his cigarette. He set off at a good clip, bouncing the wheelbarrow across the sidewalk and off the curb. Charlie trotted along behind, each step rattling pain up the bones of his spine.

"Hey," he panted. "Hey."

Jimmy stopped and looked back.

"I have arthritis," Charlie explained. "Sorry."

Jimmy tossed his cigarette onto the pavement. "Nothing for you to be sorry about. I'm the one that was walking too fast." He gave the wheelbarrow a shove and they proceeded across the street, side by side, in silence. When they reached the Quonset hut, Charlie asked, "Care to set a bit?" There was something about Jimmy that made Charlie want to speak in an old-fashioned way, not like his natural speech, which tended toward the professorial. He was thinking that he could offer Jimmy a beer, except it was only about eleven in the morning.

Jimmy grunted but not in an unfriendly way, just a sound effect to go with shoving the wheelbarrow up against the curb. He pushed across Charlie's meager strip of dead grass and parked the barrow by the steps up to the rickety porch. Charlie followed.

The Quonset hut was splotched with rust. Dead weeds and yellow grass made a front yard. An image came to Charlie's mind: a Craftsman cottage in Tacoma and his wife's flower garden. He cleared his throat. "Would you like a cup of tea or coffee? I have both."

Jimmy lit a new cigarette and gave him a considering look. "Sure." Then he stuck the butt in his mouth, grabbed a pair of jugs, and strode toward the front door. Charlie, in a burst of unusual agility, skipped around him and got the door open.

Harry, the previous owner of the hut, had been very handy at making useful things, but had lacked aesthetic appreciation, so it was easy to see what belonged to Charlie and what Harry had left behind. Charlie's things were tasteful, well-chosen, artistic, and few. Harry's things were all useful and cobbled together out of materials intended for some other purpose. The kitchen table, jerry-rigged out of an old door and some saw horses, had been Harry's. The pretty, embroidered tablecloth was Charlie's.

Despite Charlie's belongings, the hut didn't feel home-like. It was cave-like, windowless and dark. The curved walls were oppressively heavy and had a flattening effect on Charlie's mood. Trying not to feel the weight of the curved ceiling, he pumped the gas on the Coleman stove and lit the burner. The teapot, like Charlie, was left over from better days. Charlie set two mugs on the counter, both also refugees from a different life.

"Tea or instant coffee? Instant is all I have."

"Tea's fine." Jimmy unapologetically exhaled cigarette smoke in Charlie's house while examining the piles of books stacked on the floor. Charlie hadn't yet Jerry-rigged any shelving.

"I didn't buy this place. I just moved in." Charlie smiled at the thought of himself as a squatter. "I keep expecting an owner to show up and kick me out."

"Rachel won't let that happen." People were always saying things like that about Rachel: She'd take care of something, prevent something, get revenge on someone. Charlie had only lived in the town for about three months, and in that time he wasn't aware of Rachel doing anything unusual—except theft—but he was pleased to think that Rachel would want to protect him.

"I've heard that the owner was a guy named Harry who could fix things for people. Like engines, I guess."

"Harry was good at fixing stuff." Jimmy emphasized "stuff" as if implying that there were significant things that Harry hadn't fixed. Charlie considered asking what Jimmy meant, but got distracted by the sudden whistle of the teapot. He poured the hot water into the cups and dropped a tea bag into each. "Honey?"

"No, thanks."

"Let's go outside." The air outside was chilly and damp, but less oppressive than the low-hanging curve of the metal roof.

Jimmy settled into the plastic chair. He had a way of seeming both relaxed and ready for action at the same time. Charlie sat down carefully, arranged his bones for minimum pain, and reconciled himself to the fact that getting up again would be difficult. He sipped his tea and surveyed the town.

The unexpected sun of the morning was gone. Heavy clouds had been slowly gathering and now, as they sat and watched, a hazy drizzle descended on the town and blurred the shabby buildings into ghosts. The misty hills rose up behind the old buildings, gray-green with ragged vegetation, the tops obscured by cloud. It seemed to Charlie to be a metaphor for life: the brightness of his youth and the grimness of the present.

He said, speaking from his heart, "I am glad I'm old." Then he felt bad for making such a statement to a man who was no older than forty.

Jimmy said, "You seem like a guy who comes from a different time and place."

Charlie said, "Yes."

He'd been born in the mid-fifties and had come of age in the seventies. He'd been immensely interested in life and full of hope. Life had seemed–no, life had been–full of promise and opportunity. He'd majored in poetry, for crying out loud. Who would do that now? "Blest it was to be alive in that dawn, but to be young was a very heaven," he quoted.

Jimmy grunted assent, to Charlie's mild surprise. He didn't seem old enough to understand.

"So, how did it all go wrong?" Charlie asked. He meant the question rhetorically, but Jimmy answered, "It's been all downhill since agriculture was invented. This has been in the cards for millennia."

Charlie blinked, startled. He'd thought he was being obscure, but Jimmy seemed to know exactly what he was talking about. Maybe he needed to revise his understanding of Jimmy to include seeing him as something more than Rachel's redneck boyfriend.

Chapter Seven
Monday. We Was Robbed.

"They picked my pocket," Randy told Baylor. He was whispering because they weren't supposed to speak during shooting practice. Pete's orders; he liked to create tension and drama through his own words and didn't appreciate any comments from the recruits. The twelve militia auxiliary members stood in a row, pistols in hand, each waiting for their turn. They were supposed to all be focused on whoever was shooting.

"How'd they do that?" Baylor hissed back, skeptical.

"Dunno. I just know that when I got home I had no wallet. Gone."

"Huh." Baylor squinted. Odd how glary an overcast day could be. They were all standing under the long wooden roof of the shooting-range shed. Out across the wet grass, up against the line of trees, were the targets, big cutouts of male figures against a white background, pinned to a wall of hay bales. They were supposed to get a kill shot with the first bullet. No one had been successful yet, not even Baylor, who was a good shot.

A pistol discharged with a harsh pop, and a hole appeared in the white field next to the black figure.

"You missed that coon completely!" Pete yelled. "Now he's running away! Shoot him again!" Pete wanted them to think of the targets as real people. To Baylor, the targets were paper, and shooting was all about the skill of putting a hole right there where he intended a hole to be. He didn't want to think of the targets as people.

A pistol shot cracked and another hole appeared in the white field next to a black figure. Baylor leaned forward just enough to look down the row to see who the fuck-up was. Some guy named Al, older than most of them.

He was red-faced, swearing, and shaking the gun as if the fault lay with the pistol. Pete loomed over his shoulder and shouted him down. "Aim, for chrissake! Take your stance! Not like that! One foot forward, hold your arms up!"

He'll quit, Baylor thought. Al looked really pissed. Being shouted at was something they all had to endure because Pete was an asshole. Baylor was determined to get through the shouting so he could get on the real militia, which was a real job with a pay increase and benefits.

"Aw, fuck it." Pete gave up on Al. He tapped Melissa on the shoulder. "Show him how a girl shoots."

She grinned, baring her teeth. With a toss of her head, Mel went into her stance. She stilled, focused, and squeezed the trigger. A crack of gunshot punctured the air and a hole appeared in the shoulder of the target figure.

"Winged him!" Pete was pleased. "Try again."

Baylor looked across the field at his target. The black figure was short, stocky, and wore a baseball cap. It was meant to represent an illegal immigrant. They were creeping into America by the millions, according to the news. Some got in boats and went around the Border Wall, or dug tunnels under it, and some even used big ladders to get over it. They came with families, kids, wives. But there's no room here, Baylor told himself. Besides, they were weird people. Short, squatty people with lots and lots of kids.

Mel put her next bullet in the migrant's thigh.

"He's down!" Pete yelled.

It was Randy's turn. He wasn't a bad shot, but Pete made him nervous. Randy got into his stance quickly, aimed, and fired before Pete could do any backseat driving. His bullet smacked into the migrant's crotch. Not what he'd intended to hit, but a good shot since it made everyone laugh.

"Well, he won't be breeding any more raccoons!" Pete smacked Randy on the back and turned to Baylor.

"Let's see you do a head shot," he said.

Baylor stepped forward and lifted the pistol two-handed. He sighted along the barrel and out across the grass to the distant black figure. A gust of breeze made the target flap almost like the figure was trying to run. Baylor's stomach knotted. He exhaled, inhaled, and started over. It's just a piece of paper, he told himself. Just hit the black spot at the top. He squeezed the trigger and put a bullet into the target's head.

Chapter Eight
That Evening. Baylor's Mother

He stirred the frying hamburger with his mother's one plastic spatula. The thick, greasy smell of onions and cooking fat sparked tears in his eyes. The vent fanned roared, saturating the tiny kitchen with a fog of noise. He didn't like having his ears full–it made him feel frantic and claustrophobic–but the fan's incessant blur was better than the blather from his mom's TV.

She was visible over the breakfast bar that divided the galley kitchen from the dining/living/TV room, nearly horizontal in an enormous fake leather Lazy Boy, the view of the TV restricted to the space between her feet.

One of the wrappings on her legs was loose. Baylor was grateful for the smell of the cooking hamburger; it disguised the nauseating stink of leaking lymph. His mom's legs were swollen and blistered, a side effect of her unmanaged diabetes, a warning to Baylor of what the future could hold for him.

Not me, he told himself. And he dumped a goodly dose of garlic powder into the hamburger. He was never going to let himself get into the kind of condition that had been normal for his mom for as long as he could remember: obese, alcoholic, lame.

But he'd try to get some good nutrition into her. Baylor twisted the top off a jar of spaghetti sauce and poured it over the meat. Inhaling a long, deep sniff, he turned his attention to the refrigerator. The one good thing about the tiny kitchen was that everything was in easy reach. He had to back up a bit to get the fridge door open.

Ooh, ick. He should've brought his own salad makings; she had nothing but some sad lettuce and shriveled carrots. The rest of the fridge was packed with greasy bags of leftover fast food and slices of very old pizza. Baylor let the door slam closed.

He turned the heat down under the simmering sauce and checked the big pot of hot water. Almost on a boil. With the sauce added to the meat, he didn't need the vent fan anymore. Baylor checked the TV, saw a red-faced man sneering out at the world, and left the vent fan on.

He pawed through the shelves and found a can of green beans. Beans were boring, but they'd have to do. Then he dug through the drawers, looking for a can opener.

"Hey, Mom?"

She muttered something, eyes on the ranting man.

"Mom," his voice sharpened. "I can't find the can opener."

"Just look for it!" she snapped, without taking her eyes from the TV.

Just look for it. In her opinion, everything he'd ever needed in his whole life was somewhere in her trailer, so it was his fault if he had unmet needs. Well, he couldn't make beans without a can opener. Baylor made a noisy fuss out of his search and found the can opener at last. For some reason, she'd left it on a shelf behind a stack of Tupperware.

The water was on the boil, so he broke up some slightly stale spaghetti noodles and dumped them into the pot. The beans went into a bowl and then into the microwave. He leaned his butt up against the breakfast bar and watched his cooking action: sauce simmering, noodles boiling, beans being zapped by the microwave, all contributing to the wall of noise between him and the ranter on TV.

They ate in the living room, his mom in her Lazy Boy and Baylor in an elderly upholstered rocking chair. His mom's plate was balanced on her enormous gut while Baylor held his plate with one hand and tried to eat with the other.

"Mom?"

"Hmm?"

"Could you turn the TV off while we're eating?"

"Whafor?" she paused with a forkful of noodles in the line of sight between them. "I like this show."

"I don't." It was a show like all the news: some guy flanked by a pair of blondes with prominent boobs. They discussed current events with outrage. Always outrage. That evening the outrage was directed at the political party that was out of power; for some reason a mass breakthrough of illegal immigrants who breached the wall was their fault.

"Look at all them coons." His mother pointed at the screen with her fork.

The TV showed footage of a mass of people who were scrambling through an arroyo under the wall. Some were dragging or carrying small children. Baylor couldn't understand why they still birthed kids when it was so obvious that there was no future in those little countries down south. Too hot. Fires all the time. Kind of weird that the jungles were on fire, but he'd seen the footage of it. The image of a sloth struggling to cross a road ahead of a fire was stuck in his mind. Baylor winced, wishing he hadn't seen that show. All kinds of animals had been fleeing across the road, but the sloth was the saddest image, its struggles so hopeless.

Baylor stabbed his fork into the thick red sauce. What had smelled so good in the kitchen now looked like blood and entrails. He set his fork down on the edge of his plate.

Mumbling around a mouthful, his mom made more stabbing motions at the TV. "Bet those people will head right here. Everyone's coming here."

That's because western Washington didn't have tornadoes, hurricanes, drought, flood, or catastrophic fires. It just rained all the fucking time, took a three-month break for summer, and then rained again. They had landslides, that was their local disaster. So, yeah, people were moving to the Puget Sound. Some of them even moved out to Rainier where housing was still cheap.

The illegals hid out in the woods.

"Got to round those coons up and take them to the camps," said his mother with satisfaction. Supposedly the taxpayers had to pay for their keep in the camps and they got medical care, which wasn't fair when so many Americans couldn't afford a doctor. And it was a waste because the coons all got shipped back to wherever they came from, anyway. At least that was the official story. There were rumors that most of the people in the camps died. Someone had told Baylor that the camps in Idaho stank, really reeked. Only guards were allowed to see what they were like inside.

But the coons just kept on coming.

Baylor watched the clip. A young mother crawled up a steep dirt bank, her baby tied to her back. Behind her, a short, black-haired man struggled to clamber up while dragging a backpack. Baylor wondered who'd shot the footage. Someone had just stood there and watched the illegals flooding in, recording but taking no other action. If Immigration had been there, the footage would've shown the agents chasing people, maybe shooting at them. Must be one of those pro-illegal outfits took the film, Baylor thought.

The TV switched back to the outraged man and the two outraged blondes. They were in agreement that it was outrageous that people were still getting past the wall.

"Mom, we've heard all this before. Can't you at least turn it down?" She was queen of the TV control. It was her magic wand that she used to control the world. "I'm watching this," she said. "I want to know what's going on."

Well, you won't find out by the news, Baylor thought. He wondered if the clip had been filmed by the news service to give their news people something to be outraged about.

His beans were cold. His mother had eaten all her spaghetti, but had left her beans untouched.

"Mom?"

"That was good." She heaved herself to the side and set the dish down on the end table by shoving a box of tissues, a paperback, and an empty pop can onto the floor. "Goddammit."

Baylor sighed.

Chapter Nine
Day Shift at the Tavern

I don't know how much longer I can do this, Val thought. She was leaning on the bar counter because the dizziness was making her head feel like it was about to roll off her shoulders. She'd been up on her feet all afternoon. Some of that time had been spent dispensing drugs and sundries to locals while accepting what pay they could give, if any. A busy day because it was payday. Skimpy Social Security checks had been cashed in town, and the locals had been drifting in to pick up Rachel's stolen goods. Val had rested between customers and had kept herself fed and watered, but still the exhaustion was creeping into her blood. So, when Old Man staggered in with Angie at his heels, looking for a beer and meds, she greeted him without enthusiasm.

"Here's some Cyclotrine for you. It's for arthritis." Val squinted through her glasses at the label. "My guess is one a day." Since it was not a prescription, only one of Rachel's stolen bottles, there was no dosage listed. Nevertheless, Val had a sense of responsibility about handing out drugs. "Sorry. When Rachel was grabbing stuff, this is what she got. But it is for arthritis."

Old Man smiled toothlessly. "I know that one. I know how many to take."

"Good. Got your old bottle with you?"

"Yeah." He fumbled a small plastic bottle out of his pocket. "I know about Cyclotrine because the vet prescribed it for Angela."

"This is medication for a dog?" Val was horrified.

"It's for both. I used to get it from the vet for her." Old Man grinned.

"And I used to use hers because it was cheaper than what the doc gave me! It's the same stuff, just the dose is different."

Val wasn't sure she believed that, but what the hell. They were all dying and they couldn't afford doctors or vets, so they just had to muddle along.

"Well, I guess it's up to you." She refilled Old Man's bottle. The remaining pills she'd give to Charlie or Vulture if they didn't mind a medication used on dogs. Valerie didn't take any medication for herself but not out of fear of overdosing. She just didn't want to be taking meds that someone else might need. Besides, her condition was fatal.

"Wanna beer?"

"That's what I came for."

Valerie pulled a bottle out of the box on the floor. They usually didn't steal beer; they bought it by the case. Even though they got the cheapest brands, they had to make their customers pay for it. Old Man carefully counted out the exact change which Valerie dumped into the cash box. They didn't keep any kind of records, just bought supplies when they had the money and went without when they didn't.

Valerie watched Old Man and his dog shuffle the distance from the bar to a booth. She wondered how much longer it would be before he could no longer make the trip. I'll go visit him, she told herself, when he gets that bad.

A loud bang from the front of the room caught her attention. Crazy Mary was posed dramatically in the door as if expecting a joyous greeting from Old Man and Valerie. When she didn't get one, she gave the greeting herself, "And here I am! How the hell are you today, Valerie?" She was legless drunk and had to grab at chair backs and tables on her way to the bar counter.

"I got your schiz meds," Valerie informed her. She reacted to Mary about the same way she reacted to spiders: with an urge to squash. But Mary was impervious to Val's frostiness.

"And how are you doing?" she asked, with over-elaborate friendliness.

"I'm doing." Val responded.

"Thass good! And you need to keep on doing because if you don't, you're done!" Crazy Mary howled with laughter at her own wit.

The corners of Val's mouth turned down, but she liked Mary's statement. She repeated it to herself: Keep on doing, because if you don't, you're done. Maybe she could cross stitch a little wall hanging with that quote on it.

"Here's your pills, Mary."

"I don't want 'em. I'll tell you what you can get me. Get me a shot of that whiskey over there." The Jim Beam was out for the locals.

Val grabbed the whiskey bottle. "Show me the money."

"Aw, don't be like that!"

"Show me."

"Alright." Mary grabbed a handful of cash out of her pocket and dumped it on the counter. "I could just drink at home, you know."

"You should be eating, not drinking, and you need your pills."

"No, I don't. Those pills make me sick." Her voice changed, more solid, not jovial. "Give them to someone else."

"No one else needs them. You're our town schizophrenic."

"I ain't the crazy one around here."

Val sighed. "Have it your way." She poured out a whiskey.

Chapter Ten
Another Saturday Night

He couldn't see anything but rain from the backseat. Mel was up front by Pete, and that left Randy in back with Baylor. They weren't talking. They weren't even making eye contact. Randy was pissed because he hadn't done well at practice the previous day while Baylor had been a star of sorts.

They'd spent the day out on the survival course. Baylor knew enough about survival to know it was not a very authentic course. It was just a hard, messy route through some woods and marsh land, tough and uncomfortable, but only life-threatening to the terminally stupid. After all, there was a trail to follow and a warm shelter to dry off in at the finish line. Survival was just a matter of persistence. Slog along for long enough and, sooner or later, everyone made it to the end. He was the star because he'd completed the course first. Randy had struggled in nearly last, out of breath, exhausted, and dehydrated. Baylor was pretty sure he hadn't learned much from the experience.

So, Randy had been radiating resentment all evening. After the survival course, they'd all gone home, taken showers, and changed clothes before regrouping. Having noted the weather, Bay had thrown on his old rain slicker over a wool shirt over a T-shirt that said, "Defense of Freedom." And he had a wool hat stuffed in his pocket. Randy was in jeans and a sweatshirt. Mel had put some effort into her version of dressed up: pink dye on one side of her head, silver earrings on the other side, and a blue jean jacket with decorative studs that provided no protection from the chilly rain. But she looked sexy as hell.

She was radiating that sexuality across the gearshift to Pete who was responding by driving with elaborate nonchalance. They exchanged grins and comments and cigarette smoke. Baylor couldn't hear their flirting over the rain and the engine, but he could see the banter back and forth. Get a room, he thought sourly.

They were headed out to Warrentown again because Randy claimed his wallet had been stolen there at the tavern. It wasn't clear to Baylor who could've stolen the wallet. He didn't remember being near to anyone except old people. The fortyish guy who looked like a criminal had never gotten close enough to rob Randy. The black-haired woman who seemed to be the owner or manager had never been near them either, so Baylor's guess was that Randy had dropped his wallet somewhere or left it on a table where it'd been snagged by one of the oldsters.

The whole plan was stupid. They'd be better off heading for one of the bars in town. Maybe there'd be some girls to dance with. But Randy had made a big deal out of how he had no money and no credit cards or debit card and how they just had to go out there and insist that his wallet be returned. Well, someone might've handed it over to the old lady bartender, and she might've it stashed in a lost and found.

So, they were off on a run out to Warrentown in pursuit of Randy's wallet. Baylor wedged himself in the corner of the backseat, gazed out at the rain, and tried to ignore Randy's discontented mutterings. Randy wanted to be part of the interaction in the front seat, but there was no role for him but third wheel. That makes me the fourth wheel, Baylor thought.

And there would be no girls at the Raven Tavern. No young ones. Just old people, and he didn't like old people. They were the ones who'd fucked everything up. His high school biology teacher had explained it. Old people had known about global climate change since the 1970s, back when they had Earth Day events. They'd known, and they hadn't done anything because they were too lazy and cowardly and didn't want to make any lifestyle changes. They just kept fiddling away and now the whole fucking planet was burning. And now they'd finally decided to do something: promote electric cars, promote wind power, ban new plastics, whatever. *Now* they decided to act. Now that the old people were all one foot in the grave, and it was his generation that was inheriting the earth–not that anyone would want it anymore.

He stared out at the rain. Weird to think of millions of people all over the world trying to walk hundreds and thousands of miles north or south to get away from fires and drought, while there they were in Washington state with a problem of rain that crashed down in torrents. Three people had died last winter when hillsides fell on Rainier. Luckily, it was only three. His mom's trailer was safely out of the slide zone. And safely out of the tide zone, too, which was why her rent kept going up. That was another weird effect of everything going to hell: funky trailers in funky trailer courts were going up in rent because of the people trying to move out of the landslide zones and up away from the shoreline. He didn't know how long she'd be able to hold out there, but she sure as hell wasn't ever going to live with him.

No way. God, no.

Baylor stared out at the rain as if staring could somehow transport him away to a better place. But there wasn't anywhere better, at least not for people who weren't rich. Rich people bought themselves homes and neighborhoods and built walls around themselves to keep the riff-raff out. I'm riff-raff, Baylor thought. Trailer trash kid. No one gives a fuck about me, either. It's everyone for themselves. That's why Randy was so pissed about his fucking wallet. Every dollar counted. You had to claw your way to high ground, and then fight off everyone else so you could keep your spot.

He sighed, but inwardly so no one would hear. There was nothing that he could do about any of it except look out for himself. Maybe next weekend he'd tell Pete's crew to fuck off and go out bar-hopping on his own. Find a nice girl. He should've begged out of this trip.

He did have a little curiosity about the people out at the ghost town, though. That was their high ground, he supposed, the place where they were making their last stands before they all fell over dead from old age. Maybe he could stick his mom out there. Baylor grinned at the thought, then wondered if they had TV in Warrentown. He didn't think so. In fact, he wasn't sure they had electricity at all; the tavern had been lit by lanterns. They lived like a bunch of bums. He leaned back in his seat, faced forward, and aimed his thoughts at the next weekend. He'd go bar-hopping on his own.

Chapter Eleven
The Militia

"Here, Angie." Old Man slipped her a bit of bread. Dinner at the Tavern that night was ... something. He wasn't really sure what. After poking and sawing with his knife, the old man had come to the conclusion that Val had cooked one of Jimmy's boots, well covered with gravy. Luckily, there was a good side salad and some green beans cooked with carrots. Val wasn't anyone's idea of a chef, but her dinners were better than what he fixed for himself. "We're tired of mushroom soup, aren't we, Angie?" That's what the food bank had: mushroom soup. Jimmy made trips into town regularly to get everyone's ration, and he always came back with a big box of mushroom soup.

I used to run a grocery, Old Man thought, and now I have to use the food bank. Everything had gotten too expensive. Except Val's dinners. All Rachel charged was a donation.

"Have another nibble." He slipped a bit of bread and gravy to Angie, who thanked him with an ear-to-ear smile. Old Man smiled back and rubbed her head. He heard a loud bang and looked up.

Three people filled the doorway. No, four. Three in front and one a little way behind. Young people. All with short spiky hair, heavy boots built for kicking, and unsmiling faces. Militia. The atmosphere of the tavern changed abruptly, and not just because of the cold rain that swept in the open door. Old Man shrank back against the wall and hunched down over his dinner plate, with one shoulder aimed at the newcomers. Ignore them and they'd ignore him. "Come here," he whispered to Angie. "Get under the table."

Valerie braced herself against the counter. Her knees were trembling.

Shit, she told herself. Stop it. Stop it. Stop being scared. We outnumber them.

For reassurance, she surveyed the room. More locals had wandered in that night than usual. Vulture the biker and his pal Sammish Bob had emerged from their makeshift compound in the woods, a rare trip in their old-school gas-fueled pickup truck. They were relics from the Iraq War. Ancient history, Valerie thought. Did anyone even remember that war? And so poor that they could barely put fuel in their truck.

They'd brought in with them a new guy, a talkative hick named Doug who was only in his early thirties, making him the youngest settler in the area. Judging by his raggedy uniform, he was a vet from one of the overseas "peacekeeping actions." Which meant, Valerie knew, that he was probably half-crazy. You had to be, after shooting mobs of terrified and desperate people.

Crazy Mary had been entertaining them from her favorite bar stool while Charlie nursed a beer and listened in. Old Man was there with his dog, backed into a corner, quietly nibbling his dinner and sipping the one beer he'd take all evening to ingest. Even with Doug's unfamiliar face, the evening had felt warm and comfortable until the militia came in.

We outnumber them, Valerie reminded herself. The militia barged through the room, making the air vibrate, and Valerie could feel the vibration in her bones. They filled the aisle between the tables and directed their glares and stares around the room, their eyes stabbing the dim interior like the high beams on a car. The bar's customers responded with side glances or quick peeks around their beer glasses.

Valerie sucked in a deep lungful of the bar's smoky air, straightened her spine, and aimed her eyes across the room.

She picked out individuals, the better to know what she was dealing with. The big blond one was the alpha, of course. Everything about his body language–his wide-legged stance, the shoulder action, the forward thrust chin–showed his image of himself as action hero.

She shifted her gaze to the others. A suck-up girl, clutching the Dear Leader's arm while her mouth held a jeer. Val's bet was that she wouldn't be so openly jeery on her own. Nor would the pudgy wannabe guy to the Dear Leader's right. He was siphoning off significance like a thief stealing gasoline. On his own, he was just a guy in his early twenties with vague features and brown hair and baby fat. The last one, the lean one who peered into the room over the shoulders of the others, was a follower too.

This is all high school again, Val told herself. High school with guns. Val called to them, "Come on in and close the door. You're letting the cold air in." She tried for a friendly tone, but couldn't keep the knife edge of antagonism hidden.

The lean one quickly responded by reaching for the door, but the big blond one cut him off. Slowly, so as to establish dominance, he instructed the pudgy one, "Close the door, please, Randy." And he stepped out to lead his group to the bar. He kept his eyes right smack on Val's face the whole way across the room.

She stuck her chin out and tried not to wish for Rachel's help. Her fingers betrayed her by trembling. Valerie pushed her hands flat and leaned on the counter. "So, you all came back? That's long drive for our little bar."

The big blond guy said, "We came to get Randy's wallet back."

Chapter Twelve
Jimmy and Val Defend the Tavern

Jimmy reached for the shotgun. He curved his fingers around the stock, liking the cool solid feel of it. He liked the heft, too. He positioned himself just inside the storeroom door, where he could listen without being seen from the front counter. With four armed militia assholes out there intimidating Val, surprise was his only ally. And not much of an ally. He listened.

The leader guy leaned on the counter. Instead of asking for a drink, he said, "We're here for the wallet."

"Wha-what?" Valerie stuttered with surprise.

"His wallet." The big blond guy pointed at the pudgy one. "We were in here last week and when we left, Randy's wallet came up missing."

Valerie's eyes jumped from one face to another. She groped for words, "I'm sorry, but no one turned a wallet in to me."

"That's because someone stole it!" Randy thrust his face at Val. Her hands fluttered up to her face and she stepped back. "I don't think, I don't think anyone here would steal anything from you. Maybe you dropped it outside?"

The big blond guy gripped Randy by the shoulder and pushed him to one side. He licked his lips, a thinking look on his face. Behind him, the lean one lagged back, as if to distance himself. The girl watched the leader, ready to imitate him. The pudgy one had his lower lip thrust out like a little kid.

"Look around," Val quavered. She took a deep breath and steadied her voice. "Look at those folks out there. None of them could steal anything. They're all too old. Look at them."

The militia did. All four pairs of eyes surveyed the room. Charlie, deep in the darkness of the room, blinked through his glasses. Old Man was trying to make himself and his dog invisible. Vulture and his crew watched the interaction, their elbows on their table and their hands on their beer mugs. Then all four eyes swung back to Val. She could see the reluctant admission in their faces.

"Those old guys couldn't pick the pocket of a dead man," Crazy Mary chimed in. All the eyes turned to her. "Don't look at me!" she laughed. "You think I could get your wallet without you knowing it?" Randy's mouth worked. On the one hand, he wanted to say yes, but on the other hand it would make him look pretty stupid to claim that he'd been robbed by a toothless, elderly, and clearly insane old woman. He shrugged and turned away.

"Well, someone did. Not you but someone," he muttered.

"I'm sorry you lost your wallet." Val tried smiling at the militia members. No one smiled back. "Hey, I can't make up for your loss, but how about a round of drinks on us just to show we're all friends now?" She didn't wait for an answer, just turned to the row of boxes on the floor and picked up the bottle of whiskey that she'd brought out for Vulture.

"How's this?" It wasn't an expensive brand but, still, hard liquor was special compared to beer.

Big blond guy had made his decision. "Sure. Thanks." He flicked a glance at Randy, who hunched his shoulders sullenly.

"Here ya go." Val set up a row of shot glasses and splashed booze into each. She batted Mary's hand away. "Not you!"

Mary guffawed and tried again.

"Not you!" Val glared. The militia members grabbed their drinks. The big blond guy held his up in a brief salute to Val, clinked his glass with the girl, and swallowed his drink in one gulp. His efforts to suppress a cough were almost successful. The others sipped, as they should, Val thought. It wasn't tequila, after all. It was sipping whiskey.

Crazy Mary watched the militia gang with a jeer on her mouth. "You guys are lucky Rachel's upstairs."

"Oh, don't start." Val snapped. "Everything's fine now."

"Cause you bought them off with booze. If Rachel or Jimmy had been here, they'd be hightailing it out the door."

"Ignore her," Val told the big blond guy. "She's full of shit."

"You think so?" Mary cocked her head.

"Yeah, I think so."

Mary laughed. She leaned forward, addressing herself to the big blond guy. "I'll tell you what no one else in this stupid old town will tell you. Rachel isn't human." She grinned, displaying her lack of teeth. "She isn't human, and Jimmy isn't either, so you'd better not mess with either one of them."

"She's our village idiot," Val told the blond guy. "Ignore her."

The big blond guy hadn't acknowledged Mary's existence except to shift slightly so that his back was toward her. Waving a hand dismissively, he said, "Takes all kinds. Hit me again." The other three followed his lead in ignoring Mary. Val topped off his drink and pointed at a booth. "You guys can sit over there and I'll bring you some potato chips."

"Sure," The big guy nodded toward the empty booth, directing the others to follow. Surreptitiously watched by the other patrons, they swaggered their way to across the room and settled themselves on the benches.

Val turned her attention to Mary. "You shouldn't say stuff like that."

"Well, it's true. Ask yourself how come she hasn't changed in fifty years? Still looks just like she did when I was a kid."

"She just has the kind of hair that doesn't go gray. You don't remember what she looked like when you were a kid."

"Yes, I do, and she looked just the same. She can fly, too. I seen her."

Val made a noise of disgust. She cast a quick glance at the militia. Seating them at a booth had been a shrewd move; wrapped in the dimness of the tavern and back against the wall they had lost importance. A quiet murmur showed that regulars were relaxing and chatting again. Peace had not quite been restored, but Val no longer felt twanging vibrations in her nervous system.

A quiet thump alerted Val to Jimmy's presence. He was holding the shotgun below the height of the counter. She jerked, startled by the gun.

"Hey, Jimmy!"

"You took care of that good." Val felt herself blushing. Her eyes dodged Jimmy's face and jumped all over the room. Ridiculous at her age to get in a flush over a guy, especially one half her age. Embarrassing to be embarrassed by any attention from him. "They're just overgrown teenagers."

"They're thugs." Jimmy leaned against the door jam and lit a cigarette.

Chapter Thirteen
Rachel, an Hour or so Later

Rachel didn't like the way the militia had taken over her bar. At first, they'd been reasonably quiet, just drank their whiskeys at their booth like any other group. But, as they drank, their voices got louder. The girl was shrill, the pudgy guy belligerent, the big blond one a show-off. Finding the locals to be unsatisfying as entertainment, they had started their own floor show–singing mostly, sometimes singly and sometimes as a trio or quartet. They were drunk to the point of being unable to stand without help, so they propped each other up with arms around each other's shoulders–a four-headed, eight-armed, spidery monster. Rachel, Jimmy and Val watched with increasing irritation. The oxycodone they'd slipped in the last round of drinks didn't seem to be having much effect.

"Shoulda given them more," Rachel hissed.

"Woulda killed them," Valerie responded.

"No loss."

"Hey," yelled the blond leader guy, "Hey, how about we all sing 'America the Beautiful!'"

They lurched into the first verse: "Oh, beautiful for spacious skies…"

"Why aren't you all singing?" The big guy demanded. Locals glanced at him out of the corners of their eyes and hunkered over their drinks. "Why not?" he shouted again. "Aren't you all patriotic here?"

"I am," said Crazy Mary. "Go ahead and sing more for us."

"We will!" The big guy made a sweeping motion with his arm and the four-headed choir yodeled out, "From sea to shining sea!" Then they bowed as a group and staggered forward, holding each other up. The girl hip-bumped a table, spilling a drink, and Vulture snarled, "Watch it."

"Oh, sorry!" She had become increasingly flirty after each drink, and now she hung off the neck of the blond guy, swung her butt around toward Vulture's face, and wriggled. He sat back with a snort. She did a hip shake that wobbled the table, and a statue of a witch fell on the floor.

"Ooo, witchy can't fly!" Still hanging on to the big blond guy, she leaned down and, with a slow sweeping gesture, scooped up the witch and held it triumphantly aloft. "Here she goes!"

"Hey, wait." The militia guy with the baby fat made a clumsy grab for the witch.

"No, let her fly!"

"Hey, gimme that."

"No, she's flying!"

"Jesus, how old are you guys? Twelve?" Vulture grabbed his drink and shoved his bulk to his feet. "Christ, can't a person have a drink here without a lot of punks making asses of themselves?" He and his friends edged their way between tables to a booth against the wall and sat down. The militia was left holding the floor, the girl pouting. The militia guy who always seemed to be on the edge of the group detached himself and started toward the door.

"Hey, where are you going?" the leader demanded.

"Just out for some air." But there was something apologetic about his shoulders that made Rachel give him a second look. He was stumbling drunk, had to grab chair backs to stay upright, but he made it to the door and left. The big blond guy made a contemptuous noise with his lips and the girl laughed. With elaborate care, she settled her butt in the chair Vulture had vacated. The blond guy joined her but Baby Fat Boy, as Rachel thought of him, stayed on his feet. He grabbed the plastic witch, and the girl, surprised, released it. Then, witch in hand, he made his way to the bar.

"You see this?" He shoved the witch toward Valerie.

She recoiled. "Yeah, I can see it."

"This wish … wish … witch … It looks just like the one my uncle had at his store. That got robbed. His store that got robbed." He leaned accusingly over the counter. "And last time I came here, my wallet got stolen."

He twisted around on the bar stool and yelled, "You hear that, everyone? My wallet got stolen and this wish … wish … witsh … whatever … comes from my uncle's store that got robbed! This here's a den of thieves, is what it is." He finished his speech with a wave of the witch.

Valerie tapped him gently on the shoulder. "You want another drink?"

He turned to her, stared a long look into her face, and said, "Are you the thief?"

"No," she frowned. "You shouldn't be saying stuff like that."

Rachel joined them by squeezing between Baby Fat Guy and Crazy Mary. She smiled and cooed, "You're pretty drunk, aren'tcha?"

Baby Fat Guy smiled back tentatively.

"I bought that witch at Walmart in Olympia," Rachel told him. "Lots of stores have those witch images at this time of year."

"My uncle got robbed." He was still belligerent, though his anger no longer was aimed at Rachel or Val. "Sucks. People ripping each other off all the time."

"Yeah, it sucks," Rachel agreed. "People shouldn't oughta do shit like that." She could see Jimmy leaning against the door frame, his eyes slits behind a cloud of cigarette smoke. She smiled blandly at him, and he smirked back.

Then, fed up with the hassles of the evening, Rachel strode out to the middle of the room and announced, "Drink up everyone. It's getting late." With the lantern light behind her, shadows made her eyes disappear. Her hair was a glossy blue-black. She looked like the witch statue.

"Oh no," the girl whined. "No, we just got started."

"Well, take your party somewhere else. I'm closing up." She tossed her hair over shoulder and grabbed a cleaning rag.

"You can't do that." The blond guy straightened up in an effort to appear less drunk than he was. "This is a bar and we're here drinking."

Rachel slapped the wet rag down on the bar. "This is my bar, and I will run it however I damn well please. We're closed because I say so."

Rachel only came up to the blond guy's shoulder, but she stood solidly with her chin up. The blond guy swayed unsteadily. Though his face was slack with drunkenness, he tried for a sneer. "You oughta think about closing up on us."

Rachel frowned, "What does that mean?"

"It means what are you? Mexican or something? You better have ID."

Rachel took a step forward and hissed, "I was living here before you were born, honey. So, clear the hell out."

"You heard the lady. Everyone out." It was Jimmy, cradling his gun. Vulture joined him, his bulk looming in the dark smoky air. Dave and

Sammish Bob climbed to their feet and added their shoulders to the wall of men.

"Everyone on your feet, let's go." Jimmy's voice was calm, but his eyes were sharp. The locals obediently sank the last of their drinks and gathered up their belongings. The room was suddenly stuffed with bumping bodies, coats, and hats. Charlie edged past the blond militia guy, mumbling, "Excuse me, trying to get to the door."

The blond man stepped back a bit to let Charlie past. Jimmy moved forward in Charlie's wake, his eyes locked on the blond man's face. There was a pause, a moment that teetered precariously between different outcomes. Then the blond guy retreated. "Yeah, whatever." He grabbed his coat. "C'mon," he told his friends. "Let's get outa here."

Vulture pushed by, followed by Dave and Sammish Bob. The militia members, caught up in the outgoing tide of regulars, staggered off together.

"It's cold out!" Rachel slapped Old Man's hat on his head. "Gotcher flashlights? It's dark out."

There was a brief jam-up at the door, then everyone spilled out into the street. Rachel could hear the pudgy guy's voice, yammering about the witch from the pharmacy, and Crazy Mary's cackling laugh. The fourth militia guy, the one who had left earlier, was sitting on the curb.

The locals huddled against the misty rain, not wanting to leave before the militia was gone. The militia's electric car, the only car parked on Main Street, gleamed in the beams of their flashlights. The blond guy blinked the doors unlocked with his remote. Headlights flashed, doors opened and slammed closed. The lean one militia guy, the loner, was the last to tumble into a seat. Revving his engine for show, the blond guy stomped on the accelerator, and the car shot off down the street. The tavern crowd watched the rain and darkness blot out the disappearing tail lights.

Rachel felt Jimmy beside her. He said, speaking softly so only Rachel would hear, "We got to do something about those assholes."

Chapter Fourteen
The Long and Winding Road

"Well, that sucked," Mel commented. She would've been leaning all over Pete except the gear shift was in the way, so instead she slumped down in her seat and propped her boots on the dashboard. The wipers slapped back and forth against the onslaught of rain. Pete was driving slowly; visibility was down to a narrow tunnel lit by his headlights through the rain-saturated darkness.

"Let's go to Leroy's," he suggested. Leroy's featured country music and dancing.

"You can drop me off at home," said Bay from the back seat.

Mel twisted around in her seat. "Huh, why?" Her tone was accusatory but blurred with alcohol.

"I'm tired." He felt exhausted and sick. Every word spoken was a rock dropped on his head.

"That bar was a letdown, huh?" Mel sounded less sneery than usual, but she was talking to Pete, not Bay. "I thought it was going to be more ... I don't know, edgy or something."

Randy pushed himself forward from the depths of the back seat. His voice was thick and slurred. "They did steal my wallet, and I bet they know the robbers. That guy, did you see the guy with the shotgun?"

"Forget it." Pete's eyes cut briefly to his rear view mirror but most of his attention was on the road. The surface was slick and muddy. Bay heard Randy slump back down into a heap of grumbling resentment. He turned his head away and peered out into the dark. Nothing was visible except wet darkness, but he could guess that the forest was flooded. For much of its length, the road followed the river valley closely enough to get the over spill when the river was high. He hoped that the road would stay passable. *God, please, don't let us get stuck,* he thought.

"I don't know why you guys wimped out back there. They're thieves." Now that they were safely away from the tavern, Randy's belligerence had no restraint. "We should've stood up to them instead of getting kicked out."

"Stood up how?" Pete didn't take his eyes off the road. "She said she bought the statue thing. What were we supposed to do? She probably did buy it. And you probably lost your wallet yourself. Stop being a crybaby."

Bay couldn't help it; he laughed. Just a little snort quickly suppressed, but Randy heard.

"Fuck you!" he yelled "Fuck you, Bay, you stuck-up asshole!"

"Ah, shit, shut up." He turned his shoulder away from Randy.

Randy threw himself on Bay in a clumsy cascade of fists. Bay wrapped his arms around his head and hollered, "Hey! Quit! Stop it." The weak drunken blows didn't hurt, but it was embarrassing to be under attack.

Pete stomped on the brakes so hard they were both thrown against the back of the front seat. Bay found himself underneath Randy, smashed by his weight into the floor, with one leg trapped at a painful angle. Pete twisted around so he could see into the back seat and barked, "Stop that." He sounded just like someone's dad yelling at kids. "Quit, Randy, or do I have to bust you up?"

Randy grumbled sullenly as he climbed off Bay and back to his side of the backseat. "Just tell him to fuck off. Tell him to stop laughing at me all the fucking time."

Pete sighed with exasperation. "Okay. Hey Bay, fuck off, will you? Please? Happy now, Randy?"

"You can fuck off, too." Randy muttered, but almost inaudibly.

"Jesus." Pete threw the car into gear and hit the gas.

Bay struggled back up to his seat, his one leg tingling and almost useless. He turned his face to the window and stared at the passing blackness. He wasn't injured, not by Randy's fists, anyway. His pride was hurt because he hadn't gotten in a good smack back. He wanted to pulverize Randy in retaliation. Instead, he had to sit there on the same car seat, acting like the whole incident was as much his fault as Randy's. That burned.

Bay had a sudden longing in his guts for the aloneness of his own home, especially his bed. He yearned to take a hot bath first, let the water burn really deep, deep, deep. Cleanse himself of the booze and his bad mood.

Then maybe he'd make some tea and spike it with a shot for warmth and drink it in bed. He'd always been good at comforting himself. Baylor listened to the wet, grinding rumble of the car wheels on the road and thought of his bed and his home. He wished for sleep.

The car slid to the side, but Pete got it back under control. He was slumped in his seat, his arms loose, his neck wobbly, but his eyes were focused on the wet darkness. The effort to stay awake had tightened his jaw, making a muscle throb in his cheek.

"Shouldn't we be to the highway by now?" Mel complained for the umpteenth time.

"It just seems longer in the dark." Pete's voice was tight with the effort to sound patient.

Surreptitiously, because he didn't want to wake Randy, Baylor pulled his cell phone out of the pocket and checked the time. Eight after one. He stared, puzzled.

"Hey." He leaned forward. Speaking just above a whisper, he asked Pete, "Didn't we leave that tavern pretty late? Maybe around one?"

"Yeah." Mel sounded bored or tired.

"My cell phone says its still one o'clock."

There was a pause, then Mel, her voice edged with uneasiness, said, "The dash clock says it's just before one."

"That can't be right." Bay struggled forward and took a look. "That's weird. We've been driving for at least …" his voice trailed off.

"Forget it." Pete braked to slow for another pothole. "We musta left earlier than one, that's all. And I'm driving slow, so I don't dump us all in a ditch."

Bay settled back in the corner of the backseat and let his eyes close.

He woke to hear whispering from the front seat.

"What do you mean?" Mel, hissed, a stabbing sound.

"My battery is getting low." Pete made his voice light, as if a low battery wasn't a big deal.

Mel shrilled, "But you charged up when we left town! We got a charge at the station."

Pete didn't answer. Bay waited, processing the information. Low battery and the rain was pounding down. And seemed like they'd been driving forever.

"It's about five miles from Rainier to the turnoff and about fifteen miles more to get to Warrentown. And fifteen miles out again," Mel insisted. "So, where are we? We shoulda got back to the highway a long time ago."

Where are we? Baylor, staring out into the black rain, got hung up on her question. She was right. Even driving slowly, they should've reached the turnoff onto the highway back to Rainier. Heck, they should already be home. Baylor pulled his cell phone out of his pocket. The time was eight to one.

Chapter Fifteen
A Blank Spot

Baylor's heart stopped. He stared blankly at the time. Then he told himself, Don't panic. It's just a malfunction of the phone.

Slowly he punched in his mother's number. Not that he wanted to talk to her. He just wanted reassurance that he could reach the world outside the watery darkness. He hit 'send' and watched. No signal. His stomach hardened into a rock. Baylor cleared his throat. "Hey," he whispered, "can anyone get cell service?"

There was a silence in the front seat. Baylor felt rather than saw a movement from Randy. Shit, they'd woken him up, and now they'd have to listen to his bitching and grumbling.

Mel startled Baylor by suddenly screeching, "I don't have any service!"

"Calm down!" Pete snapped. "We're just in a blank spot."

"There's something weird going on!" Her feet dropped to the floorboards. "We should have reached the highway by now and you're running out of power."

"We're okay." Pete's voice was harsh, each word a rebuke. "We'll get there soon." His shoulders looked stiff to Baylor.

Mel started to speak but silenced herself. The swipe of the wipers made a loud, liquidy, swish sound. The inside of the car was getting hot, all of them sweating and exhaling. Baylor leaned forward to check the time on the dashboard. Eight to one. He huddled back into his seat with his arms clamped across his chest. This is a nightmare, he thought, a fucking nightmare. The car hit a pothole and bounced. And Pete swore. Oh please, Baylor silently begged. Don't break down. Where's the fucking highway?

He felt the car lose momentum. It rolled, hit a pothole, rolled some more, and wound down to a halt. Pete stomped futilely on the accelerator and swore. They all sat in silence as the rain pounded on the roof.

"Well, now what the fuck do we do?" Mel turned to Pete, her tone almost accusatory.

"Try your cell phones again," he said

Mel's phone had an irritating ditty. Baylor didn't try his, just waited. She said, "Goddamn it." And then, louder, "Goddamn it."

Randy whispered, "We're stuck here?" Making it a question. It wasn't a question, though. They were stranded.

Pete set the parking brake. "We will just have to wait until morning, guys." He spoke calmly, but there was an underlying anger, like he was going to make the rest of them be calm whether they liked it or not. "Someone will come looking for us, or someone from Warrentown will come driving out."

"And kill us," Randy whispered.

"What's that?" Pete asked.

"Nothing."

"Just get as comfortable as you can. Get some sleep okay? This sucks, but we're dry and warm and we just need to wait for help."

He was trying to be a good leader, Baylor realized. The voice of common sense.

"After all," Pete went on, "someone is going to miss us and come looking, right?" Baylor tried and failed to think of anyone who would miss him. But Mel still lived with her mom and dad. They'd notice she was gone in the morning. So, someone would come looking.

Mel's boots bumped on the dash and, with a loud sigh, she wedged herself between her seat and the car door. Randy was a large dark lump in the corner. Pete adjusted his seat back so far that he nearly hit Baylor's knees.

Baylor tried to resign himself to sleeping in the car. He'd been half asleep already, he told himself. He could sleep again. He could just slide into unconsciousness. After all, by mid-morning at the latest someone would be looking for them. Baylor curled up, nearly in a fetal position, and tried to keep his eyes closed.

Chapter Sixteen
Darkness, Darkness

Hours later, he was still awake. He hadn't been uncomfortable in the car until he tried to sleep. Even groggy with the worn-out after-effects of alcohol, he couldn't find a way to sit that wasn't painful in some way. The arm rest poked him. There was no way to rest his neck that didn't hurt. For some reason, his legs were aching. And he had a hot spot forming under his tail bone from being in one position too long. Baylor tried to stretch his legs but there wasn't room.

He could hear Pete breathing and Mel snoring. She was a noisy sleeper, always grunting or muttering. Probably disappointed that she was spending the night separated from Pete by the gear shift. Probably she'd planned to spend the night in his bed, Baylor thought. The idea left a burn in his mind. All his thoughts left burning trails through his head.

Baylor wished for his bed at home. He still had the same bed he'd slept in as a kid, but now it was in his apartment. Just a twin bed, kind of depressing because a bed that small was not designed to be shared–not that he had anyone to share it with. And it was not a bed of good memories. No, it was the bed where he'd learned to comfort himself when no one else would do it. Still, he wished he was home in that bed.

Being stuck in the car was kind of like being a kid again: the same bad emotions rocketing around while he tried over and over to calm himself down. He'd spent a lot of his childhood hiding in his bedroom while his mom and dad stayed up to argue with each other, yammering on and on, back and forth. Only now it was his own thoughts that yammered on and on and would not shut up.

Someone would notice them missing. But that didn't mean they'd be found. He wasn't sure they were even on the Rainier road. They'd been driving forever. They should've reached the highway. No, he told himself, it just seemed like forever in the dark. But the clocks! How could their cell phone clocks and the car clock all stop working? They were somewhere with no cell phone reception and no functioning clocks. That just wasn't right. It was weird.

The worst thing, the scariest thing, was the car running out of power. It was all charged up. Heck, he'd been sitting right there in the backseat when Pete charged it up. The car that could run for over two hundred miles on a charge had run out in a little over thirty miles. There was a sickening inevitability to the loss of power, as if the road had been sucking at them, leeching off them, until it dragged the car to a stop. As if the road itself had trapped them in the dark, wet forest. They were stuck and waiting for whatever happened next.

His heartbeat felt like a small animal scurrying around inside his chest. His arms and legs were prickly with nerves. Baylor drew in a long, shaky breath and tried once again to clamp down on his thoughts. Don't think about the weird shit, he told his brain. There's a good explanation for all of it, he told his heart. We're all just too tired and drunk to figure it out, that's all. And no one was going to come after them from the tavern and murder them. Just go to fucking sleep and morning will come. It won't be eight to one forever. Baylor shifted his butt, but the sore spot still ached.

"Hey." A breathy whisper from the far side of the car seat was almost drowned out by the pounding of the rain. "Are you awake?"

Baylor hesitated before answering, not sure he wanted to have a conversation with Randy. "Yeah."

Randy shifted in the darkness and suddenly his stale breath was in Baylor's face. "I don't see how they can be asleep," he hissed.

"Drunk," Baylor suggested. He wished he could pass out.

"Yeah."

The drumming on the roof was relentless. The road really might flood, Baylor realized. And that thought really burned through his mind.

"Hey, Baylor."

"What?" He let his voice show irritation.

"There something weird going on, don't you think? I mean the clocks all still say one o'clock. See?" He thrust his cell phone in Baylor's face. The harsh light stabbed his eyes. Baylor blinked and squinted.

"What does yours say?" Randy asked.

"I don't know." All that effort to calm down and now Randy was getting him riled up again.

"All of our clocks can't be wrong. Check the car dash," Randy whispered.

"No." Baylor shifted himself back as far from Randy as he could get. "It won't show unless the engine is on. And the battery's dead." They were trapped in a nightmare, like they never were going to get home. They'd wake up surrounded by water. They'd be stuck there with each other for a week. Stop it! he yelled at himself. Stop thinking bad stuff! Everything will be better in the morning. "Go to sleep, Randy."

"But there's something wrong," Randy insisted. "It's got to be something to do with that weird woman, the one the other lady said was a witch."

"She didn't say that." Baylor let his anger show. "Go to sleep, Randy. I'm trying to sleep."

"Well, I'm just glad I have my gun is all I'm saying. No one's going to sneak up on me." The car seat shifted as Randy moved back to his own side.

Listen to the rain, Baylor told himself, and stop thinking. He felt a shiver of fear, followed by a stab of anger at Randy. There was nothing to be afraid of. No one from Warrentown was going to sneak after them and shoot them. Where had Randy gotten that dumb idea? He forced himself to focus on the sound of the rain.

The rain had a rhythm to it. Not a steady beat, not a pattern that repeated. It pounded hard and fast, then eased off, then pounded some more. And the pounding was made up of many smaller beats, some close together and some spread out, like a room full of drummers that weren't on the same song. The rain overhead had a different, heavier beat than the rain on the window. The window rain was almost soothing, more a sliding sound than a beat.

Sometimes the rain sounded like footsteps. Baylor could hear the soft thumps: hesitant, start-and-stop. Just like footsteps, actually. Like someone approaching, taking quick steps, then stopping to listen, then stepping closer. Like someone sneaking up on them.

Baylor tensed and listened. He could picture the scary guy from the tavern, the one with the shotgun, standing out in the rain, a dark figure watching them sleep. He had an impulse to peek out the window, followed by the opposite impulse, the desire to hunker further down in the darkness of the car. More footsteps. Baylor closed his eyes and concentrated. Thump. Thump, thump, thump. It sounded *exactly* like steps, like someone maybe ten feet from the car. Baylor sucked in his breath and slowly lifted his head.

The window was black and streaked with glistening rivulets of rain. At first, he could see nothing, but gradually the darkness resolved itself into the shape of a man. No, not a man; a very large dog. Baylor blinked with disbelief and the dog vanished, leaving nothing but smears of black and silver on the window. Baylor tried to get his breath under control.

"Hey." Randy's whisper shot through Baylor's nervous system like a rocket, leaving him jangled and startled.

"Jesus!" he hissed, "Don't scare me like that."

"No, wait," Randy's voice was shaking. "Look, Bay. Out the window."

Baylor did not want to look out the window again. He didn't want to see any scary guys or huge dogs. However, he couldn't *not* look. Cautiously, so as to not attract the attention of whatever might be outside, he turned his head and peeked out into the night. The darkness was a diffuse, whirling mass of black air and water, thick and impenetrable. Other than a sliver of reflection on the glass and two points of light, there was nothing to see. Baylor studied the two points of light. They were too low to be stars and they couldn't be reflections of any light coming from the car. Flashlights? People out in that driving rain with flashlights? And then he saw a man. He was a dark blue silhouette, a lean man in a cowboy hat. His eyes were yellow. He was standing calmly a few feet away from the car, immune to the rain. Just standing and watching them.

Baylor froze. All thought stopped. He just stared. The dark blue silhouette stared back, freezing Baylor's entrails. Then the figure wavered in the rain, dissolved, and reformed as some kind of large dog, maybe a wolf or coyote. Then, with a blink of Baylor's eyes, the dog-man was gone. Baylor's whole body contracted into a crouch. His heart was up in his throat, strangling him.

"Where'd he go?" Randy hissed in Baylor's ear. "Should we wake Pete?" Baylor felt metal against his arm and realized that Randy had his pistol out, like he was preparing to shoot. The gun was wavering and jerking. Fear turned to anger, and Bay grabbed Randy's arm. "Be careful with that gun, Randy!" he hissed.

"Did you see him?" Randy quavered. Baylor realized that Randy was escalating toward hysteria. Somehow, that brought a measure of calm to Baylor. He gently pushed Randy's arm down so that the gun was aimed at the floor.

"I just saw…" He tried to put it into words, "I saw patterns in the rain. Like how you can see pictures in clouds? Like that." He was trying to convince himself as much as Randy. "Just kind of dreams."

Randy's breath was loud and ragged. They listened together to the rain. The rumbling of Pete's snoring from the front seat was reassuringly normal.

"Put your gun up before you shoot someone," Bay whispered. He could feel Randy's arm trembling. "Come on, Randy. We were just imaging stuff."

Randy withdrew to his side of the backseat, and Bay heard the scratch of his boots as he pulled his legs up. Bay felt like curling up in the fetal position, too, but his butt was sore and his knees ached. Surges of adrenaline were racketing around his nervous system. He shoved his trembling hands into his pockets and eased down into the seat with his knees against the back of the front seat, but he didn't relax.

"I saw something," Randy muttered defiantly. "You don't believe me, but it was real. I still got my gun."

'I'm trying to sleep," Bay told him. With determination, he closed his eyes. Which was mistake, because on the inside of his eyelids he could see the man with yellow eyes. Baylor's eyes popped open. He sat frozen, breathing through his mouth, too frightened to look out the window.

Chapter Seventeen
Very Early Morning in Warrentown

Valerie touched the cold floor with her toes. Twin shivers ran up her legs and she clutched her blanket around her shoulders. She hesitated, though there was no sense in procrastinating. Her house was not going to get any warmer and she might as well get moving, get up, get it over with. Every morning at four she had to pee. Regular as a clock.

Grimly, she prepared herself to stand up, then thought: Someday soon I won't be able to do this. I won't be able to get up by myself. She sat still, immobilized by the raw nakedness of the moment. She was going to die soon, having never lived. Valerie examined her long bony feet on the old carpet. She could see the blue veins that writhed beneath her thin pale skin. Blood still flowed through her body with quiet persistence, even when her will was fading. Given a choice between feeling cold and feeling nothing, maybe feeling nothing was better. Sometimes she had no appreciation for life.

Valerie sighed. She studied her toes. Calluses from a lifetime of the kind of work that required standing and walking around. It wasn't true that she had no appreciation for life. She just had no appreciation for cold feet on the floor. And peeing in a bucket. Like the old pioneer days, she thought. Chamber pot. When I get to the point that I can't empty my chamber pot, it will be time to find something in Rachel's meds to use to kill myself.

Because, she thought, I have no one to take care of me. But that wasn't true either. She was pretty sure that Jimmy and Rachel would take care of her when she got to that point. Somehow that thought filled her with bleak despair. She just didn't want to think of them hovering over her bedridden body while she wasted away. And she didn't want to think of the lonely hours when they weren't around because, of course, they couldn't attend to her every minute. Besides, the animals needed someone to look after them. Charlie would try but he was old, too.

Lymphoma. The doctor said she'd die in her sleep. Well, I wish I would hurry up and get it over with, she thought. Then she snorted a laugh. "How can I die in my sleep if I constantly wake up because I have to pee?"

"So, get up!" she told herself. "Up and at 'em!"

"At least it stopped raining." Jimmy squinted at the sky and took a sip of his coffee. Rachel yawned expansively, and her hands tightened around her mug. She had not slept well with Jimmy gone. They were standing on the porch of the tavern, enjoying the hazy gold of the moon shining through clouds. The air was cold.

"I'm just curious," Rachel explained. It had been hard to leave the nice cozy nest of her bed, but she wanted to see for herself.

"Those guys have guns."

"I won't get shot."

Jimmy took a long drag on his cigarette and exhaled like a dragon. Rachel grinned. She didn't smoke. Her morning ritual lately had included drinking their homemade apple juice warmed up on the camp stove. She figured she'd better drink it before it got moldy or something. She inhaled the scent with pleasure and let her breath out. Her breath fogged in the chill.

"Going to be cold flying," Jimmy commented.

"It was wet running," Rachel replied.

They stood in silent companionship while Jimmy finished his cigarette and Rachel finished her hot drink. Then Rachel pulled Jimmy's head down for a quick kiss and took off.

Chapter Eighteen
Morning After

The rain was dancing lightly on the car roof and spattering on the windshield, a gentle sound. The warmth had leaked out of the car, leaving a stale, chilly, dampness behind. Baylor's neck felt like it would break if he turned his head. He'd spent the whole night in one position, awake but unmoving.

The world was a soft, misty gray. They were inside a cloud that had come down to earth to rest. Rivulets of water ran down the car windows, distorting the landscape into smeary streaks of pale yellow, green, and brown. Baylor gazed out into the morning, letting his mind move slowly. He didn't check his cell phone for the time. It was early, no more than dawn, and the world looked wet and cold. There was no sign of the yellow-eyed man.

Randy was snoring, but Pete and Mel were sleeping quietly. He had to pee, and he was desperately thirsty. And his head ached, and his back ached, and generally he felt like he'd been hit by a truck. *I got to move*, Baylor thought. He shifted around and sat up. No one noticed. Carefully, he squeezed his arm between the front seat and side of the car to reach Pete's door handle. But there was no way. Even if he got the door open, he couldn't squeeze out around Pete.

"Hey, Pete." No sound. "Hey, Pete, sorry I have to wake you, but I have to get out."

Pete woke suddenly with a loud groan. "What? What?" He jerked upright, his hair on end and his eyes darting every which way.

"Sorry. I have to get out and pee," Baylor explained.

"Oh, shit. Wait." Pete rubbed his face. "Shit, okay." He opened the car door and climbed out stiffly. Baylor gave him time to stretch and get out of the way before he crawled out. They stood together, swaying unsteadily. Pete arched his back and turned to the left and right. Then he dug out a cigarette. Baylor could hear waking up noises in the car, mostly swearing.

He stumbled down the road away from the car and unbuckled his belt. Though it was no longer raining, the air was saturated with water. The ground was, too. He added a stream of pee and saw out of the corner of his eye that Pete was pissing, too.

Baylor zipped up and looked around. Water everywhere but none that he normally would have considered for drinking. But he had to drink; he was dehydrated. Baylor stepped to the opposite side of the road from his pee, squatted by a puddle, and scooped up water. The water had the taste of dirt and leaves but was delicious on his scratchy throat. He tried to measure how much he was getting by estimating about a quarter cup with each scoop. After the second scoop, his hands were burning with cold. Two scoops were not enough. He dipped his chilled fingers in the puddle and scooped up more water to his lips.

Then he froze, but not from the water. The mud puddle. The road was gravel. It wasn't supposed to be gravel. The road from the highway back to Warrentown was paved. Potholed and worn out, but paved.

By the time he got back to the car, Randy and Mel were out, Mel stretching and Randy smoking. All three were standing in a group, but not looking at each other. They looked like Baylor felt: sore-eyed, stiff, grumpy.

Baylor said, "Hey, this road is gravel."

They all looked at their feet.

"It is," said Pete. "Look at that." He was holding a candy bar, partly unwrapped.

"It's paved! I mean the road to Warrentown is paved." Baylor could hear the thin note of fear in his voice. He swallowed and steadied himself. "So what road are we on?"

Pete hesitated, then said, "It's just a gravel section."

"What?"

"Just a gravel section. It's an old road and this is just a gravel section on it." He went back to unwrapping his candy bar. "Just a gravel section that we didn't notice on the way in."

Mel stared at his hand as his fingers fumbled on the wrapper. Pete took a bite.

"Not going to share?" She tried for a teasing tone.

"I'm the leader," Pete said. "I have to keep my strength up. You guys can share the other one."

Mel glared, but not at him, at the ground.

"Where is it?" Randy asked.

"Where's what?" Pete's mouth was full of chocolate.

"The other freakin' candy bar!" Randy snapped.

"In the glove box."

Randy and Mel broke for the car simultaneously. Baylor watched their competition for the door handle. Mel won. She dug around in the glove box, and emerged, candy bar in hand. Baylor's stomach rumbled audibly. A third of a candy bar wasn't going to help any of them.

Mel said, "I'm second, so I should get more."

"Oh no, you don't!" Randy snatched at her arm.

"Stop it," Pete barked. "Give it to me." Mel handed the bar over sullenly. Pete mangled it into three pieces. Baylor's piece was one bite of caramel and chocolate. It was delicious but just made him hungrier.

Baylor didn't buy Pete's explanation for the gravel, but there wasn't much point in arguing with him. Besides, the others were focused on trying out their cell phones. No one could get a signal. Mel climbed up on top of the car's hood but couldn't get a signal even from that height. Randy began to yammer shrilly about all the weirdness of their situation: the lack of cell reception, the car dying, the gravel road. His voice was like an electric drill in Baylor's ear. Feeling sick and dizzy, he crawled back into the car, leaving the door open. He heard Randy outside saying something to Pete about seeing a man in the dark. Pete scoffed, "Way out here? In the rain? Where'd he come from?"

Randy muttered defensively, "He was that guy from the tavern. The skinny, shady-looking one."

"Bullshit! How'd he get out here?"

"He must've driven out!" Randy rapped his knuckles on the car window. "Hey, Bay, tell Pete about that guy last night. You saw him."

Baylor leaned forward wearily and spoke through the open door. He knew he was going to piss Randy off, but he said, "I think it was just … kind of a optical illusion or something." He was not about to say that the man had turned into a dog or that he had stayed awake most of the night, too scared to sleep.

"It was not! You were just as scared as me!"

Baylor sighed. "Hey, I'm too tired to argue about it. Honestly, Pete, it looked like a man, but you're right that it doesn't make any sense."

Pete threw his cigarette on the ground. "You guys gotta keep your imaginations under control."

Randy huffed with outrage, but Baylor just sat back and closed his eyes. After a few minutes, he felt the car shift as the others piled in. He kept his eyes closed while the other three chatted in a desultory way. Mel kept reassuring everyone that her mom and dad would be out looking soon. Baylor knew his mother wouldn't miss him for at least a week, and even then she wouldn't raise any alarm. She'd just be mad. Maybe she'd call and leave a whiny message. Maybe she'd call several times, but she wouldn't call the militia to get anyone looking for him. He was so tired that the voices of the others–speculating, complaining, and whining–didn't keep him awake.

Chapter Nineteen
Long Day into Night

Roused by sunshine burning through the window, Bay checked out the sky. The heavy grayness was gone. The clouds had broken into big, puffy banks with a hard, shining blue of sky in between. Heat had gathered in the car and combined with damp clothing to make a smelly swamp of sweaty air. He had to pee again, but this time Pete was not in the front seat.

He was outside with Mel and Randy, all of them leaning on the passenger side and smoking. Bay extracted himself clumsily from the back seat and climbed out into the fresh air. The forest was steaming in the afternoon sun, thick with wet moss and lichens. Baylor stretched out his back and walked around to join Pete and Mel. They greeted him with tired nods.

Bay looked up and down the road. "No help yet," he said, stating the obvious. Pete grunted, and Mel sighed theatrically. Baylor checked out the road again, this time more slowly. They were in a valley of alders and maples, all the trees mossy, old, and leaning. The ground was thick with brush and rotten wood. He could see back through the tangle of lichen-covered tree trucks to the hill sides. With a shock he realized that there was no river.

"Hey, doesn't the road follow the river?"

Pete and Mel stared first at him and then off into the landscape.

"It's just a bit far away," Pete said.

But Pete was wrong. They were in a narrow valley and there was no room for a river. A stream, maybe, but not the river.

"That's pretty weird," said Bay slowly. "We must've turned off the main road somewhere."

"Oh shit, now you think things are weird!" Randy burst out with frustration. "Everything is weird! I keep telling you all. Everything is weird."

"Calm down!" Pete snapped. "Bay's right. Maybe this isn't a gravel stretch. It's just a turnoff that we got on. It was hard to see last night."

Randy spit on the ground.

"I'm going to get a drink," Bay said

"Out of where?" Mel stared, ready to sneer. "A mud puddle?"

"Yes! We need to keep hydrated."

He stomped off. Behind him he heard Randy complaining about drinking mud and Pete answering that, yes, they did need to stay hydrated. Randy responded that a person could go for a week with no water. Mel said that, hell no, it was more like one day, and Pete snapped impatiently that no, it was more like thirty-six hours. Meanwhile, they weren't drinking anything, seemed to Bay.

He knelt down by a puddle with relatively clear water and scooped up a handful. The rainwater froze his fingers. Bay braced himself and tried again. He counted scoops, trying for at least two cups of water even though his fingers were killing him.

Somewhere far off a crow cawed. He didn't look up.

"Maybe we should start walking," Mel suggested.

"Walk where?" Randy asked disdainfully.

"That way." she pointed. "If we turned off where we shouldn't have, it would be back that way."

Baylor looked at the sky. The weather was uncertain, lots of fat white clouds. Not the kind that rained, but the kind that would accumulate against the mountains, and then pile up and turn into the kind that rained. Pete made the same calculation. "We need to stay here," he said. "The car is our shelter."

No one was happy with that. Randy's cigarettes were gone, and no one would share with him. Bay had the impression that Pete was rationing his; he'd checked his pack and put it back in his pocket several times. Mel paced in circles, sighed, leaned against the car, and paced some more. The sun had swung over to the west and was threatening to disappear behind the hills.

Since no one else had thought about doing it, Bay said. "I'm going to go get some firewood."

"Good idea," said Pete. "Help him, everyone." That got loud sighs out of Mel and Randy, but they followed Bay into the woods.

The ground was sodden and choked with ferns and mossy nurse logs. Bay stepped carefully in an effort to avoid the standing water, but it was hard to see the ground through the thick, wet vegetation. He started breaking dead twigs off low-hanging alder branches.

Mel jeered, "That won't make much of a fire."

"Fire starter," he explained. She was lifting a rotten branch about four feet long and so soggy it bent. Bay didn't say anything about its flammability. He collected an armload of tinder, carried it back to the road, and dumped it on the gravel. Pete added some small branches to the pile.

Baylor waded back into the woods. He found a spindly Douglas fir. Its lower branches were dead, so Baylor worked his way around the tree, snapping the branches off. The harsh bark scoured his cold palms. He worked in silence while Pete barked orders, Randy swore to himself, and Mel griped about her wet feet.

Together they made a pile of wood, some of which looked like it might burn if gasoline was poured on it.

"Any scraps of paper in your car?" Bay asked. He had a bit of candy wrapper in his pocket. Pete had dropped his wrapper on the road, so it was too wet to be useful. He found some receipts for car maintenance in his glove box.

"Give me your lighter." Bay used Randy's lighter to start the papers burning, slid the lighter into his pocket, and began feeding the fire.

A fragile flame danced on the paper. All four crouched to watch. Bay gave the little flame a few twigs to chew on and, hesitantly, they caught. He fed in some more, then said, "Give me some of the smaller sticks."

He laid the larger, wetter branches beside the fire to dry while he slowly fed in the smaller ones. The little flame grew in size and confidence, leaping and jumping. The paper was gone, but a small bed of coals was forming.

"Great job," Pete complimented him.

"It's not really a fire yet," Bay said. He wanted a bigger bed of coals.

"Too bad we don't have hot dogs or something." Randy leaned forward, warming his legs. His jeans were soaked from the knees down. They all had wet legs. Bay carefully placed another branch where it would heat up. He decided to keep the lighter, but didn't let himself think about why. He just hoped Randy would forget to ask for it back.

The fire grew until it was big enough and strong enough to handle the larger, wetter logs without being snuffed out. Like the others, Baylor stood as close as he could in an effort to dry out his jeans. The daylight was fading out of the sky and the forest was darkening around them. Conversation died out until Randy interrupted their thoughts with, "God, I'd kill to have a beer." Mel laughed.

A crow cawed, a harsh, startling sound. Bay didn't look up until Mel said, urgently tugging on his sleeve, "Hey, Bay you could shoot that bird! We could eat it!"

As if in answer, his stomach groaned.

They all turned and looked up. The crow was high in an alder, silhouetted against the evening sky. It was, Bay realized, an easy shot. But his pistol was in the car. He made no move to retrieve it.

"Good idea, Mel," Pete whispered. He pulled his pistol out. "Go ahead, Bay. You're the best shot."

Bay squinted at the crow. Though silhouetted, he could see every detail of its glossy, purple-black feathers. It cocked its head in a look of inquiry, and one intelligent eye met Bay's gaze fearlessly. Bay's arms were full of cement, nearly immobilized with reluctance. He said, "There's no point it shooting it. I mean the bullet will just … blow the bird up. There won't be anything to eat."

"Go on, try," Pete urged. "We'll get some meat out of it." Bay accepted Pete's gun. He got a two-handed grip and began to raise the pistol slowly.

"Bay!" Mel hissed, "Come on! Before it flies away!" The crow hopped to a new branch, making a closer, easier shot.

Bay cleared his throat. "You know if I shoot it there won't be anything left to eat. Just guts and feathers."

"There will be something," Pete told him. "Something's better than nothing."

Bay aimed. He stood still, his finger on the trigger. His finger ached and a muscle in his palm spasmed. The crow was a thing of blackness, all angles and sharp points. It cawed again, like it was jeering at them. Bay couldn't make his fingers work. He let the gun drop away. "There's no point," he said. "It would die for nothing."

Pete grabbed the pistol away. He turned his back on Bay, jerked his arms into an aim, and took a shot. The crow leaped into the air, its wings black against the sky. It vanished into the shadowy forest.

"Oh fuck!!" Mel yelled. "That was our dinner!"

"What the fuck is the matter with you?" Pete locked eyes with Bay. He was a good six inches taller, built bigger, and knew how to intimidate. Bay took a step back. "We're a team. Why didn't you … Christ! I gave you a fucking order to shoot that bird."

"It wasn't an order," Bay stuttered. "We're just … we're just out getting drunk together. This isn't militia. This is just us."

"No, it fucking isn't!" Pete let his glare jump from face to face, making them all targets. "This is a survival situation and you will all obey orders. Right?"

Mel grinned, "Aye, aye, Sir!" But not in a snotty way. She meant it. Randy mumbled his acquiescence. Bay shrugged, looked away, and muttered, "Okay." But he was thinking that no, they were not militia. They were auxiliary, not sworn in, and besides, he knew more about survival than Pete knew.

Still, he didn't know why he hadn't shot the crow. There would've been some meat on it.

Chapter Twenty
And the Next Day

Baylor was hungry. It was not the good kind of hunger, the anticipatory kind like right before the pizza comes out of the oven or that moment when the smell of French fries hits the nostrils. No, this was a cold hunger, a hollowness that felt like fear. He had a sense of impending chaos, and the feeling was somehow related to his empty stomach. Baylor curled up in the car seat and hugged his knees.

As far as he could tell, he was the only one awake. They'd sat up late around the fire, complaining of hunger and bickering about who should go get more wood. Mel had kept reminding them of how worried her parents were sure to be and how a search party was probably out looking for them. Her comments hadn't been reassuring to Bay. He just wondered why the search party hadn't found them already. They should be easy to find; just check the turnoffs from the main road. He had to fight off a creeping feeling that they were lost in time, not space.

Lost in time, not space. Stuck forever on a wet gravel road in a cold wet forest, with no one for company but Asshole, Horny Girl, and the Whiner. And Yellow Eyes, the man-dog or dog-man. Bay shivered. Then he shivered again, a deep chill that ran through his ribs, down his spine, and out his limbs. He was cold, far colder than the night air. He cuddled his chin down against his chest and closed his eyes.

He was *not* thinking about the coyote man. Actively not thinking about him, as in telling himself over and over to stop thinking about him. Those strange yellow eyes. He was *not* going to look out the window at the darkness. Baylor couldn't stop shivering. It's because I'm hungry, he told himself. They weren't in any real danger. They would be found before they starved to death and there was no such thing as a man who could turn into a coyote. He was hungry and that was making him feel scared.

The next morning, they saw a coyote. They were hanging out by the car, Randy whining for a cigarette while Pete and Mel smoked. They were all sore and cranky, their faces bruised with exhaustion. The gel in Mel's hair was stiff with dirt and lint. Bay supposed his hair looked pretty rough, too. He needed a shave, and he needed desperately to brush his teeth. He was thinking about his furry teeth and spiky hair when he saw the coyote, and his first thought was how much better the coyote looked than them.

It was a handsome animal, not flea-bitten and skinny like other coyotes. Bay remembered his biology teacher saying that the huge outbreak of fleas was a global warming thing. Somehow, that coyote had missed out. He stood silently in the woods and observed them with eyes that seemed dispassionate, maybe cynical. He doesn't like us, Bay thought.

"Uh, look!" Randy hissed on a sharp intake of breath.

"Is that a wolf?" Mel whispered.

"No," Bay told them. The coyote was almost big enough to be one, but wolves had been shot out of the woods long ago. The coyote lounged confidently, head up, ears forward. Bay felt a trickle of ice water in his spine. The coyote was not at all afraid of them.

"He's waiting for us to die," Randy shrilled suddenly, "so he can eat us!"

"Oh, shut up." Pete's hand tugged Bay's sleeve. "Got your gun?" he whispered. He'd ordered them to have their weapons handy at all times.

"Yeah, Bay," Mel jeered, but quietly. "Get your goddamn gun out."

Bay didn't move. His pistol was in his holster and he felt the weight of it on his hip. The coyote was only forty or so feet away, clearly visible, standing on a mossy log. Its eyes were mesmerizing: yellow, back lit and iridescent, like opals. The coyote seemed to be assessing them, evaluating them for some quality that Baylor was not sure he had. He frowned, wondering what the coyote wanted. Then the image of the coyote wavered and the air thickened. Bay blinked to clear his vision and a man was standing in the woods right where the coyote had been. He was lean, not tall, and had stringy brown hair. He was grinning slightly. And suddenly he was gone, and the coyote was back. Baylor realized that he had been staring for a long time but hadn't even brought the pistol up to aim.

"Come on!" Pete hissed. They hadn't seen the man. Baylor licked his lips nervously. He didn't seem to have control over his arms. The coyote's gaze turned to Pete.

Baylor felt rather than saw Pete lifting his gun in a slow arc. Pete had a Heckler and Koch G3 rifle, issued to him by the militia, which he normally kept in the car trunk. The gun was black, long, and carried enough bullets to pulverize the coyote into a cloud of blood and guts. Bay's hand shot out, slammed into Pete's arm, and the rifle jerked skyward.

"Goddamn it!" Pete yelled.

The coyote was gone. Just like that. Bay didn't see it run; it simply wasn't there anymore.

"Why the fuck did you do that?" Pete turned on Baylor, fists clenched.

Baylor didn't know. His brain fumbled hopelessly for an explanation. "I s-s-saw a m-man!" he stuttered, knowing that he was making a fool of himself.

"What the fuck are you talking about?"

"There was a man." Bay's voice wavered to a halt. No one was going to believe him. He was not sure he believed himself. "Did you see him, Randy?" he asked.

Randy spat on the ground. "No, you asshole." He looked smug and Bay realized that he was being paid back for not supporting Randy's story about seeing a man in the dark. He took in a deep breath and tried to explain, "I saw the coyote, but I thought I saw a man back there in the woods, and I thought he could help us."

"You high or what?" Pete waited for an answer, but Baylor could find nothing to say. "You frickin' let us all down. This is the second time. You're worthless." Pete's words shot out in a shower of spit. "What's wrong with you?"

Bay felt the impact of all their eyes, like they were a firing squad aimed at him.

"Jesus Christ, I didn't think you'd be the weak sister on this mission." Pete sneered.

"Yeah," Randy jeered. "You're the weak link. You keep fucking us up."

Bay stepped away from the circle of angry faces.

"If I see a deer I am goddamn fucking shooting it, and we aren't going to starve because of you," Mel announced. "I got my gun right here." She slapped her hip.

"Pete got us into this mess," Bay's voice shook. "Yell at him."

Pete drew his breath in with outrage, "I'm the one that's been keeping us together. Not you. You've been trying to push me out of the leadership over and over, and I will not tolerate it!"

Bay's mouth dropped open. "I have not!"

"Yes, you have. You have been undercutting my leadership all along. You aren't a team player." Pete glanced to the left and right, assuring himself that Mel and Randy were on his side.

"I have not." Bay repeated. Then he remembered his insistence that they should be drinking water and his suggestion that they build a fire. "Maybe your leadership sucks. Ever think of that?"

"You will obey orders, or you're not in this troop," Pete squared his shoulders and took at step toward Bay. "Got that?"

Bay didn't move. A hard anger coalesced inside his chest. "We aren't a troop. We're just the auxiliary."

The butt of Pete's gun slammed into Baylor's cheek and he reeled backward, staggered, and fell. The side of his head blazed with pain and his mouth flooded with blood. He felt, rather than saw, the others gathering around him, looming over him. Baylor scrambled to his feet, one hand clamped to his jaw.

Pete's face was clenched like a fist. "We're a troop and I'm the leader and you're insubordinate. I'm expelling you. Start walking."

Baylor stared into Pete's face and felt something click inside, like a key unlocking a door. He staggered over to the car and yanked the door open. He had to let go of his bleeding cheek to grab his rain jacket and his wool hat. The lighter, he remembered, was still lurking in his pocket, forgotten by Randy since he was out of cigs. Have a nice fire tonight, Bay sneered to himself. Of course, Pete would have a lighter, but still...

He didn't look at the threesome as he stumbled past. He didn't think about what direction he was going, only that he was on his own and moving away up the road. His legs shuffled along with the rest of him on board, amazed at the sudden change in his circumstances. Ahead he could see where the road turned, maybe the length of a city block away. He took one step after another.

"Okay, stop right there! Come back!" Pete yelled.

"No." Bay spat out a mouthful of blood.

"This is an order! Come back!"

Bay didn't think Pete would shoot him, but his back muscles tightened and his shoulders hunched anyway. He kept himself moving, one step after another along the wet gravel road.

"Go ahead and run!" Mel shrilled. "You are just a detriment to us!"

"Hey, big word!" Bay couldn't yell effectively, so he gave them the finger. Far away, a crow laughed raucously.

Chapter Twenty-One
Survival

Baylor lurched a step forward and slapped a thin willow branch out of his face. Keep on moving, he told himself. One more step.

His leg muscles were numb from the knees down, and his bones ached. He was dragging his boots through wet ferns, sinking with each step into soft, dark brown earth, too rich in plant matter to be called mud but just as slippery. Another step. There had to be an end to it somewhere.

Or did the forest have an end? The road had ended, just fizzled out into a muddy track and then died in a series of mud puddles. Impossible, but true. Somehow the gravel road had morphed into a jeep trail and then disappeared altogether. Baylor could come up with no explanation. After all, he'd left the group by moving back down the route they'd come up, so after some number of miles he should have rejoined the main road. Instead, the gravel road had ended in a soggy forest of willows and alder.

So, what to do? He had a feeling in the pit of this stomach that he shouldn't have left the car. Survival meant food, water, and shelter. Water, he had in abundance. The car had been shelter. The militia auxiliary members were a threat, unless he killed them and ate them, in which case they were food. Bay smiled grimly, then nearly lost his balance in the loose, wet ground. The left side of his face throbbed. Fortunately, he had stopped bleeding.

He needed to be careful; to be both wet and cold spelled death. Pete was right; he had not accepted leadership. He'd been quietly building up contempt for Pete and the others for quite a while, just enduring them. He hadn't fit in with the group and now he was out.

And Pete was right, too, that he should've killed the coyote. Food, water, shelter, the necessities. Sooner or later they would've had to kill something or starve. The coyote had come to them, presented itself, and he had refused. Why?

Baylor didn't know. He hadn't been stopped by the hallucination of a man. Maybe it was the coyote's eyes. Somehow the eyes had filled him with inertia rather than action, a bone-deep reluctance. He hadn't wanted to see the coyote explode into blood and guts. He'd wanted to hold out longer, wait to see if they'd be rescued, before resorting to killing anything.

"We didn't need to," he said out loud. "Not then." The forest was silent except for the gentle song of the rain, so his voice jarred on his ears, making him hyper-aware of how he didn't belong. "I'm on my own," he whispered.

Food, water, shelter, and find his way back to the road. Where the hell was it? There was a hysterical scream inside him, lurking in his throat, waiting for the chance to erupt. He wanted to yell at the forest, to punish and threaten it for hiding the road to Rainier. It was inexplicable that he was lost. There was no sense in it. There was only one paved road, which he'd driven on before, a straight shot of fifteen miles mostly following a river. How had the paved road turned into a gravel road and how had that gravel road turned into no road at all? He just couldn't understand it.

Food, water, shelter, and stay calm. Four elements of survival. The paved road was by the river. Water ran downhill. So, find a stream and follow it. Somewhere the wet woods would drain into a stream. Baylor pushed his way through the salal and huckleberries of the sodden forest.

Bay was following a crow. She flew from tree to tree, always just on the edge of his sight. The nature of the landscape had changed; now they were in a solemn, quiet forest of Douglas fir, where the walking was relatively easy on a soft carpet of needles and moss. The clouds had fallen to the ground, saturating the air with mist. Bay had no sense of being in motion. He was on a treadmill, shambling along, his bones bumping into each other, his lungs full of cold wet air, but he didn't seem to be getting anywhere. Each step brought more silent Douglas fir, the tall trunks black with moisture, followed by more silent fir trees. Bay was past thinking and almost past feeling. His numb brain had only one focus: just keep walking. A swift black shape arced between the trees. "Keep going," said the crow.

"I will," Bay answered. He and the crow had been conversing off and on since they'd first met back in the swampy forest.

He'd been resting on a fallen log when the crow first appeared, cawing from high up a big leaf maple, a harsh strident sound. His stomach had rumbled at the sight of her, but he'd made no attempt on her life. Then the crow cawed again, her head cocked, one bright eye aimed in his direction. She said, "Follow me." He heard the words distinctly, though he knew crows couldn't talk. But he'd walked for hours–from morning through midday– and was lost, confused, and in pain. So, when the crow said, "Follow me," and then fluttered off, he'd followed. She'd led him up a gradual rise to the Douglas fir forest. And now he kept on walking, one step after another, more or less following the crow since he had no other reason to go one way as opposed to another.

It was hard to tell in the fog, but it seemed like evening would be coming soon. The light drizzle had soaked through his rain jacket. He was grateful to the sheep that had provided the wool for his sweater. The sweater, his wool socks and hat, and his rain jacket were, Baylor thought, the only reason he was still alive. His knees hurt. His back hurt. His face hurt. He felt hollow with hunger. And auditory hallucinations were not a good sign. "Keep moving," said the crow, and abruptly she took off in a burst of flight.

Baylor trudged onward, one step, another step, another. He chanted to himself, "Just keep going, just keep going, just keep going." Like the "Little Engine That Could" from his childhood, he huffed and puffed stubbornly along, refusing to give up. "Just keep going." The crow was leading him somewhere, or seemed to be. Or maybe that was just something he needed to believe.

He felt a chill wind soothe his aching cheek and looked up. Ahead a pale light glowed through the thinning forest. For the first time in hours, he could see the sky. An unexpected surge of hope sent Baylor stumbling forward toward the light. He pushed through a fringe of salal and suddenly he was standing on the edge of a wide, long meadow of grass interspersed with the silvery trunks of dead cedars. The crow had become a black speck against the gray sky.

The sight of the vast sky was stunning, almost frightening, after the miles of dimly lit forest. Carefully, so as not to disturb his smashed cheek, Bay tilted his head back. The sunlight was diffuse and muted by clouds. The faint mauve of evening was just leaking into the sky over the eastern hills. His little flicker of hope died; there was no road. He was still lost. Bay shivered.

The stands of dead cedars looked like gravestones. Some were huge at the base and stabbed the air with raggedly rotting spires. A crow materialized on one ragged branch. It cawed raucously, no longer speaking English. Was it the same crow or a different one? Baylor couldn't tell; all crows looked alike to him. The crow did seem to want his attention; she was hopping and fidgeting on her branch, her head cocked. Baylor wiped his damp nose with his damp hand and thought: It's stupid to follow a crow.

But he'd been lost before the crow showed up and she had led him out of the marshy forest to dry land. And now she had led him to the end of that dry land, to the edge of a meadow. Baylor knew the general geography of the Gray's Harbor area: All streams either led to the river or to the sea water of the bay. The back of the bay, miles from the real ocean, had vast expanses of beach at low tide. If he could find a stream, he could follow it. He'd end up either at the river or at a beach. Either way would lead home, eventually, if he kept on walking.

But first, he needed to find a stream. There had to be one somewhere in the wet meadow, probably on the far side where he could see willows. The crow tipped her head back and opened her throat in a wholehearted caw.

"Okay," Bay said aloud. It was stupid to talk to a crow, but she was a companion of a sort. Bay waded into the thick, wet grass. The ground was saturated with enough standing water to seep through the laces of his boots. He sloshed forward, hating the cold water that froze his toes. With difficulty, waving his arms for balance as the dense grass snagged his feet, Baylor slogged onward. A cold wind, heavy with moisture, stirred the grass and sent shivers up and down his limbs. The delicate seed heads of the rushes and sedges bowed together, giving the impression of waves. Baylor could see glimpses of the stream itself, a dark slate blue, a smoother glassy version of the hungover sky. He staggered on.

The meadow grew wetter as he neared the stream. Baylor stopped a few feet back from the edge and watched the cold water slide silently by. He could not judge the depth. On the far side, the land rose up in a steep bank tangled with roots and brush.

Baylor's mind stirred slowly. Should he wade across, or should he follow along the edge of the stream toward the bay? The bay was probably miles away. And he'd be sloshing through wet meadow water the whole way. The stream would be difficult and cold to wade, but he could make camp for the night on the dry land on the far side. Besides, he was already cold. Wading wouldn't make him colder unless he fell and got soaked.

He'd probably die if he got wet all over.

The crow launched herself in the air with a harsh cry and a heavy flap of her wings. Startled, Baylor watched her land in a cedar tree, a green one with sweeping branches. For the first time Baylor noticed that the far bank of the creek was topped by a cedar forest on higher ground. That was odd; most of the cedars of southwest Washington had died. But Bay was too tired to think about it. The shelter of any kind of forest was fine with him.

He stepped carefully into the water. His boots sank into the muddy stream bed and the cold water bit through his jeans and into his skin. The stream was only a few strides across, but the water came up over his knees and dragged on his steps. He had to work to keep his balance, shoving his stiff legs through the heavy flow. By the time he got to the other side, his legs were aching to the bone, a fierce pain that reached up to his thighs and left him gasping.

The bank was a tangle of roots, bushes, and moss. It was not immediately apparent to Baylor how he would ever be able to climb out. But he had no choice, so he grabbed a large root, heaved himself up, then grabbed a handful of willow fronds and dragged himself up further. With one hand on the base of a sapling, the other on a root, he planted one foot on the top of a rock and lurched upwards. Then, with a sob, he got his knee up over the edge of the bank and crawled on to the forest and collapsed beneath a cedar.

Baylor curled up, aching everywhere. His fingers felt like broken glass, his legs were burning, and he was trembling from head to foot. He felt cold inside, in his guts, as if his body was turning into ice water. Even the blood in his veins felt cold. I'm not going to die, he told himself. Don't give up.

If he died, he'd never get a girlfriend. If he died, he'd never buy a little house, raise a kid, come home from work to a wife. There would be no birthday parties or Christmases, no family trips out for dinner, no sharing a pizza while watching TV. He'd never cuddle into the depths of his warm bed again. And there would be no one to look after his mother.

He shouldn't have gone into the water. He'd gotten too cold. And he had thrown away the last of his energy climbing up the bank. He had nothing left.

Chapter Twenty-Two
Mercy

"Es un hombre, Papa!"
"Shh. Niño, vienen aquí."
"Que el hombre está muerto."

Baylor blinked, tried to clear his eyes. Voices. Someone to help him. He tried to move one arm–yes, his muscles were working. He pushed himself up on one elbow to see better.

He was lying on a dense, soft mat of reddish needles under an enormous cedar. Other cedars stood solemnly, their long branches sweeping down in graceful arcs. The trees were huge, the tops obscured by the intertwined branches that protected the forest floor from the misty rain. Baylor had never seen so many living cedars before, certainly none so immense. They dwarfed the man and the boy.

They were Mexicans. The man was short, stocky, and brown-skinned with a prominent nose and black hair that stuck out in wet spikes from under a plastic rain hat. The little boy had backed into his legs as if trying to disappear. He wore a T-shirt with a picture of the Virgin of Guadalupe in red and green. Tears filled Baylor's eyes.

"I whah, I whah." Baylor's voice was not working. He cleared his throat and tried again. "Por favor, help me."

"Usted es la malicia?" The man asked. His eyes were sharp, almost feverish, and his fingers were digging into his son's shoulders. Baylor became aware of a short woman standing behind the man. She was clutching a little girl wrapped in a wool blanket. Baylor pressed one hand flat against the trunk of a cedar tree for balance and carefully climbed to his knees. He swayed, holding onto the tree, and assessed the little family. The man had a look of determination, the woman was worried, and the little boy was scared. Baylor held out one hand, fingers spread, and tried out his limited Spanish. "Mi frio. Muy, muy frio."

Now that he was up on his knees, he could smell something cooking. They had a Jerry-rigged campsite made up of overlapping blue tarps tied to branches. Baylor wanted nothing more in the world than to collapse under that tarp by the fire and drink something warm.

"I won't report you." His voice was a thin plea. The man shifted his grip on his son. "No," Baylor repeated. "I won't. I can see you're just trying to get by." His knees were trembling so badly that he could barely keep upright. "I won't tell anyone. Honest."

The woman spoke and jerked her head toward the tent. The man gave Baylor a glare of warning, then made a "follow me" motion with his chin. To Baylor's vast relief, they were inviting him into their tent.

He had to struggle to get to his feet and struggle more to stay upright. None of his muscles were working properly and his balance was shot. Baylor lurched after the little family. They stood aside to let him enter their tent.

He ducked down to get under the tarp and his body just kept going until he was on his hands and knees. No one laughed. The solemn, silent boy crawled to the far side of the fire, followed by his mother and the little girl. The boy looked like a spider, all skinny arms and legs and a round, protruding belly that Baylor could tell didn't come from being well fed. The father entered last and crouched to one side of the fire where he could reach the firewood easily.

Baylor shuffled around until his feet were near the fire and held his hands out to the warmth. The woman nudged his elbow and, to his wonder and gratitude, she held a battered mug filled with some kind of hot liquid.

"Gracias, gracias." He held the hot mug up against his chest. The little family had obviously been living in their tarp home for quite awhile. Blankets were rolled up and piled out of the way. Some plastic containers lined the back of the tent, and they had a cooler and a gallon jug of water. And they had a few canned goods. He had interrupted the woman preparing dinner.

Baylor bowed his head once to the woman and once to the man and said, "Gracias a Dios." Then he lifted the mug and took a sip.

No warm liquid slid down his throat. The man, the woman, and the little boy stared at him, motionless. He wondered why the little girl was so silent. He lifted the mug again, felt the hot rim burn his lips, and prepared himself for the bite of heat on his tongue. But when he swallowed, he felt nothing.

He looked in the mug. Nothing. The mug had disappeared and he was staring at his empty hands. No, wait, what? He was sitting under a cedar and, yes, there was a tarp, but it was not tied to his tree. The tarp was rigged up as a tent a little further into the woods. Baylor tried to get up, but his numb legs failed him. He grabbed the cedar tree and, using it as a brace, pushed himself to his feet. Then, lurching like a zombie, he stumbled toward the tarp.

There was a camp, but the fire was out. There was a skillet, but nothing in it. There were three plastic containers in a row under the tarp, but they were covered with needles, leaves and moss, like they'd been unused for a long time. The blankets were spread out on the ground, twisted around lumpy shapes.

Then he smelled it: the sickening stink of death.

"No!" Baylor yelled. They lay together wrapped in each others' arms. Rain had flattened the bodies, merging them with the ground, tattered clothes and hunks of long black hair mixed together. The mother and father were under a frayed, sodden blanket and the little boy lay by their side. The green and red of the Virgin of Guadalupe was still visible on his t-shirt.

"No, dear God." He fell to his knees. "Please no. Dear God, they were kind to me. Please, God." He rocked back and forth, curled around his empty stomach, while his face throbbed with the pain of his tears. It hurt to be alive. It wouldn't hurt much to die. He could slide into death the same way he had so often slid into sleep. His body would bloat up and be disgusting and putrid at first, but later on his flesh would sink into the ground and become moss. Plants would grow between his clean white bones. Animals would come by and sniff and move on. He'd just turn into forest floor along with the Mexican family. Maybe a hunter would find their bones someday.

His mother would not cry at his grave.

She wouldn't know that he'd died.

She'd probably think he'd deserted her like his dad had so many years ago.

A crow cawed from a nearby tree.

Baylor's face squeezed tight and he pressed the tears back with his hands. Slowly he pushed himself upright. The crow was right overhead on a cedar branch. He whispered, "Why did you bring me here?" He meant, "Why did you give me hope and then take it away?" The crow didn't answer. But he knew then that he was not going to die. He was going to save himself with the tarp.

Chapter Twenty-Three
Shelter from the Storm

The cold, wet metal of Baylor's knife burned his frozen fingers. He forced himself to squeeze the release button until the blade snicked out. Then he thrust his aching fingers into his armpits and rocked back and forth until the pain receded. His hands were nearly useless from the cold.

But he had to use them. He grasped the knife and sawed at the rope. The Mexican family's tent was tied up to at two points, with the back of the tarp held down by rocks. The family lay under the tarp. He had to smell them while he sawed. The stink was giving him the dry heaves.

Bay put his weight into sawing the rope. He watched the rope fray and begged, "Come on, come on, come on" until, at last, the thick cord snapped. One side of the tarp dropped down, covering the family. Bay walked unsteadily around to the second rope. He didn't look under the tarp. He tried not to think of the family and concentrated instead on the pain in his fingers as he sawed through the second rope. The tarp fell.

Rolling the rocks off the back edge of the tarp hurt worse than holding the cold metal of his knife. I'm paying a price for robbing them, Bay thought. If he was robbing the dead. Looting? "I need it," he told them. And he felt a sob rising up inside. "Gracias." Grabbing the back edge of the tarp, he yanked it away from the family. He dragged it off into the woods without looking back.

Food, water, shelter. Food he was not going to get. Water he could take care of later. Shelter he needed immediately.

Baylor chose a relatively dry spot under a huge cedar tree. He looked around and saw just what he needed: a large limb had fallen from a cedar.

The spray of smaller branches, twigs, and needles at the end were flammable even while damp. He made his aching fingers strip off handfuls of twigs. Then he arranged the big dead limb so that the smaller branches were lying just above the ground. He sprinkled twigs on and under the smaller branches and got the lighter out.

It had hurt to hold his metal knife and had hurt more to roll the rocks, but nothing hurt as much as flicking the trigger on the lighter. Baylor almost expected to see blood on his thumb. But no, he had a precious flame and his agonized thumb was not bleeding. He knelt beside the big cedar branch, held the flame down to the twigs and needles, and started a fire.

Baylor shambled back and forth between the fire and the surrounding trees, carrying sticks until he had the fire built up over a bed of coals. Then he spread the tarp out on the ground like a picnic blanket. He positioned himself on the front edge near the fire and pulled the rest of the tarp up over his head like a tent. By holding the front edge out over the fire, he captured the smoke and heat under the tarp.

Heat. He felt the burning on his face. Steam rose from his jeans. Warm air circulated around him but couldn't penetrate his wet clothes. He was cold deep down inside, and his back muscles were sore from shivering. The tarp was not going to be enough to save him. Baylor knew what he had to do.

He scrambled out from under the tarp and lay it down carefully so the inside would stay dry. Then he straightened up and braced himself. With no blue tarp to mark the spot, he couldn't see their camp.

His legs were barely working. He felt like he was walking on stilts. The ground swayed beneath him and ferns grabbed at his feet. He could smell the camp before he could see it.

They had three metal cooking pots with handles. The pots were mixed up with ripped plastic bags, sodden cardboard, and other garbage, probably because of foraging animals. That's me, Baylor thought. I'm a foraging animal. He gulped down a sob. It didn't seem right to take anything from a family that had so little, even if they were dead. Still, he needed one of their pots or he would die too. Baylor knelt at the edge of the cooking area and reached across the debris to the nearest pot. He kept his eyes away from the bodies. "Thank you," he whispered. "Gracias. I wish I could've done something to help you."

He huddled under the tarp by the fire as the rain filled the pot. When he had about half an inch of water, he moved the pot next to the fire. While he waited for the water to heat, he pulled his wet jeans off and exposed his wet, cold legs to the fire. His skin seemed white and corpse-like, all goose bumps. He rubbed his hands up and down from his ankles to his knees, and gradually both his hands and his legs warmed. When the chill was off the water, he pulled his sleeve down over his hand for a hot pad and lifted the pot off the fire. Carefully, since the pot itself was hot, he sipped the warm water. He was going to live.

CHAPTER TWENTY-FOUR
FOOD AND SHELTER

I enjoyed the rain last night. The banging and pounding was frightening in a way, like a monster trying to hammer its way into my house. But the metal roof held and kept me safe. That's what I enjoyed: that feeling of safety. I lay in bed and wallowed in the glory of having a roof over my head. The cats were scared, though.

Charlie now had two cats. They came from Valerie. She said that many of the people who left the town had abandoned their pets and livestock. To the extent she was able, she provided for the homeless animals. The two cats wanted to be pets, but she had six or seven inside her house already plus several that lived at the tavern and more that lived wherever they could but ate at her house. It was a relief to her to place two of them with someone.

"They're not fixed," she'd warned him. "Get them fixed quick or you will have an infinity of cats."

Getting them fixed would not be easy, but he'd do it. Meanwhile, they were winsome animals, full of purrs, who liked nothing better than to occupy his lap. He'd have to put cat food on the list for Jimmy's next store run.

Charlie's front porch was a good vantage point for observing the town even though he was down on the same level as the Tavern and downhill from where Valerie lived. Since the intervening buildings had been demolished for firewood, wiring, and anything else that could be used or sold, he could see the Tavern, front and back, and observe the comings and goings.

Rachel was first to emerge at about nine o'clock. She carried a black garbage bag which she heaved into the dumpster. She was whistling, as if she had something to be especially cheerful about that morning. Charlie slid his hand down his cat's silky back and murmured, "You wouldn't think that woman could face down a militia, would you?" The cat purred. "I need to name you guys."

Then Valerie stepped out of her front door. She was dragging a large shapeless bag. Charlie watched her bending, moving, and bending. Gradually, he figured out that she was pouring food into dishes. She must spend every cent she has on cat food, he realized. And vet bills. Finally finished with the cat food, she headed around to the back of her house. Charlie had never been back there but heard that she fed chickens and a pig.

I hope the animals had shelter last night, he wrote, his notebook awkwardly propped on the arm of the plastic chair so as not to bother the cat cuddled in his lap. *I was selfish last night, feeling so warm and safe and not thinking of those who were out in the weather.* He wondered if he could budget some of his income to help Valerie with her pets.

Get mine spayed first, he thought. Then help Valerie. *In this town,* he wrote, *we all help each other. In a weird way, it's a Utopia.*

He heard heard a sharp cry from up the hill. Charlie squinted, but his old eyes couldn't make out the source of the sound. It seemed like a cry of fear or pain but he couldn't tell if the source was human or if it was animal. He stood up to see better and listened. Was there another shout? He couldn't tell. Meanwhile he could hear the normal sounds of the village: the bleating of a goat, Maria hollaring for one of her kids, the swish of breeze through the alders along the river. After a few moments of listening, he sat down again.

I heard a strange sound but it was probably just a crow, he wrote.

Baylor crashed through the last of the huckleberries like a legless drunk, tripped, and fell into a weedy yard.

A cabin! Thank God. Baylor was too exhausted to feel joy, but a vast relief surged through his nervous system. He stared around in wonder. He saw the ordinary things that he had not seen in days: a battered old pickup truck, a garbage can, curtains in a window. A road! And, downhill, more cottages. Civilization. He was back in Warrentown and saved. Slowly, he climbed to his feet.

Then he stood, swaying, confused. Baylor's brain was barely functioning beyond the thought of food, but he could tell there was something odd about the cabin. It was wrapped in silence. No chickens, no one chopping wood, no radio on. No one hollering at their kids or talking on the phone. Maybe there was no one home.

"Hello?" Baylor called. His voice came out as a jagged squawk, interrupting the silence. He waited, then realized that it didn't matter if anyone was home or not because he'd break the front door down if he had to. He just needed to get up the front steps. The legs that had carried him so far were weak as water, and he could barely control his muscles, but he was determined to make it. Come on, he told himself. Get moving. He stumbled into motion and shambled toward the house.

And that's when a sleepy dog on the porch lifted its heavy head. A pit bull. Bay swayed to a halt. The dog rose to its feet and gazed at him through tiny eyes embedded in a blocky blunt head. It had the shoulders of a buffalo. "No," Bay whispered. "Please."

The croak of a crow ripped the silence and the dog's eyes shifted. It cocked its head, listened, and then it turned and trotted into the house. Bay stared in amazement. He tried to yell, "Anybody home?" but his voice came out in a thin squeak. "Hey!" he tried again louder. And from inside the dog barked once. A man's voice, diffuse as the air, wisped, "Hello?"

Somehow Baylor got his legs going. He crossed the muddy yard to the front porch and stopped. Three steps faced him. Baylor grasped the wooden handrail and hauled himself up. He was shaking from head to foot, almost crying, when he lurched up to the open door.

"Hello? Can you help me? I've been lost." He grabbed the door jamb for support. "I've been lost for so long."

"Lost, you say?" An ancient voice like crumpled parchment. Deep in the midst of the gloomy interior, sunk into a shabby couch, was a skeleton. An old man with thin yellow skin that hung on the bones of his face, limp as wet paper. He had an old-fashioned cotton sleeping bag tucked under his chin. The dog sat quietly at his feet.

Bay staggered in and stopped in the middle of the floor. "Can I come in?" he asked.

"Sure," the old guy said. His eyes were blue and white–but the colors were in the wrong places. He had yellow teeth and his long stringy hair was a dirty gray. "I don't get visitors much besides Rachel."

Bay was afraid to sit down, afraid that he would not be able to get back up. The old man looked like he couldn't get up either, and Bay had a vision of the two of them dying there in the dark. He said, "Hey, man, would you mind if I got something to eat? I'm starving. I mean seriously. I wouldn't ask, but I haven't eaten in days."

"Sure." The old man made a small gesture with his fingers toward a door. "Back there."

Bay aimed himself at the door and stumbled through to the kitchen. It was like the rest of the house, filthy. Cobwebs, dust, and dishes unwashed from previous weeks were mixed up on the counter with opened cans and wads of paper towel. There was no sign of recent cooking, but a paper plate containing a half-eaten meal sat on the counter. Someone had delivered a meal. Baylor hoped that didn't mean there was no food in the house. He was too hungry to feel hungry anymore. The starvation was not in his stomach; it was in his arms, his legs, his spine, his mind, his veins and blood, and his nervous system. He didn't care what he ate as long as he ate something.

Frantic rummaging through the shelves produced a box of crackers. He ripped a sleeve open and stuffed a handful in his mouth. Then he choked, coughed, and spit them out. Leaning on the sink, he wiped his mouth and tried again with just one.

The calories slid down his throat and his entire body screamed, "Food!" Bay's fingers were shaking so badly that he could hardly get the next cracker into his mouth, but he ate the whole sleeve, one cracker at a time. He could only chew on one side, but that didn't matter. Then he noticed the dog staring at him from the doorway.

"Okay, sorry, I had to do that." He started pawing through the mess in the kitchen, looking for something they could all eat, and found some cans of chili in a cupboard. Next, after opening several drawers, he found a can opener. Then he hunted for a pan, and–thank God–found one that was sort of clean. Just dusty. He didn't think he had the strength to wash any dishes. It took all he had to light a match and get a burner going on the Coleman stove. He wrenched the can opener around the can and dumped the chili into the pot. Bay stared at the pot. He was too hungry to feel grateful for the food. He just wanted it to hurry up and get warm.

"Enough there for all three of us," he told the dog. It wagged its tail and trotted back into the living room. Bay followed. "I've got chili on for all of us," he told the old man.

The old guy's eyes were closed. "Hey," Bay whispered. "I'm warming up some chili." The dog licked the old man's face and he snorted and woke with a small shake of his head.

"Oh, I got sleepy, I guess."

"I'm warming chili for all three of us."

"No need."

"I kinda do. I ate all your crackers." Baylor sank into a shabby armchair. Exhaustion oozed through his veins. He blinked to keep himself awake and told the old man, "You look like you could use something warm inside you."

The old man lay back with a sigh. "Won't help." A silence opened up between them. The dog sprawled with her chin on her forelegs. Bay sagged into the worn upholstery, immobilized, his mind moving slowly on thoughts of chili. He was just about to get up when the old man said, "I didn't think an angel would come for me."

"Huh?" Bay asked. He had his palms on the armchair, ready to heave himself to his feet.

"I didn't think a devil would, either. I ain't been a bad person."

Bay didn't know what to say. He wanted that chili.

"I ain't been a very good one, either. If you meet Rachel, now there's a good person."

Bay almost said that he didn't know any Rachel, but then the old guy would probably start talking about this Rachel and he didn't want to sit and listen to it. He started to get up.

"Can I ask you something?" The old man's hand fumbled with the blanket. Bay watched with disgust as the bony arm and curled yellow fingers reached for him. "Can I just ask you one question?"

"Sure. Okay." He realized with horror that the old man was crying.

"Will I see my dog there? Will I see her again?" The old man's eyes were aimed at the ceiling. Bay was glad that he didn't have to hide his expression. He hesitated, then gently touched the old man's decaying hand. "Yes," he said. "She will join you. You will be together."

"Thank you." The old man breathed the words out in a long sigh and his arm went limp.

Bay stood up carefully. It looked like the old guy had gone to sleep. So maybe just chili for two? He headed for the kitchen, a little steadier on his legs. The smell of the warming chili opened up a ferocious desire to stuff his face. He banged the cupboard doors in a frantic search for a clean bowl, found none, and decided that he would eat straight out of the pot.

He grabbed a spoon out of the sink and wiped it on a dishrag. Then, with some regret, he dumped half of the chili on the floor. The dog pounced and gobbled. Bay started gobbling too but slowed himself after the first bite. The chili was barely warm. Didn't matter. Each swallow sank into his blood stream like a drug. He could feel the warmth, the thick tomato flavor, and the grease seeping into his veins. Each sensual swallow was followed by the sensation of calories and vitamins. He scraped the spoon about the bottom of the pan to get the very last scrap of tomato sauce. Then he licked out what he could reach with his tongue. He didn't even notice the pain in his cheek until he was done.

"Oh, Christ, that was good." He wanted more but he didn't want to eat the old man out of house and home. "What do you think?" he asked the dog. "Another can?" But she turned and trotted into the other room. I'll fix seconds later, he thought. Make some for the old guy if he is awake. Then he thought: No, I'm going to crash. I need to sit down before I fall down. He headed into the living room, aimed at the chair, but something about the old man caught his attention.

The old guy was laying still, his head back and his mouth open. A string of saliva, like the trail of a slug, ran down his cheek. He wasn't breathing.

Chapter Twenty-Five
Valerie Meets Baylor

She was outside feeding the cats when she saw the zombie lurching toward her down the hill from Old Man's house. He was young but looked old, gray-faced and shambling as if his joints were no longer connected properly. The skin on one side of his face was purple. Old Man's elderly dog trailed uncertainly along behind him. Val dropped the bag of cat food at her feet and hurried as best she could down her front steps, her own movements spiky and awkward.

"Young man!" she called. "Young man!"

He swayed to a stop, his hopeless eyes aimed her way. A dim understanding blossomed on his face

"Can you help us?" His voice cracked. "The old guy," he gestured weakly, nearly losing his balance. "The old guy is dead."

Val hurried up the sidewalk. The young man was filthy, wet, and stank of sweat and death, but she recognized him. He was the quiet militia kid, the one she'd thought of as a follower. He swayed, and she laid a hand on his shoulder to prop him upright. After transferring her hand to his waist, she said, "Come with me." When he didn't move, she urged, "Come along with me. I'll take care of you."

He took one careful step and then the next, watching his feet and concentrating. The dog followed, her brow furrowed and her eyes full of confusion.

"That's right, one step at a time." Val included the dog in her encouragement, "Just keep moving along slowly and we will get there."

She'd never thought of the five steps up to her front porch as difficult, but now they looked like the trail up a mountain. The cats stared, appalled, and slid away to hide in her rose bushes. The young man grasped the stair rail and pulled while she pushed gently on his lower back. He heaved himself up the steps. Old Man's dog stopped on the front sidewalk, unsure of her welcome. Val got the door open, looked back and called, "You can come in, too, if you don't bother the cats."

She left the door open after guiding the young man inside. Suddenly her tiny living room seemed over-filled with dirt, water, and sweat. Val pulled the young man's raincoat off and hung it on her hall tree. Then she directed him to her upholstered armchair, the one she'd sat in for so many years while watching TV with her mom. For just a second, she wished her mother's hospital bed was still there for the young man to lie down on.

"Now, you get your boots off," she told him. "And come on in." This last comment was for the dog, who was poking her nose through the door. "Come on in so I can shut the door."

She bustled around. The wet, muddy boots she dumped on the back steps. She fired up the Coleman stove and filled her biggest pot with water from her supply of plastic jugs. Then she poured some water in a glass. Food. Something fast. She had a big hunk of cheese in her pantry, along with some cabbage from the greenhouse, some onions, and her home-canned tomatoes. Her hands shook in her hurry as she fumbled together a sandwich. She scooped some warm water out of the pot for tea.

"Here you go." Val set a tray down on her coffee table, the sandwich on a small plate flanked by water and tea. She saw the dog out of the corner of her eye. "Yes, you too." Val hurried back into her kitchen and returned a moment later with a bowl of water and a small plate of cat food. The young man was holding the sandwich up in front of his face as if it was a communion wafer. He sank his teeth into it slowly and his eyes closed.

Chapter Twenty-Six
Baylor Has a Vision

From his position up near the ceiling, Baylor watched the old woman. She was kneeling by a couch. With gentle reverence, like an offering, she raised up her moist washcloth. Fat drips of warm water splatted on her knees, but she didn't mind. Humbly, she cleansed the bruises on the body of a young man. Her hand moved slowly in circles, loosening the caked-on mud. When the cloth grew dirty, she dipped it in warm water, wrung it out carefully, and then gently lay it on the young man's skin to rub some more. To Baylor, her actions seemed close to an act of worship.

But they were not in a church. They were just in an ordinary home, shabby and crowded with old-fashioned furniture. The body was thawing, the skin bluish-gray like rotten ice. Some of the body had melted, making a puddle on the floor and the old woman was kneeling in the water. Baylor didn't think she was worshiping the blue, half-frozen body, but she was performing a ritual of some kind. Something magical was happening. From his position near the ceiling, it seemed to Baylor that the thawing body was evaporating gradually. Each time the woman's hand made a circle, a bit of skin was transmuted into blue droplets which rose in the air in a mist and glittered in the sunlight.

Somehow, he knew the droplets would sail out the window and into the air and around the world. Somewhere–maybe nearby but maybe faraway–the droplets would land on someone's hair or hand or shoulder. It seemed like a futile activity to him. There was so much world out there, so many people and animals, that the droplets could not reach them all. It was hard for him to believe that her ritual was making much difference. Still, futile or not, the old woman continued to ease away the mud with circular prayers and the prayers lifted as silently a butterflies, rose, and disappeared.

Then suddenly he was looking at Valerie. He could tell that her back was aching and her knees were cold. She thrust the washcloth into the water and wrung it out almost impatiently because she wanted to get done cleaning him up so she could get off her knees. She was only gentle because she was making herself be gentle. Baylor could hear her thoughts clearly: She wanted to finish up, but she disciplined herself to work slowly. She almost believed that some of the droplets to find their way back to her.

Baylor heard a raven whisper. "You never know. You do it because it matters."

Chapter Twenty-Seven
Baylor Wakes Up

Baylor didn't so much wake up as become conscious again. It was a gradual process. First, he became aware of a beige ceiling, grimy with smoke. Confused, he let his gaze drift and discovered walls hung with dreary old family photos. He was lying on a couch in a room crowded with the kind of furniture he associated with his deceased grandmother: smothering, overly upholstered chairs that absorbed the sitter and sapped one's will to rise and move.

He had been absorbed by the couch and a pile of hand-knit afghans, and he had very little will to rise and move. Instead, he listened to the quiet, gentle rain tapping on the roof. The air in the house was cold, though he could smell an old fire in the fireplace. A dog was snoring–and suddenly Baylor was jolted by a memory. An old man had died. Right there in front of him. Baylor struggled with the afghans and freed up his feet. He pushed himself into a seated position and gazed around the room, trying to remember where he was. Not the old man's house

Then he remembered. An old lady. And she had fed him, stripped him nearly naked, and put him to bed on the couch like a sickly child. The remnants of his meal lay on the coffee table, just a few crumbs on a china plate. God, he had been hungry. His pistol lay beside the plate, in-congruent in the old lady's house. And he remembered her name.

"Valerie?" he called softly. His voice woke the dog who lifted her sad eyes questioningly. The house answered with silence.

"She went out?" he asked the dog, who responded with a tentative wag of her tail. The remnants of her meal, too, lay beside her in a dish on the floor. Her water dish was empty. Baylor needed his clothes. He couldn't see them in the room anywhere.

Baylor climbed to his feet slowly and edged past the coffee table out to the middle of the room. He felt top-heavy, as if his head was not quite connected to his neck and might fall off. Cautiously and carefully, Baylor navigated the short distance from the couch to the kitchen door. There, with relief, he found his clothes. She'd hung his things out to dry over her kitchen chairs. Everything was damp, but he could see that she had tried to clean up his jeans; the leaves and dirt had been brushed off, leaving parallel brush marks. His wool socks were damp but would be warm.

Naked, he felt as helpless as a baby. With each item of clothing he put on—socks, pants, shirt—he felt restored, almost like he was rebuilding himself. He had an impulse to pick up his gun but rejected the thought in favor of making some coffee.

He spotted a coffee pot sitting on a Coleman stove positioned on top of the oven. Evidently Valerie's stove didn't work. Gazing around her kitchen, he noticed other oddities: a jug of water squatted in the sink, there was a lantern on the drain board, and a stack of milk crates occupied the space designed for a refrigerator. Even though the interior of the house was dim, no lights were on. She hasn't got any power, he realized. Well, then he needed matches. Baylor started poking around, opening drawers and cupboards. He found a pantry full of canned goods, cabbages, potatoes, and what looked like homemade preserves. The matches were in a drawer with the silverware.

He got the Coleman stove lit under the coffee pot and leaned against the counter to wait. After the strange days lost in the woods, ordinary things were miraculous. Walls. A roof! Furniture. Most of all, food. Dear God, there was no limit to how much he could eat. Baylor's stomach rumbled.

A cheerful voice outside the window snagged his attention. Baylor looked outside and saw a garden and a greenhouse. The garden was, he realized, formerly a yard, and the greenhouse had once been a regular house. Someone had stripped the walls off, leaving the uprights, and had wrapped the structure in plastic. That's clever, he thought.

A shout, and then a stocky man in a plaid wool shirt emerged from the greenhouse. He had a basket of some kind of greens in his arms. A little boy followed him, also lugging a basket. The boy set his basket down, revealing a T-shirt decorated with the image of the Virgin of Guadalupe.

Baylor grabbed the counter and fought off a tide of dizziness. Then he shoved the back door open and yelled, "Hey, kid!" The little boy jumped like a startled deer. "Hey!" Baylor called, again. "Hey." But he didn't know what else to say. He could hardly ask the kid if he was the same child as the dead boy in the woods. "Do you speak English?"

The boy's father, glaring suspiciously, barked a command. The boy shot Baylor a look of fear, grabbed his basket, and ran toward his father. They both disappeared around the corner of the greenhouse. Baylor stared after them until he heard the sound of the coffee pot perking.

Baylor was back on the couch, sipping his cup of coffee, when he heard voices outside. A man and a woman were coming up the steps. He set his coffee cup down, feeling a bit guilty. Valerie entered in a bustle of umbrella and raincoat. She was followed by a tall, lean, sharp-faced man who was keeping the rain off with a black cowboy hat. Baylor started to rise to his feet, but Valerie forestalled him.

"No, you just stay where you are. Oh, you got some coffee. That's good."

"Thank you. I helped myself. I hope you don't mind." His eyes were on the lean man. Bay recognized him as the guy behind the bar, the one with the shotgun.

Valerie waved a hand in his direction and said, "This is Jimmy. He's our handyman around here."

"Oh, hi," Bay half rose and held out his hand. Jimmy had a strong grip. Up close his eyes were strange, his irises almost yellow.

"Sit down, everyone." Val plopped herself down on the least comfortable chair and gave Baylor a look that mingled sympathy with assessment. Bay suddenly had a feeling of being on trial. He was still weirded out by the sight of the Mexican kid in the Virgin of Guadalupe T-shirt, and Jimmy's strange yellow eyes were even more unsettling. He wasn't afraid, but he was confused. Never before had he been unable to tell what was real and what wasn't. Jimmy stayed standing. He lit a cigarette and said, "So, you found the old man dead?"

Startled, Baylor cleared his throat. "No, sir. He died while I was there. I went into the kitchen to warm up some chili, and while I was there, he died." He checked their faces. Did they think he was at fault in some way? "I didn't know he was that bad off. I mean, I didn't know him at all."

"You were lost," Valerie said, "and his house was the first place you found."

"Yes." That answer didn't seem adequate. Both Val and Jimmy seemed to be waiting for more. Baylor felt tears building up behind his eyes. He blinked, grimaced, and muttered, "He seemed like a nice old guy. He asked if he would meet his dog in Heaven, so I told him he would."

Jimmy nodded his acceptance. "Guess we got to bury him, then. I'll dig the hole." He looked around for an ashtray, and finding none, ashed his cigarette in Baylor's coffee.

Chapter Twenty-Eight
Old Man's Funeral

The incessant rain had made a puddle in the bottom of the grave. The old man was cocooned in one of his wool blankets because they had no casket. They were putting him to rest in cold water and mud.

"Well, let's do it." Jimmy grabbed the long bundle by the front, and Baylor groped through the layers of fabric around the feet. Even thinned out by age, the old man was heavy.

"Drop your end first," Jimmy said. They didn't want to just heave him in any old way. Baylor dropped to his knees and tried clumsily to set his end of the bundle down gently. His fingers slipped, and the body fell with a sodden squelch. Jimmy grunted as his shoulders took the full weight at his end. The bundle sagged; Old Man had gone through rigor mortis and out the other side to a hopeless limpness. The rain thickened to a heavy, pounding shower as Jimmy released his grip on the wool and let the body fall.

They huddled beside the grave, Val and Rachel under Rachel's big black umbrella, Jimmy and Baylor toughing it out in just their jackets, Crazy Mary wrapped in a tarp, and Charlie hunched up inside a rain slicker.

The wool of Old Man's blanket was already soaked.

Jimmy grabbed the shovels and handed one to Baylor. He dug into the pile of dirt next to the grave and tossed the first shovel full into the hole. Baylor hesitated. He wanted to have time to think before that first smack of dirt hit the blanket, but Jimmy had a rhythm already. Dig, dump, dig, dump. Baylor stumbled around to the other side of the pile. His legs and arms felt shaky from exhaustion.

He dug out a shovelful of mud and watched it slide off the shovel onto the old man's blanket. Then he loaded his shovel up and dumped another load. He watched as each shovelful of brown mud obscured the wet, dark wool until there was no blanket to be seen.

No one spoke, though Mary shuffled from one foot to the other and sniffed. She wasn't crying; the cold made her nose run. Baylor and Jimmy reached a machine-like coordination, one digging into the dirt pile while the other's shovel swung over the grave. Then as suddenly as turning off a water tap, the rain stopped.

Rachel checked the sky: masses of gray clouds, swollen and pregnant with more moisture. The straggly dying cedars on the hillside were almost black in the evening light, but the alders were glowing yellow. She wondered if Old Man had ever felt delight in the colors of the fall, and she quickly rubbed the dampness off her face on her sleeve.

"Well, that's it." Jimmy let his shovel drop. He wiped his hands on his jeans.

They were all silent. Down the road, a goat bleated at something, probably Pig, one of their ongoing disputes. A rooster crowed, and a crow answered. Rachel lifted her head, listening. They were losing the light and the sky was beginning to leak, a sign of more rain to come.

Charlie cleared his throat. "Seems like we should say a few words." He glanced around the small half-circle of faces. "Does anyone know what religion he was?"

"He used to go to town to some church," Crazy Mary said with a shrug.

"Okay, Christian then." Charlie coughed deprecatingly, "I can quote the Bible a little."

"Go for it," Rachel said

"Ashes to ashes dust to dust," Charlie recited. "Earth to earth, we therefore commit his body to the ground; earth to earth, in sure and certain hope of the Resurrection to eternal life, through our Lord Jesus Christ; who shall change our vile body, that it may be like unto his glorious body, according to the mighty working, whereby he is able to subdue all things to himself."

"Or another way of looking at it," Rachel said, "as the Lakota saying goes: 'Nothing lives forever, only the earth and the sky.'"

Baylor shivered. It seemed to him that he would never be warm again. The dog was shivering, too.

"So, anyone else?" Rachel asked.

Baylor wanted to say something, something that would make up for the old guy dying, something meaningful about his life. But he hadn't known the old man and didn't know what meaning the old man would've given to himself. So, he just said, "He was a nice old guy. He sure loved his dog."

Charlie smiled at him through the drizzle. "Thank you for taking in his dog. I'm sure that helped ease his passing."

Baylor hunched his shoulders in embarrassment. "Well, he helped me." Then: "Hey, does anyone know the dog's name? I kind of wanted to call her by the name he used." He looked from face to face. "Does anyone know?"

Rachel said, "I can tell you a story about that."

"Make it short." Jimmy was soaked, muddy, and out of patience.

"It's a short story," Rachel said, without defensiveness. She gazed at the muddy grave. "Old Man told me how he got the dog. He found her up the road that way." She gestured. "Maybe some hunter or camper left her up there in the woods on her own. Anyway, he was just up that way fishing, and she walked out of the woods. It was a day like this, raining off and on." She looked up at the ominous sky. "Old Man, like you said, he was a church goer and he liked those old gospel songs. There's one that goes, 'Somebody got lost in the storm' and that's what he thought when he saw the dog staggering out of the woods. Somebody got lost in the storm."

Rachel paused and they all looked at the dog. She stared back, her brow furrowed.

"Anyway," Rachel went on, "he thought she was such an ugly dog and she's a pit bull and he knew a lot of people were really prejudiced against pit bulls, so he thought he needed to give her a really pretty name. To offset being an ugly pit." Rachel smiled down at the dog. "He named her Angela."

"Angela." Baylor touched the dog's head with the tips of his fingers and she leaned into his leg.

"Ok, let's get out of the rain." Jimmy picked up the shovels and they followed him down the road to the tavern.

Chapter Twenty-Nine
A Party at the Tavern

Baylor was so tired he felt like he was disintegrating. His molecules were separating and he was becoming a fog. He threw his arms around Valerie's pillow and buried his face in its soft fluffiness. Val's quilt was pulled up to his ears so that only the top of his head was visible. Angela sat on the floor, her brow wrinkled.

"Come on up on the couch," Baylor whispered. "It's okay."

Angela placed her paws on the edge of the couch. He bent his knees to create a space for her. She launched herself up and clambered over his legs. Baylor felt her circling, circling, circling until, with a damp thump, she settled down. Her weight was warm against his thighs.

Baylor snuggled his cheek against the pillow and gave himself permission to stop thinking, to just fall, fall, fall into sleep. He watched the slow circling of a star pattern in the inside of his eyelids. Then the star pattern dissipated, replaced by a view of the vacant lot uphill from the Tavern. He was seeing through his closed eyelids a huddle of wet people in the rain. They were all gray, the same color as the weather-beaten cottages and the swollen clouds. A raven ripped the air with a caw and his chest ached with the wrongness of bodies in the mud. Baylor realized that he was crying. Just sobbing like a little kid.

"Hey, I brought you a drink."

Embarrassed, Baylor wiped his eyes on the quilt. Valerie was hovering over him with a mug of something fragrant and steaming hot.

"Thanks. I thought I could just sleep, but I keep thinking."

"This will soothe you. I put honey in it, too." Baylor struggled to a seated position, careful not to disturb the dog. He accepted the mug and inhaled the rich scent. Her comment about honey implied that the drink was spiked with something else. A sip told him what: rum. Tea with honey and rum. He closed his eyes.

Valerie sat in her armchair. They were quiet together. Outside, the rain had settled into a quiet pitter-patter on her roof. Val sighed and sipped from her own mug. "I gotta ask you something."

"Okay." Reluctantly, Baylor opened his eyes.

"Are you still with the militia?'

Her question jolted him. "No!" He set the cup down and tried to speak calmly. "I mean, no. I got kicked out, but also I quit. So, no."

"It's important because Rachel has her ways. I mean, if you see anything or anyone … Rachel has her ways." Her eyes were full of warning. "I mean it."

Baylor thought of the Mexican guy he'd seen with the kid and the basket of greens. He said, "I'd like to stay here and help out here." It was true, he realized. He didn't want to leave Warrentown. He wanted to stay and be part of the community. "I don't want to go back."

Valerie nodded. "Okay, then. We're going to have a–well, not a party exactly, but a get-together this evening. You want me to wake you after your nap?"

Val and Baylor hurried through the mist toward the Tavern. Bay held an umbrella up over their heads. Val had put on her best dress and had combed her hair into a loose knot decorated with a ribbon. Baylor was still in his damp clothes since he had nothing else. He wasn't sure that he wanted to go to the get-together; his nap had not helped. He needed another week of sleep at least. Still, Val was his hostess, so he thought he'd better be her escort. He didn't like the idea of an old lady walking around in the dark even if it was just a short distance. Not while he was snoozing on the couch. So, he held up the umbrella as they hurried along.

"Look, there's Charlie." Charlie's flashlight bobbled in the dark.

"Hey, hello." Charlie had stopped on the corner to wait for them.

They entered the Tavern together, Bay last so he could shake out the umbrella. Vulture and his crew were already hunkered down around a table, Crazy Mary was on her favorite bar stool, and Jesus and Maria were seated in a booth. Jimmy and Rachel were leaning on the counter, shoulder to shoulder. Everyone had drinks, and Vulture was smoking a blunt. The atmosphere was dense with smoke, damp, and sweat.

Val joined Jimmy and Rachel behind the counter, and Charlie sat down with Jesus and Maria. That left Baylor unsure where to fit himself in. Crazy Mary cackled at him and, placing one foot on the nearest bar stool, gave it a little shove in his direction. He sat and leaned against the counter top. The room was slowly revolving. That one spiked cup of tea with Val had been too much.

The tavern was noisy, but in a pleasant way. People huddled together with their mouths to each other's ears, speaking below or through the music. Baylor had no one to talk to so he focused on enjoying the jukebox, or whatever was making the music. The selection was eclectic: some old Grateful Dead, a couple Queen stadium rockers, some blasts from the past of country music. Waylon Jennings he recognized from his childhood; his mother had been a fan of what she called "real" country. Also, Willie Nelson. At one point a clear, bell-like female voice rang out, singing about the bells of Norwich. Baylor hung on every note. He'd never heard anything like it. Then the jukebox reverted to old rock again.

Baylor's hand felt wet. He realized that he was holding a beer, but he could not remember how it got there. While his mind had gone wandering with the music, his position on the pinnacle of the bar stool had become precarious. The floor seemed a long way down, and he needed to keep a grip on the counter. The air had thickened with marijuana smoke. Vulture was acting as barman, toting drinks out to the room, while Valerie rested, leaning up against the door frame, a glass of wine in her hand.

Baylor laid his head on his arms and told himself that he was just going to close his eyes for a minute. Someone gave his shoulder a shake and he heard Rachel's voice: "Get this kid a cup of coffee before he passes out." A mug landed on the counter in front of his face. He lifted his head, expecting to see Val, but instead it was Jimmy's lean face, yellowish eyes, and feral grin. "Get some of that into you," he said.

Bay leaned on his elbows and sipped the coffee. It was hot and black as midnight, loaded with caffeine. Rachel was standing next to Jimmy, her head tilted to rest on his shoulder. They were silhouetted against the golden glow of an old-fashioned paraffin lantern. Slowly Bay's brain began to function, and he wondered how they powered a jukebox with no electricity. Rachel tapped him gently on the wrist, and he realized that she wanted his attention.

"Look at this. You made the news."

"Huh?" She was holding a newspaper, folded to show a headline. Baylor blinked but could not focus well enough to read. After a glance at his face, Rachel turned the article around and read it to him. "It says, 'Three Missing Militia Members Found–One Still Missing.' It says the police are investigating the missing member."

She stopped and gave him an assessing look mixed with sympathy. So many thoughts jammed together in Baylor's head that his brain froze up completely. He saw the rain pounding down on a muddy road, three people arguing, Pete's rage-contorted face, a big black gun. He heard the harsh cry of a crow and the squelch of his boots in a mud puddle. He felt his fingers burning with cold as he fumbled with his knife. His mind winced away from the blood red and rotten green of a raggedy T-shirt. He saw a little boy lugging a basket of vegetables, trying to keep up with his dad.

"Oh, God," he said, as his brain came unstuck. "I need to call my mother."

"Nice kid." said Jimmy. Somehow Baylor had managed to get off the bar stool and onto a chair, where he had fallen asleep with his uninjured cheek on the table and his arms sprawled out. Charlie, Vulture, and Jimmy were drinking around him.

"Yeah. I wonder what he's going to do with himself for the next decades." One of the comforts of being old, Charlie thought, was the absence of a future. Jimmy gazed thoughtfully through the smoke of his cigarette at Bay's slumbering form.

"He'll muddle along like people always do."

Charlie grunted, "Muddle along until somebody nukes us all back to self-replicating cells."

But Jimmy disagreed. "Won't come to that. No money in it. Remember how the greedy old people reacted to the prospect of the Arctic melting? Oh goody, shipping lanes! The rich knew this was coming, and they didn't care because they figured they could protect themselves and find a way to keep on making money. But there's no way to make money off nuclear winter."

"Why don't I find that comforting?" Charlie asked with heavy irony.

Jimmy shrugged. "Actually, about Baylor: I think Rachel's going to keep him. She needs a replacement for Harry."

Charlie frowned with the effort to form a question about Harry, but a loud snore from Baylor distracted him. "Do you think a young guy is going to want to live here? His generation oughta hate old farts like me."

He didn't get an answer to that question, either, because Rachel materialized behind Jimmy and leaned in to kiss his ear. "They're playing our song." she whispered.

Charlie watched them dance and thought of his wife. Not that they had ever danced like Jimmy and Rachel. A rough, raggedy cowboy voice was crooning "Waltz across Texas." Jimmy's hand was splayed across Rachel's butt, and her face was nestled against his chest. She swayed her hips, barely moving her feet, and he rocked with her rhythm. As they slowly angled away, Charlie caught a glimpse of a lascivious smile on Rachel's lips. Someone made a "woo-hoo" noise and someone else laughed. Rachel's grin widened, and her arms tightened around Jimmy's shoulders.

"Sheesh," Baylor muttered. "They need to get a room." His face was soft and shapeless with sleep.

"Oh, the dead arise." Baylor didn't smile in response, so Charlie ventured a pat on his arm. "Your day will come." And your day will go, he thought, leaving your heart broken. But, watching Rachel and Jimmy dance, he was grateful that he had once been loved.

Chapter Thirty
Goodnight, Everyone

After Rachel called time, everyone staggered off homewards. Tired as he was, Baylor half-carried Valerie up the stairs and into her house. Once inside, she lit a little forest of candles. Bay watched her shaky hands and thought that she must be older than she looked. Or maybe ill. Her cheeks were saggy, and her chin trembled. She caught him staring and gave him a quick smile.

"There now. Candlelight is so nice, isn't it?"

Baylor dropped into the couch and pulled the quilt up around his knees and chest to keep out the chill. He watched Valerie carry a candle into the kitchen and called out, "Hey, can I help you with something?"

"No, I'm just going to get us a warm drink. I always sleep well if I have a warm drink."

Baylor fidgeted. He felt guilty for staying cozily nested in a quilt on the couch. On the other hand, Val had declined his help and it didn't take two people to heat something on the stove. He was relieved when Valerie reappeared without her candle and carrying two mugs. Baylor stood up and took the mugs while Valerie leaned down, braced herself on the arm of her upholstered chair, and fell the rest of the distance into its soft embrace. "Oof," she said and smiled that quick, reassuring smile again.

They both settled down, holding their mugs of hot apple juice. Baylor raised his to his face and inhaled the warm scent. "Smells good," he said.

"Umm, yes, this was an experiment. There's an old tree out back. The apples are all wormy and small but, boy, the taste! It was a lot of work, getting the cores out."

A lot of work. She didn't look like she was going to be up to much work in the future.

"You know…" He stopped, unsure.

She raised her eyebrows with inquiry, with a brave smile that looked fake pasted on her face.

"I could help out at the bar." Baylor watched her expression hopefully. "I could spell you. I can cook, too." He didn't want her to think he was trying to steal her job and the income she needed. He studied her face, unsure of what he was seeing. The fake cheerful smile faded but whatever real emotion was going on she kept muted. Then she said, "You know, I think that would be nice sometimes."

"I can chop wood and help out with the animals too. I like animals."

A comfortable silence lengthened between them. Baylor sipped his drink and enjoyed the both the scent of the warm liquid and way it slid down his throat. He felt at home with Val, as if they were related. He felt that way about the whole weird little town.

"That was a nice party, wasn't it?"

"Yes, it was." A real smile lit her face.

"I liked the music. I hadn't noticed the jukebox before."

Val looked puzzled. "Jukebox? I thought that was…" Her voice trailed off. Then she added, sentimentally, "I love Frank Sinatra. Even as a kid. He was kind of a secret vice since I was supposed to love Kurt Cobain."

Baylor's eyebrows lifted in surprise. Not at the professed love of Sinatra; that seemed to suit what he knew of Val. It was the reference to hearing Sinatra at the tavern that confused him. "I don't remember any Frank Sinatra songs." He grinned. "Tell the truth, I don't remember much of that party. I think I passed out for a lot of it."

"Oh, I loved him singing "One for the Road," to see us off when Rachel called time." Val raised her mug of hot apple juice. "Here's to getting shitfaced and passing out."

Baylor barked a laugh of surprise. "Here." They clinked their mugs.

Valerie sipped her last, set the mug down, and pulled her afghan up over her thin chest, exposing her feet. Her eyes closed. She looked, Baylor thought, completely spent, like she might simply slide away into the night air.

"We need to get you to bed earlier," he said in a jokey tone. "We were out too late and it's cold in here. I can chop up some firewood for you tomorrow. Bring it in and warm up the house."

"Jimmy does that. But we're trying not to burn anything if we can avoid it." She spoke without opening her eyes.

So that's why the house was so damn cold, Baylor thought. Saving on wood. Or not wanting to add to the carbon. His imagination drifted; he saw himself in one of the cold cottages. He'd insulate the heck out of the windows for starters. And he'd heard of people using car batteries for electricity. He could get himself and Val set up that way. Baylor took a sip of the juice and felt the warmth spreading out through his blood. He'd get his mom out there, too. Not to live with, hell no. But set her up with her car battery and candles and so on.

He checked Val. Her eyes had opened. "Does anyone here have TV?" He asked anxiously.

"No." Val raised her eyebrows in surprise.

Baylor explained, "I was thinking of bringing my mom out here. It would do her good to get away from the TV. Maybe she'd start reading books again." His few memories of happiness as a kid were of her and him sitting on his bed with a shared picture book. He could get magazines for her to look at, too. Maybe she would make some friends.

He smiled tentatively at Val. Her hands were trembling. It occurred to him that she might drop dead like that old guy. "Hey," Baylor threw the quilt off his lap. "Let me help you into your bedroom. We both should be asleep."

Writers write, but they can't do that with nothing to say. Charlie paused because that was his problem: He was sure of nothing and didn't expect his thoughts to have any value to anyone other than himself, but he still wanted to speak past the grave. He wanted to have something to say after all his years of life.

He was out on his porch with one of the cats, enjoying the rainless night. The stars were out, a rare sight in cloudy southwestern Washington. Charlie tilted his head back. One advantage of living in a town that had no power was no streetlights and lots of stars. Huge numbers of stars, in fact. The sky was littered with them. *I don't look at stars enough,* Charlie thought. He loved the stars, and even more, he loved the sense they gave him of a vast, endless eternity. Charlie wrote:

Why isn't there a religion focused on the worship of stars?

Of course, maybe there was one and he just didn't know about it.

Maybe the Druids sought comfort and meaning from the stars and the infinite expanses of universe around them. A bit of doggerel from his childhood popped into his head. Charlie wrote:

Starlight, star bright
First star I see tonight
Wish I may, wish I might
Have this wish I wish tonight.

He paused, looking up at the stars, not sure what he would wish for if he believed in wishes. The night sky was so gentle and calm, the stars so very, very far away. Would his wish be answered if he made one? He wrote:

Do all the children safe in bed
Have an angel overhead?
For every child that died in fear
Is there an angel's quiet tear?
And is there somewhere up above
For all who died without love?
In this dying world so wracked with grief
How can anyone have belief?
So, star light star bright
The first star I can see tonight
Wish I may wish I might
Have the wish I wish tonight.

Well, what drivel, he thought, and I used to be a poet. The sight of his scribbles on paper made him smile; he could just imagine the reaction of his former colleagues or students. Old Charlie's gone senile. Yet, the little rhyme did sum up how he felt. He did yearn for belief in something, some kind of justice, some kind of comfort, something to make the sufferings of the world meaningful.

Charlie wiped his eyes on his sleeve and sniffed. "I'm allergic to you," he told the cat. He sniffed again, then leaned his head back the better to see the stars. To what, he thought, do we owe the honor of this cloudless night? Then something swept across stars, briefly obscuring them. Maybe just a smear on his cornea, maybe a wisp of cloud? Charlie blinked to clear his vision. Whatever it was, continued in a leisurely circle round and round, circles that seemed to be climbing upward. But it was hard to track something that could only be seen by the sudden absence and reappearance of stars.

"Can you see the stars?" he asked the cat. But she was purring, too grateful for the warmth of his lap to look at the sky. He warmed his hands in her thick, soft fur. "Good girl."

I love my cats, and my cats love me, he wrote.

Time to go in. They'd all pile under the quilts together, him and the grateful, happy cats. Charlie took one last look at the sky. Whatever he'd seen, it had ceased circling. The stars were undisturbed in all their glory. Charlie shook the stiffness out of his neck. Then, gently, he scooped his cat up into his arms and carried her into their home.

Epilogue

Raven

There were many things that the people of Warrentown didn't know about Raven. They didn't know, for example, that she was as much a creature of darkness as of daylight. They didn't know that she loved the night and she spread its soft comfort over the ravaged forest to hide the sins of mankind from the stars.

Yes, every night she stretched her wings out, fanned her feathers, and a soft gray mist rose from the forest of dead cedars. She did a pirouette and the back side of the sunset–the eastern side–deepened from lavender into blue. With a flip of her wings, the sun dipped and sent one last long arm of glittering gold across the ocean before drowning in the horizon. She spread her wings out, fanning the tips of her feathers, and the air thickened into blackness all around the Salish Sea.

Finished with her work, Raven let the wind lift her high into the nighttime sky. She circled once over her place, her bend in the river, and gentle dew fell on the alder and maple leaves, on the fir trees, and on the needles of the few remaining cedars. The roots of plants wriggled down into the soil and sipped the water. She gave a hard flap and shot up in the sky.

Raven rejoiced in the feel of wind under her wings. She climbed high up in the night sky until she was invisible from the ground, almost as high as the stars. There she slid easily through the black air, canting from side to side just because she could. She sailed in long, slow spirals and, as she flew, she gazed upward at the sky.

She cleared the clouds away, so she could see the stars spangled in a vast array from horizon to horizon. She thought about the stories humans had made up about pictures they saw in the stars: The Big Dipper, the Great Bear. But in her opinion, the stars themselves—so long-lived and far, far away—were remarkable beyond belief or understanding, making stories unnecessary. So amazing to think that some of the stars were visible to her eyes, even though the star itself had nova'd out in a blaze of glory.

Sometimes she liked to fly upside down, so she could see the stars. No one knew Raven could do that. Upside down, she slid in long, slow circles through the night sky.

But no one, not even Raven, can stay in a state of exultation for long. She rolled right side up and dropped altitude.

The misty black air obscured the town below her. Only small pricks of light, like little stars, could be seen. One for Val, her Coleman lantern burning. She was curled up in her armchair with a couple cats and a book. Angie was sprawled on her couch. That new young man, Baylor, was staying in her spare room. He'll be useful, Raven thought. Val was going to change her will to make Baylor be the inheritor of her animals. Another star was for Charlie, inside his home, surrounded by purring cats. Jimmy wondered what use a poet was to them, but Raven wanted to have a witness, someone who might tell their story someday. No star shone for the Old Man, but headlights flickered through the trees for Jimmy. He was on his way toward Olympia to forage for supplies. Raven's heart lifted when she thought of Jimmy; she was grateful that she was no longer alone. The light in the window at Jesus's house was warm and bright, his family all tucked in bed, warm and dry. A faint star twinkled out in the woods for Vulture and his crew, probably stoned or baked or whatever term people used to mean high. There was even a little spark for Crazy Mary, passed out on her couch.

And one bright star for home: the lantern in her window. She did one last circuit for the night, then spiraled round and round and down until, guided by the light of her home, she lit on the roof of the Raven Tavern.

A Mountain in the Air

The Third Novella

Prologue

On a sunny morning in 1991, grunge guitarist Pete Wallis walked off into the flower meadows on Mt. Rainier and never came back. He didn't die—at least not in the way people normally think of death. But he never came back.

Forty-three years later, in 2034, he said, "I think I'm going to have visitors soon." No one answered, but Pete didn't care; he'd gotten used to talking to himself. Besides, he'd lost all sense of time and had no idea how long he'd been on the mountain.

Mt. Rainier hadn't been much affected by climate change back in the nineties when Pete went for a hike and vanished. On the morning of his disappearance, it'd seemed like half of Seattle was up wandering around on the flower meadows while paying homage to the mountain's cold blue and green beauty. Herds of people roamed everywhere, snapping photographs of each other posed against the snow or the flowers.

The parking lot had been jammed. Pete managed to wedge his old Honda into a space by running his wheels up over the curb into the thick green grass of the sub-alpine meadows. "Parked so close I had to get out the passenger side," he recalled.

"It was a madhouse this morning," Pete told the flowers. "I should probably be getting back." Faces of his fellow band members drifted into his mind. He'd be missed from the daily rehearsals.

Yeah, they'll all be pissed when I get back, he thought distantly, but the thought didn't stick. Instead his mind floated back to the parking lot, to his struggle to get out of the Honda. The moment his boots landed on the ground, he'd felt the power surge. The hot, subterranean energy of the earth under the surface coating of parking lot had shoved its way right up his spine and into his head. Now his spine was connected to the mountain, part of a larger nervous system.

"Yeah," Pete told the mountain, "I feel you." The feeling was solid, as safe as eternity. As Seattle native, he was used to heavily vegetated hills, but the mountain was different: exaggerated, hyper-real. The steep tilt had thrown him off-center, making him see and hear things that he'd never noticed before. He hadn't been a flower guy or much of a nature nut before his trip to Mt. Rainier. He'd come to the mountain out of a need to think and, instead, he'd lost himself into noticing.

Flowers. He'd never seen so many flowers in his life. Clumps of fat red flowers, spangles of yellow daisies, secretive cups in dark blue that lurked in the wet grass, a haze of tiny white stars in between the rocks, spikes of blue that shaded into lavender. The flowers grew in patterns. The blue spikes stood tall in drier areas, but the almost-hidden blue cups grew upright out of the trickles of water that drained down the slope, making miniature streams through the meadow. The fat red flowers seemed to like being near the trees.

And oh! the air smelled sweet. The sharp, almost tingling scent of sap and needles floated over the moist, heavy smell of the grassy meadow. What kind of trees were they? He didn't know their names, but he'd grown to know each tree intimately. They were conifers with sharp blue-green needles and rough scaly gray trunks. They looked stunted, bent under the memory of the winter's snow, and were full of twittering birds.

Birds everywhere! His ears had opened up to their music, and he spent hours listening to the interplay of their voices. Small gray birds ruffled their wings and clicked their beaks as they hopped across the rocks in search of bugs. With loud caws, ravens lifted their wings and flapped into the sky. Clouds of kinglets buzzed in the sun. Every sound was like a tickle in his ears.

"It's all so beautiful," Pete thought. "I could sit here forever." There was a comforting warmth on his shoulders, but he could feel the underlying chill, the memory of winter. The contrast between summer and winter was everywhere: the ice-cold glacier run-off that trickled through the warm grass; the trees bent over from vanished snow; the marmots busy with their brief, intense searches for food. Poised in that space between cold and warm, his body felt tingly and excited, and his mind felt clear, almost transparent, without thought. He inhaled the trees, the flowers, the snow, the summer that still felt like winter, the hard blue sky.

I'm at the tree line, he noticed. He was in a transition zone—a liminal space, though he was not familiar with the term. Even though he was hiking distance from the snow—a very steep hike—the snowfields still looked as far away as heaven. Untouchable, unworldly, not a place for humans. He knew that people walked up to the top of the mountain all the time. It was a climb that required endurance, not skill. Pete had thought about signing up for one of the treks to the top, but the idea of joining in with a group of people and being stuck with them all day...Besides, it seemed to him to be a desecration. He wanted to think of the snow fields as being up there above him, out of reach of ordinary life. He didn't want to stand on top with a bunch of people taking pictures and congratulating each other.

No, he didn't feel like being around any crowds. Come to think of it, where were the crowds? The noisy families with their cameras and their kids had evaporated into the bright, cool air. The parking lot and his Honda had disappeared too. It seemed like he hadn't seen any people in a long time. Years maybe. No, not years, he'd only been on the mountain for an hour or so. Or had he been there for years? "It seems like years," he told the mountain. "It seems like I've been here forever. I should get my ass in gear and go home, but I don't want to. I don't want to go yet."

Besides, he could hear an old lady's voice, wispy and exhausted, whispering in the breeze. "I'm tired," she said. Then, "Move over." Pete obliged with a sideways shift of his weight before realizing that the voice was not speaking to him. "Oh, I'm tired. I'm just going to close my eyes for a bit."

A face flickered into Pete's memory: a woman with sad, hungry eyes. Where had he seen her? Some tavern, probably. Yeah, her face was in the dancing crowd. He couldn't recall exactly when or where, but he did remember that he'd classified her immediately as not fuckable. She was too old for the venue, and besides the transparent longing in her eyes was...sad. He hadn't wanted to be tied down by anyone's neediness, so he'd looked out at the other girls, the ones who laughed and shook their hair with abandonment, and he sang for them.

Why did he remember a sad woman who couldn't dance? Yet he could feel her nearby, and somehow he knew her name.

Pete sat up to better scan the mountain meadows and the clear blue sky. "Hey," he called. "Hey, come on up here." There was no answer but the breeze and the trickle of melt water. Pete tried again. "Hey?" he called, "Are you out there?"

"Valerie?"

Chapter One
The Rip Van Winkle Experience

"You know about Rip Van Winkle, right?" Coyote Jim was getting exasperated with the Big Buy security guy. Sure, it was hard to explain magic to someone who didn't believe in it, but not any harder than explaining religion. Anyone who believed in God should be able to believe in shape-shifting nature spirits, he thought. "What happened is just like the Rip Van Winkle story. We're in a different reality."

Security Guy was slumped at the base of the cedar tree, shell-shocked and silent.

"Hey, say something." Jim snapped his fingers in Security Guy's face. "React. Come on."

Security Guy blinked rapidly, opened and shut his mouth a few times, and finally squeaked out a question, "Where are we?"

"I keep telling you. Same place we used to be. Different time." Shit, Jim thought. He wanted to get back to the Big Buy to help out with the burglary. "We're in the Big Buy parking lot but somewhere in the past." Jim waved one hand at the nighttime forest surrounding them. Immense, silent cedars loomed in the moonlight, and the dark air was thick with the scents of moss and recent rain. He was knee deep in damp ferns, and Security Guy was getting his butt wet from sitting on the mossy ground. "I'd say pre-Columbian. Maybe earlier. Or maybe it's a different reality."

He checked Security Guy's face. He was open-mouthed, on the verge of panic. Jim squatted down to get eye level. "Wanna cigarette?"

After a few tries, Security Guy was able to mumble, "I don't smoke."

"You do now." Jim handed him a lit cigarette. "You're going to sit here under this tree for about an hour. That's all. Okay?"

Security Guy held the cigarette like it was a lit firecracker.

"See, the thing is, there's more to life than what you grew up knowing about," Jim explained, trying to keep the impatience out of his voice. "So you gotta just accept it. I'm a shape-shifter, and we're in a different reality than the one you're used to. You aren't crazy, and nothing bad will happen to you." Actually, Jim wasn't certain about that part. It was likely that the Van Winkle experience would end with Security Guy getting fired.

Back when it was normal for people to believe in fairies—or elves, the fair folk, pucas, orisa, and so on—it was also normal for humans to fear kidnappings by magical forces. In the old days, the kidnap victims could recount their experiences when they returned and be believed. However, with the advent of public education and the long, slow murder of nature, belief in magic had diminished to the point that few people who disappeared were willing to be truthful about what they'd experienced. They made up cover stories by claiming amnesia or by accusing someone of drugging them. They didn't say they'd met up with a magical being and got zapped into an alternative reality.

If a middle-aged security guy in Rainier, Washington, in 2034, disappeared while the Big Buy store that employed him was being robbed, he was likely to be fired on his return. No one was going to believe that a coyote shape-shifter had taken him to a different reality where there was no Rainier and no Big Buy store. No one was going to believe that he'd sat under a cedar and smoked a cigarette with the shape-shifter while the shape-shifter's friends robbed the store. Jim very, very rarely sent people over to the other timeline. Robbing stores was a necessity for survival, but he didn't want to fuck up anyone's life if he didn't have to.

Security Guy was panting with fear. He was a large, lumpish man with a soft, shapeless face, a man who'd expected to spend the night shift at the Big Buy store reading magazines and eating candy bars. He'd fantasized about what he would do if someone tried to rob the store, but Security Guy had always known in his heart that he was no hero. His plan had been to call 911 and let the militia take care of crime. However, Jim hadn't given him a chance to call anyone. Jim had sneaked up on him, aimed a gun at his head, and said, "Calm down and listen to what I say."

The security guy hadn't calmed down. His eyes darted around frantically as he tried to make sense of his surroundings. Instead of the back door of the Big Buy store, he was crouching by a huge cedar tree, bigger than any cedar anywhere near Rainier. Instead of looking out over an asphalt space surrounded by a chain link fence and lit by halogen lights, he saw trees looming with menace in the darkness, lit only by a pale misty moon. Instead of being alone, he was with a lanky, dark-haired guy who had freaky yellow eyes and talked about time travel and shape-shifters.

Security guy wasn't an out-doorish person, and he was afraid of the dark. "Where am I?" he asked again.

"You're okay. That's all you need to know. You gotta watch?"

"Uh, yeah." Security Guy pushed his sleeve up. "Yeah."

"What time is it?"

"It's, it's three. Three in the morning."

"I'll be back by four at the latest. You just sit right here and watch the minutes go by." Jim hoped that staring at the watch would give the guy a focus, something to cling to. "I'll be back in a little while. Don't move or I won't be able to find you."

"What? You're leaving me?" Security Guy was afraid of Jim but even more afraid of being stranded alone in the magic forest.

"I'm going to disappear now."

"Please no." The cigarette wobbled in his fingers.

"I gotta go. You watch your minute hand, okay? And don't wander off anywhere." Jim wondered if he should just whack the guy over the head with the gun and knock him unconscious, but rejected the thought. He didn't want to accidentally kill the security guy. He should've thought of bringing a rope so he could tie the guy to a tree.

"Don't move," he repeated, backing his words up with a little magic. *Calm down and sit still.* "I'll be back in an hour."

Chapter Two

The Robbery

"How're you guys doing?" Jim materialized on the asphalt at the back of the Big Buy store. Reality shifting always made him dizzy, so he staggered a step before regaining his balance. He swept a glance around, taking in the two trucks and the robbery crew. Baylor was jamming an ax into the back of a pick up that was already crammed with shovels and rakes, lawn furniture, and a stacks of plywood. He grinned when he saw Jim and waved. Baylor was a normal person, without magic. He was in his twenties, strong, and seemed to be enjoying himself.

Rachel waved, too, but she wasn't grinning. As he always did, Jim took a few seconds to admire her feral raven beauty. Then he sauntered over to her and kissed the top of her head. She was just the right height to fit under his arm. He gave a gentle tug to her long, thick, black braid and smiled into her black eyes. "You guys about done?"

The other truck was full of boxes. Big boxes. Charlie was at the truck's door ready to leave. "We got five solar generators!" he announced gleefully. Charlie was a retired professor of poetry from the University of Washington. He was elderly, frail, near-sighted, and delighted with himself for being one of the drivers in the raid on Big Buy.

"Better scoot then," Jim told him. Jim had done enough robberies to be unthrilled. He just wanted to get the job done with a minimum of fuss.

"Yeah, Charlie, go ahead and leave." Rachel spoke in a loud whisper, not wanting to attract attention. The Big Buy was on the outskirts of town in an area where in previous years people had chopped down the forest for development in hopes of attracting light industry or shopping opportunities. Years of failure had followed, and now most of the sites were abandoned or occupied by storage companies. There wasn't much risk of being overheard, but the risk did exist. Some of the sites had been colonized by homeless people, and some of the sites had security guards to keep the homeless out.

"Okay." With geriatric jauntiness, Charlie climbed into the pick up truck. He fired up the engine, gave them a wave, and rolled out the exit.

Jim didn't watch him leave. Instead he strolled up to the second truck and looked it over. "Just about done?"

"Yeah. I just found these." Baylor hefted a box on to the pile of stuff in the back of the truck. The side of the box was adorned with a colorful picture of a skill saw ripping through a wooden plank. Baylor slapped the box cheerfully. "It's a wrap, folks!" His tone was insouciant, but Jim could see the nervous twitch in his cheek. Baylor was anxious to get away.

Rachel pushed an errant strand of hair back from her face, ran a matter-of-fact glance over the truck, and said, "Yeah, let's go." She gave Jim a quick kiss and headed for the driver's seat. Like Charlie, Baylor waved good by as they rolled out the gate.

Jim was left in the dark silence. Overhead a pale moon filtered pearly light through the cloud cover. The natural scents of grass and trees wafted in on the breeze and competed with the oily stink of wet asphalt. Jim heard the faraway swish of a vehicle on the rain-slick highway. Time to go back and rescue Security Guy.

That's when he heard a thin female voice float in on the night air: "Did you just rob this place, Jim?"

Okay, that's a complication, Jim thought, with a surge of irritation. What the fuck was he going to do with a witness?

"What?" he asked the darkness. "Who are you?"

"It's me." He heard the crunch of footsteps on twigs and gravel, and a skinny wrath appeared in the open gate of the chain link fence, a small blond figure in jeans and an over-sized sweatshirt. Her long tangled hair was tied back from her face with a bandanna. Even though he hadn't seen her in two years, Jim recognized her immediately.

"TJ?"

"Yeah." She approached him cautiously, but her nervousness was directed around the Big Buy storage area, not at him. "Are you guys robbers?"

Jim didn't answer. He assessed her, noting the clothes that were stiff with accumulated dirt and her thin, wasted cheeks. The TJ he remembered had been unattractive, mostly because her rage at life had been visible in her stiff shoulders and sharp voice, but she hadn't been ugly as she was now, ugly with despair and defeat. He was afraid to ask her how she was doing, so he just said, "Yeah. We stole stuff."

"Cool." No spark appeared in her dead eyes. "I always thought you were a cool guy."

"I take it that you aren't going to cause any trouble for us?" he asked.

She shook her head. "No. But I wouldn't mind if you got some stuff for me. I've been trying to figure out how to get in here. I didn't know someone could just drive up in a truck and take stuff."

"There was a little more to it than that."

"I thought there was a security guard." Something about the way she said "thought" gave Jim the impression that she'd met the security guard and had failed to seduce him into giving her access. Jim could see why her offer of a blow job hadn't worked; too much like sex with a zombie.

"TJ," he said, "I got to wrap things up here. Where are you living these days?"

She pointed over her shoulder with deliberate ambiguity. "Got a place that way." Her shoulders hunched defensively.

Okay, so she didn't want him to know where she was living. Jim said, "I can't talk now. You want to catch up later?"

Maybe a little spark lit her eyes or maybe it was just his imagination. She tilted her head and said, "Sure."

"Follow the fence down to the road. I'll meet you there." He thought about it. "How about at three on Tuesday? I mean in the afternoon, not at night." Jim rarely knew what time it was or what day it was, but he could stick to a date if he had to. "I'll see what I can do for you then."

"Okay." She stared at a spot in the air somewhere near Jim's knees.

"But I gotta finish up here now, TJ."

"Uh, okay." She shifted from foot to foot, then jerked her body into motion. At the gate, like Baylor and Charlie, she gave him a small wave. "You promise," she said. Then she vanished into the darkness.

Jim said, "Shit." He dropped his cigarette on the asphalt. He didn't worry about DNA or fingerprints, partly because there was no file anywhere on him and partly because he didn't think the militia could investigate it's way out of a paper bag.

He time shifted back to the ancient cedar forest of the other reality and discovered that Security Guy was gone.

"Well, fuck." Jim turned in a slow circle, looking for clues. The night was shaping up for maximum annoyance. He should've known it. Just the fact that they were doing a big steal meant big complications. Two trucks, four people, using the Van Winkle trick to get rid of the security guard—it had all offended his sense of the right way to rob. Enough weird things could go wrong with a quick in-and-out at a roadside EV station/store. And now he had to go find the idiotic security guy.

"HEY!" Jim yelled. "I'm back!" He listened. A breeze stirred the branches over head and tiny feet rustled in the leaf litter.

"HEY!" he yelled again. "Where the fuck are you?"

Was that snapping noise the sound of human feet on ground litter?

"Do you want to get home or not?" Jim stared into the darkness in the direction of the snapped stick. His night vision was excellent but not good enough to penetrate very far into the dense blackness between the cedars. His ears, blessed with the excellent hearing of a coyote, picked up a faint voice.

"I'm coming. I'm trying." The voice sounded plaintive and was followed by the crash of a body tripping and falling into a huckleberry.

"Shit! Goddamn it!"

"Keep heading toward my voice," Jim shouted. The security guy sounded like an rhinoceros crashing around in the underbrush. Jim heard more swearing, more sounds of a human running into trees in the dark, and finally a gasp of relief: "I'm coming."

Security Guy, his hair full of twigs and his uniform wet and dirty, stumbled through a huckleberry and nearly ran into the cedar tree. He fell to his knees.

With a lurch, Jim shifted them back to the present. They arrived in the Big Box back parking area, with the security guy kneeling in a puddle of rain water. Jim could tell from the movement of the moon that they'd been gone about an hour of real time even though it had been only ten minutes or so in the other reality.

Security Guy was crying.

"Look, hey, listen up." Jim tapped him on the shoulder. Security Guy sucked in his breath and tried to control himself.

"You're going need a cover story," Jim told him. "No one is going to believe what really happened. They'll think you were in on the robbery."

"What robbery?"

"It doesn't matter. This is what matters. A guy with a gun put a bag over your head and drove you away for a few miles and left you. You got the bag off and walked back. You didn't call anyone because the guy took your cell phone. Give me your cell phone now."

"Uh." Grunting, Security Guy dug into his pocket and produced a phone. Jim snatched up.

"Got it?" Jim asked. "Got your story straight?"

Security Guy nodded.

"So now you need to go inside, find a land line, and call the militia."

"You want me to call the militia?" His eyes were big and cow-like.

"I don't *want* you to do it, but you better or you're going to get fired and maybe arrested." Jim was fed up. "So get your shit together. I'm leaving."

And he left, though he didn't wave good by at the gate. Instead, he jogged down the gravel road toward the highway. Once he was out of sight of Security Guy, he stopped and listened in case TJ was lurking in the scotch broom somewhere. Then he popped the sim card out of the phone and smashed it under his heal. He quickly shed his clothes, shoved them behind a bush, and tossed the old sneakers after them. Naked and cold, he shook his head, then his shoulders, and fell on the ground, four-legged. He shivered deeply and tensed every muscle, then relaxed as his fur warmed his body. In his coyote form, Jim sat back on his haunches and pointed his nose at the night sky. He let out all of the irritation and impatience from the robbery in a series of staccato yips. Then he howled out his angry joy at their success. Then he let his howl die away into a low growl of worry. What the hell was he going to do about TJ?

Shit. Jim set off for home at a trot, knowing he had a long ways to go. He was grateful for the distance because he needed to work off his bad mood and think.

Chapter Three
How TJ Met Jim

"I can give you a blow job. A good one. You don't even have to stop driving."

TJ remembered saying that to Jim two years previously. He'd picked her while hitchhiking, her second time at running away from home. Not that anyone at home had been chasing her. So, not really running away. Just leaving.

Morosely, TJ kicked at the gravel in the road. The black night arched over her head, full of clouds and pregnant with rain. The cool air chilled her; she had no body fat and her clothes were damp from crouching behind the fence, spying on the thieves. It was a good thing that no one from the homeless camp had come over to watch. Some of the people were crazy.

TJ shivered. She didn't really like any of the people at the camp. In fact, she was afraid of some of them. And she despised them all. But they were her friends.

Lights in the distance caught her eye. She was near the corner where the road to the back of the Big Buy lot met the highway, sitting in the dark because she hadn't wanted to go back to the camp. TJ watched the yellow lights, blurry with distance and damp air, as they got larger and brighter and nearer. Then suddenly the lights passed and she was alone in the night. She huddled within her damp sweatshirt and thought about Jim.

He'd turned her down flat for the blow job. Most guys liked having a girl's head in their crotch. It made them feel macho or something. Jim was pretty macho anyway, in her opinion. A bit scary-looking but not too scary. Older than her, but she liked that. She wasn't sure what he was. Mix of some kind. Maybe part Native American? Or maybe just Italian. His eyes were weird. Gray and yellow. She'd never seen eyes like that. He'd been hard to read, too, harder than most men. But she'd thought he'd go for a blow job, if she offered, since she'd owed him for trying to jack his wallet.

But he hadn't. He said, "I don't do sex with kids." Bastard! Son of a bitch! Two years had passed, but the memory still stabbed her in the guts.

"He could've been nicer," TJ said aloud, just to hear the sound of her voice. She felt stunned by his unexpected reappearance in her life. Their reunion had to have some significance beyond coincidence. It was a perverse trick of karma, a left-handed miracle. The universe was fucking with her. She let her mind go back to the summer day two years ago when she climbed into Jim's truck and rode up the coast with him.

She knew immediately that he was not just another middle-aged guy who'd picked up a hitchhiker, hoping for sex. She kind of wished he was looking for sex because he was cute in a way. Lean, almost bony, dark-complected, with strange eyes. She settled into the passenger seat and prepared for a ride that might be enjoyable.

But it wasn't. He didn't talk. Guys talked! They made little forays of conversation, feeling her out. Where was she from? Where was she going? Not that they were interested. They just felt like they had to do some build up before suggesting whatever kind of sex they thought she owed for the ride.

But not Jim. They rode side by side for what seemed like hours of silence. That pissed her off, so she decided to rob him, if she got the chance. The chance came when he stopped to pee. She got his wallet out of his jacket pocket and tucked it into the pouch of her sweatshirt. Then, when he stopped for a charge up at an EV station, she seized the opportunity to flee with his money. A couple of old assholes in a van had finished their charge up and were about to pull out onto the highway. She jumped out of Jim's truck, grabbed her stuff, and ran over. But the old guys didn't let her in right away. While they were arguing, Jim caught her at the van and demanded his money back.

TJ hunched her shoulders, cringing at the memory. Really, really stupid. She shouldn't have done it. Stupid.

After her half-assed robbery attempt, they got back on the road and headed north. He drove in silence on his side of the truck while she rode in silence on hers. Trees flashed by. An abandoned house. More trees. They drove up the Oregon coast right by the ocean, but she couldn't see the waves. The sea rolled by on his side of the truck while her head was locked in position, staring inland.

More trees flashed by while the silence hardened into a wall. She huddled, her arms around her knees, unable to find a focus for her thoughts. First, she pictured Jim's yellow eyes, then winced away. Then she imagined her brother's house but winced away from that too. She tried to distract herself by watching the view from the truck, but all she saw was trees, trashy houses, and more trees.

Then she felt the truck slowing down. Tightening her grip on her knees, she shot a glance at Jim. He pulled over to a wide spot beside the highway. Over a fence, cows grazed in the long grass of a pasture. In the distance, a shabby house with a blue tarp roof was nearly buried in blackberry vines. Nervously, she set her hand on the car door handle.

He said, "Food. We're stopping to eat. You eat, don't you?"

"Yes." She glared at him. He didn't have to be a jerk.

"First I want to get something straight between us."

She tightened her face into a mask.

"I want you to stop bullshitting me." His words slapped the mask right off. Her mouth opened, but she was too startled to say anything.

"My guess is you ran away from somewhere. Nod or something."

"Yes!" She glared.

"So where are you going?"

"My brother. I'm going to live with my brother in Rainier." She tilted her chin defiantly, but was unable to keep her anger from draining away.

"Does he know you're coming?"

Her eyes dropped.

"No?"

"I had to just leave home! He wasn't listening to me! I had to leave!" She felt the tears pushing at her eyes and pushed them back with her hands.

"Okay, whatever. I'm not getting in the middle of that fight." She heard his loud, impatient sigh. "Look, I got no problem driving you to your brother if he's a real person who is really there in Rainier."

"He's really there. He'll take me in." She tried not to sniffle. Jim wasn't kicking her out of his truck. He didn't want sex. He was going to give her a ride and feed her. She might get all the way to Rainier, if she played it right, so she sucked her breath in and braced herself for what she had to say. "I'm sorry I stole your money. I shouldn't of done that."

"Okay." He paused, then asked, "What's your name?"

She'd defused him. He wasn't mad anymore. She said, "Tamar Jean. TJ." Then, "It's a stupid name. My mother made it up."

"TJ. I'm Jim."

She shot him a brief glance, caught his strange gaze, and quickly turned away. Talking to her hands clenched in her lap, she said, "I really did have to leave. I started hitching in Eddina, California." She lifted her chin and said straight into his gray and yellow eyes, *"Most guys want something. You know. Something."* He made no comment. *"And I have done it before. Lots of times. I can pay for my ride and lunch and anything else that comes up. I'm not a kid."*

"You don't owe me anything for the ride," said Mr. Weird Eyes. "There's no obligation."

TJ shrank back in her seat. His words weren't exactly a slap to her pride, but close. Then he said, "You owe me for trying to rip me off. You can pay me back by phoning your brother. Let's make sure he's going to be home when we get there. I don't want to be dropping you off on the front steps like a Fed Ex package."

TJ sat up straight. Okay. She could do that.

TJ bent over and wrapped her arms around her stomach. She was very aware of the moist, black nighttime air and the hard gravel grinding into her butt. A wisp of breeze brought the scent of moss and conifers along with the stink of garbage, asphalt, and the campfire. All the other homeless people were either crashed out in their tents or slumped around the fire. She didn't want to crawl back into the damp, stinky hell of her sleeping bag. Not with Micheal there. Not for another round of the constant fighting that was their relationship.

On the ride up to Rainier, she and Jim had almost become friends. She'd been reluctant to leave him, but the good bye had felt inevitable, as if he was bound to drive out of her life as randomly as he had driven into it. She hadn't wanted to climb into her brother's truck, driven by her bitch of a sister-in-law. Her eyes had stayed locked on the rear view mirror until, with one last secret little wave, Jim vanished from her sight. Only then did she turn her eyes to the road ahead, the main drag through Rainier, clogged with traffic and awash with rain. They hadn't even gone a block away from her last glimpse of Jim before her sister-in-law had started nagging.

"You didn't ride the bus up here, did you? You hitch-hiked."
"I rode the bus."
"Don't lie. I know what you did to get here."

TJ jammed her palms up against her eyes to hold the tears back. Then she wiped the drip of snot off on her sleeve. "I *always* ugly cry," she whispered. With all the shit she had to cry about, it really sucked that she was ugly when she cried. Fiercely TJ wiped her eyes and told herself to stop the fucking crying, like crying ever did a bit of good because it didn't. Crying was as useless as praying.

She let her breath out in an angry huff. In the silence that followed, a coyote barked a series of high pitched yips. TJ lifted her head and listened. The coyote was nearby. It changed its song to a long, angst-ridden howl, a cry from the gut, as if the coyote was speaking for the whole sad world. She listened as the howl wound down into a growl and faded away. Then she whispered a little "owoo, woo, woo," of her own.

Chapter Four
Baylor's Morning After

Baylor lived at the top of the hill in a rundown cottage with a little front porch that overlooked the decaying ghost town of Warrentown. The village had once been a prosperous timber town, and he could see the remains of the prosperity from his porch: a row of red brick buildings across the road from the river. The decaying roof tops, buried in leaf debris, told a story of abandonment. The timber company had over-harvested their land, and climate change had killed off the remaining cedars and the hemlocks.

The only remaining business in town was the Raven Tavern, and it was more of a club or community center than a business. Located on the corner of the Main Street and the street leading up to his house, Baylor could see the blocky nineteenth century brick structure sticking up above the rest of the town. It looked like a memory, an old time photo. There oughta be Model T's and ladies with parasols, Baylor thought.

The shabby, decaying town wasn't a place of memories because the people who remembered were all gone. Dead or moved away. Baylor lived in the house once owned by the guy who had run the corner grocery. The grocery had died along with the other businesses when the sawmill shut down. That was back before Baylor's time, and he knew little about it except that he had acquired the old guy's house and, along with it, the old timer's dog.

"Right, Angela?" He fondled the over-sized head of his chunky pit bull. Angela slobbered all over his fingers with joy. She was made for love.

"Too bad about the old guy." Baylor often thought of the old man whose house he now inhabited. The house was a dump with no power or water, but the roof was still good. Baylor had spent hours scrubbing the floors, the cabinets, even the walls to rid the place of mold. He was still using the old man's furniture, and he'd left the old man's pictures up on the wall. Since he couldn't bring himself to sleep in the old man's bed, he used the couch.

"I know he ain't here haunting the place," he told Angela. "It just doesn't seem respectful." Besides Angela slept on the bed, and it smelled both of elderly incontinence and dog farts.

It didn't matter that he was sleeping on a couch. He had everything he needed in the cottage for himself and Angela. Baylor sipped his coffee—brewed on a campstove—and felt contented. No, he felt more than that. He was happy. Better than Christmas, Baylor thought, because he was the Santa Claus. Him, Charlie, Rachel, and Jim as a team. The thought warmed him.

After the raid on Big Buy, they'd parked behind Rachel's tavern. Then they'd all split up to go home and catch a little sleep. Now everyone was getting up, and some were already headed for the tavern to open their presents.

From his perch at the top of the hill, he could see Charlie yawning in front of his Quonset hut down by the river. The hut had once been an auto repair business, but Charlie had converted it to a hobbit burrow. Baylor had seen the inside and knew about the stacks of books, the embroidered table cloth, the good china, and the other artifacts from Charlie's previous life as a college professor. Charlie had several cats, and they were lounging on his plastic lawn chairs, soaking up the morning sun.

Just up the hill from the Quonset hut, old Valerie was carefully descending her front porch steps. She was a squatter, too, and she'd made an abandoned cottage into a home. Hours of weeding had rescued the rambling roses along the picket fence, and the goats kept the lawn mowed. The interior of her house resembled a pioneer homestead where she did canning, dried fruit, made granola snack bars, and even dried meat for jerky. During the day, she ran the tavern. "At least for now," Baylor thought. Like everyone else, he was worried about Valerie's health.

The grumble of an old time gas vehicle caught Baylor's attention. A battered pickup made the turn from the front street between the Quonset hut and the tavern and pulled in beside Jim's truck. Baylor recognized the fat old man who heaved himself out and landed unsteadily on his feet. It was Vulture, head of a secretive crew of old bikers that had their own community out in the woods somewhere. Baylor was mildly surprised to see Vulture without his armor of intoxication. Normally Vulture and his old gang members were high on something, often multiple somethings.

"I guess I better get going," Baylor told Angela. He chugged the remains of his coffee and jumped to his feet. "This is going to be fun!"

By the time Baylor and Angela arrived, a small crowd had gathered in the alley behind the Raven Tavern. Baylor looked around, checking the faces he knew. Crazy Mary wasn't there, but Jesus and his family were in a little huddle near the back door of the tavern. Jesus and his wife were a matching set: shorty, sturdy people with thick black hair and golden brown skin. Their children, a little boy and his slightly older sister, were shy and stayed close to their parents. Baylor could never look at them without a sense of wonder. He'd seen them dead out in the woods a couple years previously, yet there they were, giving the appearance of life. He'd never asked anyone about the ghost family. Rachel, he thought, would be the one to ask, but there were some strange things about her too.

Old Valerie was propping herself up against the wall of the Tavern and Vulture slouched beside her—an odd combination since Valerie was thoroughly respectable and Vulture had been a drugged-up criminal all of his life. Baylor watched as Vulture dug a crumpled pack of cigarettes out of one of his many pockets. Politely he proffered the pack to Val and grunted, "Want one?" Valerie tried to disguise her recoil by shifting her position and shook her head shyly. Baylor felt a kinship with Valerie; he, too, was afraid of Vulture.

"Someone just got out of bed." Baylor jumped, startled. Rachel smiled, her black eyes narrowing with good humor.

He grinned, embarrassed. "Yeah, me." Even though she appeared to be only a decade older than him, Rachel always made him feel like a teenager.

"Well, let's get going." Jim's brusque indifference made Baylor feel even younger.

"Okay." Baylor grabbed the tailgate and jumped up on the truck. He looked at the jumbled pile of boxes, unsure where to start.

"How many did you get?" Vulture asked.

"Not sure." Rachel answered. "We were just grabbing stuff."

Baylor seized a box and hefted it. "Solar generator for home use," he read off the box. It was heavy. He pivoted and handed the box down to Jim, who set the box on the ground. Baylor handed off three more of the same type box to Jim, who set them in a row.

Rachel looked over the small audience. "That's four. One for Val; one for you, Baylor; one for Vulture; and one for Charlie. Jesus, I'm sorry but you're stuck with chopping wood unless we can go back for seconds."

"Okay." He waved one hand cheerfully. "I chop wood."

"I don't need one. I can chop wood too," Baylor said. He thought the generators should go to older people first.

Rachel shook her head. "Your mom, Bay."

He'd told everyone that he wanted to bring his mom out, but he hadn't figured out where to put her. Living with him was out of the question, and most of the houses were decrepit.

"Thanks, Rachel, but I don't know if I'm going to get her out here."

"We'll figure something out."

"I have an idea," said Valerie. "Why not have your mom live me with, Baylor? I have two bedrooms that I'm not using."

Baylor discovered that it was possible to feel both relieved and appalled at the same time. It was a huge relief to be spared the need to prepare a house for his mother when he didn't have the time or the money. On the other hand, his mother was hard on people.

So he hedged, "Uh, I don't know. I mean, thank you, but you don't know my mother. She can be..."

Valerie shook her head. "She can have the house after I'm gone."

They all knew that Valerie was dying, but no one had said so out loud before. Baylor was left speechless. His eyes jumped from face to face, frantic to find someone who could say whatever the right thing was to say.

It was Rachel who spoke up, "That makes sense, Val. You always think of other people more than yourself." She turned to Jesus, "That makes one for your family."

Baylor found himself tearing up. He blinked rapidly, hoping no one had noticed. "Thanks, Valerie. I hope she won't be any trouble."

Jim said, "Grab one of those big boxes. Let's get this job done."

So all of a sudden the problem of finding a home for his mother was gone. Baylor turned to the task of unloading with new energy. "Hey, Jim," Baylor asked, "can you help me with the composting toilets?"

Jim climbed up and they hoisted the toilets into the waiting arms of Vulture and Jesus.

"Five," Rachel counted, after all the toilets were unloaded. "Valerie for sure. Charlie. Vulture?"

"Sure," he said. Baylor had never seen their compound, but he assumed that it was pretty funky. Even funkier than Warrentown.

"Baylor, there's one for you. That leaves one for the tavern and for Jesus and family."

"Let's get rest of this stuff handled," Jim said.

An hour or so later, the trucks were empty and the stolen goods were distributed. The plywood was stacked behind the greenhouse under a tarp. Jesus and Maria had toted the lawn furniture off to their place. They all trooped into the Tavern for some brunch.

Once inside the Tavern, Valerie had to sit down. "Give me a minute," she said.

"I'll get you some coffee," Rachel said. Jim fired up the Coleman stove and got the coffee going. Valerie closed her eyes. A few minutes later, when the coffee was done, she was asleep. Rachel and Jim got busy frying eggs for everyone.

"I found someone to help Val," Jim told Rachel.

"Yeah?"

"She's a mess, but she might work out."

"Hey, come and get it!" Rachel shouted. "Okay," she added quietly to Jim. "Val's going to need help. So will Bay's mother."

Chapter Five
TJ's Morning After

TJ fumbled in her sweatshirt pocket for her little packet of powder. She carefully poured out a dose onto her palm and snorted it up. As soon as the meth hit her sinuses, the familiar surge electrified her brain and burned through her nervous system, igniting her arms and her legs. "Oooh," TJ mumbled. "Okay." She let her breath out, shook her head, and fumbled her way out of her tent and into a tired, hot day.

The little encampment was quiet except for the thin cry of Tina's baby. It was always crying, a reaction to life that TJ understood and shared. Tina herself was a heap of rags in an old lounger, her white feet stuck out in the sun from under a battered blanket. She was either asleep or passed out with the baby on her chest.

Whatever. TJ didn't care. She looked around at the random assortment of tents. It was hard to tell who else was there. The campers were mostly creatures of the evening and night. Sometimes as many as thirty people gathered around the fire pit in the late evening, and they would all stay up drinking, talking, and snorting meth until the small hours.

Every morning was the morning after.

TJ rubbed her eyes to get them open. Then she dug her fingers into her hair and yanked out a few tangles. The sun was well up. In fact, it was probably sometime in the afternoon. Maybe as late as two o'clock. No wonder it was so quiet. Mid-afternoon was the in-between time, too early to gather around a fire pit, too late to for those who had jobs to leave for work, and too early to return for those who had gone to town to panhandle or hit the food bank.

Micheal had gone out foraging, and she'd missed her chance to go into

Rainier with him. She'd heard him waking up but had faked being asleep to avoid dealing with his pissy mood. He was always at his worst in the morning, crawling around in the tent snarling at her. Farting. Micheal owned a truck, and someone had been outside the tent yammering about needing something from town.

She'd listened to the grumpy mumbles, the shuffle of feet on the ground, and the sounds of coffee being made. Then Micheal had poked his head in the tent and said, "Hey, get up."

She'd pretended to be dead.

"Hey, TJ, get up. We're going to town."

Nope. Not her.

More shuffles of feet and retreating mumbles. Someone said, "Fucking bitch."

Micheal never hit her. She could say that about him. He never hit her, and he did get his act together about basic survival stuff more than some other people. He even worked sometimes.

"Doesn't matter," TJ whispered to herself, "He's still an asshole." But all of that morning crap with Micheal had happened hours ago in a different reality. She'd fallen asleep after he left, and now she was awake.

TJ shifted her weight from foot to foot. The meth had given her the energy to get up and be active, but there was nothing that she wanted to do. She felt something soft brush against her leg and nearly jumped out of her skin.

"Oh, Buddy!" The tabby cat purred at her. TJ felt a stab of guilt. Missing the trip to town meant she wouldn't get to pick out what she wanted from the food bank. She could usually get some cat food or, at least, something a cat could eat like canned stew or corned beef hash. Micheal wouldn't think about the cat.

Buddy stared at her with expectation. "I'll find something," she said with irritation. She didn't want the buzz kill of a hungry cat.

TJ crawled back into the tent and poked through their food supplies. Not much left. Peanut butter but no bread. Mushroom soup. Chicken noodle soup. That would have to do. She rooted around in their housewares box and found a can opener. After crawling back out into the over-bright sun, she opened the can and dumped the soup into a plastic bowl. Buddy sniffed the yellow sludge and nibbled at a bite of chicken.

"I'll get you some water." She had two bowls for the cat, a red one for food and a yellow one for water. TJ checked their water jugs. Most were empty. She poured out the remains of the last jug into Buddy's bowl and thought about Micheal's reaction if he came back and found the jugs empty. Well, shit. Micheal had forgotten to take the jugs with him to fill at an EV station, and he'd blame her for the lack of water when he came back.

So she'd better go get some from the woods. TJ watched Buddy to make sure she was eating. The cat had goo stuck to her whiskers. "Okay," TJ told her. "I'll get you some food when we go to town next trip." She gathered up two empty jugs and started off through the woods toward the stream.

The homeless encampment sprawled long the edge of the woods behind the empty buildings of a wannabe shopping mall. The developer hadn't been ambitious—the mall consisted of only four stores—but even that modest effort had been too much for Rainier, and no business had ever lasted long enough to stick in TJ's memory. To her, the mall had always been dead.

The campers couldn't use the buildings because the militia wouldn't let them. All winter long, in the constant cold drizzle, they either hunkered down in their tents or crouched, sodden and cold to the bone, around the fire pit. The militia came by regularly to yell at them, to tell them what losers they were, and to warn them that they'd get busted if anyone broke into one of the empty buildings. They usually made the campers hand over their weed, meth, or whatever else they had. The militia shits were bigger druggies than the campers.

"Fuck them," TJ told herself. What total assholes to make a point of denying them shelter when they needed it. She kicked a stick out of her pathway.

The pathway was hers. She'd created it by walking into the woods, following the same route each time. The others mostly walked down along the edge of the woods to the old pasture where young trees competed with scotch broom. There was a big hole back in there where someone had started digging a foundation and had quit part way through the job. It was their shit hole now. The campers used coffee cans for toilets and lugged their crap down to the pit. It wasn't far.

TJ used the pit like everyone else. Her trail into the woods was for a different purpose.

Chapter Six
TJ Has a Vision

The stream wound its way through fourth growth timber down from the foothills of the Olympic Range. It began, she supposed, up in the mountains where there used to be glaciers. There was still snow in the winter but nothing that stayed into summer anymore. Climate change. "Too fucking hot," TJ grumbled. Still, she was grateful that the winter snow melted and combined with nine months of rain every year, which meant the stream never completely ran out of fresh, cool water.

Tina said people could get beaver fever from the water. She meant some kind of bug or parasite. TJ had heard the phrase "beaver fever" before, but thought it meant some guy being totally horny after girls. Either way, she'd been drinking the creek water for nearly a year, and she hadn't gotten sick from it. At least she hadn't gotten any sicker than she already was from other things.

It was hard to get to the stream because it ran between steep banks choked with thickets of young trees. She had to crawl between the stems and branches to get to the edge, and then she had to scramble down through the roots and dirt to get to a perch on a rock by the water's side. Once she got to her rock, she was cut off from the real world.

TJ settled her butt on the rock and set the water jugs down. A ray of sun warmed her shoulders. She let her eyes follow the flow of water over rocks into the pool at her feet. She always felt peaceful on her rock.

The water was lovely. Pebbles, colored like jewels, gleamed in its depths. Orange rocks, rust-colored rocks, even blue rocks. Some kind of emerald green plant adorned the stones at the edge of the stream. Maybe it was moss. She didn't know the names of plants. She just knew that

A Mountain in the Air

something moss-like grew under the water and she enjoyed the vibrant color.

TJ's shoulders relaxed. She leaned forward, resting her chin on her arms, and let her eyes close. The water glugged and slurped as it swirled into the pool. Like music, she thought. The shifting breeze overhead was a soprano voice, swaying in harmony with the water's song. She could imagine her own breath as part of the music—in and out, in and out. The gurgle of the water, the sigh of a breeze, and the rustle of willow leaves made a wall that shut out the sounds of the world. TJ's mind drifted.

She became aware of a boy dancing on a boulder. No, not a boy. He was twenty or so but dressed in a way that announced his decision to not be an adult. Skinny, in jeans and a T-shirt, with a bony face made dramatic by dirty blond hair rasta'd into twists like snakes, he was joyfully hopping and twirling all by himself. TJ wondered vaguely where they were. They seemed to be on the slopes of a mountain, up high, near the top. Above her fields of jumbled stones merged into snow and the snowfields expanded sky wards until they merged with clouds. She was looking around at the wildflowers when the young man noticed her, stopped dancing, and called out, "Valerie?"

She looked around, wondering who the young man was calling to.

"Is that you, Valerie?"

He was suddenly closer. His eyes were bright and friendly while his lips hesitated between a smile of greeting and one of embarrassment.

"No," TJ said. "I don't know any Valerie."

"Oh." His smile collapsed into disappointment. "I was kind of expecting someone else."

TJ started to stand up, when a softness against her elbow startled her awake.

"Oh!" Suddenly she was back by the stream, sitting on a rock. Buddy, tail aloft, was rubbing her head on TJ's elbow.

"Buddy?"

The cat purred.

"Wow. You shoulda seen the dream I just had. "

Buddy leaned into her hand and TJ responded by scratching behind her ears. Then Buddy turned and climbed up the bank. Her departure was determined, almost as if she'd heard a directive to leave. TJ sat back on her heels and thought about it. Maybe it was time to go.

Jim!

It was Tuesday! She'd tried to track the days, but had gotten confused. The robbery had been on a Sunday, then came Monday, and that meant it was Tuesday and Jim was going to come back! How had she managed to get mixed up about that? She might miss him!

In a burst of nervous energy, TJ held first one jug under the water to fill and then the other. Full, the jugs were heavy. She screwed the tops down, heaved the jugs up to the top of the bank, and shoved them back against the willows away from the edge. Then she grabbed the thin trunk of a young tree, planted her sneaker on a big root, and hoisted herself up. Her knee hit one of the jugs and it tumbled down, smacked the rock where she'd been sitting, and tipped into the water. The top popped off and the water spouted out.

TJ felt her insides tilt and tumble with the jug. Just moments ago she'd been happy but now the water was spilled, and Buddy was heading back to the camp, leaving her panicking and in a hurry. Fuck, fuck, fuck. She had to go down and get the jug! TJ twisted around to get her feet aimed downwards, slipped, and tumbled, landing on her knees. She fell forward and her palms landed in the water, sending a shock of cold up her arms. TJ jerked herself back away from the stream and ended up curled on the gravel next to the spilled jug. She felt broken, smashed, as if she might fall so far that she could never return.

A meow from up the bank called her back. Buddy was asking her what she was doing. TJ carefully pushed herself upright and brushed the dirt off her sweatshirt. Her knees hurt. Her palms were scraped raw. She was bleeding from the base of one finger. She wondered what the hell had just happened. She had gone from the sweet happiness of the singing stream, to hurrying to make her date with Jim, to broken and battered at the water's edge.

Had the stream done that to her? Or Buddy? No, it was the jug. The jug had jumped into the stream, and she had fallen trying to retrieve it. Fuck it. She wasn't going to retrieve it now. She was going to fucking leave it right there to rot or be nagged at by the water until pushed downstream somewhere. Fucking no good useless...Stop crying, TJ told herself. Stop it.

Buddy meowed anxiously from the top of the bank. "I'm coming," TJ told her. "Give me a minute." She squinted up at the sky. A lot of sun. It had to be mid-afternoon. Jesus! "Oh shit, Buddy." She scrambled up the bank, grabbed the remaining jug, and tried to hurry on her sore legs down the pathway.

Chapter Seven
Jim Makes an Offer

She stumbled into a run as soon as she cleared the trees and entered the camping area. Her run was lop-sided and awkward, but she moved as fast as she could back to her tent. There she dropped the jug. Then she set off at a trot around the abandoned shops to the weedy expanse of cracked asphalt that had been intended for parking. The gravel road that led back to the Big Buy storage ran parallel to one side of the parking area, separated by a mess of scotch broom. Jim's truck was parked right where he said he'd be.

TJ's heart jumped and she broke into an awkward, lop-sided run while waving her arms. Then she stopped, dropped her arms, and set off at a walk. It was pathetic to run. If he didn't see her and left, then he left. Big deal, she told herself. But she kept her eyes on the truck as she limped through the scotch broom.

Jim watched her slow arrival through the exhalations from his cigarette. TJ had time to contrast him in her mind with Micheal and find Micheal wanting. Jim was sexy. He always looked like he'd just rolled out of bed. His weird yellow eyes made him scary in a good way. Micheal was young, tough, and was trying to have a life, but he was an angry, mean person and scary sometimes in a bad way.

She haled Jim when she got in range. "Sorry, I don't have a watch."

"No problem." He dropped the cigarette onto the gravel.

TJ finished her approach, her steps slowing. She became aware that she was wearing the same clothes as the night of the robbery. Plus she was wet and had mud on her knees and butt. "I fell in the creek," she said and disliked the defensiveness in her voice.

"You okay?" He looked her over.

TJ shrugged. "Yes. Except I skinned my hands." She held her palms out.

"Ouch." A silence fell between them. On TJ's side the silence was uncomfortable. She rummaged around in her mind for something to say and remembered Jim's promise. "Did you...you said you'd bring me something. Something from the robbery."

"Yeah." He shifted his weight from one side to the other as if in preparation for what he was going to say. "I don't have any stuff for you. I have an offer."

TJ squinted at him. She didn't think he was working up to hitting on her.

"An offer to come out and live at Warrentown where I live. The lady that owns the property there will give you a place to live."

She was so surprised that she could think of nothing to say. The word "lady" was reassuring. A thought struck her.

"Is she your girl friend? The lady?"

Jim seemed surprised at the question. "Yes, as a matter of fact, she is. She's kind of the mayor."

"The mayor?" Weird.

"It's a ghost town. Nothing fancy. No power but we're working on solar. No water except at the tavern or the river. But there's empty houses there that can be fixed up to be better than living here. Rachel will expect you to be helpful around the place. Everyone helps everyone else."

She'd been offered places to stay before but only in exchange for sex. "What kind of being helpful? What does that mean?"

He shrugged. "Just doing what needs to be done. Carry firewood to someone. Wash dishes after supper. Most of us eat at the tavern. There's a big garden and a green house, and there's always something to do there. Look after the animals."

"Are you guys farmers?" She was incredulous.

Jim grinned. "Sort of. We raise a lot of our own food." He shifted around, sniffed the wind, and grimaced. TJ became aware of the smell of garbage and distant sewage.

She hunched her shoulders, aware that she, too, smelled bad.

"So what do you think?" TJ examined Jim's face trying to read what was behind his eyes. He didn't look kind or pitying. He didn't even look particularly friendly. He looked patient, like he could hang out there leaning on his truck waiting for her answer until the middle of next week. For some reason, that patient neutrality was exactly what TJ needed.

"I've got some stuff," she told him.

"Sure."

"I'll go get my stuff."

"Okay."

She hurried away through the tangle of scotch broom, not wanting him to follow and help because she didn't want him to see the camp. She crossed the parking lot and rounded the corner of the empty building, nearly tripping over Buddy who had been waiting for her.

"Oh, Buddy," TJ said, stepping around the cat. "Sorry." She trotted past the campfire and the huddled coffee drinkers just waking up under the hot afternoon sun. TJ dived into the tent and grabbed her backpack. Hands shaking, she snatched up her scattered clothes. She realized that she was shivering even though the inside of the tent was hot. What the fuck? Her fingers trembled on the zipper to her sleeping bag as she struggled to disconnect it from Micheal's. She had to hunt for a piece of twine to tie it in a roll. Then she sat back and tucked her hands into her armpits.

"Stop it, stop it, stop it." TJ tried to steady her breathing. "You're being a fucking idiot," she whispered. She needed to think, get organized, not leave anything important and not take anything that wasn't hers. She wouldn't take any of the cooking stuff because Micheal would need it. She wouldn't take the peanut butter or the mushroom soup. He'd be pissed off when he found her gone because he was always pissed off, but she wouldn't give him a reason to call her a thief.

"Okay, now you're ready," she told herself. "Calm down." She didn't want Jim to see the her stupid shivering. TJ hauled her backpack and sleeping bag out of the tent and stood up. The coffee and alcohol drinkers around the fire were watching her. TJ struggled into the back pack and lifted up the sleeping bag.

"Going somewhere?" Tina called.

"Yeah, I'm leaving."

She started off while they watched.

"Yeah? Going where?"

TJ ignored the question. As she neared the corner, she saw Buddy unfurling her tail and arching her back in greeting.

"Bye." TJ didn't bend down because of the pack on her back. "You be

288

good now." She couldn't take a cat with her. She had no crate or pet carrier. Not even a box.

Buddy didn't say anything. TJ set off, heavy-footed under the pack, even though it was just clothes and didn't weigh much. Holding the sleeping bag made her steps awkward. Even though the ground was flat, she felt as if she was pushing her way up a steep grade. Jim's truck seemed a long way off with all she had to carry. Huffing in her hurry, TJ crossed the asphalt and pushed into the scotch broom. She kept her thoughts aimed at Jim and didn't look back. With a final push, she extricated herself from the brush and stumbled up to the truck. Then she dropped the sleeping bag.

"That's all?" Something in Jim's tone stabbed at her. She shrugged her way out of the backpack and set in on the ground. She started to say that, yeah, she'd brought all of her stuff, but a pressure was building up in her chest and she could feel tears stinging her eyes. Instead she said, "Can I bring my cat?"

"Sure."

She ran back to get Buddy.

Chapter Eight
House-cleaning

Baylor leaned on the broom and looked around. He wasn't heartened by what he saw. Jim had asked him to clean up the insides of a funky old cottage for a newcomer. The amount of work facing Baylor rose up like a tidal wave. He yawned prolifically, wiped the sweat off his face, and said out loud, "I'm *almost* done."

Which was a big fucking exercise in sarcasm. He was done with the living room and the hallway but had barely started the bedroom. Jim had headed off somewhere to pick up the newcomer, leaving Baylor alone with a filthy house and a broom. While Baylor agreed that it was a good idea to straightened things up a little, he felt a bit resentful too. No one had helped him clean up the house he'd moved into.

"Stop being childish." His voice disrupted the dusty silence. Some unknown person was going to walk into this hellhole of spider webs, and he should be thinking about that, not about the work he wanted to do on his own place. Baylor took the broom and whacked at the spider webs that hung in dusty strands from a bent curtain rod. Gross. He ran the broom along the edge of the ceiling all the way around the small bedroom. Then he stuck the broom out the hole in the broken window and shook it vigorously.

The room had once been a child's bedroom and felt haunted. The bedding was still on the bed, the pretty pattern of roses on white obscured by layers of dust and mold. The wall paper was pink and featured a border of cartoon characters tumbling along just below the ceiling. A small dresser that used to be white had been left with it's drawers open, frozen in the moment when all the clothes had been scooped out and packed for departure.

Someone had loved the kid, he thought. Painted the room. Put up the tacky decorative border and bought the flowery bedspread. Then the sawmill closed and everyone left.

Well, fuck. Shit happens. Truth was, people in Western Washington were a hell of a lot better off than people on the coast where the rising ocean was wiping out seaside communities or in the dry states where everything was on fire or in the tornado belt with their annual round of apocalyptic storms. And no matter how bad off Americans were, people in other parts of the world were in way worse shape. Starving. Dying of thirst. Desperate to find refuge somewhere, but turned back, shot at, walled out, deported. Like Jesus and his family. They had tried to find refuge in Washington but had hidden in the woods out of fear of the militia. And died there.

Ghosts. At least, he was pretty sure they were ghosts. Weird things happened in Warrentown.

With that ambiguous thought, Baylor pulled the old bedspread off the bed, wadded it up, and shoved it out the broken window into the backyard. The sheets beneath were filthy, so he wadded them up and tossed out them after the bedspread. That left the twin size mattress looking pathetically small and naked without the bedclothes—and still haunted by the missing child. He could almost see a little girl cuddled up all snug and sleepy, dreaming. Or maybe the kid had cried at night. Mostly likely the kid had done some of each. Either way, the kid was gone now. No toys or homework or anything else left behind.

Focus on cleaning this dump, Baylor told himself. Probably the child was now an adult, lived in Rainier, and was grateful to be living where it wasn't a forty minute drive to get to a store. Wherever the family had gone, they'd left the house behind to be lost to unpaid taxes. And the bank didn't want the house either. Very few people *wanted* to live in Warrentown. We're freaks and weirdos, Baylor thought, because we want to be here.

An engine rumbled outside. Jim had arrived with the newcomer. Another freak to live with us weirdos, Baylor told himself with a grin. He glanced around the bedroom. He hadn't gotten much done. With a wry grimace, he propped the broom up against the wall and hurried to the front door. He arrived in time to see a small blond girl push the truck door open and slide out while awkwardly clutching a cat to her chest. She was so thin that she appeared to be a collection of sticks wrapped in a dirty sweatshirt.

Jim sauntered around the truck—in Baylor's view Jim was always strolling or sauntering—and stopped to light a cigarette. Once lit, he pointed at the girl and said, "TJ, meet Baylor. Baylor, meet TJ."

The cat wriggled and Baylor said hurriedly, "Come on up." He didn't want the cat to bolt and disappear. TJ clumped up the stairs, heavy-footed, still clinging for dear life to the increasingly wriggly cat. Jim followed, cigarette in one hand and a backpack in the other. Baylor held the door for them.

With three people inside, the living room felt crowded. The cat sprang out of TJ's arms and landed with a thump on the ancient rug. Her tail was up, her eyes bright with curiosity. TJ surveyed the room with less confidence. "No one owns this place?" she asked. Her voice was gravelly, as if she wasn't used to speaking.

"The bank does," Jim said, "but they never come out here. Rachel doesn't let them."

"Oh." As she looked around, Baylor saw the old house through her eyes. It was just a cottage. The front door opened into the living room with no closet or entry for hanging a raincoat. The windows were the old-fashioned kind with leaded glass, and had the potential to be charming, but the curtains were filthy beyond redemption. The kitchen, visible through an arched doorway, had been painted yellow once but was now a sour mustard color, edged with black mold.

"I've been cleaning a bedroom," Baylor said. He was trying not to feel like a real estate agent peddling a dump. After all, he didn't have any stake in the house or the girl. Still, he felt like he had to find some virtues in the decrepit mess. "Back here," he said, leading the way.

TJ and Jim followed him down the short hallway to the bedroom.

"The window's broke, but this room's better than the other one because the roof leaks over there."

She said, "Oh" again. Just the one syllable, as if she didn't know what she felt or what she wanted to say.

Jim said, "We'll get a tarp on the roof, and we can nail plastic up on the window. That'll get you through the summer."

Baylor shrugged apologetically. "There's only so much we can do without spending a lot of money. We all basically just camp out in houses. My house up the hill has a hole in the floor in the bathroom." Which didn't matter since he never used the toilet or the sink.

The cat pranced into the room, purring, and rubbed on TJ's leg.

"Your cat likes it here," Baylor pointed out.

She almost smiled. "Yeah."

"You probably have mice," said Jim. "The cat will like that,"

Chapter Nine
Valerie is Too Tired

"I don't know how much longer I'm going to hang on," Valerie told her cats. They were curled up like throw cushions on her couch. Only one responded. Her oldest female cat, mother of millions until Charlie got her spayed, blinked her green eyes and murrowed softly.

Usually Valerie followed up her statements of worry with statements of reassurance, telling the cats that Charlie would look after them and they'd be fine. That day the words didn't come to her mouth. She knew it was true; Charlie *would* care for the cats. And the chickens and the pig. For a former college professor, Charlie had proven to be very adaptable, but she didn't have the energy to summon up any reassurances. She could hardly keep her eyes open.

"I need to get up," she said, more to herself than the cats. Food. She needed to get down to the Tavern and start dinner for everyone. Now that they had the solar generator and a small refrigerator, Rachel was going to get more interesting food for her to fix. Everyone was sick of soup and peanut butter sandwiches. Valerie leaned forward, planted her feet, shoved down on the arms of the chair, and carefully stood up. The room lurched, and she grabbed at the wall for support. Windows tilted sideways and blurred. Valerie made herself breath carefully, one breath after another, until the room righted itself.

"Steady yet, old lady?" she asked herself. She had a sudden image of her own body laying in a lump on her floor. Her old plaid work shirt and dirty jeans would fade right into the worn, faded rag rug. When they find me dead, Valerie thought, they'll say my body matches the decor.

"I'm dying," she told the cats. The calendar on her wall said 2030 and was four years out of date. Valerie felt like she was decades out of date. Years and years. She could remember back when life had bloomed with hope, back when she'd been young enough and dumb enough to expect a future that included love and some semblance of economic stability. Now she was old, and her personal future had arrived with the finality of a door slammed in her face. She was content with her friendships, her animals, and the roof over her head, but she was aware that she had no future where dreams could come true. She only had a past where they hadn't.

She didn't want to die. In spite of her old age, death was coming too soon. Valerie looked around her shabby living room. This is it, she thought. This is where my story ends. In a rundown cottage in a nearly abandoned town, surrounded by cats.

"I probably stink," she told the cats. "I should wash some clothes." They didn't care. The tabby slowly rose to her feet, stretched her back, and purred an invitation. Val let go of the wall and wobbled the short distance to the couch. She tried to lean down to pat the cat but fell forward and barely got herself turned around in time to land butt first. She sank down, defeated. "I'm tired," she said. Then, "Move over." The cat stared at her blankly. "Oh, I'm tired," Valerie explained, giving the cat a shove with her hip. "I'm just going to close my eyes for a bit."

Cuddled in the cozy embrace of the couch, Valerie relaxed into the sun's warmth. A yellow glow lay over her shoulders, her lap, and the field of flowers that spread out all around her. Even the sky was yellow and softly glowing. So pretty, she thought. Funny that she'd never noticed the flower meadow before. She thought she knew the area around Warrentown pretty well, and it was mostly dead cedars or fourth growth Douglas-fir.

But there she was sitting on a rock in a meadow of flowers and butterflies.

"Are you Valerie?" A young boy—he seemed like a young boy to her but was probably in his twenties—was smiling at her, a smile that was friendly but unsure. He was perched on top of a boulder and it, too, was suffused with a gentle, warm yellow.

"Hello?" Valerie's uncertainty made the greeting a question.

"Hello yourself," he said, grinning. "I'm expecting a visitor. Are you Valerie?"

"Uh." Valerie wanted to chat with the young man, but the distance in years seemed insurmountable. He was skinny, wiry. His bones were like tree branches, his hair like lightening, and his smile had the wattage of the noon day sun. And yet he seemed to be part of the boulder, as if he and the boulder had grown into each other some way. She perched gingerly on her rock and tried to find a position that didn't hurt her butt.

They were on a mountainside, she realized suddenly. Mt. Rainier.

"I can't see Seattle. I thought you could see the city from here," Valerie chattered nervously.

"Sometimes I can," he said. "And sometimes I can see totem poles and long houses instead." He shrugged and a fat spliff appeared in his fingers. "Want some?" he asked.

Suddenly she knew who he was. He turned the full wattage of his smile on her, a feral grin that had shot a bolt of pure sex into her clitoris when she was in her forties. Now he just made her feel old. And shy and embarrassed. Her eyes dropped to the clasped hands in her lap. She saw with shame her fragile elderly skin, swollen knuckles, and yellow fingernails. Her face, she knew, was as wrinkled as old laundry.

"Hey," he spoke gently.

Valerie didn't answer. Something was banging on the inside of her head.

"Come on." His tone was wheedling. "Relax. Want some weed? It might mellow you out."

She wanted to meet his eyes and take the joint from his fingers, but the banging in her head was getting louder. Somehow she had floated away so that she was looking down at herself. She saw a sick old lady sitting on a rock on a mountainside. The young woman she'd been was long gone, dead and buried beneath day after day of getting by, doing what needed to be done. She'd never been the type to let go, let those endorphins loose to run free. The young man was dancing on his rock, and she wanted to join him, but the bang! bang! bang! was driving her nuts.

"Stop that!" Valerie shouted. And she woke up, startled and confused in the silence that followed her yell. There was no banging noise. The cats were staring at her as if she'd lost her mind.

TJ stepped back from the door, hugging herself. There was no reason for anyone to shout at her. Baylor had *told* her to knock on that door. Well, fuck you, she thought. Fuck you sideways and up and down and just fuck off.

She stomped down the steps. Baylor, standing in the yard, watched her angry descent and frowned. A young goat saw her, bounced straight up in the air, and hopped over the fence into the yard. TJ froze, disconcerted by the unexpected friendliness of the little animal. It had strange devil eyes, yellow with horizontal black slits, but its face was soft and full of fun.

"Hey," said TJ. "Look, a goat."

"Yeah, Val has lots of animals."

"She *yelled* at me."

"I heard her." Baylor squinted at the house, puzzled. "I wonder if she's okay. I mean, that isn't like her. Yelling at people."

The baby goat decided to show off with a series of vertical jumps, followed by some bounces off the steps, off the wood pile, and off TJ. With a cry of pain, TJ staggered sideways.

"Hey, don't do that!" It's little hooves were sharp.

"Oh, go away!" The same voice that had yelled at her earlier was shouting again. An old woman was leaning out the door. Her thin gray hair stood stiffly upright on top of her head but was flat against her ear on one side. She was wearing a man's plaid shirt that hung off her thin frame clear down to her knees. Bony white feet protruded from the bottom of her jeans.

She saw TJ and Baylor standing in the yard and said more calmly, "I meant the goat. Tell him to go away. He eats my roses."

TJ saw with surprise that there were pink roses struggling to bloom along the fence. She hadn't noticed them on her way in.

"Go away, goat," she said ineffectually.

The old lady grimaced and came all the way out on the porch. She hung onto the porch railing for balance. Even though she was skinny and weak, she had a big voice. "GO AWAY!"

The goat stopped bouncing and stared at her.

"Go now!"

The goat complied by leaping the rose-covered fence. In a series of hops, he disappeared down the street.

The old lady asked, "And who is this new person?"

"This is TJ," Baylor answered. "We're trying to clean up a house for her, and we wondered if you had any buckets or jugs we could borrow."

Chapter Ten
Water of Life

Water was available from a faucet in the backroom of the Raven Tavern, but that was for drinking. Armed with plastic jugs from Val, Baylor and TJ walked across the road to the river. Getting water again, TJ thought. Her trip to the stream earlier in the day seemed as remote as an event in her childhood, almost like some other person had dropped a water jug and had fallen down a bank onto rocks. Her skinned palms were stigmata, a reminder that she was, in fact, the same person as TJ from the homeless camp.

Baylor and TJ scrambled down to the river's edge. It was a lot easier to get down the river than it had been to reach the creek. There was no brush in the way and someone had rolled the bulkhead rocks around to make a landing place at the water line. Green water, heavy with silt, moved slowly between low banks choked with willows on the far side. Near the willows, the river was shadowed and dark green, but the reflections of clouds and sky made wavering patterns of white and blue midstream. TJ dipped her hand in the water. It wasn't as cool as the stream, but the strong, steady current felt reassuring, as if the river wanted to hold her hand.

Baylor crouched down on the rocks, dipped a jug into the water, and held it down until it was full. Finished, he plopped the fat, wet jug on a rock. TJ grabbed it and scrambled up the rocky bank to the road. When she returned, Baylor had another jug filled but he held her off from picking it up. "Your hand is bleeding."

"Oh, yeah." TJ shrugged and looked away. She didn't want to tell him anything about the homeless camp, not even that she had fallen down after spilling a jug of water. "I can still lift things."

"You don't have to."

"I want to." TJ made a grab for the jug and, reluctantly, Baylor let her have it. He filled the remaining jugs and helped TJ lug them up to the road. Together, they piled the jugs into a wheelbarrow. Baylor grabbed the wheelbarrow handles and started pushing the water up the hill to TJ's new home. About halfway up the hill, they reversed the wheel barrow so that Baylor could pull it by the handles while TJ pushed. They arrived at TJ's front yard sweaty and hot.

"Well, that was good exercise!" Baylor grinned at TJ and she tried to smile back.

Valerie had supplied them with a couple of scrub brushes, rags, and some old towels. They hauled the water into the kitchen and there TJ slumped, exhausted already. The ugly yellow cabinet doors opened to scary interior spaces where spiders lurked in the mold.

"Maybe we should clean this place by burning it down." Baylor said, deadpan. At the sight of TJ's thin, tired face, he added, "Joking."

TJ smiled, briefly.

"We could rip some of these cabinets out. You aren't going to need all of them."

"How can we rip them out?" TJ was feeling disconcerted. She had rocketed out of her familiar life of sleeping late and getting wrecked all night into a strange place where everyone said things like, "We'll fix your roof" or "We can rip those cabinets out." Micheal had been an active guy, in his way. He shuffled off to work when he could and came home exhausted and mad. He said things like, "Why haven't you cleaned up the tent?" and "Why don't you ever wash your hair?" even though he never washed his. He'd shaved it all off. Micheal, she realized, was drowning. Thrashing around, trying to save himself, but drowning.

Baylor was about Micheal's age and about his build, but his mind was different. He looked at the old cottage, suggested actions, and then got started even though it wasn't his house. She felt like a little kid running along behind him. She also felt like she wasn't going to be able to keep up.

"Jesus has some tools. We'll get some hammers and some wedges and just pry them out." Baylor peered under the overhead the cabinets, examining as best he could how they were attached to the wall. Then he climbed up on the counter and poked his head into one of the top shelves.

"Yuck," he said, jumping down. "You aren't going to want to go up there."

"Maybe we should just leave it," TJ suggested. She was hugging herself and looked very small. "I don't have anything to put in cabinets anyway."

"You'll get stuff. Food, water, a campstove."

TJ suppressed a yawn and thought about the white power tucked in her pocket. "Where do I go to pee?"

Baylor grinned. "Well, we're putting in composting toilets, but right now I'd say go around back and fertilize your yard."

"Okay."

"I mean just for now. We have outhouses over on the north side of town. Most people have a bucket in their house, and they empty it in the outhouse."

"Okay," she said, edging away.

She found a hidden spot in the weeds behind the house and dug out her little plastic packet. Only a tiny amount was left. It was going to be hard to get more. Maybe Baylor would drive her into town? Probably not. He didn't look like the type. Jim wouldn't, that was for sure. If she stayed in Warrentown, meth wouldn't be part of her life.

Maybe that was a good thing?

Stupid question. Of course it was a good thing. Right?

TJ examined the unfamiliar landscape of her new life. For some reason, someone had thrown some blankets and sheets out on the ragged weeds of the backyard. Evening was shading the blue sky with lavender, and shadows were forming around the broken-down houses. A woman's voice, singing in Spanish, floated in the breeze and some children laughed. Ambling down the alley, a pig stopped to sniff some yellow grass. A raucous rooster announced himself with a loud "Ar-ar-ar-oo," and a man yelled "Shut up!" The bratty little goat popped up out of the weeds, daisies dangling from his mouth. Their eyes met. TJ couldn't read the meaning behind his slit-eyed stare. Then, with a cheeky kick of his heels, the goat bounced away down the alley after the pig.

Buddy was going to like living in a house, TJ thought, and her heart fluttered with something almost like hope. She took a long deep breath of the heavily scented air. Roses and pig shit. TJ grinned.

"No more of this shit." She waved the baggy at the soft evening air. "This is the last." Carefully she opened the tiny plastic packet, shook the powder onto her wrist, and inhaled sharply.

"Ohhh." She closed her eyes, anticipating a spurt of pleasurable energy. Instead the drug had a bitter bite that left her feeling jangled but tired. "There wasn't enough," she told herself. It sucked that her last hit was no fun. "Fuck," TJ said aloud. She pinched the packet open and shook it over her wrist. Nothing. Then she licked her finger and rubbed the dust off the inside of the packet. The dust made her finger taste bitter but had no other effect. That's that, she thought. I'm done.

TJ shoved herself upright. Insects hummed in a tangle of blackberries. A quiet, soothing chuckle caught her attention. First one hen, then two more, then parade of hens were clucking and pecking their way down the edge of the alley. Each hen stopped, eyed her, accepted her, and moved on.

"I don't know," she told the hens. She was having another weird attack of shivers, like the shiver attack she'd had in the tent that morning. "Stop it," she told herself. She needed to settle down before she got back to Baylor. Breath in, breath out. When her hands had stopped shaking, she whispered. "Okay. Let's go clean some shelves."

TJ waded through the long grass and weeds around to the front of the house and trudged up the steps. Baylor was hard at work, scrubbing the counters. She picked up a brush, dipped it in the water, and started in on one of the lower shelves.

Chapter Eleven
A Party at the Raven Tavern

TJ collapsed into a plastic lawn chair. A small crowd had gathered behind the Tavern where Rachel was roasting a hot dog over a fire pit made out of an upside down metal garbage can lid. The old lady Valerie was arranging condiments on top of a battered plastic cooler. The evening sun was blocked by the solid mass of the Raven Tavern. TJ was grateful to sink into the cool shade. Her meth jolt had dissipated, leaving her feeling frazzled.

"Here." Val materialized beside her, holding a glass of water.

"Huh? TJ jumped, startled by Val's sudden appearance.

"Water," Val told her. "You look like you might be dehydrated."

"Oh, thanks," TJ would have preferred a beer. Most of the people gathered around the fire with their willow sticks and their hot dogs were drinking something alcoholic. But water was what she'd been given, so TJ took a sip. And then a long gulp. Yes, she was dehydrated. Water was what she needed.

"Hey, TJ," Baylor called.

"Huh?" She was startled again.

"What do you want on your hot dog?"

He held the hot dog in its bun over the table of condiments. TJ stuttered with embarrassment, "Anything. Anything's good."

"Mustard?" he asked. "I hate this yellow food bank shit."

"Okay, skip the mustard."

He eased his way through the small crowd, carrying a plate heaped with food. In addition to the hot dog, the plate held a pile of potato chips and some lettuce slick with salad dressing.

"There you go," He handed her the plate and went back to the fire to fix a hot dog for himself. TJ held her plate carefully in her lap while she took another long drink.

"You're the new neighbor." A gnomish old man, his plate teetering in his hand, carefully lowered himself into a chair beside her. "I'm Charlie." He smiled, poking his face forward like a turtle. "I heard that a house is getting fixed up for you."

"Yeah." TJ set her empty glass down. "Me and Baylor are cleaning it up."

"And now you have your food, water, and shelter." He had a kindly look, like Santa Claus or someone's granddad. Not like *her* granddad, who was a wife-beating martinet, but an ideal granddad like what a child would imagine. "All of your lower Maslow needs are met now."

Whatever that meant. TJ didn't respond because she didn't like obscure utterances that she didn't understand. Besides, she was hungry.

With a thump, Baylor landed on the other side of Charlie. He took a big bite of his hot dog and mumbled through a mouthful of bread, "So what're you talking about, Charlie?"

"Maslow?" Charlie shoved his glasses up his nose. "Just commenting that our new neighbor is getting her basic Maslow needs met."

Baylor leaned forward and said to TJ, "Charlie is a college professor. He knows all kinds of stuff."

"I can be a bore, too, though," said Charlie apologetically.

"I don't think so." Baylor chomped though his hot dog in a series of big bites. He wiped his mouth on his hand and grimaced. "I never learned much in school. I wish we had some napkins."

Charlie grinned. "What I miss most about civilization is a flush toilet."

"Yeah. Hot water on tap would be nice too."

"I guess we all have different ideas about what's essential." Charlie paused to take a bite of his hot dog. "But food, water, and shelter, those are *really* essential."

"I know about that. Needing food, water, and shelter. Everyone does." TJ's voice sounded defensive even to herself. She took refuge behind a handful of potato chips.

"I know about that for sure. I almost died two years ago." Baylor leaned across Charlie to talk to TJ. "I almost died of hypothermia out in the woods. Here's to food, water, and shelter." He raised his hot dog up in a salute.

"And good company." Charlie raised his hot dog in a toast. "Maslow says that once your basic needs are met, you can work on getting your other needs. That's belonging, creating, and self-actualization."

"Here's to that." Baylor toasted again but using his beer. TJ hunched over her plate. She didn't know what self-actual-whatever meant and she had no intention of asking.

Chapter Twelve
Dancing in the Dark

"She's a lost soul." Jim could tell that Rachel wasn't altogether pleased by his decision to being TJ to Warrentown. He wasn't altogether pleased either and for the same reason. "I thought that ignoring her would be like ignoring a stray cat. Maybe I fucked up."

"I don't know." Rachel took a slug of beer. "We'll see."

They surveyed the tavern together. It was after dinner. Valerie had fallen asleep in her chair behind the bar. TJ, prompted by Jim, had washed and dried the dishes for Rachel to put away. Unprompted by him, she'd wiped down the bar, rinsed out the bar rags, and draped them over the counter edge to dry. She had a broom and was sweeping the back room. She was paying them back for the big bag of supplies that sat waiting to be taken home for her and her cat.

Most evenings, once dinner was eaten, the Tavern emptied. Other evenings, as if a call had gone out, more locals showed up, ready to hang out well into the night and even into the next day. That evening was shaping up to be a social occasion.

Vulture and his crew of old bikers had rattled into town in their ancient gas-guzzling pickup truck and had taken over a table for a poker game. Charlie had joined the game because they weren't playing for real money. If the stakes had been higher than bottle caps, he never would've run the risk.

Baylor had planted himself at the table by the door, a good place for watching everyone while quietly drinking. The ghost family—Jesus, Maria and their kids—were relaxed together, talking quietly. The kids were sitting on the floor playing with the baby goat.

"That baby is a pain in the ass," Rachel commented, "and he's never going to grow up."

Jim grunted agreement. The children rolled a ball toward the baby goat. Puzzled, the little goat sniffed the ball, then with sudden burst of obnoxiousness, head-butted it across the room. The ball bounced under the table and collided with the feet of the card players. Vulture made grumpy noises while Charlie reached down and tapped the ball back across the floor.

"They'll be playing soccer with that goat in a few minutes." Jim grinned.

"What else do you want done?" TJ appeared beside them, frowning nervously. Her eyes searched through the room and found Baylor.

"You're fine," Rachel said. "Thanks."

"Have a beer," Jimmy invited her. "Hang out."

"And here's Mary!" A screech jangled every ear in the room. A scrawny old woman, too drunk to stand upright without help, was swinging from the door lintel. "And let the party begin!"

TJ carefully navigated her way across the room, carrying her beer while dodging the card players, the goat, and the children. She dropped into the chair at Baylor's table and answered his grin with a quick, nervous twitch of her lips.

"You look beat," Baylor said.

TJ took a long slug of her beer. "Yeah, didn't sleep much last night." To avoid a lag in the conversation, TJ hunted around in her mind for something more to say. "So do you like living here?"

"Yeah." He seemed surprised by her question. "Yeah, I like it a lot. I'm bringing my mother out here tomorrow or the next day."

TJ was silenced. She could find no point of connection between her life and the life of a young man who cared for his mother. Baylor, slumped his chair, was probably tired and maybe a little tipsy, she couldn't tell. He seemed content to just sit and nurse his beer. Maybe he didn't want to talk.

TJ let her eyes roam the darkening room. Someone had set out a Coleman lantern that beamed out a pleasant glow. Golden light reflected off the collection of oddments that Rachel had used to decorate the walls. TJ noted old license plates, broken china plates, dream catchers, and other objects chosen for their reflectivity. And mirrors, lots of mirrors. The tables, too, were decorated with light-catching junk, mostly old vases of the kind found in a second hand store. Plastic flowers. Tacky ashtrays. TJ's table sported a small sculpture of a beagle wearing tennis shoes and a glittery hat. The glowing lantern and sparkling walls gave TJ a feeling of disconnectedness, as if nothing was quite real.

She cleared her throat and attempted conversation. "Rachel has some weird stuff here."

"Oh, you don't know half of what's weird about Rachel." The old drunk lady had been standing with her back to TJ while back-seat-driving the card game, but TJ's remark snagged her attention. She turned unsteadily, leaned on their table, and dropped into an empty seat.

"Mind if I join you?" She smiled with drunken flirtatiousness, revealing gaps between her yellow teeth.

Baylor grinned back at her. "Do you care if we mind?"

"Not at all." She waved her hand dismissively. "So..." She smirked salaciously at TJ. "Young blood in town, eh? He needs someone his age." She leered at them, leaking drool.

TJ hunched her shoulders. "Jim brought me here."

"Oh, he did, did he?" The crazy lady reared back in her chair, waggling her eyebrows histrionically. Then she leaned in and nudged TJ's shoulder. "I'll give you a little advice, girl. You better leave Jim to Rachel, honey, because if you try to take him away from her, well..." She paused dramatically, then tapped her finger on the table for each word, "I. Would. Not. Do. That."

Still grinning, Baylor said, "Mary, this is TJ. TJ meet Mary."

Mary looked TJ over, grunted ambiguously, and asked, "And where might you be from?"

"California." TJ lifted her chin and met Mary's eyes.

"California," said Mary disdainfully, "And how did you get up here?"

"I hitch-hiked."

"To Warrentown?" Mary gaped in exaggerated amazement. "Rachel let you do that?"

"No." TJ frowned. "I told you. Jim drove me."

"Oh, that explains it. Because Rachel controls the road, you know."

"What does that mean?"

"It means you can only get here if she lets you, and you'll leave if she wants you to go."

"I'll leave if *I* want to leave." TJ felt her insides tightening up. "No one can make me stay if I don't want to leave if I want to." Somehow her words had gotten tangled up. She frowned, and tried again. "I mean, if I'll go where I want to go."

Mary laughed, "HA! Go where? Where's a little waif like you going to go? Because no matter where you go, that's where you are, right? It don't matter where you go."

"Words of wisdom," said Baylor. "Hey, I really like this song." TJ could tell that he was changing the subject on her behalf. It worked. Mary began to howl along with the thumping rhythm, and Baylor joined in, singing about playing the eights and aces. TJ had never heard the song before. She joined in with whisper as Baylor yelled out a line about taking a long shot gamble and heading out to someplace with a lake.

"Bob Seeger," he told TJ. "I like the oldies."

Eventually the crazy old woman staggered off to the bar to get more booze. Shortly afterwards, Baylor stood up and explained, "Gotta drain off the beer." TJ watched him cross the room, nodding at people, being greeted and teased. Everyone seemed to know everyone else.

She slid down in her chair to wait for his return. The card players were hunched over their game, shoulder to shoulder in a circle. All old men, with bodies that had once been muscular but now gone to fat, they wore heavy wool shirts as if they lived in a permanent winter. Smoke filtered out from inside their circle along with grunts, snorts, and the occasional laugh. TJ's vision shifted and for a moment she saw them as musk oxen, the cigarette smoke transmuted into hot breath on cold air. TJ blinked and the card players returned, hunched and hairy but human.

Charlie had abandoned the card game and was sitting quietly at the same table as the illegal immigrants. In the dim evening light, his face was a vague as a ghost and his eyes inward-looking. TJ watched his mouth moving. Was he singing to himself? Or praying? It was hard to tell. Glimpses of phrases tickled the edges of her vision. Glittery words. Colorful words, carefully chosen to have just the right effect. TJ leaned forward, concentrating, but the words seem to vanish as soon as she looked at them. She blinked her eyes and the gleaming words were replaced by the shine off a mirror on the wall. Wow, that was weird, TJ thought. Charlie continued to chant or whatever he was doing.

The illegals didn't seem to be paying him any attention. They were relaxed, side by side, comfortable in their togetherness. The two children were curled up on the floor, sleeping like puppies. Nice family, TJ thought vaguely. All of her thoughts were floating on the air, wandering on their own like helium balloons at a party.

Rachel and Jim were two-stepping gently to the music. TJ watched as Jim lifted a strand of hair from Rachel's face and leaned in for a kiss. Then they tightened their arms around each other and slowly revolved. Soft voices crooned against the the background of guitar and harmonica, and the melody flowed through the room and around the quiet forms of the people. Charlie was nodding his head or maybe nodding off to sleep. The air was full of the sway of the music.

TJ slid down in her chair and let herself melt. Country was not really her thing but that evening, tired and drunk, she was ready to lose herself in a sentimental tune. Her eyes were closed so she didn't see Baylor's return, only felt his presence as a shift in the air as he sat down.

"You sleepy, TJ?" he asked gently.

She opened her eyes. Now Jim and Rachel were dipping and twirling slowly, making her hair swing out in a black cloud. A rich golden voice was singing something about saving the last dance for...TJ pictured herself dancing with Baylor. Then she rejected the thought. Then she remembered the song from earlier in the evening, the song about the reckless abandonment to chance. The long shot gamble.

"You wanna dance?" TJ asked. What the hell, she was drunk, right? Go for it.

Baylor looked startled but willing.

"Okay." He stood up and, with old fashioned grace, offered her his hand. She took it and he pulled her up into a loose embrace. TJ, who had never danced the two-step before in her life, hung onto his shoulder like a lifeline. Her legs were wobbly, partly with drunkenness and partly with sudden rush of horniness brought on by the smell of Baylor's T-shirt and her close up view of his chest. She avoided making wrong steps by not stepping much at all. Baylor's hand in the small of her back felt warm and firm, and his crotch was swaying, right there, inches from her belly. He smelled of sweat, wood smoke, and hot dogs.

The music morphed into waltz and TJ found herself swaying and revolving slowly as a gravelly voice remembered Texas and waltzing under the stars. It seemed natural to lean her head against Baylor's chest and close her eyes. She slid her hands around his sides and dipped her fingers down the back of his jeans.

What the hell. Take that long shot gamble. "Wanna go home with me?" she murmured. "Try out my bed?"

Chapter Thirteen
TJ Shares a Secret

She didn't know why she was disappointed. It wasn't like sex had ever been all that good with any other guy. Mostly just grunting and sweating. And they *all* leaned on her hair sooner or later, nearly scalping her. She didn't know how prostitutes or girlfriends or anyone who had to fuck regularly could stand to have long hair. Sooner or later *every guy* would get in that position on top, grunting and lurching while leaning on their hands or elbows, and they never noticed that they were leaning on her hair. It *hurt,* but she knew from experience that there was no point in telling them to stop. They just got pissed.

Sex was a transaction. Why had she thought Baylor would be any different?

Probably because they'd gotten drunk together at the Tavern. No, she'd been drunk with guys before. Maybe because he was cute? Even dirty, like they all were, he had a kind of freshness. He was always planning things, and then he went out and actually did the things he planned. His constant activity had made him muscular and lean. Not super good-looking. Not hot sexy like Jim. Jimmy, now *he'd* be a good fuck. She could tell by the way he touched Rachel. Yeah, the way he touched Rachel. Like she was the whole world to him. Like he wanted to explore every inch of her. Like she was wonderful, precious.

Stabbed by jealousy, TJ glared at Baylor's sleeping form. Why hadn't any guy ever looked at her the way Jim looked at Rachel?

"Hey, Baylor."

"Hmmm?"

So he wasn't been asleep. Just ignoring her because he was done.

"That wasn't your first time, was it?" She knew Baylor, like all men, would be embarrassed by any hint that he had been less than a total stud.

"Huh? No!"

She'd gotten a reaction. She waited, expecting his anger, anticipating him saying something snide, something hurtful. Then she'd strike back.

"I'm just kind of drunk." He rolled over, facing her. Gently, he lifted a lock of her hair away from her face. "I'm sorry if I wasn't very...I'm sorry."

TJ's mind went blank with surprise and then her insides fell apart.

"Maybe we can do it again slower in the morning." He stoked her face with gentle fingers.

She struggled for words. "I just..."

"You didn't come, then?" he asked. She could barely make out his face in the darkness, but he didn't look angry. He sounded sad.

"No." Then she added, trying to pull herself together by showing a little contempt, "I never do."

"How come?" Innocent surprise. With one finger he traced her hairline to lift a stray lock away from her eyes. She usually did come, though. Easily. And often messily. Not with Baylor, which was weird. She couldn't understand why she hadn't had an orgasm with him. She'd tumbled into bed with some anticipation, with a vague hope that something different and special might happen. It was strange that her body had refused to respond when she'd responded to guys she was indifferent to or even hated. Even the ones who pulled her hair.

"I don't like sex." Total lie. Why had she said that? She did like sex! Sex gave her power.

"You don't?" His voice was warm with concern.

"No." She rolled away from him so that she was on her back, staring at the ceiling. He was acting all sweet but that wouldn't last. On a surge of anger, she began to talk. "My first time was with my stepdad. And my second time and my third time." She grinned, letting some laugh leak into her voice to show him that she could talk about it without getting upset. "He said he was teaching me how to do it, so I'd know how."

"Jesus, Teej." No one else had ever called her "Teej." "What an asshole. Is he in prison now?"

"Prison? No. Why would he be...oh, you mean because I was a kid? No."

"Why not?" Baylor was pissed. "Doing that to you. Why didn't he get locked up?"

"Because no one reported him."

"Did your mom know about it?"

TJ did laugh then. "Yeah. She was pissed. At me, not him. For breaking up her marriage. Except their marriage didn't break up. She stayed with him and I left."

"Oh shit, TJ." He gave her shoulder a squeeze. "That's the worst thing I ever heard off."

"It wasn't that bad." But it had been that bad, and she felt an ache behind her eyes.

"Yes, it was!" Baylor leaned across her, grabbed a handful of her unzipped sleeping bag, and pulled it over her. "No little girl should ever be treated that way. Fucking asshole ought to be in prison."

"Well, you can go down to California and tell him that." TJ felt another another attack of shivering coming on. She clenched her jaw muscles to keep her teeth from chattering.

"He oughta be locked up. It's not fair if you..." He changed his mind about what he was going to say. "It's not fair to you to get a bad start in life like that. My parents were," he shrugged, "not great people, but they didn't treat me mean. Not like that."

TJ's mother hadn't been mean. There had been birthday parties and family trips to the ocean. When TJ got a head cold, her mother had fixed hot rum totties. TJ had always started out the school year with a few new outfits. Her mother had family photographs framed and placed for show around the house. Maybe that was the problem; all that mothering had been for show, as if her mother had been playing house. Here's the mommy and here's the daddy and here's the little girl, everyone happy in their little house on the edge of town.

And all completely fake. The town was a dirty mess of angry white people, fighting for low-paying jobs while trying to keep themselves above the level of farm workers. The fields were toxic with pesticides and herbicides, and the heat was remorseless and sometimes fatal. Her mother's curtains had always been tightly closed against the burnt-up brown grass of the front yard and the hot radiation of the sun.

TJ had hated everything about her life in California. The sex with her stepdad was bad, but so was the rationed water, the stray dogs that died of heatstroke in the streets, and the underfunded school that didn't have enough desks or computers but did have armed guards in the hallways.

People like Jesus and Maria were treated like they were a different species. "Don't talk to them. Don't stand near them in a store," her mother had said a million times. "They only come in to shoplift." Her mother had been relatively nice about the farm workers compared to what other white people said—like the claims that they used drugs and trafficked young girls. No one called them "farm workers" or "Mexicans." Instead, there was a whole list of slang words for them just like there were words for black people or Asians or people who lived in San Francisco.

Though she'd been taught all of her life to fear the brown-skinned, black-haired people, as a kid she'd never thought of them as scary. It was their lives that frightened her. The poverty. The hard work. The blistering, baking, suffocating heat. They were trapped at the bottom of the social order, an object lesson that life could be a lot worse. The horror of their suffering had made her grateful for the safety of her family's house with its air conditioning, regular meals, and working class respectability.

Her mother had been proud of her step dad's job as foreman of a crew in a packing plant. They ate off matching china plates, had a dining room table, and even had a tree in the backyard. They went to church, and her mother had believed fervently that God was on their side against all those other people who went to other churches or didn't go to church at all.

TJ hadn't left home because of the sex. The sex had stopped when she got high school age and her stepdad lost interest. He switched to teasing her about her conquests with high school boys and started leering at the kids he saw at church. No, she left because of a fight over family rules. Entering high school had triggered something in TJ that made it impossible for her to do anything her mother asked. Clean up her room. No. Clean up after herself when she'd used the bathroom? No. Fuck off, Mom. Wash the dishes after dinner. Yeah, like that was going to happen. The last straw landed when her stepdad entered a fight on her mother's side. He said something about respect which made TJ explode into a tantrum of throwing things and breaking things.

"TJ?" Baylor whispered..

She jerked, startled, then pulled herself together with a handful of sleeping bag tucked under her chin. "What?"

"Are you okay?" He tried to stroke her, but she was hidden beneath the sleeping bag.

"Yeah, I'm okay." She was suddenly completely exhausted. "Let's go to sleep, alright?"

After a pause, he said, "Okay."

TJ rolled over on her side with her back to Baylor. She hugged herself tightly and focused her thoughts on the blackness of closed eyes. After awhile, the shivering stopped.

Chapter Fourteen
Another Morning After

TJ stayed curled into a little ball with her eyes squeezed shut. Baylor had rolled out from under the covers and was sitting quietly on the edge of the bed, probably watching her. She concentrated on breathing in slowly and then out slowly, in slowly and out slowly, aware that she was reenacting her last morning with Micheal but grimly determined to refuse Baylor any kind of greeting. She didn't want to meet his eyes or hear what he had to say, not while she was ignoring the traffic jam of her own thoughts and feelings. Breath in slowly, let the breath out slowly, she told herself. Go. Leave. Baylor, fucking get out of here. She felt a soft pressure on her shoulder. His hand. No, a soft smacking sound. He'd kissed her.

Her breath caught but she managed to keep her eyes closed. Slowly, she told herself. Breath out. Now slowly in.

The bed creaked and shifted. He was up. She tracked the sound of his steps down the hall into the living room. There she heard a mumble of greeting. He was talking to Buddy. Then the door opened and closed.

TJ stayed curled up. She didn't want to uncurl. She wanted to burrow deeper into the bed, deep into the mattress, to be lost in the darkness behind her eyelids. A thump and a sudden weight on the covers meant that Buddy had joined her. TJ wriggled one arm loose and reached down to touch Buddy's soft fur. A purr vibrated on the morning air.

"Come up here." TJ patted Buddy into motion and guided her up to the pillow. The purr settled into a deep thrum by her ear. Breathe slowly, she told herself, breathe with the purring. In and out and in and out.

After a while her breathing steadied and her muscles relaxed. She floated in a soft, warm, gray cloud over the green hillside of Warrentown, holding Buddy tightly against her chest. The misty air was the same gray color as the rooftops and the dead cedars in the forest above the town. TJ felt cool water on her cheek and tightened her grip on Buddy. If it started to rain, she would stop flying around and go back to the house.

But she couldn't go back because Buddy was loose in a wide green meadow under a perfect blue sky. Frowning, TJ looked around. Where was she? Outside her house in Warrentown? But she couldn't see any houses, not even her own squatter's shack.

"Hey, up here!" a male voice called. Expecting to see Baylor, TJ's shoulders tightened defensively. She scrambled to her feet and then, just as suddenly, sat back down. She was naked! Frantically she searched around with her hands, grabbing at items of clothing strewn in the grass. None of the clothes were familiar. She tried to find a blouse or T shirt, but the clothes were uncooperative, kept slipping from her hands or morphing into towels.

"Hey, don't worry," the male called to her. "You look good!"

TJ clasped a towel against her chest. The guy on the rock was naked too. He looked to be in his twenties and had spikey hair.

"Who are you?" TJ challenged.

"Me?" His mouth hung open and his eyes went blank. "Uh...you know, that's kind of a good question." He inhaled a long toke on his spliff and added thoughtfully, "I've been up here for a long time." Then he looked harder at TJ and said, "Hey, you aren't Valerie. You're the other one."

"Huh." Too flummoxed to respond, TJ just started blankly. The young guy's hands wove words in the air, words to the song that Baylor liked.

"What does that mean? What are you saying?" TJ called. Frustration gripped her. She wanted to dance over the grass of the flowery meadow but movement was impossible. In fact her body had disintegrated and morphed into a damp smelly blanket. She was embedded in a sweaty old mattress and there was no mountain, no music, and no one dancing.

She dragged herself out of bed to face a worn out, faded day. Carefully, moving slowly, she pulled on her jeans and T-shirt. Buddy greeted her as she stumbled into the kitchen. There, TJ leaned on the counter and fought off a dizzy spell. Her feet seemed to be a long way down near the floor, and her head was rolling around near the ceiling. Somehow she managed to fill Buddy's water and food bowls without falling on her face. Leaning on the counter, she watched her cat eat, but didn't want any breakfast for herself.

Rachel had been kind enough to give her a bag of cat food, but the only human food she had on hand to give away was peanut butter. TJ pushed herself away from the counter, stumbled out to her front steps, and sagged down into a heap to look out at the day.

The baby goat was playing with a chicken. Annoying a chicken, actually. They were joined by several more chickens who ganged up on the goat, clucking at him and stamping their feet. TJ watched the little drama distantly, not caring who won. The baby goat bounced off to find someone else to bother, and the chickens went back to pecking in the dirt and clucking their grievances to each other.

Maybe she should head down to the tavern and get some coffee. She was two blocks up and just around the corner on a side street, not a long walk and all down hill. TJ made the trip in her mind and imagined herself at the back door of the Tavern, hearing voices inside. Rachel and Jim sharing breakfast, sharing little glances and quick grins. And Baylor would be there.

TJ's mind stopped functioning. She couldn't imagine meeting Baylor down at the tavern over coffee and eggs. Most of her sexual experiences hadn't involved meeting up the next day. There had been lots of next days with Micheal but most had been a continuation of low level irritation. Like a marriage, TJ thought bleakly.

The sex with Baylor hadn't amounted to much, but the after-sex had been different in a way that left her feeling like an open wound. TJ remembered his hand gently brushing her hair from her face, and her arms and legs contracted into the fetal position. No, she couldn't go down to the tavern. She didn't know what she was going to do with herself all day, but she definitely wasn't going to go looking for Baylor.

Chapter Fifteen
Baylor's Mom

Baylor set the box down on the floor with a thunk. The thin whine of his mother's voice reached him from the back room of Valerie's shabby little house. "Where's my TV?" she called. She owned a huge flat screen that wouldn't fit into her new bedroom. All she watched was the worst junk on the air: reality shows strident with fake drama, the fake TV news station that was all screeching outrage all the time, and fake educational shows about Sasquatch or serial killers.

He'd *told* her that the TV wasn't making the trip. He was going to sell it to one of her neighbors in the trailer court. She was getting moved with a minimum of her stuff.

Valerie said, "I can make some tea. And I can make some sandwiches."

Baylor wiped the sweat off his forehead. He was only twenty-three but he felt older, which was probably self-pity or maybe a hangover. Either way, he was feeling worn out. He stayed up all night robbing a store, then got drunk a couple nights later, and then stayed up late with TJ. TJ.! Baylor's thoughts crashed into a car wreck. He didn't know what to think about his night of sex and confidences. He'd replayed their conversation over and over in his head, and every time it came out differently. Sometimes he saw himself as a lousy fuck who had come way too fast, sometimes as the hero who had received the blessing of confidences from the heroine, sometimes...what? He didn't do one night stands. At least, not often. He didn't like the stale, sour feeling of sex followed by a quick good by. He shouldn't have gone to bed with TJ. They hardly knew each other.

But she'd told him about the sex abuse, which he was pretty sure she didn't talk about to just anyone. So she must like him. Right?

"Baylor?" Valerie was hovering in front of him, blinking her weak eyes.

"Oh, yeah, thanks. A sandwich would be great. If it's not too much trouble."

"No trouble." Valerie smile was full of worry. Baylor knew that it *was* trouble to make a sandwich. Everything about living in Warrentown was a lot of trouble. Taking care of his mom was going to be a lot of trouble. Baylor was coming up on the two year anniversary of his arrival in Warrentown and, so far, he'd learned how to run a lap top off a car battery, how to build an outhouse, and how to rob a big box store. He was also learning how to live on very little money. Now he needed to learn how to take care of an old lady, and that scared him more than robbery.

"I can help in a minute," he said.

"No, no." Valerie's hands fluttered her rejection of his offer. "You just keep helping Gale, and I'll get a snack for all of us."

"Baaayyloorr," his mother called. "Where are you?"

I can do this, he told himself. "Just a minute, Mom."

Baylor's mother Gale had flooded the bedroom with her presence; she was an immense, sprawling shape that nearly buried her recliner. One fat red arm slopped over on the end table by the bed, threatening the stability of the Coleman lamp, while the other hung like a ham over the armrest. Her legs, wrapped in white bandages, lay inertly on the foot rest, oozing lymph and thin trickles of pale blood. Her round face bobbed like rubber ball floating on the swell of her belly and chest.

Her recliner was jammed into one corner of the room next to the windows. Along the wall was her bed, queen-sized in a kid-sized bedroom, covered with layers of blankets in discordant colors. The closet was so crammed with clothes and boxes that the door wouldn't close. Other belongings had been shoved under the bed.

Baylor's mother had brought smells into her new home. Her perfume—which to Baylor was reminiscent of bug spray—the mothballs she'd packed with her clothes, and the sickening reek of her lymph-saturated bandages, combined into a stink that gave Baylor claustrophobia.

Baylor had swept the floor and scrubbed the one window in preparation for his mother. He'd put up colorful pictures cut out of a calendar to cover the places where the wall paper was stained with dampness and had washed the ancient curtains. All of his efforts to make the room pleasant had disappeared, negated by the presence of his mother.

"Hey, Mom," Baylor said, "Val's making us some lunch. You should come out and join us."

"I ain't going nowhere." She slapped the end table to register her disgust, and a box of Kleenex fell on the floor. Baylor stooped and picked it up. Their eyes met briefly and he saw her tears.

"Mom. Really. This will work out. Val's really nice."

"I'm sure she is." Gale wiped her face on a Kleenex and looked around for a wastepaper basket. Baylor took the Kleenex from her and put it in his pocket. "I'm too tired to get out of this chair," she said. "It took all I had to get up them steps."

Getting his mother out of her house trailer, into the truck Baylor had borrowed, out of the truck again, and up the stairs to Val's house had just about wiped Baylor out, partly because of the sheer strength needed—his mom was three hundred and fifty pounds, easily—but also the emotions had been a burden. She had bitched her way out of her house, and had screamed with rage and embarrassment while being hoisted into the truck by Baylor and Jim. The whole drive out to Warrentown had been a nonstop stream of complaints, recriminations, and demands. The stairs up to Val's porch had been the last straw; Gale started crying and didn't stop until they—Baylor, Jim, and Valerie—finally dumped her into her recliner.

Then Jim left and the full enormity of the what he had burdened himself with fell on Baylor's shoulders—an d his work wasn't done. Now that he had moved her, he needed to care for her.

"Mom," he said, "I know it isn't perfect, but... Please try to get used to being here." He hadn't dumped her in a nursing home. They couldn't afford a good one, and the local one in Rainier was a crowded, understaffed, dirty deathtrap. She should be grateful to be here, Baylor thought.

Gale glared. Baylor leaned against the door frame and waited. Then Gale sighed and turned her face away. "I'm going to take a nap." Her voice sharpened and she added, "And I want my TV."

Baylor shoved himself into motion. She wasn't going to get the TV. No one in Warrentown had a TV. She was going to have to live without it just like she was going to have to live without junk food. She'd been a book reader back when he was a kid, so his plan was to provide her with reading materials. Baylor returned to the living room where Val was standing holding a tray of sandwiches.

"Is Gale hungry?" she asked. If I don't care for my mom, Baylor realized, Val will. That meant he'd have to look after both of them.

Chapter Sixteen
Strange Days

TJ wasn't looking for Baylor, but she was imaging him looking for her. He was an eye and a voice at the edge of her mind, watching and commenting. She felt his eye monitoring her as she huddled on her front porch, squinting at the blue sky of a new day, and she heard him wondering what she would do with her time. His eye judged her because she wasn't doing anything.

TJ got up, hesitated, then drifted down the steps. She was greeted by humid air packed with the sun-warmed smells of grass, goat poop, and roses. Baylor's eye judged her as she dithered uncertainly and approved when she turned her attention to her yard.

The grass was yellow and grew in unruly tufts. Here and there flowering weeds were getting ready to spread seeds in a silent war with the grass. Straggly bushes flanked her front steps and a broken trellis tilted against the drain pipe at the corner of her house. A rose bush! Twisted and straggly, a rambling rose was struggling to stay alive.

TJ waded through the grass and weeds to the rose. It had managed to produce one small pink flower. She touched the flower gently. Insects had been nibbling on the dehydrated petals. The leaves, too, were dry. In fact, whole plant looked tired and stressed.

TJ knelt down, grabbed a handful of grass from near the base of the rose vine and pulled. With a poof of dust, the roots popped out of the dry ground. She dug her fingers into the dirt and grabbed another handful of grass. A grunt from behind startled her. She turned and found herself face to face with the baby goat.

"I'm trying to weed here," she told it. "Maybe you could help. Do something useful." The goat blinked at her, then kissed her nose. TJ sat back abruptly, wiped her face on her sleeve, and almost laughed. "I meant eat some grass or something."

The goat bounced back toward the road and disrupted a small gathering of hens.

"Okay, don't help." She yanked another handful of grass out of the ground. A minute or two later, her hands were sore from the stiff stems and her arms were coated with dirt. TJ sat back on her heels. Without a trowel, she really wasn't going to make much headway. Besides, what the rose really needed was water. "Later," TJ promised. Meanwhile, since she couldn't pull weeds, she stood up and stomped on them instead. After marching back and forth in front of the rose several times, she succeeded in giving it some living space, but at a cost. Her face, arms, and legs were covered with sweat and dust, and her hand was bleeding again.

"I'll get you some water," TJ said. She noticed that the goat and the chickens had taken their argument down the street and were gathered at the corner by Val's house. She could see no humans around anywhere. She couldn't hear any voices either. TJ stumped wearily up the steps into the house. Buddy was up on the kitchen counter and greeted her with a purr.

"Hey, Bud." She ran her fingers down Buddy's back, thinking that cats were lucky because they always seemed clean. "I can't lick myself off." She felt grimy. Her chin was sticking to her neck and her hair was stuck to her cheek. Her armpits felt like they were slick with mud. She felt Baylor's eye noting her dirty appearance.

A bath meant water. Her jugs were nearly empty. If she watered the rose, she would have very little left for herself. TJ found herself dithering again. Water the rose or not? It seemed like a hugely important decision, even though she didn't know why. Maybe she could get more water, enough for the rose and herself. TJ made the mental trip down to the river in front of the Raven Tavern where Jim, Rachel, and Baylor were probably all hanging out. Nope. Not going there.

The rose was going to have to take care of itself a little longer. She dug through her backpack and found her towel and washcloth. Neither was very clean but that didn't matter. Using the last of her water to wash her face, the back of her neck, and her armpits, TJ felt a little better. She felt Baylor's eye on her again, and he was wondering what she would do next.

"I don't *know*," TJ said defiantly.

With no more water, she couldn't clean her house or wash any clothes. She didn't want to go out and weed any more because it was too hot and she didn't have the right tools. Going down to the Tavern, meet other people? No.

She went back to bed. She imagined Baylor watching her and the thought made her curl up in the fetal position with her eyes squeezed shut.

An hour or so later, she'd lost all sleepiness. Bored and a little lonely, she got up and drifted out to her front porch. Yeah, she told the imaginary Baylor, I'm going in a circles. Bed to porch to yard to bed and now to porch again. So far living in Warrentown was a bust. She didn't have any water, didn't have any food, and was going to be out of provisions for her cat pretty soon. A thought came into her mind: I need a little bump. I'd feel better.

"No!" TJ said, startling Buddy.

"No," she repeated more calmly.

Just a little bump, said her mind. She could go back to the camp and get some from Micheal. She didn't have any money but she had other ways to pay if he was in the mood.

TJ's legs retracted of their own accord and her shoulders hunched until she was seated almost in the fetal position again. How could she get to the camp? Hitchhike? There was no traffic in or out of Warrentown. With some relief, she realized that going back to the camp was out of the question. Too far to walk and she'd have to ask someone for a ride. And she wasn't going to do that.

So what was she going to do? Baylor's eye reappeared, watching her sit there, dirty and hot, bored and thinking about meth. TJ jumped to her feet. Buddy jumped to her feet, too, and scampered down the steps.

"No, you stay here," TJ said. She wasn't going to think about meth. She was going to get cleaned up, really cleaned up, from her hair down to her toes. TJ went back inside and rounded up an armful of the plastic water jugs. She carried the jugs out to the wheelbarrow, tossed them in, and then stopped to think. It had taken her and Baylor working together to push all the filled jugs up the hill, which meant it would be a hell of a job for her to do by herself. TJ took two jugs off the pile, leaving four, and grabbed the handles of the wheelbarrow. She set off for the river, but instead of turning toward Val's house to go downhill by the Tavern, she went the opposite direction on a different route. Buddy followed her to the corner and sat, watching her.

"I'll be back," TJ promised. The river seemed a long ways off, way down at the bottom of the hill. Coming back up was going to be hard, but the only alternative was to go back to the house and sit there, all dirty. TJ shoved the wheelbarrow around the corner. She had to struggle to hang onto the handles as it dragged her down the steep, decaying side street to the main road. At the bottom of the hill, she looked both ways, not for traffic but for people. No one was hanging out in front of the Raven Tavern. She was both relieved and disappointed that the street was empty. TJ shoved the wheelbarrow into motion and crossed the street.

There was no pathway through the rocky embankment and no convenient rock to perch on at the water's edge. TJ scrambled from rock to rock down to the river, balancing precariously while holding her water jugs. At the bottom of the embankment, she parked her butt on the pointed edge of a rock. In that uncomfortable position, she held a jug under water. It took both hands pushing to keep the jug submerged. The water made heavy gulping noises as she was drowning the jug.

TJ heaved the filled jug onto the rocks by her side. Careful not to replay her mishap at the creek, she settled the jug firmly between two rocks. She screwed the cap on and grabbed the next jug. Once she had the four jugs filled, she toted them back to the wheelbarrow one at a time. The whole operation was difficult and stressful, and her hand started bleeding again.

Difficult, stressful, but somehow satisfying. Now, she thought. Uphill.

She set off with determination, but it didn't take long for her to realize that she wasn't strong enough to push the wheelbarrow uphill, even with the reduced load of just four jugs. She stopped and turned the wheelbarrow around. Then she put herself between the shafts like a mule and started the long trudge up. She could see her corner, two blocks away uphill. The distance seemed immense, but each step took her nearer. TJ tromped along steadily and was just settling into her stride when the wheel dropped into a pot hole, yanked her backwards, and she lost control of the wheelbarrow.

"Oh *fuck*." The falling wheelbarrow had twisted her arm, making her elbow hurt. It lay on its side, its wheel spinning pathetically, looking like a dying animal. Her jugs had spilled out, and one had rolled down hill. Impeded by its handle, it hadn't gone far, but any steps downhill were steps she'd have to take back uphill again.

"Oh *fuck*. God*damn* it!" TJ yanked the wheelbarrow upright and jerked it uphill past the pothole. An angry glance at the jugs showed that the caps had stayed on and no water was spilled. TJ was furious anyway. She stomped downhill to the errant jug that had rolled the farthest. Grabbing it, she had a sudden memory of the plastic jug that had fallen into the stream just before she fell, too, and skinned her palm. The memory felt old, like something that had happened in a different lifetime. She had abandoned that jug because she'd been in a hurry to meet up with Jim.

She didn't have any plan to meet up now with anyone. She was avoiding other people.

TJ stood still, her hand extended down to the jug. None of this would be happening if Baylor had come by to help me, she thought. Out loud she muttered, "Fuck the jugs." She could just dump everything in the street. Just leave it all and go back to that funky no good house and... She didn't know what she would do back at the house. Cry? Go to bed?

TJ bent down slowly and grabbed the jug by its handle. She hoisted it up and trudged uphill to the wheelbarrow. The distance was only ten feet or so but felt longer. She set the jug down in the wheelbarrow carefully so as to keep it balanced. "Don't you *dare* fall over again," she snarled.

"Hello? You need help?" Startled, TJ turned around. She saw a short, stocky man standing the front of his house, holding a shovel. Two small black-haired children stood beside him quietly. Three pairs of warm brown eyes observed her.

TJ felt a touch of fear, an automatic response, but the fear quickly fled, leaving her feeling embarrassed. She gestured at the pothole. "I had an accident. Sort of."

Jesus said something that sounded like "help you" but she wasn't sure because his gravelly voice was heavily accented. He handed the shovel to the little boy and started across his yard toward TJ, grinning shyly as he approached.

"Water?" he asked.

"Yeah, I'm trying to get some water home." She shifted nervously from one foot to the other.

He picked up two jugs as easily as if they were full of air and set them in the wheelbarrow.

"This road," he told her, "bad." He settled the last jug in. Then, before TJ could thank him, he grabbed the handles of the wheelbarrow and started striding uphill.

She jumped to follow, saying, "I can help."

A Mountain in the Air

Jesus just smiled and kept marching along, his short legs pumping like a machine.

TJ had to huff and puff to keep up with him.

She said, "Just to the corner's good. I can take the rest of the way."

He nodded, smiling, and kept powering on uphill.

At the corner, Buddy spotted them and minced in their direction, tail waving. Jesus dropped the arms of the wheelbarrow and parked it by the curb. He pointed. "You cat?"

"Yes. Her name's Buddy."

"Good cat." He smiled hard at her as if his smile could make up for his lack of words.

TJ took a deep breath and said, her shoulders hunched awkwardly, "Thank you. A lot." She smiled, too, but shyly. "I really mean it. Thank you."

"No problem." Nodding and smiling, Jesus, strode off downhill.

By the time she'd lugged the water jugs into her house, she was ready to go to bed again. Instead, she plugged the kitchen sink with her wash cloth and filled it with river water. From the bag of supplies Rachel had given her, she found soap and shampoo. Then she pulled her clothes off and, using her towel for a washcloth, she scrubbed her skin from scalp to toes, scrubbed until her skin was red. Finished with her skin, she unplugged the sink and let the water drain out. Then she hauled a jug up on the counter, stuck her head in the sink and dosed her hair with cold river water.

"Owww oh boy, oh boy!"

It felt good, savagely good. TJ dumped shampoo on her head and scrubbed and scratched with her fingernails until her scalp was burning. Then she wrung her hair out and poured water on her head over and over until the sink was full of foam and her hair was slick and clean.

Her towel was too wet and too dirty to use for drying herself off, and her clothes were too dirty to put on her precious clean skin. TJ revolved slowly in the kitchen and gloried in the feel of cool air prickling her body. Then she wadded up the towel, threw it on the floor, and told Buddy, "Now I can go to sleep!"

She lay on top of her sleeping bag, hoping to have another dream about the dancing guy with the weird hair. This time, since she felt clean, maybe she'd be able to dance with him. TJ tried to bring the dream back to her mind by picturing the weird guy. Skinny dude, she remembered. Pasty white skin. Not an outdoorsy guy, but he'd looked pretty happy on the mountain. Mt. Rainier, probably. She'd never seen the mountain since it was far away over on the other side of the Seattle/Olympia metro complex. She'd never seen the cities either. All she really knew about Washington was the southwest corner and that was mostly dead trees. Climate change had killed off the cedars. Where had she learned that? Probably her brother. There were plenty of other trees, but the dead trees everywhere really stuck out. Depressing.

At least it wasn't as godawful hot as California in the summer. Washington rained. A lot. But now she had a house so she'd be all cozy and dry during the winter rains. A tentative thought cautiously crept into her mind; maybe she was going to like the weird little village of strange people. TJ focused on the thought, poked it, looked it over from every angle, and checked under and behind it for possible dangers.

She was a little disappointed that Jim wasn't paying any attention to her. Not that she was going to compete with Rachel. She'd just thought that maybe...but he hadn't bothered to check in on her. Just dropped her off and that was that. Not like Rachel, who had been helpful with cat food and shampoo. And the cleaning stuff! She needed to get that stuff back to Valerie.

What about the other people of Warrentown? She wasn't sure about Charlie with his lectures on whatever. And the family of illegals. Her mother would just shit to know she'd been to a party with them as if they were neighbors. And she'd actually met one of them and talked with him a little. Well, they *were* neighbors! And it was obvious that everyone liked them. She wondered how often the townsfolk got together and partied at the tavern.

And Baylor. TJ's heart stopped. She pictured herself in bed with him, telling him about her stepdad, and him wanting to get on his silver steed and rush off like a knight in armor. That was sweet. But after that, nothing. He'd disappeared. All day he'd been on her mind but he hadn't so much as dropped by for one minute.

Fuck him. He didn't count. TJ squeezed her eyes shut and pressed her palms against her face. All day she'd imagined him watching her, and he probably hadn't been thinking about her at all.

She'd spent the day with animals. Buddy, always by her side, the annoying baby goat, the little gang of chickens always gossiping and bickering. TJ pictured herself out in the yard the afternoon sun, kneeling by the rose bush. She watched her hands grabbing up dry yellow grass and pulling. She remembered how the baby goat had shoved his intense little face over her shoulder as if he was asking her what she was doing. The chickens had wanted to know, too. I'm going to make this rose grow, she told herself. So far, the goat and the chickens were her best friends in the weird little town besides Buddy. Buddy was happy because she'd never had a home before. She lay on the bed, stretched out along side TJ's leg. Her purr was a deep comforting thrum, and her fur was soft as a warm breeze. "Oh, Buddy," TJ whispered.

Then she remembered her promise to the rose. "I never watered it. I should have given it some water."

Chapter Seventeen
Coyote Run

"I need to go for a run," Jimmy said. He'd been human too long and felt stiff and tired.

Rachel sighed. "I need to fly." Her raven nature needed to cut loose every now and then. Sometimes she flew while Jim ran, raven and coyote off in the woods together, but most of the time one or the other had to keep an eye on things in Warrentown.

That evening Jim and Rachel were behind the bar, watching Vulture and his friends get drunk. Everyone else had gone home earlier. Charlie was gone because his solar generator allowed him access to electric light in his house which he was using to revive his interest in painting with watercolors. His cats participated by walking on his paintings and trying to drink from the water he used to rinse his brushes. Crazy Mary had tried to get home but had only gotten as far as the foot of the hill that led up toward TJ's house. She was propped up against the wall of the deduct corner grocery store where she had a good view of the moon as long as she could keep her eyes open. Rachel knew she was out there, and knew the night was warm and she would be okay. Stiff in the morning from sleeping on cement, but okay. Jesus and his family had been among the first to leave. They rarely stayed more than a few minutes past dinner because the kids needed to be taken home, bathed, and put to bed. Besides, Maria had to make her nightly check on the chickens, and Jesus liked to go out to the garden and commune with the cabbages. Once everyone was settled and safe, he and Maria had a few quiet drinks at home.

Rachel wasn't sure what TJ was up to. She was new enough to be a bit of an unknown quantity. Mainly she seemed to be keeping herself to herself.

"You need to check on her," Rachel commented.

Jimmy grimaced. "I don't think she has much longer."

"Huh? Oh, I meant check on *TJ*. Not Valerie. But you're right."

"Yeah, well..." Jimmy shrugged. TJ hadn't established herself as either an asset or a liability, but Valerie was a friend that would be missed badly by everyone who knew her.

Rachel added, "We need to help her get ready."

"Yeah." He finished his beer and set the mug down with a thump. "I need to get out in the woods. And I'll check on TJ."

He kissed Rachel on top of her head. "Don't worry about Val. See ya in a bit."

"Go for it. I'll go out when you get back. I like flying in the dark."

Jim headed for the back door of the Tavern. Once outside, he quickly stripped off his clothes and dropped everything into the back of his pick up truck. The air was sweet and cool, the sky darkening to lavender. Later on, he knew, the moon was going to be full and spectacular. He was going to do some howling that night.

Valerie and Gale were sleeping, both restless with dreams. Gale's nighttime was a tumble of incongruities without narrative: wads of bandage soaked with pus, a dead cat, the air in her bedroom pulsing with heat, a disjointed image of Valerie as a skeleton, a sense that Baylor was outside when he ought to be in with her. She rolled her head back and forth in her sleep, restless and angry. She didn't try to escape her dreams. She wallowed in them.

Valerie was dreaming of a mountain floating in the air over Seattle. White glaciers that shaded into green-blue forest and then faded into the robin's egg blue of the hazy sky over the city. Valerie was up on a flower meadow, knee deep in moist green grass, surrounded by cool crisp air and birdsong. She was holding her hands out as if about to dance.

"Valerie?" a voice called. His face open with friendliness, Pete was on a boulder. "You came back! Come on up."

Valerie's arms drooped. Shyly, she wrapped her arms around herself, very aware that she was wearing an ugly old bathrobe. Thank goodness she wasn't just in her nightie. Too humiliating to be a scrawny old woman, but at least she could hide her skinny legs and varicose veins.

"Hey! Come on up. The view's great from here!" Pete bounced on his toes like a little kid.

Hesitantly, Valerie stepped into the grass. Her feet were bare and the ground was rough with twigs and cold with dew and damp dirt. She trod carefully, partly to protect her feet but mostly to avoid the flowers. Flowers bloomed everywhere in the simple, direct colors of a Disney movie. So many! Her arms lifted and, without meaning to, without thought, she began to dance. Tentatively, careful of her old bones, she swayed over the grass, just high enough so that her toes trailed harmlessly through the blossoms.

"That's the way!" the young man called. He waved his arms and swayed his body, though more rigorously than Valerie.

I'm dancing, Valerie thought, and immediately her body grew heavy. No! She told herself, Dance! She tried a slow twirl, holding her hands on her thighs to keep her bathrobe from fanning out. Laughing, the young man pirouetted, impossibly nimble on his boulder.

Valerie did a series of careful spins. Is this what it feels like to be happy? she wondered. But she could feel a heaviness dragging her downward. Val sank into the meadow, her feet smashing the grass.

"Hey, don't go!" the young man called to her. "I want to ask you something."

Val whispered, "I want to stay." She took one last look around the flowery meadow before waking up.

"I want to go back," Val said to her dark bedroom.

It felt good to lope freely with no sense of going anywhere in particular, just moving for the sake of moving, sliding though the cool air of night like a fish though water. The road was lit by moonlight, bright but diffuse, a glow that saturated the air with silver mixed with darkness to create a pewter glow. The road shone with reflected light while the forest was dense with black shadows. The night sky was blue black over the trees but pearly near the moon. No stars, but the moonlight marbled the clouds with shades of gray and dull silver. Between the banks of black forest, the road was like a river and he was a swimmer in the moonlight.

Effortlessly, he loped onward. His muscles felt long and limber and he enjoyed the deep breaths that fueled his movement. He had no sense of getting any place and it was possible that he wasn't. Sometimes the road led out to the highway and on to Rainier, and sometimes it turned on itself and lead back to Warrentown. Sometimes the road was long, stretching out for hours, and other times it contracted, making travel quick and easy. That night, he knew he could run as long as he wanted to run and still have road ahead of him..

A shift in the darkness told him that the trees had changed back to the old growth before timber companies and climate change. The air dampened and thickened. He could smell the sharp tang of the cedars. A hoot-hoot-hoot far off marked the territory of a spotted owl. Jim was grateful for the road; he knew that the old forest had been no place for a coyote—too dense, too dark. No, it has home to those who could fly or climb. Catch a mouse for your children, he thought to the owl.

Jim wasn't running to hunt. He had to run sometimes because, if he didn't, he got cranky and impatient. Earlier that day he'd snapped at Charlie for being so damn morose in a poetic way—quoting someone about how the world would end, fire or ice being the choices. Jim knew the world was fucked and, for the most part, he thought humans were getting what they deserved. They were certainly getting what they had brought on themselves. No, he saved his sympathy was for animals and plants.

However, because he was a spirit and had lived for a long, long time, he chose to not dwell on the suffering. He tried to find something each day to live for. The alternative, in his view, was to just die already and get it over with without whining. Getting morose over a beer and quoting cynical depressing poetry was not how he chose to cope. He didn't take his existence for granted. Humans, so fragile and transitory, pissed away their lives on pointless dramas, competition for things of no value, or inflicted suffering on each other. He really didn't understand why they repeated destructive behaviors even while killing themselves. Maybe humans didn't live long enough to learn from experience. Each generation made the same mistakes.

He sometimes felt an intense nostalgia for the natural world that had been trampled and torn to shreds by human activity. What he missed most was the sense of time, the sense that animals would be born, feed, procreate, and die in long cycles of time into the future. He, like many humans, avoided thinking about the future since he didn't believe that life was going to get better. People, he knew, had immense power, but they often didn't use the power for good. Not for themselves and not for any living things. Most of them didn't even realize what they had destroyed except in terms of how it affected them. They didn't notice the animals that starved or drowned or died of thirst or were no longer able to raise babies. They only noticed when humans suffered—and even then most didn't care unless the suffering was their own. All he and Rachel could do was take care of their little corner of the world.

He wasn't sure why Rachel had wanted Charlie for their community. Mostly she wanted help. Was Charlie helpful? Well, yes he was. He'd do anything you asked him to do, including helping to rob stores. He contributed. Jimmy wondered how well TJ was going to fit in and thoughts of her led to thoughts of Valerie. Valerie was their cornerstone. She was their beating heart. What were they going to do without her?

Jim realized that he had started thinking and the old forest had vanished. He was back to the cool night air and the luminous road. He stopped, panting a bit.

Yes, Charlie was helpful. Was TJ going to work out? Since he was responsible for her presence in the town, he'd be the one to kick her out if she became a liability. And no matter how much people annoyed him, he didn't really like being unkind to them.

He'd better check up on her. Realizing that his run was over, Jim turned back and trotted down the road to the village.

Chapter Eighteen
The Night is Full of Wonder

She lay awake in her sleeping bag for a while but her heart was racing, so she got up and groped around in her backpack for some clothes. She must've slept the whole evening away because now it was dark, so dark that she had to chose her clothes by feel. Once she'd pulled on some jeans and a T-shirt, she got up and groped her way though the darkness into her living room. Buddy, rousted out of bed by her departure, followed, purring happily. It was fine with Buddy to be up in the dark.

TJ peered out her kitchen window at the nighttime sky. "Let's check out the night," she said to Buddy. After all, there was nothing to do in her living room. She had no light, no Internet access, and she'd already found out that her phone couldn't pick up a signal. "Come on." She led Buddy to the front door and they stood together and looked out into the night.

The moon was fantastic. An immense, flat, silvery disc, gleaming with white gold and touched with faint swirls of blue, it loomed over the distant forest. The dark sky was ultramarine blue and lit with patterns of moonlight on the clouds. The little town was shrouded in black shadows.

TJ stared, transfixed. "Buddy, look at that," she whispered. It's that special moon, TJ thought, when the moon got extra close to the earth and looked bigger than usual. She tried to remember what the special moon was called. Tiger moon? Blue moon? The moon needed a beautiful name because she'd never seen anything like it in her life.

"I'm gonna call it a..." she rummaged around in her mind for the right word, but none came close. "I can't think of what to call it. Maybe a dreaming moon?" She did feel like she was dreaming. The soft damp air was full of potential, lit with a pearly moonlight that hinted impossible possibilities. TJ rose up on her toes as if she was about to fly, then settled. Hesitating, her hand on the door jam, and she peered out into the moonlight.

Off in the distance, the forest was a woolly black darkness, mysterious and forbidding, but her street, what she could see of it from her porch, was full of invitation. The moonlight had given the pavement a soft pewter glow. Yellow brick road, TJ thought. Could she venture out? She shoved her bare feet into her sneakers and stepped carefully down her front steps, holding the railing and feeling slightly off balance because the moonlight and darkness had knocked her depth perception off kilter. At the bottom of the steps she stopped and looked up and down the street. She wasn't afraid, exactly, but her heart was a jumping jack and she could feel a tremble in her fingers.

But there was nothing scary about her street. The weird glow of moonlight lit the asphalt of the street and made the gray weathered paint of her cottage look luminous. Unable to see much detail, TJ became very aware of smells. The scent of dirt mixed with a trace of sweetness tickled her nose. Her rose! She needed to water it! Maybe if she watered it more, it would flower more and she could come out at night and inhale its fragrance.

TJ turned so quickly that she nearly tripped on Buddy. "Going to water the rose," she explained. Enough moonlight shone through the kitchen window to light her way back to the jugs lined up on the counter. She pushed the empties aside and hefted the one jug that still contained some water.

She couldn't give the rose all of the water because Buddy would need some in the morning. "I used too much on me," she said, with regret. Her hair was light, soft, and clean and felt good on her cheeks, but she should have saved some water back for Buddy and the rose.

"I'll give the rose half," she told Buddy. Buddy was underfoot again, purring.

TJ paused on the porch to take in the sweetness of the night air. Something else smelled good. She breathed deeply, almost tasting the heavy, thick, moist scent. Compost? Maybe. Jesus's garden was just across the street. She was probably smelling his vegetable crop.

The darkness was very quiet, but not silent. Faintly she could hear the sound of the chickens gossiping and complaining. Their nighttime voices were a low chuckle, soft and sleepy. No wonder the chickens and the goat were always around; her house was across the street from the greenhouse and one down from Valerie's backyard.

A Mountain in the Air

The darkness allowed her to look around without feeling watched or evaluated. She padded quietly across her lawn to the rose. A soft brush of fur against her leg told her that Buddy had joined her. TJ tipped the jug and let the water slide down into the dirt at the base of the rose vine. The water disappeared into the dry soil.

"Still thirsty? I'll get you more tomorrow." Shoving the wheelbarrow uphill was going to be a daily task. She'd get stronger over time. TJ set the jug down on the grass.

Buddy said, "Muuroow?"

"I don't know," TJ answered. "Let's walk around a little."

The night was full of odd angles and disconcerting tilts. It was hard to tell in the dark which way was vertical, especially since the hillside disappeared upwards to one side of the road and downwards on the other. She couldn't see the houses or trees nearby well enough to use them for orientation, even though the moonlight allowed her to see for miles out over the forest across the river.

TJ drifted out to the middle of the street. The moon had grown larger, filling the western sky with gleams of silver, making the undersides of the clouds glow. On impulse, TJ leaned her head back, held out her arms, and slowly did a spin like a slow motion dancer. Grinning at Buddy, she made a series of gentle swoops from one side to the other, letting her hair swing. I wish I could fly, she thought. It would be wonderful to fly. But, unable to fly, she settled for making circles, round and round until she nearly tripped over the curb.

"Ooof. Almost fell," she said to Buddy.

Buddy was staring fixedly down the street. The rigidity of her posture was a warning. TJ followed Buddy's gaze and saw a coyote standing silently at the corner where her street joined the road downhill. The coyote had been watching her dance. A big coyote. Almost as big as a German Shepard, but lean with rough fur and a long pointed face. Even from thirty feet away, TJ could see that it's eyes were yellow. She stared, stabbed by fear.

"Come here." She grabbed the cat up. Clutching Buddy against her chest, TJ hollered at the coyote, "Go away."

It didn't move. TJ began a slow sideways shuffle toward her house. Buddy squirmed in her arms and TJ whispered, "Hold still."

"You aren't getting a cat to eat," she yelled defiantly at the coyote. Thinking of the chickens and the baby goat, she added, "You go away.

Don't eat anyone here." Her voice sounded weak and quavery. She cleared her throat and tried for some volume. "I mean it! GO away!"

The coyote turned and strolled downhill out of sight behind Valerie's house. TJ, still hugging Buddy, kept her eyes fixed on the empty intersection. When she was sure the coyote was gone, she turned, hurried up the steps, and dropped Buddy inside her house. "You stay right there," she said. She closed the door on Buddy's meows of protest.

Then she ran down to the intersection and stopped. She looked down the hill. The street fell before her, silvery in the moonlight, the cottages on either side obscured by shadows. The brick wall of the Raven Tavern loomed solidly black except for the yellow light in one upstairs window. TJ wondered who was up. Rachel, maybe? Or Jimmy? Should she go down there and tell them about the coyote?

TJ dithered at the intersection. Even though the tavern was only two blocks downhill, the distance was beyond what she could imagine walking in the darkness. She looked back over her shoulder at her street. Her cottage windows were completely black. No warm yellow light in the window for her, though her cat was waiting for her in the dark. Downhill, the moonlight was glittering on the river. She wondered what it would be like to sit on the back and dip her toes in the water. Maybe go swimming? That would be awesome, swimming under the beautiful moon! She hadn't been swimming anywhere in forever. The coyote was probably gone, she told herself.

Just to be sure, TJ peered down the hill, looking for the coyote. There was nothing on the street except moonlight. The shadows around Charlie's yard seemed empty and harmless. Across the street, the alley behind the tavern was impenetrably dark. Maybe the coyote was hunting mice or rats back there, TJ thought.

So what should she do? Go down to see the river at night? Go home? She stood at the intersection, fidgeting from one foot the other. And then something moved in the alley behind the Raven Tavern. TJ's insides froze. The coyote! No, the figure was too tall. A spark of light floated in the air. A man stepped out into the moonlight.

Chapter Nineteen
Coyote Moon

Jim watched TJ dancing in the moonlight. She was holding her arms out like wings, her head tilted to one side, curving her body into slow pirouettes. At first he thought she was flying low to the ground with her toes just inches above the pavement. Then he saw her stumble a bit when her foot hit the curb. She landed near her cat.

The cat was staring down the street at him. He saw TJ follow the cat's stare until her eyes locked with his. Then she grabbed up her cat and shouted, "Go away!'

Oh, of course. She was seeing a coyote.

"Don't eat anyone here! I mean it!"

Jim trotted off down the street. Interesting, he thought. She was out dancing in the moonlight. Good for her. When he arrived at his truck, parked behind the Tavern, he took one last look at the moon with his coyote eyes. He tensed and relaxed his shoulders, straightened up on his legs, and shook his fur into hair. He grabbed his clothes and boots out of the back of the pick up and dropped everything on the ground. Briskly, he got dressed. The night was warm, so he left his socks in his boots and padded barefoot out to the street. Up at the top of the hill he could just make out TJ's shape in the moonlight. She looked small and fragile and she was dithering, taking a few steps out into the intersection and then retreating. He lit a cigarette and waited. He watched her freeze, stare, then begin the walk down the hill slowly, cautiously. When she got within in haling distance, he called out softly, "Hey TJ."

"Hey Jim," she said ducking her head shyly. "Insomnia?"

"I like being out at night."

"I couldn't sleep."

"It's the moon," he said.

"Yeah. It's amazing." She took in a deep breath and babbled nervously, "Amazing. I've never seen the moon look like that. What do they call a moon like that?"

Jim shrugged. "I don't know." He paused, examining her thin, hunched figure. "You okay, TJ? Haven't seen you down here getting anything to eat."

"I'm okay." Quickly she changed the subject. "I saw a coyote. Big one. Right up there." She pointed back uphill. "I'm afraid that it might get the baby goat or the chickens."

Jim shook his head. "Don't worry about that."

TJ tilted her head and challenged him. "Why not?"

Jim dropped his hand away from his face. He knew his eyes were still brightly lit and yellow with his coyote nature. Looking straight into her face, he gave her the full beam of his strange eyes and said, "The animals won't be bothered."

She swallowed but didn't speak.

"There's a lot of weird shit in this world, but some of it's good weird shit." He spoke kindly, but TJ didn't look reassured. She started backing away slowly.

"Come down here to eat tomorrow," he said. "I've got a job for you."

TJ struggled to get her voice working, "Okay." She turned, took three fast steps up hill, then turned again. "Good night, Jim."

"Good night, TJ."

She hurried up hill. At the corner to her street, she stopped to look back down. The astonishing dreaming moon still glowed over the distant black forest. TJ hung onto the corner post of Valerie's fence and let the damp air fill her lungs. Had Jim practically told her he was the coyote? "He couldn't have meant that," she whispered to the darkness. Her imagination was on overdrive, but she kind of understood what he meant by "good weird shit." All around her the little town of Warrentown seemed suspended in a moment of magic, swathed in moonlight, poised between night and dawn, and lit with silver and gray that gave the rundown cottages and cracked sidewalks a gentle glow. Her nerves were tingling, but she was no longer afraid.

Chapter Twenty
TJ's Job

"I'm going down to the Tavern for breakfast today," TJ told Buddy. Buddy was munching her breakfast daintily. "Jim's expecting me."

At least that's what she was telling herself. He'd wondered why he hadn't seen her. That meant he'd been looking for her.

TJ wasn't sure how she felt about Jim anymore. The yellow eyes were creepy. "But there is no such thing as a shape-shifter." Buddy gave her no reassurance, being uninterested in TJ's comments. "I never believed in stuff like that." Not even as a small child. TJ had never liked fantasy books or fairy tales or the Bible for that matter. None of it had anything to do with real life. As a kid, she'd wanted answers. She'd wanted a protector. Now she thought that all of the fantasies about God, fairies, unicorns, and happy ever after were just stupid.

But...what had Jim said about the world being full of good weird things?

"Some weird good things and some shitty bad things." Buddy sat back and wiped her face with one paw. Then, tail aloft, she minced her way across the room to the open door. There she settled on the top porch step to contemplate the early morning sun.

She's got her food, shelter, and water, TJ thought. She's enjoying herself. She was glad that Buddy was safe. While living in a tent on the edge of the woods, Buddy's safety had been a constant worry. TJ joined Buddy on the porch.

The fantastic moon had vanished without a trace, replaced by the tender light blue of early morning. The hens were enjoying the warmth of a sunny spot on the side of the road. They huddled into the grass, clucking at each other, as if settling down for a game of cards. TJ looked around for the baby goat, almost missing him, but no random outbreaks of high spirits were going to interrupt her or the chickens that morning. TJ ran her fingers through her hair one last time and squared her shoulders.

"You just stay right here, okay?" she told Buddy. "Don't follow me."

She bounced down the steps and set off briskly down the street. She was just rounding the corner when a thin shriek from Valerie's house startled her.

"I don't want that!"

The shrill voice was jarring on air of the quiet morning. TJ froze, staring at Valerie's cottage. The curtains were pulled back and the windows open, but TJ couldn't see Valerie.

"No!" The voice packed a lot of annoyance into one syllable.

"I don't want any help." Less shrill, but still nasty.

Someone's in there, TJ thought. Yelling at Valerie.

TJ had intended to drop by Val's house in hopes that Val would eat breakfast with her since she didn't want to enter the Tavern on her own. Now she wanted to stomp into Val's house and tell the unknown psycho bitch to shut up, but, instead, she chewed her fingernails and listened.

"Tell him to get up here!"

Val mumbled something.

"He isn't busy. What's he got going on? He hasn't got a job."

Her voice was full of sneer. Bitch, TJ thought.

"He's just busy doing nothing," grumbled the voice.

Val's screen door open with a screech of rusty hinges and Val called out, "See you later."

TJ launched herself into a causal stroll around the corner and down the hill. She timed her arrival just right; Val saw her from the front porch and sang out cheerfully, "Good morning, TJ." She smiled.

TJ's mouth formed a smile in return, and her hand made a little wave. She stopped at Val's gate and waited as the old lady navigated the five steps down from her porch. Val arrived at her garden gate looking breathless and dizzy. She pushed her gate open and TJ caught her by the elbow.

"Thanks," said Val. She stood tilted to one side, eyes closed. TJ held on to her arm, feeling panicky. Val's skin was papery and fragile. Tiny blue lines wriggled under the white hairless arm. TJ was afraid to touch Val for fear of bruising her but afraid to let go for fear she'd fall down.

"Are you okay? Who was that yelling at you?" she asked. Please be okay because I need you to be okay because I don't know what the fuck to do if you aren't, she prayed silently.

"Yes." Val blinked, sighed, and gently pulled her arm away from TJ's grip. "I'm okay. I just get dizzy sometimes if I move to fast."

TJ didn't know what to say to that so she didn't say anything.

"That's Baylor's mother. She's living with me now." Valerie tried to smile. "She's...trying to settle in. Well, let's get down to breakfast." They started off down the street slowly, with TJ matching Val's steps and watching her feet, afraid that Val would stumble.

"I haven't seen you in a while." Val commented.

"Uh. I just...I've just been cleaning my house. Taking care of my cat."

Val's face lit up. "I have five cats, a baby goat, seven chickens, and a pig."

"They're all yours?"

Valerie laughed, "They belong to themselves." She saw TJ's look and added, "They were all abandoned, so they don't really belong to anyone but I look after them. That dratted baby goat."

They reached the alley and Val angled toward the back door. She said, "I didn't know they took so long to grow up," just as Baylor opened door.

TJ and Baylor stared into each other's faces. Then Baylor stepped backward, red-faced and mumbling, and TJ quickly sidestepped behind Val, ducking her head to cover her blush. Val, her eyebrows raised, chattered on, "Hey, Baylor, TJ's here. Since Baylor's mom is living with me now, TJ, we were wondering if you could help out some." She beamed a smile from Baylor's face to TJ's.

TJ said, "Huh?" Her hands seemed to have developed a life of their own. They fluttered in front of her face, then fled down her sides, and then hid in her pockets. Baylor, too, seemed off kilter, with his eyes aimed first over their heads and then at the floor. Valerie made little shooing motions and said, "Let's get breakfast and talk about it."

Rachel and Jim were cooking pancakes on the Coleman stove. Making little clucking noises like one of the chickens, Valerie herded Baylor and TJ into the tavern. Several tables had been shoved together for the morning breakfast eaters. Charlie was sitting next to a thin man with a mottled purple scar on his cheek who poked at his pancake as it if was asleep and needed to be waken up. He seemed to be friends with Charlie, but, to TJ, everyone in town seemed to be friends with everyone else. Jesus and his wife were seated across from Charlie and they both smiled greetings as TJ, Val, and Baylor got seated. Charlie politely asked the thin guy to pass the pitcher of water.

"Here." The thin guy's hands bobbed up and down as he aimed them at the pitcher. TJ watched uneasily as he lined his hands up and pushed. Once the jug was across the center line of the wooden table, Charlie grabbed it.

"Thanks."

Over the clink of forks against plates, TJ could hear Rachel and Jimmy making quiet comments to each other as they cooked. Then Jimmy stuck his head through the door and called out, "Hey, everyone, how're you doing for pancakes?"

"We're good," Charlie said, looking around. "But Val and TJ just got here."

Jim appeared carrying a plate and a spatula. He dropped two pancakes on Val's plate and two on TJ's

"You back for more?" he asked Baylor.

"No." Baylor shook his head. He shot a nervous look across the table and added, "I just need to ask TJ something."

"You?" Jim asked the thin man.

"I'm done, thanks." He tried to mop his mouth with his napkin but missed. Everyone treated his shaking as normal, but TJ watched him out of the corners of her eyes.

"More?" The smell of Jim's pancakes was warm and soothing.

"Yes, please." Jimmy added three small round discs to her plate and called out, "All done here," as he headed back into the tavern's makeshift kitchen.

TJ was aware that she and Baylor were sitting side by side and not talking. She felt shy and was embarrassed by the shyness which made her feel more embarrassed in spiral of confusion that was unfamiliar and scary. She stabbed her pancake and made herself eat a bite.

She heard Baylor clear his throat. She stabbed another piece of pancake and made herself eat another bite.

Baylor cleared his throat again and Val burst into cheerful chatter, "Did I tell you Baylor's mother is staying at my house?" She blinked her faded eyes at TJ and smiled nervously.

A Mountain in the Air

Baylor finally got his voice working, "That's what's kept me so busy. Moving my mom."

Oh, TJ thought. Couldn't come by for one second?

"But Gale is all settled in now." Valerie was still trying to be sweetness and light.

"Except she needs help," Baylor said. He looked tired. "I'll help, too, but I need to get a job so I can pay for supplies and stuff."

There was a small silence. TJ felt pity for whoever had to help Baylor's mean old mother. Then she realized that Val and Baylor were staring at her. She froze, her fork in the air.

"Do you think you could help me a little, TJ?" Baylor asked.

Chapter Twenty-One
First Day at Work

"I've always wanted to go to Mt. Rainier," Valerie said. "Did you know Pete Wallis died there?" She was trying to make conversation to distract everyone from the painful process of changing Gale's bandages. Baylor and TJ were kneeling on the floor at Gale's feet like acolytes at the feet of a big fat goddess. They were surrounded by medical supplies, all neatly laid out on paper pads Rachel had stolen from a pharmacy. Rachel sat on the couch next to Valerie.

"I kind of know about that," Baylor mumbled distractedly.

"Who?" TJ's voice was thin. She was staring fixedly away from Gale's leg.

Valerie was surprised. "Pete Wallis? You never heard of him?"

TJ shook her head.

"I never heard of him," Gale said from far away on the other side of her immense chest.

"Well, he was only locally famous," Val agreed. "I guess you had to see him play in person to really get to be a fan. Excuse me for saying this, but he could give a girl an organism just by making eye contact."

Baylor gently tugged at the edge of the bandage, peeled it back, and revealed a patch of blood mottled with yellow and green clots. TJ screwed up her face into a scowl of disgust. Gale's leg looked like it had been chewed up by a bear trap.

"That music was from a while back," Valerie added hurriedly. "But the greats you don't forget."

"Like Elvis." Gale's eyes were closed.

"Some people become gods," Rachel observed, "if they are remembered long enough."

That brought the conversation to a halt. Gale's eyes were clenched closed. TJ stared hard at the wall. The stink from Gale's leg went right up in Valerie's nose and down the back of her throat, making her gag.

"I don't imagine that many people remember Pete." Valerie knew she was babbling but anything was better than watching Baylor wipe disgusting goo off the open wound. "I guess not many people will remember me either." Gale emitted a groan.

"Hold still." Baylor dabbed at the bloody leg.

Val reached for Gale's hand, and Baylor said to TJ, "Hand me some more of those wipes."

TJ fumbled some small white squares of gauze out of a package, her hands made awkward by gloves and disgust.

"Anyway," Val said, still trying to get Gale's mind off her leg, "I'd like to go to Mt Rainier. It was a weird place for Pete Wallis to die."

"How come?" Baylor asked, to help out with the distraction.

"Because he was an urban guy. The kind of guy to get his picture taken because he was in a bar fight."

"See, what I'm doing is cleaning," Baylor told TJ, "I don't rub. I just pat. Here." He dropped the blood soaked gauze into the wastepaper basket.

"He wrote songs about all kinds of things. Not just love songs," Valerie told them. Gale gripped the chair arm, making her knuckles white. "Like...he wrote about being trapped in a rut or wanting to, to...get away. Anyway, I wasn't the only one who thought he was a god. Lots of girls did back then."

"How'd he die?" Baylor kept his eyes on the wound. He gently sopped the last bit of green slime. Gale gasped. Her face was scrunched up and she stared fixedly at the ceiling. TJ's face was scrunched up too, partly because of the smell and partly in sympathy with Gale.

Valerie launched into the story. "He was basically front man for a really good bar band that got a record contract. I used to have the album. I played it over and over. This was way back in the nineties, I guess. Well, anyway no one knows how he died. Or if he died. His car was found up at Paradise on Mt Rainier but he was never found." She shrugged. "There was a search. It was a big deal at the time."

"Are you done?" TJ asked Baylor. Her voice was small. She felt like she might need to run off somewhere and puke.

Baylor examined Gale's leg. "Yeah, almost. Hanging in there, Mom?"

Gale grunted.

"Teej, hand me those wipes. Those right there."

TJ found the medicated wipes and handed a small packet to Baylor. He tore off his gloves, changed to a fresh pair, and opened the packet.

"Almost done," he said. "Now I'm going to wrap her all up again."

"Where did you learn all this nursing stuff?" Val asked.

"Oh, the visiting nurse taught me." Baylor shrugged. "They used to send a nurse out, but budget cuts or something so I had to learn. It was that or go to a nursing home."

TJ picked up the scattered used gloves and ripped packaging, dumped them into the wastebasket, and carried the trash out to the kitchen. Valerie's eyes tracked TJ's departure, her return, and followed her as she picked up the basin of water and headed for the back porch. *I must not backseat drive,* she told herself. But she couldn't help thinking that TJ was young and inexperienced and probably not reliable, whereas she, Valerie, was right there in the house and experienced in caring for sick people. She'd cared for her mother for years.

But it's TJ's job, she told herself firmly. Baylor had asked her to look after his mom. So back off, old lady! She turned her attention to Rachel, who was holding one of Gale's hands. To Valerie's surprise, Rachel began to sing softly with her eyes closed, nodding her head with the gentle rhythm of her tune. Val listened but couldn't make out the words. She thought of asking, but kept quiet. After all, Rachel might be praying and prayers were private. She wondered if Rachel would say a prayer for her when she died and a sudden vision of a flowery mountain side appeared in her mind. She felt the hot sun on her shoulders and could hear the buzz of insects. Clear sweet water trickled over stones between the flowers. The vision was so real that Val went rigid in her seat, her heart full of yearning. *I really, really want to go there,* she thought. Then she found herself back in her cramped living room. Rachel was watching her with sad affection.

Valerie wanted to say, "Promise me you'll take me to Mt Rainier before I die," but she didn't. Instead she asked, "How's Gale doing?"

"She's asleep. She'll rest for awhile."

TJ returned carrying the basin. She set the basin down and started packing the medical materials away with shaky hands.

Rachel said, "This is a liminal space."

She spoke with a tone that got everyone's attention.

"What's that mean?" Baylor asked.

"Transition space," Rachel explained calmly. "Like a crossroads. Crossroads can be very strange places."

"Strange?" Baylor frowned. Something tickled at his memory, some story about a guy who learned to play guitar from the devil at a crossroads. Or maybe learned the fiddle there? "You mean like people making deals with the devil at a crossroads?"

Rachel said. "Sometimes just choices. Like in a nursing home, that's transition from life to death. That's what this house is like right now. It's a powerful liminal space."

"You can't choose not to die," Baylor said sadly.

"You choose how you handle it."

TJ wrinkled up her nose. "It's depressing. And..." She shrugged, not wanting to say that death was scary.

"That's you feeling it." Rachel's eyes had a measuring look. "There isn't much difference between life and death for humans, if you think about it. Like between each heart beat, your heart stops. Between each breath, you aren't breathing."

TJ muttered, "I don't like being near blood and pee."

"That's your job, if you can handle it." But Rachel was done. She finished her beer and turned her gaze toward the rest of the room. Valerie's living room was lit with pale sunlight. Out the windows, the sky was a friendly blue, promising a pleasantly warm summer day. Valerie's eyes followed Rachel's and she thought of taking a walk. Then she thought that no, she'd rather take a nap. And Baylor had been wise to get TJ to help out.

She smiled at TJ and asked, "Honey, would you mind coming back this evening and help me make dinner?"

CHAPTER TWENTY-TWO
DAILY LIFE

TJ woke feeling a complete absence of enthusiasm for the day. With some annoyance, she reviewed the previous afternoon and the hours she'd spent in the company of the two old ladies. Baylor had not stopped by, at least not while she was there fixing dinner and washing dishes. She hadn't seen Baylor much at all except when other people were around, and then he acted like they barely knew each other. Which should have been fine since fucking some guy didn't mean anything except maybe getting some help—drugs or a ride of something—and besides she hadn't fucked Baylor to get paid back later. She'd fucked him because...the truth was she'd done it out of jealously because Rachel and Jim were so beautiful together. And she'd been drunk.

So forget him. Except that now she had a job taking care of his mother! She was supposed to go over to Valerie's house and check on Baylor's mother twice a day so that he could go off and find work in town. And what she got out of it was a place to live and meals at the Tavern

It was almost like Jim had tricked her to get her there.

Well, he *had* said something about everyone helping everyone else. And someone had left a big bag of cat food on her porch for Buddy along with a jar of peanut butter, some jam, a loaf of bread, a box of sundries, and a Coleman campstove. Someone was thinking about her. Probably Val.

She'd gone through the box of sundries like it was a treasure chest. Toothbrush. Toothpaste. Hand lotion. Shoelaces. Not that she needed shoelaces, but still someone had thought she might need them. Band aids and a tube of Neosporin. Aspirin. Tampons. A box of baking soda.

She'd have to ask Val what she was supposed to do with the baking soda.

TJ stared at the ceiling. The box of goodies was nice, but she was still in a shitty mood. Why was she so pissed off? It wasn't about having a job. She didn't mind doing things to help out so that others would help her. She didn't even mind Baylor's mean bitch of a mother since mostly her job was to help Val. Val was sweet. The job wasn't the problem.

Baylor. That was the problem. *He* had dumped *her* and it was supposed to be the other way around.

"Well, fuck," TJ told the ceiling. Then she sat up, startling Buddy. "Hi ho. Hi ho. It's off to work I go," TJ sang sarcastically. Buddy blinked her green eyes. "I'll feed you first," she promised.

"Hey, Valerie." TJ gently cracked the door and peeked in.

"Come in." Val called from the kitchen. TJ entered the living room, scouted the chairs, and realized that there was nowhere to sit down without disturbing a cat. Gale was enthroned on the couch and took up most of its length. She had a cup of coffee in her hand and a look of dissatisfaction on her face.

"Good morning," TJ said.

"What so good about it?" Gale asked.

That was so close to TJ's feelings that she had a brief flash of kinship with Gale.

"Yeah, I had trouble getting out of bed this morning," she said.

Gale grunted and shifted her bulk to a slightly different angle. "I didn't get any sleep and there's no TV here." She glared as if it was TJ's fault.

"No, I guess not."

Val poked her head out the kitchen door. "Oh, hi, TJ, I'm glad you're here. Want some coffee?"

"Sure. Thanks."

Val disappeared.

TJ sat on the coffee table. She felt awkward around Gale. It was hard to fake friendliness to someone she heartily disliked. In a tone light with false cheeriness, she asked, "How are your legs this morning?" The wrappings looked good. Baylor had already come, wrapped, and left.

Gale's lips thinned into narrow pink line. "What do you think?"

TJ's shoulders hunched. "I see Baylor got them changed already."

Gale sniffed loudly.

To TJ's relief, Val entered the room, carrying a tray. She set the tray down on the coffee table next to TJ and said, "I got hot water started in the kitchen for Gale's bath."

"Okay." Since she was supposed to help this disgusting mess of mean old lady, TJ slugged down a mouthful of coffee and got up. "You ready for a bath, Gale?"

"Yeah, as ready as I'll ever be." She flopped her arm down on the couch.

Val said, "I'll help."

"I can do it." Gale grumped.

"I'm here," Val smiled.

"What are we going to use to..." TJ looked around. Giving someone an old lady a bath seemed insurmountably complex when there was no bathroom plumbing. TJ was taking her baths while standing by her kitchen sink, but she didn't think that method would work with Gale.

"I'll just set this down here." Val spread a towel over the coffee table. "Will you get the water please?"

TJ fetched and carried as directed by Val until all the fixings for a bath for Gale were in place including a complete change of clothes, washcloth, two basins of water, and soap. No shampoo, but Gale said she didn't need it. All preparations complete, TJ smiled at Gale, expecting some approval. Gale looked the supplies over and hefted her substantial bottom forward on the couch. Then she snapped, "Well, you two aren't going to watch, are you?"

TJ stepped back quickly. Val put her hand on TJs shoulder and said, "Let's go take care of some things out back, okay? Give Gale some privacy."

They retreated through the kitchen to the back door. As soon as they were out of earshot, TJ hissed, "What's *with* that bitch?"

"Pain." Val smiled sadly. "Pain can do that to people."

"She takes it out on everyone!"

Val shrugged, "She's miserable. Maybe if we can make her a little happier?" She shrugged again and said, "You go first. I just need to lean on you a little bit."

"Sure." TJ took the porch steps carefully, Val's hand pressed down on her shoulder. Once in the backyard, she said, "That bitch just kicked you out of your house."

Val sighed, shook her head, and laughed. "Baylor did warn me. But, hey, since you're here, you can help me with some things."

"Sure." TJ found some eagerness inside herself. She looked around, "You want this all cleaned up back here?" The yard was lumpy with animal poop.

"That would be wonderful! I can't bend down much anymore or I tip over."

"What should I do with it?"

"I was thinking I'd try mulching it."

TJ had never thought of herself as a shit-shoveller but the job was actually enjoyable. Armed with a shovel, she stalked the poops wherever they could be found in the open grass or tucked under the bushes. She tossed each scoop on top of the moldy weeds Val had dumped in a pile in a corner of the backyard.

"I don't compost food," Val explained, "It all gets eaten by either Pig or that dratted baby goat."

Val's goal was to intersperse layers of goat and dog poop with layers of weeds and grass. Under Val's guidance and armed with a pair of lopers, TJ attacked the weeds growing along the fence. Then she helped Val dig weeds out from around the foundation of the house. By the time they were finished, the mulch pile was knee high.

"We'll see if it works," Val said. "Well, I mean you'll see if it works. I won't."

"Okay," TJ said, puzzled but wanting to be agreeable. The yard looked much better, though the smell of animal poop lingered.

"Hey, she hasn't called for us," TJ commented. "Should we maybe check?"

Back in the house they found Gale asleep. She had changed her nightgown into a billowing Hawaiian print blouse and a pair of blue cotton pants. TJ pitched the water out the back door while Val added the washcloth and towel to her pile of laundry. Gale snored.

"TJ," Val asked hesitantly.

"Huh?"

"Would you mind sweeping the floor and dusting for me? I'll fix us all some lunch when you get done."

TJ started in Val's bedroom. She worked slowly so she could look around. Val's room was like a museum with exhibits from The Most Boring

Life Ever Lived. Most of the exhibits were pictures: Val as a baby, Val as a child with her mother, Val dressed up for church, Val posed with her mother in front of a gravestone.

TJ studied the gravestone picture for a while. There was a strong family resemblance between Val and her mom. They both were pale skinned, freckled, and had plain, square faces. The mother looked mean but that was probably an effect of squinting into the sun. The grave was unadorned. They weren't wearing black. TJ puzzled over the photo, unable to figure out it's meaning.

Then she moved to Val's dresser to examine the photos there. All were in decorative frames, but the photos themselves were just snap shots of ordinary life. Judging by the photos, Val had spent her time going to church with her mother and gardening around their trailer. TJ wondered where Val's dad was. Maybe he took the pictures?

There were no pictures of Val as a teenager. The missing years, TJ thought. The rest of the photos had been taken by Val. She had framed up pictures of cats and dogs, her flower garden, pictures of the sky, and lots of pictures of her standing or sitting by her mother. The pictures showed them getting older and older and older.

None of her dad, TJ noted.

"TJ," Val called. TJ jumped guiltily. She hadn't gotten much done.

TJ sat across the table from Val and sank her teeth into the cheese and tomato sandwich. The bread and cheese were from the food bank, but Jesus had grown the tomatoes in the greenhouse.

"He's a genius with plants," Val said. She had a bit of salad dressing on her nose.

"You talking about one of them illegals?" Gale called from the couch.

"I don't think he's illegal," Val said in a soothing voice. And she winked at TJ.

"My son said there were some of them living here."

"Jesus and his family keep us in veggies almost all year round," Val kept her tone light, refusing to acknowledge Gale's negativity. "And they've been looking after the animals too, now that it's harder for me to get around."

Gale snorted. She had dropped some of the cheese on her chest but hadn't noticed. Her little eyes were squeezed by the fat cheeks masticating the sandwich. It put TJ right off her food.

"Honey, you probably got things to do of your own," Val said. "Thank you so much for helping out."

"I don't mind." TJ was surprised that she really meant it. "I'll come by this evening. Hey, I need to get some clothes washed. Can I wash some of mine with some of yours?"

"You bet." Val smiled. "That would be a real help."

Gale set her dish down with a bang, signaling that she was done

"I'll clean up." TJ jumped to her feet.

"Oh don't. Leave it. I wash the dishes once a day, so I'll do it tonight after dinner."

"Okay." TJ got up to leave but hesitated by the door. Val looked tired and and her hands were shaking. "You sure?" she asked. "I can do them, no trouble."

"Go on, honey," Val said. "We're going to nap for a while." Gale had already leaned back into the couch, eyes closed and mouth open.

Chapter Twenty-Three
Val's Memories

After TJ left, Val gathered up the dishes and dumped them into a plastic basin in the sink. She stood still and listened to Gail's mutterings, wondering if Gail would bark out a command and wondering if she had the patience to respond kindly if Gail did. The mutterings and grumblings morphed into the sproing of couch springs adjusting to Gail's massive butt. With a final grunt, Gail went silent.

Good! Relief flowed through Valerie's nervous system. Her hands were shaking a bit but otherwise she was okay. After wiping her hands briskly on her apron, Val returned to the living room. She was heading toward the bedroom when Gail's voice snagged her.

"That little girl is no good."

Val went rigid, frozen mid-step.

"Skinny little thing. Where'd you guys find her?"

Val turned slowly. As usual, her face responded to conflict by trying to produce a smile. Inside her chest, her heart was sproinging like the couch springs had under Gale's weight. Her mind fought visions of shouting, of a fist, of blood, of boots kicking her puppy, of her mother on the floor.

"Gale," she said carefully, " I am very grateful to TJ for her help."

"Baylor ought to here." Gale's voice descended into a whine.

"He's working. He got a job."

"He shouldn't have quit the militia. He used to make good money regular." Now that Gale's voice had calmed a bit, Val took a peek at her face. Gale was crying.

"Oh, honey." Val stumbled in her haste to get across the rug to the coffee table. There she lowered herself carefully. Gale's bulk was distributed

A Mountain in the Air

across the couch like a series of big hills. Her head made the smallest hill. Tears were leaking from her eyes.

Val said, "I am so sorry that you are in pain."

Gale moaned, "It just goes on and on and on."

"I'll ask Rachel for some pain meds."

Gale huffed to show how little she thought of that idea. "I got some. From my doctor. No good."

"Rachel might have something, and if she doesn't, she'll get it. She had some morphine derivatives when I turned my ankle last winter."

Gale brightened just a bit. "Can you get something for me? All the...useless doctor...says he can't give me more..." Laying on her side was making her pant.

"I'll ask her." Val thought of the walk down the hill and wasn't sure she could make it. She was too tired. But if she didn't go, Gale would be in pain. She ought to go. Come on, old lady, she told herself. Get moving.

Gale let out a long gurgling snore. Val sat still, amazed. How could she fall asleep so fast? Maybe she wasn't in pain from her legs so much as she needed to let out her anger, like squeezing pus out of a wound. Anger gone, she slept.

Val eased herself off the coffee table and slowly stood up. She moved carefully toward her bedroom door, partly for fear of waking Gale, but also for fear that her legs might give out and she might fall. Relief that the incident was over had left her feeling weak. She managed the short distance to her bed and flopped down on the sagging mattress. There she lay until she had the strength to kick her shoes off and roll toward the center of the bed. Valerie let her eyes close and allowed herself to fall deep into sleep.

She found herself once again on the flowery mountain side. This time it was Val who called out to get Pete's attention. "Hi! Hello, Pete." She was too shy to shout, so her voice evaporated on the bright mountain air, but he saw her and jumped up to greet her.

"Hey, Valerie! You came back! How's it going?"

She knew it wasn't a real question, but her mind groped for an answer anyway. "Okay. No, not okay. Some okay and some not okay." Weightlessly, her body drifted up the mountain side until she was hovering over the grass just below Pete's boulder.

"Come on up," he said, with a wide gesture of his arm. "Welcome to my abode." He grinned, mocking his own silliness.

Val, suddenly aware that she was floating, began to sink. Also aware that her awareness of floating was dragging her down, she got caught up in a complicated effort to not think about floating while trying not to think about not floating. She floundered.

"Hang on! I'll get you." Pete dropped to his knees on the boulder and reached his hand down. Val grabbed his hand and he lifted her up to the rock. She landed beside him with a soft thump.

"There you go!" The laugh was gone from his eyes, replaced by an almost paternal concern that made Val feel very old and very vulnerable. She was conscious of a yearning to be like Pete—happy, active, seemingly free of pain both physical and emotional. To her embarrassment, her eyes filled with tears.

Pete settled beside her and put one arm over her shoulders. Val shrunk beneath his touch. Her body, she believed, was as appealing as a dried out mummy—all bones and wrinkled papery skin.

"Val," Pete whispered, "What's wrong?"

"He killed my puppy." She had no idea why of all the answers to "What's wrong" that one event from her childhood was the one that jumped out of her mouth.

"Who did?"

"My father. My asshole nasty father." Val spat out the words. "He kicked my puppy to death right in front of me because she wasn't house broken. I hate him."

"Shit, yeah, Val. I hate the fucker too."

That made Val laugh a little. Then she sighed. "Then he beat my mom so bad that she was never able to take care of herself. I took care of her."

And that was how her father had sentenced her to a lifetime of television, urine-saturated sheets, and solitaire games played on the kitchen table while she listened with one ear for her mother's trembling voice. Her life was a long list of experiences she didn't have because she'd spent her life caring for her mother.

She'd run away every now and then but never far and never for long. On one of those escapes, she drove to Olympia to a tavern where Pete's band was performing. There, immersed in the audience of drunken rowdies a good twenty years younger than her, she'd cut loose and danced until three in the morning when the tavern finally closed. She'd kept her eyes on Pete the whole time, sucking up into her heart every detail of him from the sweat on his cheekbones to the way the muscles moved in his arm as he changed chords on the guitar. Oh, she had yearned for him, yearned to be noticed in the crowd, yearned for him to see her and think about her.

After the set was over, Pete and his band mates jumped into the crowd. They were mobbed instantly, of course. Everyone who wasn't already near them tried to get closer. Valerie got shouldered and shoved and squeezed back up against on wall of the tavern. From there, all she could see was bobbing heads and thrusting shoulders. She dug into her purse—she was the only woman there carrying a shoulder bag—and found an old receipt and a pen. After smoothing the receipt against the wall, she wrote "Dear Pete, I love your music. It keeps me alive," and signed it with her name and phone number. Then she scratched the phone number off.

And then she left. One of the first to stumble out the door, she found herself alone in the parking lot. And there, parked way over to one side, she saw the band's van. It was probably an old mail truck, but they had painted it dark blue with their name sprayed on graffiti-style. Valerie carried her scrap of paper over to the van and tucked it under the windshield wiper on the driver's side.

She remembered the note now. Torn between humiliation and wonder, Valerie whispered,. "Do...do you remember me?"

Pete shrugged, looking a bit sheepish. "I saw you in a bar somewhere. Didn't you leave me a note or something? I always thought the note was from you."

"Yeah." Val turned away to hide her blush.

"It was a real sweet note." At the time, he'd thought her gushing statement of fandom was pathetic. "You said something about us making you feel alive."

"Yeah."

"But, hey, I got a question for you." His eyelids flickered as if he was embarrassed.

"What?" she asked. With an effort, she faced him.

"Uh," he groped for the right words. "I don't want to be rude or nothing, but didn't...I don't remember you being that much older than me. Like you are now."

"Pete," she said with some asperity, "forty years have gone by."

"Forty years?" His eyes got an inward look.

"At least forty." Puzzled, Val studied his face. "This is a dream, you know. My dream. I'm dreaming."

He blinked with surprise, and laughed. "This ain't a dream." Then he added seriously, "I don't know what it is."

"Well," Valerie hesitated, then took the plunge, "everyone thinks you died."

They gazed at each other. Then Pete said, "I don't remember dying. I'm here because...I don't know. I like being here."

"I like it here too."

Valerie's eyes suddenly opened and she found herself wide awake, staring at the ceiling of her bedroom.

"Wow," she whispered. That was one hell of a dream. She could still see the flower meadows like a transparent curtain between her and the faded, damp wallpaper of her bedroom. She blinked and the flower meadows vanished. Instead, she was snuggled deep the embrace of her quilt, her body as relaxed as a smooth flow of water. The sweet, gentle yellow of the afternoon sun lay across her bedroom floor and, from outside, she could hear the comfortable sounds of the village people going about their business. A rooster crowed and Maria yelled, "Shut up!" With a quiet rumble, Baylor's electric motorcycle rolled by. A voice, probably Rachel's, called out something and was answered by a quick, friendly bleat from the bike's horn. Someone was tapping softly on her front door. TJ! TJ was there to help with Gale and the evening meal.

Val pushed herself in to a seated position and slid her legs off the bed. "Coming!" she called, making her voice sound cheerful, but her mind was full of her conversation with Pete. He's becoming my secret best friend, Valerie thought. She laughed to herself. How silly!

Chapter Twenty-Four
More Strange Days

"She could use someone there all the time," TJ told the baby goat. She had finished up her another day of work and was out in her yard watering her rose. The baby goat had more or less moved into her yard and was mowing her lawn. Jesus had seen her petting the baby, so he'd tried to communicate with her about the goat's food needs. After a lot of futile playing of charades, he simply gestured for TJ to follow him back to his house. There, stacked on pallets and protected by tarps, Jesus kept bails of hay. He showed her the goat's shed with a wire manger for a daily breakfast. TJ understood that now the goat was hers to look after.

"What's his name?" she'd asked.

Jesus had learned a basic vocabulary in English but could understand more than what he could say

"Nombre?"

That sounded like name to TJ. "Si, nombre." She nodded eagerly.

Jesus laughed. "Espiritu."

"Spirit?"

"Si, yes, si."

TJ was doubtful but maybe the name came from the baby's spirited, bouncy attitude. "Okay, Spirit, then."

But "Spirit" had quickly morphed into "Squirt."

Squirt was mowing the lawn while TJ was watering the rose when she heard the sound of a motorcycle. She glanced over her shoulder and saw Baylor roll by. He was going to the tavern. She'd been happily planning to take a sponge bath to get rid of the sweat and dirt of the day, but the glimpse of Baylor interrupted her mood. She hadn't seen more than a glimpse of him in several days.

Her feelings about that were so prone to sudden change that she couldn't say for sure what she felt. He'd fucked her and dumped her. No, he hadn't because she'd fucked *him* and had dumped *him*. She'd thought they'd be friends, but he'd just wanted someone to look after his horrible mother. Well, what was wrong with that? She had fucked guys to get rides or food or shelter or those things Charlie talked about, so what was wrong with one time sex to get help for your mother...and so on.

She'd just expected to see more of him. She wanted to see more of him.

She'd seen plenty of his mother, though. Poor Val living with her. Baylor should just go ahead and put his horrible mother in a nursing home, TJ thought. But they probably didn't have any money to pay for it and, if you couldn't pay, those places could be real hell holes. She knew because her grandma had spent her last years in one. "Shoot me when I get old," TJ said aloud.

She let her breath out with a huff and told the goat, "That's enough for today." Buddy was sitting on the front porch. TJ climbed the stairs and plopped down beside the cat. Squirt bounced up and joined them.

"Hey, you guys." She petted Buddy with one hand and fended off the goat's kisses with the other. "Hey, you silly guys."

"Looks like you got a friend."

It was Baylor. On foot. Sneaking up on her. He looked exhausted, dirty, and so tired he was walking tilted to one side. He climbed the steps and dropped down beside her, pushing the goat's nose away from his face.

"I got a job doing roofing," he explained. "We finished up today."

TJ fumbled in her mind for something to say "So that's where you've been?"

"Pretty much."

"Are you working tomorrow?"

He shook his head. "They don't have anything lined up right now. Things are really bad when you can't even get a roofing job."

The sweat on his face reminded TJ. "You need a drink of water?"

"Yeah, in a minute." He flashed a grin. "I just want to sit for a minute."

"I'll get it." TJ jumped up and hurried into the house. She felt disoriented by the sudden appearance of Baylor. He'd been in her thoughts so much that somehow he'd become a fantasy, and it was jarring to meet up

A Mountain in the Air

with the real him. Also, she had only one drinking glass and was lousy at being a hostess anyway. Well, her used glass would have to do. She filled the glass, noted the diminished water in the jug, and headed back outside.

"Here." The glass was plastic, decorated with orange flowers, probably the last survivor of a set. Val had given it to her.

"Thanks," said Baylor with real gratitude. He drank all of the water down at once long gulp, then wiped his mouth on his sleeve.

TJ looked around for something to talk about. "That goat. Jesus says his name is Spirit. I've been calling him Squirt."

Baylor's mouth opened, closed, and opened again. He asked TJ, "Can I tell you something and you won't think I'm nuts?"

"I don't know." She shrugged, puzzled.

"Well, that goat." He stopped, glanced at her, and said, "I don't know if this is a secret or not but Jesus and Maria and the kids are ghosts."

She stared at him with surprise. "Ghosts." TJ dragged the word out to show skepticism.

"Yeah." Baylor gave her a quick glance. "I know this for a fact because I saw their dead bodies."

"Where?" TJ asked, trying not to sound too challenging.

"Out in the woods. I got lost and, yeah, I know I had hypothermia and could've been hallucinating, but I wasn't. I saw their dead bodies, and then like two days later I met them here. They're ghosts."

"Maybe you saw some other Mexicans? I mean you hear about the illegals trying to hide in the woods."

He shook his head. "It was them. Little Miguel has that Virgin of Guadalupe T-shirt. Besides it was two years ago that I met them, and the kids haven't grown at all. Kids that age, they grow fast. Like they get bigger every year."

TJ pictured Jim's yellow eyes. If ghosts were real...She shivered.

"And that goat," Baylor pointed. "That damn baby goat is still a baby like he was two years ago too. He's a ghost too."

TJ laughed.

"Serious. He'll never grow up."

"Uh, maybe that 's a good thing? Aren't billy goats really smelly and mean?"

Baylor shook his head. "Don't know. Never met one. But ghost are real."

362

"Yeah, okay." TJ grinned. If Baylor wanted to believe in ghosts, that was okay with her. She shrugged and added, "You know, there's something strange about Jim."

Baylor barked a laugh, "No shit, Sherlock!"

She winced away, hurt.

"I mean, I'm sorry, TJ. I shouldn't laugh because I know I've been here longer than you. Yeah, Jim and Rachel are both something special. Not ghosts. I'm not sure what but something." Her shoulders were still hunched up defensively. "You, me, Charlie, and Valerie are the only normal people here. And my mom. And Crazy Mary."

TJ turned her face toward the setting sun. Long shadows stretched across the street. She could feel the nighttime coming. She said, "This is freaky stuff."

"It took a while for me to believe it. I think I saw Rachel turn into a crow once. I mean a raven." He glanced at her. His defensiveness made her feel a bit better.

"A raven," she said skeptically.

"Yeah, I know. I was pretty freaked out." He took a deep breath and plunged into his story. "I saw her in the upstairs window. You know she lives above the tavern? I saw her in the window, and she changed into a really big raven and flew away. She didn't see me."

The fact that Baylor believed really stupid stuff made TJ feel a little more confident about her side of the conversation. She said, "Jim said the world is full of weird stuff that's good. Good weird stuff."

"Yeah, it is." Baylor took in a deep breath. "TJ, I've been meaning to say something to you."

A chill seized TJ. She braced herself. "What?"

"Change of subject." His mouth jerked into a quick grin that didn't meet his eyes. "I just," he paused, squinting into the sun. "I just want to say that I don't do one night stands usually." Then he added quickly. "I was drunk. We both were."

She felt a door close in her heart. So it's my fault we fucked, she thought. He's making it my fault.

"I don't want you to get the wrong idea."

So don't get any wrong ideas about liking each other. "Yeah, well, I didn't get any wrong ideas. It was just a one time thing," TJ snapped. "And don't get the idea that I want to do it again."

"I, hey, wait," Baylor protested.

"You just wanna be friends," she jeered. "I do one-night stands all the time."

Baylor stared at her. "I wasn't going to say that."

"Well, what were you going to say?"

"I, I, I was going to say that I wanted to..." Baylor's voice stumbled to a stop.

"What?"

"Shit, TJ! I wanted to ask you for a date!"

TJ's mouth fell open, then closed. She was a shattered glass, a window with a rock through it. It was her turn to stutter. "A d-date?"

"Yeah." Baylor was blushing. He tried to hide the red in his cheeks by rubbing his tired eyes. "So we can get to know each other better. I mean if it's okay with you?"

TJ heard herself say, "Yes." Then, "Where can, how can we go on a date here? What kind of date?"

"I got an idea about that."

TJ tried to get a grip on herself. She screwed her face into a grimace and said flatly, "You won't like me if you get to know me. No one ever does."

Baylor stared at her. "I like you."

"You don't know me."

"Well, you don't know me either. Not really."

TJ hugged herself.

"I might be a total asshole," Baylor said. She laughed.

"For real." He tried to read her face. "But," he shrugged, "seems like we get along pretty good. What the hell, right?"

TJ let her breath out. She felt like she was walking off a ledge, risking death from a fall from great height, but she stepped out into the air anyway. "Yeah, okay, what's this great date, then, that you're going to take me on? Because I can't dance and I don't have any nice clothes."

"I thought maybe we could go on a picnic."

TJ had to look away. She didn't know if she wanted to laugh or cry or run away or kiss him. A picnic. *A picnic.*

She rolled her eyes skywards and said, "Okay." A picnic.

"Yeah, I thought we could go to Mt. Rainier."

Chapter Twenty-Five
Putting the Pieces Together

"So we're going on a picnic, to Mt. Rainier," TJ explained. She was whispering to keep her news from Gale's ears. She and Val were cleaning up the kitchen after lunch. Val, TJ had noticed, was pretty good about keeping pots washed but hadn't dusted any of the pantry shelves in forever. Plus the counters all needed a good scrub, and the floor really needed to be mopped. TJ arms pistoned as she rammed a damp rag in and out of the cupboard over the counter. Val stood beside her, ready to put dishes away once the shelves were clean.

"Mt. Rainier! What a lovely idea."

She sounded so wistful that TJ nearly blurted out an invitation for her to come along. Instead she asked, "Have you ever been there?"

"No. I've just seen it. Sometimes it looks like it's floating in the air. It's a very dramatic mountain. I think it's fourteen thousand feet."

"How come you never went to see it? I mean aren't you from around here?"

"Yeah, Rainier born and bred." Val's tone was sarcastic. "I guess I never got around to it."

TJ tossed her damp rag into the sink. "All clean now."

Val started handing TJ dishes, dealing out the plates like a deck of cards. TJ stacked the dishes neatly and then arranged the coffee cups in rows. Finished, she slid off the counter and stepped back to view her organized display of Val's random collection of mismatched dishes.

"Beautiful!" said Val. She was leaning on the counter, TJ noticed, and her forehead was damp.

A Mountain in the Air

"Well, maybe we should use some of those cups for some coffee," she suggested.

"Gale?" Val called. Her voice started off loud, and fizzled into breathlessness. "Do you want a cup of coffee?"

Gale's response was a mumble which TJ took as an affirmative. "I'll make it," she told Val. "You go sit down."

Val hesitated. TJ saw the droop of her mouth, the deep lines in her cheeks, and the tremble in her hands. "Go," she said. "Go sit down before you fall down."

"I'm just a little tired."

"So go already!" TJ grabbed the coffee pot. Val, with a soft laugh, transferred her hand from the counter to the door jamb. As Val made her way into the living room, TJ moved briskly around the kitchen. She knew where everything was stored since she had reorganized the pantry. She knew how to use the Coleman stove since she had cleaned the burners, and knew which jugs had river water and which had water from Rachel's tap since she had labeled them. While the coffee perked, she selected from the colorful array of coffee cups the one she knew was Val's favorite—white with a pink floral design—and her own favorite which was decorated with cat faces. For Gale, she picked an ugly boring brown mug.

With a sense of satisfaction, she pulled a tray out from a freshly cleaned shelf, and set it down on the recently wiped counter. Then she poured the coffee and arranged the coffee cups in a neat triangle on the tray. They had no milk or creamer, but Val did have a small bowl with sugar.

"Here I come!" With some pride, TJ carried the tray in and settled it on the coffee table.

"How lovely!" Val inhaled the scent of her coffee before taking a sip. TJ watched Gale, looking for some sign of pleasure or gratitude. Gale grunted as she leaned forward and grunted again as, cup in hand, she sank back into the couch. Holding the cup against her chest, she closed her eyes.

TJ decided that she didn't care if Gale liked the coffee or not. Val liked it, so that was all that mattered.

Gale's eyes popped open. "I used to do jigsaw puzzles in the afternoon," she said. "Listen to the radio and do a puzzle. Would you girls like to do one with me?"

Val looked surprised. "I don't have any puzzles." She sipped her coffee, then added, "I do have a radio. Baylor showed me how to run it off a car battery."

"Honey, go in my room and look in my closet. There's six or seven puzzles in there."

It took a few seconds for TJ to realize that she was the "honey" Gale was referring to. Surprised and pleased, she set her cup down and jumped to her feet. "In the closet?" she asked.

"Up high. I think he put them up high."

"Okay."

In addition to puzzles, Gale had a flat black board covered with felt, designed as a surface for puzzles. They set the board down on the coffee table and spilled the pieces out. Gale propped the puzzle up so they could see the picture. Val got the radio hooked up and TJ asked, "What kind of music are we going to listen to?" She was pretty sure they'd hate anything she liked, and she'd hate anything they chose.

Val said, "We probably don't all like the same kind of music." It looked like they were faced with a dilemma, but TJ suggested that they cycle through stations at about fifteen minutes each. They set the volume low so they could chat and got started.

The first station was country. Wincing, TJ tried to ignore the music. Instead, she stared at the board. The chaotic pile of pieces was overwhelming. She didn't see how anyone could ever get a puzzle put together, but Gale and Val both seemed confident.

Gale pawed her way through the chaos and gathered the pieces into small piles. She hunched over the game, eyes alert, poised like a heron about spear a fish. TJ watched her hands dart out, snap a piece into place, hover, and dart again. Each dart of her hand was followed by a grunt of satisfaction.

"How do you do that?" she asked, a bit annoyed by Gale's success

"Just pick part of the picture like this flower here," she explained, "and then find all the pieces that have that color in it. See? And then fit them together."

"My strategy is to do the edges first." Val, too, had the alert about-to-pounce look of a heron peering into a stream

TJ scanned the welter of colorful pieces and studied the picture on the box. Three gamboling puppies had been photographed in the act of escaping from a basket. TJ decided to focus on the blue pieces which, put together, would make the table cloth in the picture. Her fingers dug around in the pile of pieces, finding and grabbing the blue ones. In a few minutes, she had a small pile of pieces to match up.

While she examined her pieces, Gale and Val muttered comments and encouragement to each other. With a flourish of triumph, Gale snapped the last piece that completed the face of a puppy, and Val said, "Oh, I think that matches up with this over here." A picture of a puppy began to emerge from the pile of puzzle pieces.

TJ tried to fit one piece to another, and to her surprise, she succeeded. She sorted through her pieces and tried another match. No good, but there was a likely match in front of her...It worked!

Gale, in charge of the radio, switched stations when the news came on.

"The world's still going to hell in a handbasket," Gale observed.

"I've gotten so I just don't want to know," Val agreed.

TJ kept her black cynicism about mankind to herself and continued to fit pieces of blue together. The trick, she realized, was to look at the details of the shapes. Gradually, her part of the puzzle enlarged. After the fourth or fifth time the news came on, TJ was surprised to notice that the room was darkening. Val twisted back and forth in an effort to ease a pain in her back.

"I can't sit much longer," she said.

TJ pulled her mind out of the tiny world of blue puzzle pieces and watched Val roll her shoulders. She's in pain, TJ realized. On impulse, she said, "Maybe you should go for a little walk? Just to loosen up? Me and Gale will be okay."

"I'm fine. I just need to get the kink out of my back."

TJ sat back. She met Val's eyes and said, "You should go down to the tavern and get a beer and hang out for a while. Me and Gale can get some dinner here." She was a bit nervous about staying with Gale, but Val looked like she needed a change of scenery. TJ, remembering Val's duties at the tavern added, "After I get something fixed for Gale, I'll come down and help cook at the Tavern." She added, because she didn't want to leave Gale out, "Maybe you'd like to come down with me?"

Gale shock her head. "I think I'll just sit here for a while and finish up a bit more of this puzzle. You two take off."

"You need some dinner," TJ objected.

She shook her head. "I'm not hungry. If I get hungry, I'll get some crackers and peanut butter. Go get the crackers and peanut butter for me. Then you to take off."

Val and TJ walked together down the hill. The intense rays of the evening sun burned a fierce yellow in contrast to the dense blue shadows between the ramshackle houses. The heat of the day was receding, and a pleasant breeze brushed TJ's hair. Charlie was settling into one of his plastic chairs in his weedy front yard, a cat at his feet. He lifted one hand in greeting and TJ waved back. She felt very aware of each step on the uneven sidewalk, partly out of concern for Val, but mostly because she felt very alive, very aware of all the details of the moment. I'm happy, she thought, and a sense of wonder filled her heart.

One of Jesus's roosters crowed raucously and Maria yelled "Shut up!"

TJ grinned at Val. "That rooster sure is noisy."

"Yeah," said Val. She, too, was looking around, enjoying the evening. A small smile lifted the corners of her mouth.

"Are you okay?" TJ asked.

Val stopped, inhaled deeply, looked around, and said, "Yes, I'm okay."

It was a statement that seemed to mean much more than the words. She smiled at TJ and said, "It's a lovely evening, isn't it?"

Chapter Twenty-Six
Val is Dying

Valerie was sitting on the boulder next to Pete. She felt comfortable there, as if she belonged. She asked, "Do you still think this isn't a dream?"

He hesitated, then laughed. "I think I'm part of this mountain now. I think I'm like one of the rocks or one of those trees over there."

"Weird."

"Yeah, because I didn't notice time passing before you started coming up here. Forty years is a lot of years to not notice, right?" He laughed.

Valerie didn't laugh. She was thinking that her forty years had been years of frustration, loneliness, and drudgery that had gone largely unnoticed. Just day after day of day dreaming and TV. Her mother hadn't appreciated Val's help much. Her mother had wanted to die. But that misery had ended when Valerie found Warrentown. Her life there was alive with well-loved animals and friends. Images floated into her vision of her garden, her little house, the cats and the pig and the baby goat. Rachel and Jimmy. TJ. Even Gale sometimes. She would be missed and not just because she was useful. Val felt a swelling in her heart as if she was about to cry or pray or hug someone.

"Hey, look at you all serious. Whatcha thinking about?" Pete asked.

"I was thinking that I've been pretty happy lately. Did I tell you that I'm going to die soon? I have lymphoma."

"Oh, shit, Valerie," Pete patted her awkwardly on her shoulder.

She smiled and said with sudden realization, "I don't really mind."

To his own surprise, Pete said, "I wish I'd met you a long time ago." He was surprised because never in his life had he been the least bit interested in females as people, and he certainly had never been interested in an old one. But he'd missed out, hadn't he? A whole universe of females that he hadn't explored except for quick sex. But now he was friends with Valerie. "But, hey, let's not be sad. Take a hit off this."

He handed her the spliff. Valerie held it awkwardly. She was familiar with marijuana, everybody was, but she'd never liked it much. Marijuana seemed to trigger intense thinking in her, and that was mostly intense thinking about her failures and her missed opportunities. She shook her head and said, "I think I'll just sit here and look at the scenery."

And she did. Faraway across the Salish Sea, the blue peaks of the Olympics were silhouetted against the yellowing sky. Overhead, the sky was blue, shading into lavender, and below them, the water of the Sound glittered silver and black. She felt like she was floating in a sea of color.

"I have always wanted to be up here," she told Pete.

"Me too," he said, "Even when I didn't know it."

"Baylor and TJ are coming up here for a picnic. Maybe you'll see them?"

He shook his head. "I don't see people much. Mostly you."

Then he cocked his head and listened. "I think someone is calling you."

"Oh." Valerie leaned forward, listening. Probably someone in Warrentown needed her. No, not needing. Someone was thinking about her.

"Come back when you're ready." Pete told her. "I'll be waiting."

"Hey, Val, wake up." Jim patted her shoulder. Val was asleep in her chair behind the bar.

"Closing time," Rachel said.

Val blinked vaguely and moaned.

"Come on, honey. Wake up and then we'll get you up and take you home."

Val mumbled, "I'm back," but her eyelids drooped.

"Val, honey, wake up."

This time Val's head jerked and her eyes snapped fully open. She stared blankly. Rachel and Jim watched consciousness return to her eyes.

"Oh, boy, did I ever have a dream." Val rubbed her eyes and shook her head. She felt like she was still halfway dreaming.

"Yeah?" Rachel asked. "Tell it to us quick before you forget."

Val shook her head. "I'm not going to forget this one."

"Here." Rachel handed her a glass of water.

Val took a sip and wiped her mouth with her hand. "I dreamed about Mr Rainier," she said. "I dreamed that this musician I used to have a crush on was up there." She paused, sipped some more water, and grimaced. "When I say it out loud it just seems silly, but it's almost real. I mean, I've been up there to visit him four or five times now, and we always talk." She laughed, embarrassed.

Rachel said, "You dreamed it, so it must mean something to you."

Val looked inward. "That's just it. I mean dreaming about a guy I had a crush on being still there up on a mountain... It's just that it seemed so real and I keep going back. That's all, I guess. It just seemed real." She rubbed her eyes, then dropped her hands into her lap. "We were having fun. I think I sort of...we got to talking about Baylor's date with TJ."

Rachel and Jim exchanged looks, and Jim asked, "Baylor is dating TJ?"

"Yeah, he's planning to take TJ up to the mountain and have a picnic." She paused, and added, "I think I'm a little jealous."

"This guy," Jimmy asked. "This guy on the mountain, he seems real, right?"

"Yeah." Valerie examined Jim's face. "Almost real anyway. I mean it can't be real that someone has been sitting up there for forty years and didn't even know it."

Jimmy's eyes met Rachel's and she said, "People used to believe that fairies—what they called fairies, I mean—could transport people to a different reality."

"Rip Van Winkle. Remember that old story?" Jimmy watched Val's face.

Val said, "Sort of."

"Well, the story is that...fairies...made this guy go to a different reality for a while and, when he came back, years had gone by." Jimmy shrugged dismissively. "The story is wrong in places. Humans don't understand this stuff."

"Well," Val said slowly, "that's what my dream is like." She frowned. "You're talking about this like...like you..."

"That explains it," Rachel interrupted. Suddenly brisk, she went on, "About your idea of going up there to the mountain. We can do that. All of us can get in Scotty's old van. Charlie can take care of Gale while we're gone."

"I've never been there," Jim said.

"Neither have I," said Val, "but I've always wanted to go. But not on Baylor's date."

"No problem." Rachel wiped her hands on her dishtowel and dropped in on the counter. "We'll go to different places on the mountain. Plenty of room up there."

Chapter Twenty-Seven
The Spirit of the Mountain

They piled out of the van into the parking lot and looked around. Jim reached in to give Valerie a hand. She climbed out, stood tilted off balance with her hand on the van's door, and said, "Everything's slanted." The slant was doing something to her mind, putting her off-kilter in a way that was deeper than just being slightly dizzy.

"Yeah, it's a mountainside." Jimmy took her elbow. "Let's look around."

They drifted in a little herd toward a sidewalk that led in the direction of the lodge. The landscape was disconcerting. Besides the slant, Valerie was confused by the incongruity of people, cars, asphalt, noise, and the vividly green mountain meadow. She could see the top of the mountain where the remaining glacier gleamed under the sun. She could smell the sharp, resinous scent of the conifers at the bottom of the meadow. The mountain was there, but obscured, like a photo of a shopping mall over-laying a photo of forest and meadow. She hung on to Jimmy. He seemed to know what he was doing.

They made their way up the sidewalk toward the lodge. It was a sprawling, old building built out of logs, cabin-style but on a much larger scale. Very picturesque, the building looked like something a child would make out of pretzels. People were gathered in little clumps in front, posing for photos.

TJ said apologetically, "I have to use the bathroom."

Baylor said, "I'll wait with you, Teej."

Rachel told them, "You two go take a walk, okay? Look around for a while. We're going to find a place to sit."

"Okay."

Valerie watched TJ and Baylor disappear into the lodge. She envied them. Oh, to be young and energetic! She just wanted to sit down somewhere. Jim gave her arm a gentle push and steered her onto a footpath into the meadow.

"Look at all the flowers," Valerie was awe struck. The voices of the crowd had disappeared. She was alone with Jim and Rachel in a long slanted meadow, fringed with trees at the bottom and boulders at the top. The trail was a thin passage for their footsteps between thick green masses of grass interspersed with flowers. Without the trail, it would've been impossible to walk without stepping on the blossoms that enlivened the slope with color: red, blue, yellow, white, and purple against the dark green of the grass.

"It's unbelievable," Val whispered, not wanting to intrude her voice on the meadow. The sky was a smooth robin's egg blue decorated with big fluffy white clouds. The conifers were a silvery blue with scaly gray trunks.

"Like a painting." Or a poem, she added to herself. Each part separate but each woven into the others. "A tapestry." She felt Rachel's fingers on her hand. "It's just like my dream."

"Let's go up to those rocks," Rachel suggested.

They made their way single file along the pathway, stopping frequently to look at the flowers, to feel the breeze, and enjoy the sun. They were almost to the top of the meadow when a voice called out cheerfully, "Hey! I thought someone was coming up here today."

A young man lounged on top of a boulder. He sat comfortably with his legs dangling over the edge and grinned down at them. Valerie's mouth opened with surprise. It was Pete. Not the Pete of the album cover photo. This Pete was softer somehow. Still lean—almost bony—still pock-marked, pasty-faced, and deliberately ugly, grinning to show off bad teeth, but also friendly and relaxed. It was the Pete of her dreams. "Come on up," he called.

Valerie felt her hands and knees trembling. Rachel took her by the elbow and smiled reassurance. "Careful," she said. "I'll help you."

They climbed up the steep bank of rocks and settled themselves in a row on top of the boulder. Pete grinned at each of them, playing the host. "So hi, Valerie, we meet again, but how about the rest of you? And why'd you come up here to visit me?"

Rachel did the introductions, adding "This trip was Valerie's idea."

"I didn't know you were up here for real, Pete." Val said. Seen up close he was a like a little boy, full of eagerness and delight. Oh, wait a minute, she thought. How can he still be so young in real life?

"Hey," Val said slowly, "Am I dreaming again?"

"I don't think so," Pete said. "There's something about being up here that messes with your head in a good way." He kicked his heels against the boulder. "Like I said, I think I'm part of the mountain now." He shrugged.

"It's so beautiful. I could sit here forever." Abruptly, she turned to Jimmy and asked, "Do you know why...Pete's still young? I mean how he can he still be young if this isn't a dream?"

"This is a different place," he answered. "Pete's right; this place plays by its own rules." He shrugged and added, "Why not just enjoy it?"

"Like these flowers," Pete said. "I never paid much attention to flowers before I found this place."

They all contemplated the flowery meadow. Valerie's thoughts wandered around in her head. Could dreams come true? She wondered why she wasn't frightened, then wondered what there was to be afraid of. She didn't understand what Jimmy meant by it being a different place with its own rules, but she wasn't upset either. The trembling was gone from her fingers, but her heart felt fluttery, as if she was poised on the brink of something deeply desired.

"I liked your records with I was young," Valerie said. "You sang about things I cared about."

"Angst." He laughed. "Teenage angst. The meaning of life!"

"I thought you were a big success."

"Yeah, in a way I was." He shrugged. "But it was...I don't know. I write a whole different kind of song now."

"Could you play something for us?"

"Sure." His guitar was in its case, propped up against the boulder. He pulled it out, plucked the strings, did a little tuning, and began to play.

Jim shifted his butt on the hard surface of the boulder. He was not blissing out into a mountain high like Valerie and Pete. Rachel wasn't either, though she gave no signs of impatience or discomfort. Like Jim, she was listening to the music but mostly listening to Valerie's shallow breathing and the long pauses between her heartbeats.

Pete didn't sing. He played ripples of notes that wove through the grass like the rivulets of glacier run off. He hit chords that resonated with the boulders, then switched up to fingerings that fluttered over the flowers like butterflies. Jim thought about adding a howl or two, but before he could start, Valerie began to sing.

She didn't have much voice, just a thin soprano, and she didn't have any words. Pete grinned encouragement and added his gravely baritone, popping out nonsense syllables playfully around her "ooo's" and "la, la,la's." Jim grinned at their silliness. Then Pete broke off his playing to laugh. He and Val smiled into each other's faces and Pete said, "I'm glad you came to visit. You're fun."

Rachel stood up. Jim joined her. He felt immensely tall, standing on the boulder, looking down the sweep of the meadow to the tree line. Far out in the distance, the Salish Sea was blue, the waves glittering silver under the sun. The foothills were dark and thick with trees. He couldn't see any longhouses or totem poles. No Seattle, either.

"Time to go?" Val asked.

"Yeah," Rachel said. "We need to head back."

"That's too bad." Pete set his guitar down. "Couldn't you stay a little longer?"

"Val can stay as long as she wants," Rachel said.

"What do you say, Val?" Pete asked.

"Yeah, I'd like to stay." She blinked back sudden tears. "But I'll miss you guys. Rachel and Jimmy."

"No, you won't." Jim said, "You'll be having too good a time up here."

"Wait a minute. Don't leave yet." Valerie struggled to her feet. She stood in front of Rachel and Jimmy, hesitating. Then she asked, "Is any of this real? Or am I dead? Or dreaming?"

"You aren't dreaming," Jim said. "It's real in its own way."

Chapter Twenty-Eight

Birthday

TJ left the bathroom and hurried out through the arching logs that framed the entrance. A quick look around, and she spotted Baylor. Then she froze, immobilized by a rush of wonder and fear. He was waiting for her. That guy with his bright face, his lean build, his air of competence. He was a healthy person—healthy in his mind—and he was out there waiting for her, the sick person, the person who had been fucked up all of her life.

TJ pushed herself into motion out the door and across the entry plaza. As she moved, she tried to figure out how she would greet Baylor. Smile? Say something about the view? Say she was sorry for taking time to use the john? She was still groping around for something to say when Baylor turned, saw her, and smiled. TJ's heart did a pirouette in her throat.

"Hey," Baylor said and held one arm out. Blushing and embarrassed by her blush, TJ walked into a quick side embrace. Then he released her and asked, "You okay?"

"Yeah, I'm good. Let's..." She looked around. "Let's go that way."

They joined the crowd of tourists who were wandering up a paved trail toward a meadow. The irritation of having to match the slow pace of other walkers helped TJ recover her equilibrium. When the couple walking in front of them abruptly stopped, forcing Baylor and TJ to stop as well, TJ let out a huff of annoyance.

"Let's try to get away from the people," Baylor suggested, "as soon as we get a chance."

When the paved trail sprouted an unpaved side route, they turned off. The new trail wasn't wide enough for them to walk side by side, so TJ fell in behind Baylor. They walked into a grove of spruce trees, and TJ felt a lurch, a brief attack of dizziness. Suddenly the sounds of people disappeared. TJ stopped in her tracks and looked around. The air was alive with the flits of small birds. The trees were bigger. She turned around, her eyes searching first uphill and then down.

"Weird," Baylor said. "Something like this happened to me once before, I think,"

"What?" she demanded, annoyed because he didn't seem concerned.

"I don't know." He was almost smiling. Then he saw TJs expression and added quickly, "It's okay though. It won't last long."

"What is it?"

He shrugged. "I don't really know. Hey, let's sit down." He led her by the hand to a sunny spot in the meadow, and they settled into the grass. Bugs flew up into the damp air.

"We can't hear people anymore," she said.

"No." He squinted at the sky. No jet trails, just a few wispy clouds. TJ felt herself settling down, calming. The cool air felt good on her skin, and Baylor's body was warm against her arm. "Isn't it weird that we can be so close to people, but it seems like they aren't there? Life we're somewhere else?"

"Like time travel," Baylor suggested. "Like we're back before cars or something."

He smiled at her and she smiled back. "Hey," he asked, "ready for our picnic?"

"Sure." He twisted around and pulled his pack off. "I got...let's see. A sandwich for you and one for me." He handed her a peanut butter and jelly sandwich. "And I have some lemonade." He set a thermos down carefully in the grass. "And chips." A small pack for each of them.

TJ took a big bite out of her sandwich. The sparkling air, the scent of the trees, the green grass, the extravagant beauty of the mountain all combined to make her hungry.

"Here." He handed her the thermos.

"Thanks," she said, and took a sip.

They passed the thermos back and forth in a silence that felt comfortable. Then Baylor said, "I've been up in the Olympics lots of times. You and me should go hiking there too."

"What's it like?" She didn't really care. Her whole body had melted into contentment.

"Completely different from this. Not as as heaven-like, I guess, because of the mountains not being as big. More forest." He shrugged. "Still it's good to get out in the woods, you know?"

She nodded as if she knew, but getting out into the woods was a new and unfamiliar experience. Except for her trips to the stream to get water, she'd had very few interactions with nature. Despite the unfamiliarity, she was loving the picnic, she realized. Loving it. She felt a flood of gratitude for Baylor. He was sweet and kind, unlike the people she'd previously known. In fact, except for her experience with Warrentown, she'd had very little experience with people who were kind. In Warrentown, she'd found people who cared for her, and she wanted to care for them.

She thought about getting high but not seriously. Not as something she really wanted to do.

"Hey, Baylor, looking after your mom isn't that bad. We did a jigsaw puzzle. I've never done one."

"Yeah, she spends hours on those puzzles." He sighed ruefully. "She's my mother, but...she can be hard to take."

"Valerie just ignores her when she's being nasty and is nice to her when she isn't. And anyway, it's a job."

Moving with sudden decisiveness, TJ set the thermos down in the grass and wedging it in so it wouldn't fall over.

"I'm going to tell you something, and I don't want you to laugh," she said.

"Okay."

"I want to change my name."

Baylor laughed and then slapped his hand over his mouth. "Sorry, TJ. Really! I only laughed because I thought you were going to say something really serious and solemn or something. Changing your name, sure. I mean, is there a different name you'd like better?"

"I said not to laugh!" But her feelings weren't hurt. Not much. "Yeah, I hate my name."

"TJ? You don't like initials?"

"I hate my name because it's what my mother named me. I don't want to have anything to do with my old life. I want this to be my birthday."

"Okay." Baylor wasn't laughing anymore. "So any thoughts about your new name?"

She shook her head, a little embarrassed. "Not really." Then she added,

"I'd kind of like something that... that would be part of..." Her voice trailed off.

"All this?" Baylor asked.

She wrinkled her nose. "Yeah, but naming myself 'mountain' or 'flower' or something would be just stupid."

"Well, since this is your birthday, maybe name yourself for the month? I mean girls get named for May and June so why not July?"

"July," TJ said quietly.

"People are going to call you Julie."

"July," she said. "I'll correct them if they say it wrong."

Jimmy and Rachel saw Baylor and July sitting on a bench in front of the lodge. Both jumped up as they approached, and Baylor said, "We thought we'd missed you somehow, but the van was still here."

"Sorry." Rachel checked the sky. It was evening, They'd been gone for hours. "I hope you guys didn't get too bored." She grinned at their shy smiles and the way their eyes fled so they were looking away from each other—while still holding hands.

Jim snorted. "Had a good picnic, I see."

July took one step away from Baylor. He took one step toward her and put his arm around her shoulders. Jim laughed out loud.

Baylor, red-faced and embarrassed at his own embarrassment, quickly changed the subject. "TJ has an announcement to make. I mean...You tell them."

July squared her shoulders. "I decided to change my name. I decided to be named 'July' because today is my birthday."

"Oh, hey, that's great!" Rachel gave her a quick hug.

"Your birthday?" Jim asked. "That's cool."

"Not my real one. I just decided that today is my birthday because.. I want today to be my birthday." Something about Jimmy's face made July pause and look around. "Where's Valerie?" she asked.

Jim and Rachel didn't answer. They let Baylor and July think about it.

July whispered, "Is she at the van already?"

Rachel said, "Val's not coming back with us."

"But don't worry about it," Jim told them. "It's a happy ending."

Baylor's fingers tightened on July's hand.

"It's okay," Rachel said. "Kind of perfect that she left on your birthday, July. Let's go home now."

Epilogue

Pete and Val watched the sun set. The sky was glorious, banded with colors that merged into each other, gold at the horizon fading through oranges and reds into lavender and dark blue.

"The stars will be out soon," Pete commented.

"I hardly ever saw stars when I was alive."

"I didn't either. Light pollution." And too much time indoors. He hadn't even tried to see stars.

They let a long silence grow between them. A breeze lifted, stirring Val's hair, but she wasn't cold. For some reason, the obnoxious baby goat came into her mind. He was probably out bumbling around, head-butting everyone.

" So this is what death is like," Val said.

Pete nodded slowly. "Yeah. For us anyway."

"I used to be afraid of dying, but I think it was because I felt like I hadn't lived."

"Do you still feel that way? Like you never lived?"

"No," said Val. "I found Warrentown and the people there. My friends and my animals. It took awhile for me to kind of relax, you know? And realize that I was happy." She laughed. "I didn't realize that I was happy because I wasn't used to it, I guess."

"Yeah," Pete said. "I didn't realize I was unhappy until I got up here and sat around for a while. Then I could see it. You know, looking back."

"We spend a lot of time not knowing ourselves. Humans, I mean." Valerie wondered if maybe most people were unhappy. Either quietly miserable or actively and obviously miserable. Well, given the ravages of climate change, they had reason for misery.

"I hope everyone will be okay." Valerie hugged herself.

Pete said, "Well, you know, mostly they won't be. I mean if you think in terms of the whole world. Mostly people and animals aren't going to be okay. But your friends are better off than most."

"That's true." There were no guarantees of safety in life. "They have each other," she added.

She hoped that TJ and Baylor were kissing each other. Maybe Gale would start reading books again. Charlie was probably writing in his journal or maybe composing poems. Crazy Mary. Val almost missed her cliches and drunken snippets of unintentional wisdom. Jesus and Maria would be putting the children to bed. Maybe TJ and Baylor would be putting each other to bed, if they had gotten that far along. And Jim and Rachel, she hoped they were in the tavern waltzing to a country song, working up to a night of love-making. Her cats and the chickens, the pig and the goat would all be looked after and happy. Valerie realized that she really didn't miss anyone. She was just glad they existed and were helping each other.

"Good night," she said to the air and the mountain. "Good night, everyone."

Other books by Laura Koerber

Wild Hare

WILD HARE IS LISTED ON KIRKUS REVIEW AS ONE OF THE BEST INDY BOOKS OF 2019

"Wild Hare is a fast paced work of apocalyptic and dystopian fiction penned by author Laura Koerber. Combining such varied concepts as fantasy and magic with climate change and political domination is no mean feat, but the plot of this adventurous tale does just that," Readers' Favorites

Starred review in Kirkus Review:

"The story manages to weave together a complex tapestry of themes, from climate change to poverty to what qualifies as morality in a world that's facing catastrophe. The prose is clear and concise throughout, giving readers a sense of each scene and character through the protagonist's eyes. A wrenching, complex novel that any fantasy fan would do well to pick up."

In the year 2032, the US is a one party kleptocracy and the forests are on fire from climate change. Bobby Fallon, half human and half nature spirit of the wild hare clan, fights to protect his little part of the North Woods in Wisconsin.

Available at Amazon here: Amazon.com: Wild Hare eBook : Koerber, Laura: Kindle Store

Wild Hare's Daughter

"My mother would never tell me who my dad was, but I found out anyway. In a town of only eight hundred people, most of them not in the right age range to be my dad, how hard was it going to be?

That was back before I started flying. I was obsessed with wondering who Daddy Dear was until random incidences of spontaneous levitation changed my perspective.

So…before I started flying, I thought the militia was just a bunch of assholes who were spreading rumors about magic to cover up their incompetence, but once I started flying, I saw things differently. Flying meant that magic was real, and therefore it was logical that magic was involved in the jail break and the congressman's disappearance. And that meant I was not the only one who had magic. *Someone else in my town had magic too.*"

Set in a dystopic near-future, Wild Hare's Daughter is a story about secrets, trust, and family. This novel is a sequel to Wild Hare, which was listed by Kirkus Review as one of the one hundred best indy books of 2019.

Available at Amazon: Amazon.com: Wild Hare's Daughter eBook : Koerber, Laura, Thayne, Tamira: Kindle Store

The Eclipse Dancer

Honorable Mention 2018 Reader Views Literary Awards

"The story line is simple in that it is easy to follow, yet intricate as layers unwind with a seamless, melodic flow. And, while the author excels at getting inside the heart and soul of her readers, the connection garnered by what remains unsaid is remarkable. The writing is descriptive and artistic, without being flowery or overdone, and leaving just enough room to incorporate snippets of one's own imagination. Some things are just not taught and Koerber's writing is one of those things–she has a gift. " Reader Views

Available at Amazon: Amazon.com: The Eclipse Dancer eBook : Koerber, Laura: Kindle Store

The Dog Thief and Other Stories
Written as Jill Kearney

"Decrepit humans rescue desperate canines, cats and the occasional rat in this collection of shaggy but piercing short stories."

Listed by Kirkus Review as one of the best books of 2015, this collection of short stories and a novella "explores the complexity of relationships between people and animals in an impoverished rural community where the connections people have with animals are sometimes their only connection to life."

According to Kirkus Review: "Kearney's prose is elegant and unfussy, with threads of humor and lyricism. She has an excellent eye for settings and ear for dialogue, and she treats her characters, and their relationships with their pets, with a clear-eyed, unsentimental sensitivity and psychological depth. Through their struggles, she shows readers a search for meaning through the humblest acts of care-taking and companionship.

A superb collection of stories about the most elemental of bonds."

Available from Amazon: The Dog Thief and Other Stories - Kindle edition by Kearney, Jill. Literature & Fiction Kindle eBooks @ Amazon.com.

Printed in Great Britain
by Amazon